FOUND AND LOST

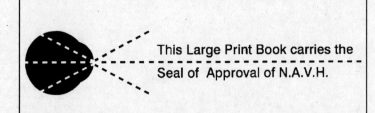

FOUND AND LOST

AMANDA G. STEVENS

THORNDIKE PRESS

A part of Gale, Cengage Learning

GALE
CENGAGE Learning·

Farmington Hills, Mich • San Francisco • New York • Waterville, Maine
Meriden, Conn • Mason, Ohio • Chicago

GALE
CENGAGE Learning

Thorndike Press® Large Print Christian Mystery.
The text of this Large Print edition is unabridged.
Other aspects of the book may vary from the original edition.
Set in 16 pt. Plantin.

LIBRARY OF CONGRESS CATALOGING-IN-PUBLICATION DATA

Stevens, Amanda G.
    Found and lost / Amanda G. Stevens. — Large print edition.
      pages cm. — (Haven seekers ; 2) (Thorndike Press large print Christian mystery)
    ISBN 978-1-4104-8144-3 (hardback) — ISBN 1-4104-8144-1 (hardcover)
    1. Cults—Fiction. 2. Church and state—Fiction. 3. Large type books. I. Title.
PS3619.T47885F68 2015
813'.6—dc23   2015014424

Published in 2015 by arrangement with David C Cook

Printed in Mexico
1 2 3 4 5 6 7 19 18 17 16 15

Now unto the King
eternal,
immortal,
invisible,
the only wise God,
be honour and glory
forever and ever.
Amen.
1 Timothy 1:17, King James Version

"It is well settled law that the First Amendment does not protect speech that incites violence. As we noted in *Jennings v. California,* the evidence considered by the California State Legislature was sufficient to support the Legislature's conclusion that the speech of 'archaic' bibles (as defined in *Jennings*) incited violence and thus that the California statute banning possession of archaic bibles was constitutional.

"Similarly, we have long separated the social evil of hate speech and fighting words from protected freedom of expression, limitations of which do not 'creat[e] the danger of driving viewpoints from the marketplace.'

". . . And so we hold today that Iowa's Statute, which classifies attacks steeped in the philosophy of or quoting the text of archaic biblical translations as hate speech, not to run contrary to the First Amendment. Affirmed."

Carmichael v. Iowa [citations omitted]
Supreme Court of the
United States of America

1

It wasn't every day a man embarked on a criminal career. No wonder he couldn't stop checking his mirrors. He leaned toward the handlebars of his Kawasaki Concours 14 as the warm wind slid over his arms. In less than a week, the calendar would hit summer, and nights like this would suffocate on Michigan humidity. He should relax. Enjoy the ride.

Right.

So far, Clay's life as a lawbreaker was limited to misdemeanors. Take his latest crime, for example. Accepting ownership of two Bibles counted as mere possession.

He would cross the felony line in a few minutes.

He coasted the bike into the turn lane and signaled left. Straight ahead, the sun hung a few inches above the horizon, glaring just enough to impede his vision. Hard to tell how fast that granny car was approaching.

Fine, he wouldn't pull out. No matter what his wife said, Clay didn't have a death wish.

Then again, he *had* agreed to help Abe distribute illegal Bibles. Only for one night, but still.

He could have turned. Granny was doing about twenty-eight in a forty-five. Clay flexed his hands on the contoured grips, shifted his weight and the bike's from one foot to the other. The car whooshed past. He revved the bike and passed a lighted subdivision sign to his left, then a row of trees, backlit in pink by the sunset. A low billboard to his right portrayed a young woman with a somber expression and a book in her hands. Leather cover, gilt-edged pages. Bold, red words on a black background: *"No Fear. Just Call."* Across the bottom, *"Michigan Philosophical Constabulary"* and the number for the anonymous tip line, emblazoned in orange.

Last week, that board had advertised a hotline against child abuse.

Clay's phone vibrated in his jacket pocket. Not now. He turned right into the dark parking lot of Shelby Physical Therapy, a slate-gray structure with an asymmetrical roof. His headlight caught the weathered siding on the front of the building. Even without full daylight, the less-faded pattern

10

was unmistakable. A cross had hung there — not in six years, of course, but for a long time before. Clay sighed. Repurposed churches always held melancholy around them, like gravestones of freedom.

Or maybe he'd been reading too much Poe this week. Who was next on the Lit Philes group syllabus? Willa Cather?

As he and his bike rounded the building, headed for the Dumpster behind it, the phone stopped buzzing against his chest. Then it started back up. Could be Khloe, which could be an emergency. She and Violet wouldn't interrupt a sleepover to call him unless the house had burned down. He worked the phone out of his pocket, praying not to drop it, and glanced at the display. His world tilted into surreal territory.

Marcus Brenner. The man just happened to call while Clay was on his first and last anti-Constabulary mission.

He opened the phone and pressed it to his ear. "Hello."

"Eyes on you. Get out of there."

The call ended.

Eyes . . . Constabulary eyes. Clay's heart leaped like an engine on nitro. He leaned into a U-turn, as if he'd pulled in only to turn around.

Fight or flight? Option two, please. He

11

could gun the bike all the way to the highway. The Constabulary could send a whole battalion of squad cars after him there. They were welcome to choke on his dust. But no. He would head home at the same pace he'd ridden here. After all, the Constabulary had no reason to wonder if the side case of a random motorcycle contained Bibles.

If Marcus hadn't called, Clay might be explaining to Constabulary agents right now why he was leaving Bibles in a Dumpster. *"See, I was just throwing them away."*

He turned left. A mile later, the adrenaline rush caught him, buffeted his senses like too much air curled around a windscreen. He was stupid. He'd been minutes away from re-education. But now he sped away from their eyes. The sound that escaped him fell between a chuckle and a sigh, and the wind grabbed it, hurling it back into his face.

Wait a minute.

Marcus had been watching him. How else would he have known to call? Clay mentally rewound his path through the subdivision, trying to recall a dark-blue pickup. As far as he knew, Marcus never drove anything else.

He hoped no one in the Bible business would search that Dumpster for the backpack, not while the Constabulary had it staked out, anyway. Clay braked for the light. No turn on red. Nice.

"Hey."

He jumped, half-swiveled on the bike, and stared up at the red truck to his left. Yelling across the cab at him, through the open window, was Marcus.

"Home Depot, up at Twenty-Six," Marcus said.

Clay nodded.

"Pull in there."

The light turned green. Marcus drove straight, though that wasn't the route to Home Depot. Clay made the turn toward Twenty-Six Mile Road. Adrenaline still zinged through his system. He darted around a few cars, then glanced at the speedometer. Ought to ease off the gas. But the traffic plodded along, and his bike glistened and flitted, a dragonfly among a herd of cows. He passed a stodgy sedan and swerved into the Home Depot parking lot.

He shut off the bike, kicked the stand into place, and leaned back. His heart rate settled. He waited.

After ten minutes, the sun dipped away. Dusk smoldered in a purple haze at the roof of the store and darkened higher into the sky, where starlight poked at the clouds.

Clay dismounted the bike and leaned his hip against it. Maybe he should call and ask Marcus what the heck he was doing here. Maybe he'd go home, before Natalia got back from that scrapbooking thing. He'd concoct a story, just in case. The truth was not an option. *"Nat, you know that illegal church you wish I didn't go to . . . Well, the illegal pastor asked for help distributing some illegal Bibles."* She'd throw her scrapbook at his head and have every right to.

He flung a leg over the bike and reached to turn the key. No reason to loiter here and tempt fate. Abe would have to take the Bibles back and find someone else for this job.

The red pickup pulled into the parking lot. Marcus parked a few spaces from him and got out of the truck. The guy hadn't changed, still possessed a Neanderthal bulk that warned slim literature teachers not to provoke him. But to irritate him — that could be entertaining.

Marcus crossed the parking lot with a deliberate gait and eyed Clay with a familiar, earnest look. "Where is it?"

How much would Abe want him to know about the distributing?

"Where's what?" Clay tightened his lips against a grin. Marcus's glare hadn't

14

changed either.

"The Dumpster's the drop point. You were going to leave it." Marcus glanced toward the bike. Yeah, not too many places to hide something there.

"So you're still in contact with Abe?"

"Abe?"

"He's the one to talk to," Clay said. "Broke an ankle at his granddaughter's birthday party. I'm just filling in."

Marcus paced, one hand curved around his neck. "I didn't know Abe was doing this."

He said it as if he should have. Clay dismounted the bike again and folded his arms. "How did you know I was?"

"Your bike." Marcus angled his glare at the Kawasaki. "It's yellow."

"Yup."

"Hard to miss."

"Yup." Kind of the point. Clay rubbed a thumb over the handlebar.

"But I wasn't sure. I hoped, and then you left when I told you to, so . . ." He shrugged. "Had to risk it."

Risk? Oh. If Marcus had followed Clay and been wrong, the real Bible bringer would be under arrest right now. See, thoughts like these didn't grow naturally in Clay's head. He did not belong here.

"You've got to find a new spot," Marcus said. "They've been patrolling the neighborhood, might have noticed a pattern."

"How do you know?"

Uncertainty furrowed between Marcus's eyes. "Well. You know. This is . . . what I do."

Aha. The words confirmed the speculation that had spun around the little church group for a month or two last winter, when Marcus first vanished. Apparently, only Janelle had managed to talk to him before he snipped his life from everyone else's without warning or farewell. Clay figured he'd grown busy or disillusioned. When he'd remarked to that effect, Janelle had snapped at him. *"You don't know Marcus at all if you think he doesn't want to be here."*

Clay cocked his head and stared at the big guy in front of him. Marcus met his scrutiny with a point-blank gaze.

"You know, a lot of things make sense now."

Marcus nodded.

"But if you didn't know about Abe's little distributing operation, you must be part of something else."

Marcus stepped past him and eyed the bike again. "I should take the stuff with me."

16

"Marcus, come on. What's going on with you?"

He sighed. "I don't deal with . . ." Habit dropped his voice. ". . . Bibles."

"Then what do you — ?"

"People."

"Fugitives? You help them — you move them?"

Marcus studied him, then nodded, one hand clenching his neck again.

"Those network people are the craziest . . . Who sweet-talked you into that mess?"

Marcus blinked. "Nobody. Never mind."

"You what, just decided to . . ." He finally got it, all of it, in one gleaming moment. The timing. The recent lack of Constabulary success stories on the local news. The rumors that someone was warning people before search warrants could be executed, moving people over the state line into Ohio, where Michigan Constabulary agents had limited jurisdiction.

Marcus circled the motorcycle as if he might be inclined to buy it. He jabbed a finger at the left side case. "In here?"

"Level with me, man. Are you saying you're the ringleader?" The mastermind of an entire network of fugitive-hiding criminals was someone Clay knew personally. Unbelievable.

"I didn't mean to lead anybody. It just grew."

"Janelle knows, doesn't she?"

"She kept . . . poking. Figured it out. Anyway. You've got to give me the stuff."

"I'll see what Abe wants done with it."

Marcus paced the length of the bike. "You can't take it home. You've got a kid. Is it in a bag or something?"

"Backpack."

"Good."

Danger prickled Clay's scalp. He paused with one hand on the side case. "Hey, won't we look suspicious handing off a backpack after dark in a parking lot? On the security cameras, I mean."

Marcus's mouth twitched. "They're off."

"How do you know?"

"This is where I stock up. For work. I've talked to some of the freight guys."

"They turn off their cameras for you." For Pete's sake, the guy had turned into a con man or something.

"Not for me. Security just never turns them on."

Well, okay then. Clay's heart hammered as he popped open the side case, grabbed the backpack, and brought it into the open. Only a few cars dotted the parking lot. The store would be closing soon. No one paid any attention as he relinquished his cargo, transferring ownership of federally prohibited literature.

My First Felony, a memoir by Clay Hansen. Might have a ring to it. Or the clanging of a cell door.

"So this is the latest Constabulary brainstorm — Bible busts."

Marcus looped a strap of the red backpack over his shoulder. "Tell Abe to find a new site."

"Will do."

"Thanks." Marcus turned toward his truck, then slowly turned back. "Um, how's . . . everybody?"

Clay shrugged. "Fine. Phil and Felice got married last week."

Marcus's smile revealed creases around his eyes. "They went to the justice of the peace?"

"Well, yeah. But Abe married them too, that secret ceremony thing, 'a covenant before God and these witnesses' . . . We all took communion, and they fed it to each other like wedding cake. Janelle was there, and a Christian friend of Phil's. It was nice."

Marcus nodded.

Hungry quiet spread between them. Clay's mind stretched to remember the tidbits that

19

floated around their midnight meetings, bits and pieces, the lives of friends. "Janelle's sister-in-law is pregnant again, and the baby seems healthy this time. Oh, and last week some stupid teenagers broke into the store, pried the door apart —"

"She should've let me replace that door."

"She's got a new one now. They didn't take much. The cops think they didn't realize it was just a little country store when they broke in. No idea how they missed that detail, since the sign's right there: 'J's Little Country Store.' "

"But she's safe? Everybody's safe?"

"So far, so good."

Marcus nodded. "How's your family?"

A single guy couldn't understand how enormous that question was. "We're going up to Mackinac next weekend. My daughter wants to draw the fort."

Another nod. Marcus shifted his feet. "Thanks. For the update."

"You could come back." Sure, the man was dangerous company these days, but he was still a friend.

"No. But thanks."

He walked back to the truck. Unlike his old blue one, it didn't stand tall enough for running boards. Clay followed him, clapped a hand on his shoulder, and Marcus turned, surprise drawn into the arc of his eyebrows.

"Look, if you're ever short-staffed in this crazy network of yours, let me know."

Words he shouldn't say, despite the nobility of this work. He could walk away from it all if not for . . . well, the something that tugged between him and Marcus. Brotherhood, maybe, of a sort.

Marcus shook his head. "It's not safe."

"I get that, and it doesn't bother me."

"Right." Marcus looked past him at the Kawasaki. "You're not even wearing a helmet."

"Oh, please."

"I mean — the thing's loud, and yellow. At least wear a helmet. So they can't ID you."

Yeah . . . so Clay really didn't do this covert ops thing well. "Maybe I'll think about that."

"Okay."

"So, uh." Clay shrugged. "Take it easy, man."

Marcus nodded. "Sure."

"Stay out of jail."

The guy didn't even twitch a smile, only nodded again. A sense of humor would really improve his personality. Clay grinned for both of them, hopped back on his bike, and left via a different exit. Of course, if

Marcus was right about the cameras, nothing they did out here really mattered.

The wind and the miles rolled by.

Would he really help Marcus's crazy network if the guy called him? Maybe. Helping imperiled believers was the least Clay could do for a God who had died for him. Besides, if Marcus could pull this off, so could Clay. Loud, yellow motorcycle and all.

He coasted up his driveway. Most of the house sat in darkness, but Khloe's lamp was on. Through her window, he glimpsed the lavender wall — no, iris, she insisted. She and Violet must be in there, draped across the bed side by side, discussing guys and movies and jewelry. Using his credit card to buy more charms for their bracelets. Nah, Violet wouldn't go along with that anymore.

Khloe. His sassy, spoiled little miracle. He parked the bike in the garage and let himself into the house. Here was his true responsibility — home, his wife, his daughter. Noble or not, his first instincts were right. He should leave saving people to Marcus. Let it go. Then again . . .

He'd hand it to God. If Marcus called, then maybe Clay was supposed to join him.

2

Violet had spent the eleven-minute bicycle ride to the Hansen house rehearsing how to bring up The Topic. Then she'd stepped into Khloe's bedroom, plopped down in the blue beanbag chair, and lost every planned word. Small talk took over for an hour or two and then gave way to silence. She slouched into the beanbag chair. They had to talk about it. She had to mention it. Somehow.

Khloe sprawled on her stomach over the blue carpet, stretched out to her full length of four-foot-eleven. She always extended even her feet, as if to take up as much room as possible. Her hand swept a flesh-colored pencil over the sketchpad paper. A woman's profile began to take shape.

From the dresser, her sound system emitted a low stream of music, some artist from at least a decade ago. Violet couldn't figure out what Khloe had against current music. *Come on, no dodging, just ask her.* Best friends didn't need a smooth-edged speech. Shouldn't, anyway.

Khloe glanced up and rolled onto her back. Her strawberry blonde ponytail fanned out to the left of her face.

"I'm going crazy here. Just spill it, Vi. I want every detail."

Violet swallowed. "What?"

"You didn't text me all day, even when I sent you that link about the aquarium. You should've been bouncing up and down and planning a field trip and stuff. I was afraid you weren't coming over at all."

She should just say it. But with Khloe poking a pencil in her face, not a word squeaked out.

A grin cracked the rose-petal line of Khloe's glossed lips. "I could guess. You could just nod or shake your head."

"Khloe . . ."

Khloe pushed up from the floor and knelt close. "Fine, leave out some details, just tell me. How far did you get?"

Oh . . . "This has nothing to do with Austin."

The smile inverted. "You guys still haven't — ?"

"Khloe, I know. About your dad. I know what's going on."

A story-weaving wrinkle gathered between

Khloe's eyes. She couldn't possibly think she'd get away with the first lie in a decade of friendship.

Violet ran a thumb over her charm bracelet. "Thursday, when we made carrot cake, he wasn't at that pub like you said he was. At first I thought he must have lied to you about it, and you didn't know, but . . . you did. And you know where he really was."

"He was at the pub like he said. Like *I* said."

No way. Violet looked away from her, up at the fixed smiles of age-old singer/songwriter posters tacked on the wall over the lavender-quilted bed.

"Just so happens my dad was there," she said to the image of Carole King. "And I asked if he said hi to yours."

The colored pencil in Khloe's hand dropped to the carpet.

"I figured it out." Violet crossed her arms. "I never, ever thought your dad would, but . . . Khloe, why didn't you tell me?"

"There's nothing to tell."

Oh, fine. She'd say it. She faced Khloe and unfolded her arms. "He's having an affair. Right?"

"What! Of course not!"

The surge of red in Khloe's cheeks had to

be real indignation. But she knew. Didn't she? In the Hansen family, people paid attention to each other. How could Khloe not know?

Or maybe it *was* something else. Something disastrous enough to make Khloe lie, knowing she would be cutting threads in their friendship.

Khloe jumped to her feet and plopped onto the bed. "Okay, whatever, you hit the bull's-eye. It's an affair, and it's embarrassing, and I didn't want you to find out."

When lying fails, get snarky? Who did Khloe think she was talking to, her mother? Violet jumped up and planted hands on hips. And gosh, she must look kind of motherly.

"I'm not stupid, Khloe."

Khloe tried to glare but instead ducked her head. She scooted back on the bed and pressed against the wall.

"So?" Violet said. "Where was he really?"

"I wish he was cheating on her. I wish he was cheating and lying and . . . and robbing banks."

A chill breathed over Violet. She crossed the room and reached for Khloe's right hand with her left. Their charm bracelets clinked. Together.

"Okay." Khloe sucked in a breath. "Vi,

you know Dad goes to our church."

Of course she knew. He drove them every Sunday.

"Well, um, Elysium isn't the only church he goes to."

For a stupid moment, Violet didn't get it. Having two churches was a little weird, and there weren't many others in the area, but there were a few. Maybe he liked to hear various speakers. Then understanding smacked her in the face.

Clay's other church wasn't a *real* church.

"Yeah," Khloe whispered. "That's where he was. One of their meetings. Dad's . . . a Christian."

No way. He wasn't.

Or maybe he was. Maybe knowing him for two-thirds of her life didn't mean Violet really knew him. Her legs rubberized. Maybe she should sit.

Oh, come on. Of course she knew him, and he wasn't dangerous or violent or even harmlessly demented. "Khloe, are you sure?"

Khloe scuffed her small foot along the bed frame. "He's been bugging Mom to go with him. And me."

Uncle Clay. Not related by blood, and usually just Clay in her head now (though she'd probably always call him Uncle to his

27

face). He couldn't be a Christian. He was too normal. Too safe.

Khloe buried her face in her knees. "They meet on Thursdays. Eleven at night. They can't meet in daylight like a real church, of course. And Mom says . . . we, um . . . we're going."

Violet's spine prickled. "No way, Khloe, you have to tell her no."

"She used to worry about him, but he's been going for like a year now and nothing's happened. She says if we go one time, maybe he'll get it out of his system."

Wait a minute. A year? "You haven't reported him in a *year*?"

Khloe's gaze snapped back up. "Report him? Why in the world would I?"

"He needs help. Good grief, Khloe, he's your father."

"Exactly."

"What, re-ed? You can't just ignore —"

"Call me selfish, but I'm not going to re-ed. So he's not, either."

Violet's thumb found the silver bracelet around her left wrist and rubbed her starfish charm like a genie lamp. Khloe had a point. She was a minor. She'd get slapped with automatic re-education, as if she were seven, not seventeen. As if she couldn't recognize dangerous beliefs.

Re-education would destroy Khloe's senior year. Her GPA. Her life.

And good grief. It was Clay. Violet didn't need to report him. He was harmless.

Christians aren't harmless.

"Okay, at least tell me you're not going to that meeting."

Khloe's lip wobbled. "Trust me, I'd rather have a hundred MRIs. If I get caught . . . gosh, can't you just hear me? 'My dad dragged me here, I'm not a Christian, honest.' The con-cops will be like, 'Yeah, right, little girl.' "

"Would your dad take me with you?" The words popped out of Violet's mouth before she tried them on, but yeah, they fit. Khloe shouldn't be stuck in this alone.

Khloe's green eyes lit. "Really?"

"Of course."

"Oh, Violet, I'd owe you . . . my life, or something."

"Nah. Besides, you'd come with me. If it was my dad."

Khloe bit her lip. "Actually, no, I wouldn't. Vi, if we got caught . . . Well, I'd kill myself. Since my life would be over anyway. And your parents — who knows what they'd do."

Change the locks, probably. Her mom would finally have an excuse to renounce motherhood. Well, so what? Violet would be eighteen in three months. All she needed was a livable apartment at a retail employee's salary. But none of this was the main point.

"Khloe, I don't know if it's right. Ignoring this. Re-education would help your dad. And all of them, whoever they are."

Khloe swiped at her cheeks. "This is why I didn't want you to know. You'd be all honor-bound. But, Vi, you can't turn him in. Please. I'll do anything. I just don't want to go to re-ed."

Violet inhaled the chilled air and leaned back against the wall. Would it be so wrong to pretend she didn't know? The light from the ceiling fixture offered no answers.

Khloe held up her wrist, and zircon-spangled charms glittered: a pink heart, a purple flip-flop. "I know. We'll put one of mine on your bracelet. A pledge of silence. Or, if you want to keep up your theme, I saw a new sea-life one on the website. An octopus. I'll buy it for you."

"Khloe, really."

Her voice fell. "Will this . . . will we change now?"

"No." But how could they not?

"I don't want stuff to be awkward. You get it, don't you? Why I'm not turning him in?"

Violet crossed the room and collapsed

onto the bed. She pulled her knees up to stare at her coral-red toenails, a color she'd borrowed from Khloe. When the quiet started to push in close, Violet nodded. *I'm not lying. I do get it.* But the nod was more — a promise that seams weren't unraveling.

"I should've just told you," Khloe said.

"Yup."

"And I've been contemplating your future husband. Don't you think his hair's a little fuzzy?"

"What?"

"Austin. He should use some sort of product in it."

Violet released a sigh loud enough for Khloe to hear, but she was years past conversational whiplash. If she had gone through something as bad as radiation treatments at five years old, maybe she'd act like Khloe did when a crisis tried to knock her down. Face it, sure, but not for too long.

Actually, Austin's hair was silky, not fuzzy. Smooth and soft and fine as gold. Not that Khloe needed information like that, especially if she still believed all Austin and Violet did was flirt.

"If I'm ever his actual wife, I'll tell him, 'My best friend recommends the ultra-hold, Mohawk-inducing, mullet-defeating —' "

"Who said mullet? Did I say mullet? I said fuzzy."

Violet flopped onto her back with all the drama she could force and glared at the ceiling.

Laughter squealed from Khloe, the guinea-pig-at-feeding-time shriek that had been easy to mock since second grade. "You couldn't mope for real for a million dollars."

She could probably pull off brooding, though. Violet grinned, turned onto her stomach, and let Khloe's voice slip into the background of her brain. They wouldn't talk about it again tonight, maybe ever, but silence wasn't much of a problem solver. For Khloe, Violet should go to that meeting, watch out for her, and bury the whole skeleton of secrets. For Clay, Violet should make a phone call, file a report, and pray that re-education saved his mind from the lies he believed.

She couldn't do both.

She breathed in Natalia's favorite citrus room spray and let herself shiver in the overzealous air conditioning that Clay turned down when his wife wasn't looking. Just a few hours ago, she had stepped into this house and left her blue flats in the same corner of the mudroom she'd left them in a thousand times before. She thought she had prepared herself for whatever was going on in this home. Her home.

Hardly.

"Okay."

Khloe's voice broke off midsentence. "Okay what?"

"I'll just . . . pretend I don't know."

"You just now decided that?" Khloe fiddled with her bracelet and slid a charm free. "Hold out your arm."

"You don't have to —"

"Shut up, I want to." She secured the charm to Violet's bracelet, a pansy with an amethyst center. "There. Pledge of silence."

Violet rubbed the tiny silver petals. "Pledge of silence."

3

Trees blurred at the edge of the floodlight, a flash of green-and-yellow swing set. Violet tilted her head back. Even the stars and the clouds rotated, high in the inky sky. She tried to focus on Austin as he raced the merry-go-round, pushing it faster and faster. The floodlight made a halo around his blond head. His calves flexed with the effort of running the merry-go-round into motion, and Violet's heart galloped.

Austin jumped up onto the platform and clung to one of the metal handlebars. Violet pushed aside thoughts of where she'd been less than an hour ago. Measuring Khloe's sleeping breaths beside her, then wincing at the sliding sound of the window in the track. If only she could tell Khloe everything, but . . . no.

She and Austin spun and spun, bent nearly double, then straightened as the ride's momentum spent itself. They crept to a standstill, but the trees continued to spin. She leaned on the handlebar at the same time Austin did, and his arm branded hers. Just arms, but the heat rushed all the way to the back of her neck.

Austin staggered a dizzy step back, and the grin took over his face. Not a grin, *the* grin. The one that curled her toes.

Maybe he would want more tonight.

Violet wobbled one step back and nearly fell off the merry-go-round. Everything tilted and whirled. Austin's hand shot out to catch her, and his other hand netted her shoulder. Now neither of them gripped the handlebar for balance. They half tumbled onto the weathered wooden platform. Violet pushed herself off him, except . . . no point in that. When he propped up on his elbows, she wrapped an arm around his back and smiled.

"Violet, we can't even see straight."

"Whatever."

His lips found her chin, coffee and butterscotch on his breath. Violet leaned in and bumped her head on the handlebar.

"Ow. Wait."

He pulled back. "What?"

"Nothing, just — this." She ducked the bar and pressed her lips to his.

The world slowed its spinning while Austin's long fingers glided from her hair, to her cheek, down to her neck. They caught in the loose gather of her peasant-neck top. They tugged the mauve cotton down an inch at a time, until Austin's breath tickled the bareness of her shoulder.

Violet's face flushed. She slid her lips along his jaw the way he'd taught her, and her heart cartwheeled. She slung her legs across his lap and angled toward him. His lips traveled. She raised her arms, an invitation, and her shirt came up, over her head. He tossed it aside. The humid night stuck to her skin. She fumbled behind her for the bra clasp.

"Mmm, no." Austin stilled her fingers with his. "Don't."

"We could —"

"Not out here."

When his hands fumbled downward, Violet pressed closer. Yes. Tonight. But he turned away seconds later.

Humiliation warmed her face now. She gripped the merry-go-round's handlebar, hoisted herself off his lap, and jumped down. Her top lay in a wrinkled heap in the grass. She shook it out and slid it over her head.

"Violet."

"It's fine. I get it." *You don't want me.*

He curled his hands around the edge of the merry-go-round's platform, a ring of metal that held the old boards in place. It and the handlebars had been painted and repainted over the decades, the last a coat of bright blue that was starting to wear away.

Austin let out a sound halfway between a moan and a growl. "You're seventeen, babe."

"I should've said I was twenty."

"No, you shouldn't have."

She would, though. If she could go back to the moment he asked. She sat down next to him on the merry-go-round and trailed a finger down his arm. "What's a month or two?"

"Or three."

Good grief, why couldn't he be one of those boyfriends who forgot birthdays? "You really want to stay like this for three months."

"Yes. I want to. Although you make it almost impossible."

Well, that was something, anyway. She wasn't completely undesirable. She tried to hide her smile.

"Violet, I mean it."

His lips feathered on her temple, and her whole body quivered. She settled a hand on his chest. They sat for a minute, as close as

Austin would let them be. For now. She snuggled into him, and his hand cupped the back of her head.

"I bet you put it in writing somewhere. 'Both parties must be legal adults before certain activities are allowed.' And then a list with bullet points."

Austin chuckled. "You could try appreciating my restraint. I am a guy, after all."

Love shouldn't be ruled by the stupid calendar. She pressed her palm into his chest, and he sighed.

"Babe, I want to do this right." He withdrew the embrace, leaned back on his hands, and tilted his head toward the sky. "You said you wanted to talk tonight. What's the hundred-dollar topic?"

Fine. They could talk. She did want to, just . . . later. She kicked her wedges away from her and inhaled the scent of fresh-cut grass and geraniums. "I have two questions. Mammoth-sized."

"Fire away."

Nerves stiffened her shoulders. How stupid. She could ask Austin anything. Still, easy question first. "Do they pay you to lead small group at Elysium, and if they do, do you want to do that forever? Or do you have another goal, and what is it?"

"That's . . . four questions, I think."

"Four facets, one question."

"Hmm. Let's see. No, they do not pay me. If they did, I'd still have other goals in addition to leading small group. The first being a doctorate in philosophy."

"That's a ton of school."

"Exactly."

"Why philosophy?" She swung her feet in an alternating rhythm and joined his stargazing. So many pinpoints of light, peeking down at Earth for millennia.

"I want to understand people. What makes them believe certain things or act certain ways. And I want to be able to teach them the right way to believe."

"Like you do now, at church?"

A breeze wafted over them but didn't cool the air. "Yeah, like that. But with more education, I'll be more effective."

"Will you be allowed to read the original Bible translations? Since your degree's in philosophy?"

Austin nodded.

"I think that's an amazing dream." And the perfect transition to her second question, if she could spit it out.

Austin shrugged, but his eyes settled on her, and he smiled. "If number one had four facets, I'm afraid to ask about number two."

Violet ran her thumb over the silver shark

fin fastened to his wrist with a black leather cord. When she gave him the charm off her bracelet, he'd said the cord would keep it from looking like girl's jewelry.

"Violet?"

Just ask. Out here, nestled close on a kiddie ride washed in floodlight, even the crickets and cicadas wouldn't hear her words. Still, her lips froze.

"Come on." Austin nudged her shoulder. "You can ask whatever you want."

"It's a . . . a theoretical question."

"Let's hear it."

"Suppose . . . for the sake of discussion . . . a person knew someone for a long time without knowing something dangerous about them and then discovered it. And this thing could hurt other people . . . and maybe the police really should know about it . . . except if they did, that would affect another person too. Maybe hurt them."

Maybe make them suicidal. Not literally. Khloe was the world's best exaggerator. But still.

The pansy charm seemed to burn Violet's wrist. She burrowed against Austin's arm for courage. "Would the person who discovered this thing be . . . obligated to report it?"

Austin stood up and reached down a

40

hand. "Let's walk a bit."

She let him tug her to her feet. They retrieved their flashlights and Violet's purse and shoes from the ground, then meandered to the concrete walking path. Austin followed its direction but stayed on the grass. Beneath the choir of cicadas, a bullfrog thrummed a one-note bass. A pond rested beyond the tree line.

The silence sweated from Violet's pores and dripped down her back. She shouldn't have asked, even abstractly.

"I think the answer lies in the results of each possibility," Austin finally said.

"Okay," she said. "In the first possibility, someone goes to re-, um, jail."

Austin's feet froze on the path. "You should have said re-education, to begin with. That changes the question."

Violet glanced up at him. Contemplation creased around his mouth and between his blond eyebrows. Ambling through the dark, garbed in a scholar's scowl, he looked older than twenty-one. How did she look to him?

"So you know a Christian."

"Um . . . I . . . might." She traced a five-point star with her flashlight. The beam swung up, down, across, back.

"The answer's yes. It's your duty to report them."

"But, Austin, this person's not dangerous. They'd never hurt anyone. They're just . . . messed up when it comes to God."

"Are you hearing yourself? Violet, some Christians live quiet, legal lives for years and then one day walk out their door, buy a firearm at Walmart, and go on a shooting spree."

She almost laughed at the image of Clay toting a tommy gun like a 1930s gangster. But if that reality lurked in his head for real . . .

"Re-education would help this person," she said.

"Would save this person," Austin said. "Maybe save others."

He resumed walking along the sidewalk, beneath maple trees whose leaves barely whispered in the still, hot night. They circled the whole track, back to the merry-go-round. Austin perched on the edge of the platform, but Violet's legs folded before she got there. She sank to the damp grass.

"I don't know how," she said.

"How?" Austin propped his elbows on his knees.

"You know, how to report someone. Who to call. I know the emergency number for the con-cops" — of course, everyone knew the universal number: three digits, like 911

42

— "but this isn't that kind of emergency, and anyway, I don't have proof, unless I go to the meeting."

Austin's eyes seemed to drill right into her brain. "You got invited to a Christian meeting?"

What must he think of her? A Christian would trust only his closest friends with an invitation like that . . . probably only his Christian friends. "It's not like that, Austin, really. I just have to go. Or maybe I shouldn't."

"No, you shouldn't." Austin sprang up from the merry-go-round and dropped to his knees in front of Violet. "I should."

"What are you talking about?"

"A buddy of mine is a field agent with the Constabulary. He's spent half a year trying to find this network that's hiding Christians. Nobody can figure out who they are, how they know each other, how they communicate, but you — you got an invitation."

A sudden breeze slithered over Violet's arms. "I don't think it's like that. I think it's just some people meeting for . . . well, for church."

"We need to find out. Somehow."

He was right. She could make a difference. "I'll go. I'll find out where they meet."

And report them. Report Clay. If she could.

"Not you. It's too risky," Austin said.

"I think my friend would notice if you go in my place."

He huffed and raked his fingers through his hair.

"I'll play along, Austin. They won't do anything to me."

His mouth crimped, and he closed his eyes. When he opened them, the frown remained, but his eyes shone with . . . respect, maybe. For her.

"I'll give you my buddy's work number. As soon as you get there, find a way to text the address to him. He can send in a team to bust them."

"Okay. See, it'll be fine."

"Wherever they meet, you don't go inside. Come up with whatever excuse you have to, but stay out."

"Right."

He huffed again. "This is madness."

Ever the scholar. Her lips tugged into a smile. She ducked her head and twisted blades of grass around her fingers. One of them snapped. A mosquito landed in the crook of her arm, and she smacked it.

"Do you know," he said, "sometimes you amaze me."

"Because I killed a mosquito?"

"Because you're willing to do something like this. You've got this . . . this tough thread, running under the softness."

No, she didn't. But this mission didn't require toughness. It only required love.

The Hansens would hate her when they found out.

Maybe they didn't have to. Ever.

Austin enclosed her in his arms. "We have to plan this out."

"Didn't we just do that?"

"I want you to know exactly what you're doing before you get there."

"Are you going to teach me kung fu or something?"

His lips moved over her hair. "If only I knew kung fu or something."

"I'll be careful. The most careful I've ever been in my life."

"That doesn't make it —"

"Talk later." She kissed him and, with each breathless second, resolved to do her duty. Duty to Clay, to Austin's Constabulary friend. To the group of dangerous, misguided people who needed help. *Khloe, I have to. For the good of everyone.* Violet would wear the pansy charm on her wrist forever, a pledge of silence to herself.

"It's the right thing," she whispered

against Austin's mouth.

"I know."

Austin lowered her to the soft grass. Yes. Through her clothes, his hands surveyed her body as if he hadn't already mapped most of it. *Please want me.*

"Violet."

She kissed the thumb that traced her mouth.

Austin lowered his head to the crook of her neck, and his sigh warmed her collarbone. "Three months, babe."

4

Maybe it was last night's near encounter
with a Bible bust that caused Clay to soak
up the voices floating in from the kitchen.
Buoyant voices. Violet and Khloe had no
idea their conversation carried so far.

"Wow, she actually looks sexy with her
hair blowing around her face."

"She said she was worried about the
breeze at first, that it would make her look
messy, but Mom was like, 'Nature's fan, it'll
look great.' "

"I can't wait till your mom does *our* senior
pictures."

Someone let the oven door fall open with
a *thump.* A cookie sheet slapped onto the
counter. Sleepover details had evolved as
the girls grew up. They made cookies from
scratch now, no more refrigerator dough,
and their film of choice transitioned from
girl-meets-horse to girl-meets-guy. The gig-
gling remained a constant. Tonight, the

safety of that sound loosened his inner knot of reproach, but the accusations still muttered. *You could've been arrested last night. Your family could be sitting in a Constabulary interview room right now.*

Clay settled into one of the stuffed chairs, woke his laptop from hibernation, and signed into his email. Yup, seven new messages in the Lit Philes thread. The newest one showed up first, less than a paragraph from Zena. *LOL. No way. Prof Hansen will confirm my viewpoint.*

Oh, excellent. His students were squabbling. He clicked Omar's email, the last one sent before Zena's.

How can you place limitations on deconstructionist theory? The definition of the theory precludes limitation.

Clay cracked his knuckles over his keyboard and grinned at the screen. If only these bubbling, blossoming English majors knew how they prevented job withdrawal over the summer. The group had picked up a few new students every year for the last three. Right now, they numbered eleven, including him as facilitator. He clicked on the oldest unread message. Apparently several of them were already well into reading *My Antonia,* not the ideal work for deconstructionism. Then again, Omar applied deconstructionism to, well, everything.

Khloe barreled into the den and flopped down on the sofa, her frame barely stretching across all three cushions. Violet followed at a stroll and perched on one arm.

Khloe half buried her face in the cushion. "Dad, can we claim the TV now?"

"Don't you want to wait until the cookies are done?"

"Can't you smell them?"

He inhaled and noticed the aroma that had resided in his subconscious for a while now. "Oh, yeah. They don't smell burned or anything."

Khloe threw a pillow at him. "They're not."

"I'll trade you the TV for a few cookies." They'd been making the same bargain since Khloe and Violet's first batch of Pillsbury, spooned from a plastic tub of premade dough, baked with Natalia's eye on the timer, and presented to Clay with great ceremony.

"It's a deal," Violet said.

Khloe turned her head toward Violet. "Let's make smoothies, too."

"You'd better wash the blender," Clay said.

"Or Mom will disinherit me!" She flailed on the couch like an overturned turtle.

"And kick you out."

"For my own good, to teach me responsibility, because a clean blender is a sign of character."

Clay stood and stretched, drawing the motion out with all the drama of his daughter. "I'm just saying I'm not cleaning it this time. To teach you responsibility. Would I like the movie?"

"Nope," the girls chorused.

He gave a mock bow and carried his laptop under his arm, through the kitchen, past the paper plate on the counter. He swiped two warm cookies and stuffed one into his mouth. A melted chip smeared his thumb. Mmm. Sweet and a little gooey. Natalia's laptop sat a few feet from the cookies, still cycling through the slideshow of Britney Yokomoto's senior pictures. The girl stood in an orchard, a line of trees blurring behind her. The tilt of her mouth and the lift of her glossy hair lent an almost provocative aura to some of the pictures. For Pete's sake, she was only eighteen.

Clay ambled out to the deck with his cookies and his laptop. He'd texted a few buddies, thrown together a bowling night, but nobody was free before nine-thirty. So he lounged here in an Adirondack chair, typed an email to his lit students, and listened to the girls' laughter from inside the house. Something like nostalgia rolled over him for the days when Violet stood as high as his hip and Khloe six inches shorter than that, and neither of them cared to look sexy.

Enough old-man thoughts. He wasn't even forty yet, though the unsettling number loomed only months away. Just as Clay signed his email and hit Send, his phone trilled through the screen door. He hopped up, opened the door, and reached through to grab the phone off the table. Not a local area code.

"Hello?" he said.

"You know who this is?"

Marcus. "Twice in one —"

"Shut up."

Clay dropped back into the chair. "Shutting up."

"I need help. A . . . delivery. Tonight."

Delivery of a fugitive? A Christian on the run, an active target? Danger hummed in Clay's head. *Don't agree to this.* "Okay."

"I wouldn't ask, but I'm too far away."

Probably not even in Michigan. Probably carting around some imperiled people in the bed of his pickup. A sense of the bizarre dripped into this conversation. "I'm in. What's the —"

"Fifty-four-sixty-three Indian Trail, half an hour. I'll call back. If you've got the item, I'll give you the delivery address."

"It's a plan."

"If you can't do it, tell me now."

"I just said I'll do it."

"Don't take the bike."

"Got it."

"If they don't believe I sent you, tell them I've been awake since last Thursday."

"Okay." An inside joke? Last Thursday. He couldn't forget that detail.

"Okay. Um. Thanks." The line went dead.

Clay stepped back onto the deck and woke his laptop. The slideshow screensaver disappeared, replaced by desktop icons over a photo Natalia had taken last year of Niagara Falls. Clay pulled up the Internet and searched for directions to 5463 Indian Trail. Twenty-three minutes from here.

He could leave now without an explanation. The girls knew he was going bowling tonight. But how long would he be gone? How far would he have to take this person? He went to the living room and stepped in front of the TV.

"Hey." Khloe sat up straighter.

"Mute, please," Clay said.

"Pause." Khloe aimed the remote and hit a button, and the TV at his back went silent.

"A friend of mine needs help with something. I'm not sure when I'll be back, but tell your mother not to wait up if she doesn't want to."

Khloe drew her feet under her and sat up straighter. "What kind of something? What about bowling?"

"Classified kind of something. More important than bowling." That would really send her into a curious frenzy. Oh, well.

"We'll be fine, go ahead." Violet swished her hand toward the doorway, but her eyes lingered on Clay, then darted away. Strange.

Khloe must not have noticed. She crossed her arms, but the drama was deliberate now. "We'll eat all the cookies before you get back."

"Possibly, but I'll try not to be gone long."

In the garage, he stroked the Kawasaki's handlebar, then hopped into the Jeep. Not the roomiest vehicle, but at least it had a backseat. He pulled out his phone and started a group message to Yul and Brandon, and oh yeah, to Scott DuBay. Clay's history with Scott didn't go back to college the way it did with the other two guys. Technically, he'd known Scott for ten years, and he'd tried a few times to get to know the guy, if only to be sure Violet had a decent father. Not that Violet had said anything to make

53

him suspect otherwise. Anyway, he and Scott had never really clicked. He'd offered another invitation tonight expecting a pass, but Scott had surprised him.

He typed a group text. *Rain check tonight. Something came up.* His thumb froze on the Send button. What was he doing?

The right thing. He pressed the button. Marcus had actually called. God must want Clay to help him out.

5

Any minute now, Khloe would come looking for her. After all, a girl only needed so
long to use the bathroom. Violet tugged
open another desk drawer. Empty. There
had to be something dangerous in Clay's
study, anything to justify her planned . . .
betrayal. Really, that was the only word for
it.

She slid the desk drawer shut and ran her
fingers over the book spines sandwiched in
the shelf behind the desk, careful not to
knock over the framed picture. Six-year-old
Khloe grinned at her, wearing strawberry
blonde ponytails and a glittery purple shirt,
perched on a dappled gray carousel horse.
On the shelf below, she and Khloe waved
from another picture frame, thirteen years
old and standing on either side of the Fort
Mackinac sign. If she'd been born to him,
Clay would have a picture of Violet as a toddler too. Or even a baby.

If she were his daughter, would she have turned him in by now?

She moved to the next shelf. Most of Clay's books were classics, from Richard Adams at the top left to Tennessee Williams at the bottom right. All the stuff teachers thought would enhance your worldview. Violet skimmed more titles, but none of them shrieked a warning. Of course, even if Clay did own a book called *How to Bomb the Wicked* or *Killing Pleases God,* he probably wouldn't shelve it next to *The Glass Menagerie.*

Where, then?

She rolled the desk chair over to the oak bookcase. Small items could sit on top, blocked from sight. Gripping the edge of a shelf for balance, she stepped up one foot at a time. She teetered as the chair swiveled under her. She reached over the top of the case. *Please, no spiders, no spiders.* Her fingers bumped the smooth square edge of a picture frame, and . . . a book. The cover felt like textured leather. A journal or something. She brought it down.

A Bible. Black leather cover, silver-edged pages. A name engraved in the lower right corner: *Clayton Michael Hansen.* Violet flipped it open and turned to the copyright. Thank goodness every kid learned by third grade the fastest way to identify an illegal Bible. And there the words were, inarguable. *New International Version.* Her stomach knotted.

"Hurry up, Vi! He's about to toss her into the lake!"

Violet shoved the book back into its place, jumped down from the chair, nearly falling as it spun. She dashed across the toffee-colored area rug and shut the French doors behind her. She backtracked to the bathroom and stared at her pale straw-haired reflection. Five minutes ago, she'd been ready to call Austin and tell him the whole thing was off. Clay might not be her father, but he was like her father. Almost her father. And he was a good one.

Austin had texted a phone number to her this morning, followed by instructions. *When you get to the meeting, text address to that number. Then you run. They can't find out you're a spy.*

Spy. She'd had all day to ponder that title, to break it in. It still blistered, like the narrow-toed pair of heels she'd had to squeeze her feet into yet bought anyway.

What'll they do if they catch me? she'd nearly texted back but stopped herself. Austin was already on the edge of forbidding her mission.

Which she didn't want him to do. Right?

The knock on the bathroom door almost wrenched Violet's heart from her chest.

"You're missing all the best parts," Khloe said from the other side. "Want me to pause it for you?"

"Be right out." Violet turned on the water and splashed her hands through it, breathed deep, and opened the door.

6

He might be taxiing one person or a whole family. Clay drove north, and suburbia melted farther away with every minute. Oncoming traffic thinned. He switched on the radio.

"— with a high of eighty-four degrees and a thirty percent chance of rain for the next . . ."

Clay tuned out the voice for now. News after weather. The top stories would loop in a few minutes. He could get his news online like most people these days, but radio was an untraceable alternative. Probably a lot of other Christians used it too. Had the Constabulary figured that out yet? Could you monitor a person's car radio?

Now in rural territory, Clay switched on the high beams. Ditches and culverts replaced sidewalks, and space grew between houses. Insect kamikazes pelted his windshield.

"And in the top story this hour, Senate Resolution Eight-Six-Three did pass with a vote of seventy-six to fourteen with ten abstentions . . ."

Clay's stomach knotted. Seventy-six senators voted for that pile of crap.

". . . requiring state Constabularies to comply with federal audits of case files and success percentages, among other new protocols. The president has already stated that he plans to sign this into law immediately. He's expected to do so sometime next week."

The first step. Eventually, they'd end up with a single federalized Constabulary. Clay heaved a helpless sigh and switched to a classic rock station. Led Zeppelin, perfect. For now, he'd drive. And try not to think too much.

Right.

Indian Trail proved to be a wide unpaved road pocked with eroded holes. The address from Marcus had to be on the right, since the left side of the road held nothing but fallow fields. There it was, fourth house down. He pulled into the driveway and shut off The Who in the middle of a guitar solo. The Jeep coasted to a stop while he gazed at the house — no, the mansion, and that wasn't hyperbole. This place had to be . . .

Clay couldn't begin to guess the square footage.

He pulled the Jeep up a twisting gravel driveway and parked on the slab of cement in front of the unattached garage. Its door was open, as if expecting Clay. Then again, someone *was* expected. Just not him.

Approaching the back door might seem like skulking, and out here in Farmville, half the residents probably kept loaded shotguns on their mantels. Okay, front door, then. The porch wrapped halfway around the house. A basket of ferns hung from the center, and a flowered vine curled around the lattice on the north side. Clay's footsteps seemed to echo in the quiet that encased this place. No traffic noises, no neighbors talking from across the street, no radio station hollering from somebody's car in the carport. No neighbors or carport at all, actually. The closest house was nearly a mile down the road.

He thumbed the doorbell, and it chimed a four-note melody inside the house. A minute later, a lock clicked, and the door swung open. A lively Southern twang embraced Clay before he even saw the speaker.

"Now, son, you know better than to come to the front door like a . . ."

At the doorway, she stood still. She was

61

portly in a matronly way, clad in jeans and a short-sleeved green sweater, sixty or so years creased into her face. She blinked and smiled.

"So sorry. I thought you were somebody else. How can I help you? You didn't go and break down out here, did you?"

"Actually . . ." A shrug lifted his shoulders. "Marcus asked me to come."

The gregariousness faded from her eyes. "Who? You must have the wrong house."

His heartbeat jolted into overdrive. Had he written the address wrong?

The woman pushed blonde-from-a-bottle bangs off her forehead and began to shut the door. "You have a good night, now."

"Wait." Clay held up a hand. "Please. He said to tell you he hasn't slept since last Thursday."

Her mouth opened, closed, and opened again. Then a laugh burst from her, and she opened the door wide. "My heavens, that man can still surprise the stuffing out of me."

Clay stepped inside, and she shut the door, then bolted it as a sort of afterthought.

"I'm Belinda, and my rude husband is around here somewhere. Chuck! Get your rear in here and acknowledge we've got a guest!"

"Guest? Aren't you always saying he's family?" A gray-haired man walked in from the hall, built like a tree trunk with a beer belly. Under his arm he held a baby in the classic "football" carry. He swung the boy close to the carpet, eliciting a squeal, then spotted Clay.

"Huh. Guess we do have a guest."

"He sent me," Clay said. "Marcus."

Chuck hooked the thumb of his free hand in his belt loop, to one side of his paunch. "And how do we know that?"

"He said to tell us that he's been awake since last Thursday," Belinda said.

Chuck cocked his head.

"There's no way this man —" Belinda broke off to settle her eyes on Clay, as if she hadn't fully noticed him before now. "What's your name?"

"Clay Hansen."

"First names only," Chuck said. "If you're feeling paranoid, make one up, but I'm guessing you didn't."

"Um, no."

The baby beat his heels in the air and arched his back. Chuck set him on his bottom on the runner that connected the hallway and the foyer, and the baby lurched to his hands and knees and crawled toward Belinda's feet.

"So what's the joke?" Clay said. "About being awake since Thursday?"

The couple shared a grin, then Chuck spoke. "Belinda here, she usually makes great coffee, but last time Marcus came by, it turned out a little strong."

"He drank it, though," Belinda said, "and I told him he'd be awake until his next birthday. He just had one last week."

Chuck crossed the foyer to stand closer to his wife. "So, Clay Hansen, did Marcus tell you why you're here?"

"I'm here for . . . an 'item.' "

Belinda's smile buckled. "Oh . . . but . . ."

"Now Pearl," Chuck said. "You knew it was tonight."

She latched onto her husband's arm and nodded hard. "Got everything all packed up, even. But you can't ever be ready, you know?"

She spoke the last words to Clay. He shook his head. "I don't know what — who — I don't know anything about the item."

The baby used Belinda's leg to pull himself to his feet, then toddled over to Clay.

"There's your item," Chuck said.

Whoa. No wonder Marcus told him not to take the bike.

The baby wobbled a moment, then

latched onto Clay's jeans. He looked up for the source of the new legs, discovered a stranger, and let go with a shriek. Belinda scooped him up and rocked him.

"He's right around eleven months now," she said. "We don't know his birthday, but we have an estimate of how old he was when . . . well, when he came here."

Clay's brain tried to keep up. He was here to rescue an eleven-month-old fugitive already in the care of an able, attached couple.

"Marcus should be calling me. He's supposed to tell me where I'm taking . . . What's his name?"

"Elliott." Belinda tugged up the baby's blue-and-white-striped shirt to plant a blustery kiss on his tummy. He smiled, toothless.

"And you don't know where his parents are?" Well, that was obvious. They must be in re-education.

"Nobody knows who his daddy is," Belinda said. "His mother passed away, right before the holidays."

Clay's cell phone chirped, and he dug it out of his shorts pocket. Different number, same area code.

"Hey."

"Yeah," Marcus said. "You got everything?"

Just call me the Toddler Transporter. "Yup."

"Okay. You're going to seven-eighty-two Lochmoor . . ." Marcus gave him the nearest intersection, name of the subdivision, and directions to the street. "It's about twenty minutes from where you are now."

"I know the area," Clay said. "Anything else?"

"They'll probably think you're me. They shouldn't ask any questions, but if they do, just say you can't answer them."

"Um, if they —"

Belinda waved, mouthed something, mimed taking the phone.

"Hey. Be —" *No names.* "Someone here wants to talk to you."

"Tell them later. And thanks."

Before Clay could determine if that meant gratitude for him or for Elliott's caretakers, Marcus hung up. Clay pocketed his phone and shrugged at Belinda. "He said he'll talk to you later. And I got the feeling he wants me to leave now."

"I'll go get the stuff," Chuck said and returned in a few minutes with a diaper bag and car seat.

Belinda settled Elliott inside and chattered as if words could hide the tears that dripped down her face. "It's been harder than we thought, keeping him hidden. Once our

66

neighbor showed up, toting some extra garden vegetables she couldn't use, and I just about forgot to take him up to the playpen before I answered the door. Now, picture explaining that one. She knows none of my grandbabies are that young."

Once she'd finished fastening buckles and straightening straps, she stayed kneeling on the floor and gazed at the baby, who fussed at the confinement.

"I'll make sure he gets there safely," Clay said to fill the throbbing silence.

"Of course you will." Chuck leaned down and half lifted his wife to her feet. "C'mon, now, time for him to go."

Belinda nodded and buried her face in his red shirt, sure to leave a dark smear of tears. Awkwardness piled on more heavily with every second.

When Clay hefted the carrier, Elliott's squirming abated. Clay tossed the diaper bag's strap over his shoulder, and Chuck nodded over the top of his wife's head, then tipped his gaze toward the door. As Clay stepped onto the porch, Belinda shattered into a loud sob behind him. He held the screen door to ease it shut and bore his cargo out to the Jeep.

Young-father instincts could rust but not disintegrate. He installed the base and lifted the carrier into the Jeep, facing Elliott toward the seat, and his hands remembered securing Khloe into their old minivan. They'd bought a vehicle big enough for a small flock of babies. He tossed the diaper bag onto the passenger seat and headed toward Elliott's new family.

The turn into the subdivision revealed small, identical brick townhouses with dark-red siding and narrow walkways to their front doors. Cozy in any other context, now almost claustrophobic compared to Chuck and Belinda's plantation. In a community like this one, a baby might be big news. Thank goodness the drive had lulled Elliott to sleep. Clay pulled into the open garage, his headlights illuminating a mountain of boxes along the back wall.

He switched on the dome light. The diaper bag had tipped forward and dumped a bottle adorned with T-rexes, a mint-green blanket . . . and a plain, legal-sized envelope. He stuffed the blanket and bottle back into the bag.

Across the envelope, someone had written *Elliott*. It was unsealed, the gummed flap tucked to the inside.

An explanation?

None of his business.

He slid his finger under the flap. Ouch.

Paper cut. Really none of his business.

No. He was putting himself on the line here. He was allowed to ask questions. He drew out the folded page, torn from a notebook, blue-lined and red-margined. The same handwriting marched within the lines, small and block and black. Masculine.

Dear Elliott,

I'm writing this because I knew your mom and you should have something of her since you won't remember her. I didn't know her well though, only for a weak. But I learned enough to tell you some things. Your last name is Weston. Your a baby right now, five or six months old I think. Your mom has been gone a couple months.

I guess you'll never see a picture of her, so Aubrey was kind of short and had long brown hair. In case you ever wonder about that. She talked alot, and she could get stubborn. I know now that usually she was stubborn about the right things. Especially you. She lost you for a few days, the Constabulary took you from your grandparents and she was very stubborn about getting you back. She loved you alot. When you weren't there, her face was empty, and when she got you back her face filled back up.

When she saw somebody hurt, she wanted to help them. She helped me a few times.

She tried this crazy thing to trade herself for you, to save you from the Constabulary. She went through re-education and knew how bad it was, but she would have went back if it would save you.

A few other things, less important. She couldn't flip eggs without breaking them. She liked to clean. She liked to read, and she thought it was really important that kids have books growing up. Maybe you'll like to read once you learn how. That would have made her happy.

She died because she wanted you to be safe. I think you were the most important thing in her whole life and she couldn't lose you again or see you get hurt. She was a brave person and I wish she could see you grow up and you could know her.

MB

In the dim overhead light, Clay read the letter twice and tried to ignore his fingers' itch for a red pen. His inner grammarian

70

cringed, but the misused words weren't important.

Elliott was Aubrey Weston's baby. So Aubrey Weston was dead.

What the heck happened?

Of course, he remembered Aubrey. Karlyn Cole's best friend, a member of the Table for the first half of her pregnancy, until she somehow got herself arrested. Her fate was mostly alluded to at subsequent Table meetings, prayed for and discussed in the most abstract terms. Karlyn alone indulged in the grief. Everyone else seemed to slog through the same mire in which Clay found himself: relief that their first arrest casualty was someone else, guilt at the relief, and of course, fear. Always fear, but heightened now. If the Constabulary would prey on an unassuming pregnant girl, they'd not hesitate to grab a thirty-nine-year-old lit teacher who occasionally rode a yellow street bike to clandestine Christian gatherings.

A month later, the fear began to go stale, and Aubrey returned, older behind the eyes, more swollen around the middle. And timid for the first time. After only a few meetings, she dropped off the edge of their little world. Each of them bore some fault for that. When Janelle and Abe questioned the wisdom of welcoming Aubrey back after a denial of faith — Janelle not waiting until Aubrey wasn't around — Clay had tried to remain neutral. Maybe he should have joined Karlyn in fighting for Aubrey.

How had she died?

"MB" had to be Marcus. The next time Clay saw the man, he'd ask him.

A second sheet of paper was folded against the letter. A birth certificate. For Elliott . . . Sobczek. Marcus must have gotten to know some shady people in the last few months.

The Jeep's automatic dome light shut off, encasing the garage in darkness. Light from a street lamp shone through the single window. Funny that no one in the house had opened the door. Maybe they hadn't seen or heard Clay pull in. He retrieved his fugitive's diaper bag, then the slumbering fugitive himself, and stepped up to rap on the screen door's wooden frame.

The door on the other side swung inward to flood the garage with light. Small brown moths fluttered toward the screen door, collided with it, and hung there. A man pushed it open and swiped at the light switch on the wall.

Two long fluorescent fixtures hung from the rafters with fine chains. They flickered on and buzzed above Clay.

"Here he is," the man said. Eyes level with Clay's through bifocals, he stared down at Elliott. He held the door open with one outstretched arm but didn't motion Clay inside.

Protocol did not exist for this situation. Clay lifted the baby carrier into his arms and held it out like a postal delivery. *Just sign here for your new bundle of joy.* What he really needed was a stork suit.

The man took the carrier, took the child, and a strange twinge passed through Clay's chest. He was transferring guardianship of a child from one home to another as if he knew where this child belonged.

The man set the carrier onto the mudroom floor. Clay handed him the base and diaper bag, and he set them down inside as well. He leaned down to cup Elliott's soft shoe in his hand, then turned back to Clay and smiled, ignoring a moth that fluttered past his head into the house.

"We're on schedule, leaving tomorrow morning around six. No one will ever know he was here."

Clay scrambled to decipher the subtext that, as Marcus, he should clearly know. Leaving tomorrow . . . a stack of boxes in the garage . . . Clay peered over the man's shoulder as surreptitiously as he could. The mudroom was empty. Not even a rack of coat pegs hung from the walls.

They're moving. And taking this child with them.

Before the pause could loiter, Clay smiled. "Perfect."

"Thank you for everything you've done. We're so happy to give him a home."

What would Marcus say? A question Clay never expected to ask himself. "I know you'll take care of him."

"We surely will, sir. Thank you."

Clay nodded. *Escape now.* Before his ignorance exposed itself and destroyed this entire operation. "Good luck."

A nod, a smile, and at last a closed door. Clay dashed the several steps to the Jeep and fled. No more of this. Pretending to be someone else, wrenching kids from place to place like some omnipotent social worker. That baby's father might still be searching. No, surely Marcus had attempted to find him. A vague queasiness knotted Clay's stomach. What he'd just done . . .

In the rearview mirror, green lights rotated.

Run.

As if there was any point. But he had to try. The Constabulary squad car gained fast, rode his bumper, and . . . passed him. It

74

rocketed down the road. Cars ahead had already pulled over. Clay's hand slipped on the wheel as he jerked the Jeep to the gravel shoulder.

"What was that, God? A warning? Or are You just cracking up from Your heavenly throne right now?" He leaned back against the headrest and swallowed hard. The air in the Jeep suddenly tasted sour. "Okay, whatever it was, I got the message."

7

Khloe leaned across the Jeep's backseat to whisper in Violet's ear. "I seriously owe you."

Violet shrugged. Her stomach was balled so tightly, she could barely sit up straight. She felt like Jekyll and Hyde. Her Jekyll half wanted to march into this terrorist church and text the address to the Constabulary. Her Hyde half wanted to confess to the Hansens. Or maybe dash off into the night.

Clay parallel-parked on the left side of the street and turned off the ignition. Silence seized them all, him and Natalia in the front seat, Violet and Khloe in the back.

"Okay," he said. "Everybody out."

Violet hopped down to the blacktop and held back as she shut her door, but the noise still sounded too loud. She jumped as Khloe's door slammed.

"Oops," Khloe whispered.

"Shh!" That was Natalia.

They followed Clay single file across the empty street, over to the next block. Violet brought up the rear of their stiff and silent parade. Unseen traffic passed a few streets over, a muted whir, normal people driving to and from legal destinations. Violet glanced back in the direction of the main road, just in time to glimpse a white flicker in the clouds above the horizon. Then another. No thunder, though.

Khloe appeared at her side. "Heat lightning."

"The air got cooler on the way here," Violet said. "Maybe it's a storm."

"Nah, just looks like one."

Ahead of them, Natalia beckoned with a quick, taut motion. They jogged a few steps until they caught up.

This street, Apple Lane, dead-ended into a main road a few hundred feet ahead. Clay had brought them in the back way. They hadn't left the residential neighborhood, but a few of the houses on the left appeared to be used for businesses. Sweet Serenity Massage Therapy, read the sign in one front yard. The next, hung from the porch awning, read Debra's Salon. Clay veered toward the final house, up a redbrick walkway to the door. A black-lettered whitewashed sign stretched above the doorway: J's Little Country Store.

The Christians met here?

He knocked on the door, then glanced over his shoulder. His smile caught the streetlight. Right, because he thought he was helping them find the truth or something.

Violet turned a circle in search of the house number. There, the mailbox: 5682 Apple Lane. She dug into her purse for the phone.

The door cracked open, but no light shone from inside. A female whisper seeped into the night. "He prepares a table."

"Before us," Clay whispered back.

"In the presence."

"Of our enemies."

The door eased open further, still without spilling a bit of light. Clay slipped through the opening into the blackness, and Natalia followed him.

Austin's voice yelled in Violet's head. *"Do not go inside."*

Khloe tossed a glance over her shoulder: *Don't leave me.*

"Come on in, Violet," Clay whispered from inside.

She had to. She scaled the two steps up into the black lair. She'd find a way to leave as soon as she sent the text: 5682 Apple Lane.

The door sealed behind her, and she was lost in a cocoon of darkness and scent. This country store sold candles. Lots of them. A warm hand slid into hers.

"Dad says be careful not to bump into stuff."

Khloe tugged her along, and Violet followed, almost stepping on Khloe's heels. They must have crossed the whole length of the house by now, or maybe the darkness made the seconds feel like minutes. Ahead of her, someone opened a door. She was tugged forward again, into a warmth that suggested this room was usually closed off from the air conditioning.

"Careful — stairs," Khloe said, a second before Violet would have pitched to her death. She gripped a wooden railing and descended one silent carpeted step at a time until Khloe's heels clicked on tile.

Someone flipped a switch, and a bare bulb overhead flooded the room with light. The basement was a storage room piled with boxes, some still sealed with packing tape, others with open flaps poking upward. People clustered, seven including her. Too many for the space in the center of the room, connected to the stairs by a narrow cleared path.

"Welcome, Clay's guests." An older woman, fifty or so, beamed at them. "I'm Janelle."

Aunt Natalia stepped forward, prodded by decorum as always. "Natalia. It's a pleasure to finally meet all of you."

Violet pulled her stare away from Natalia's convincing smile. "I'm Violet."

"Khloe, with a K," Khloe said.

"Say, brother." A young guy with dyed-black hair and an eyebrow piercing stepped forward. "Thought you only had one kid."

Clay laughed as if the guy had made a joke. As if he'd talked to this twenty-something man too many times to count . . . which he probably had. His rolling stride met the younger man halfway, and he shook the outstretched hand with that signature Uncle Clay, life-is-awesome grin. He was as comfortable as Violet had ever seen him anywhere.

"Violet's my adopted niece — Khloe's best friend. I could practically claim her on my tax return."

Not much of an exaggeration, especially during the summer.

"Aha," the man said. "Glad to have you all. I'm Phil, and my beautiful bride is Felice."

Felice couldn't be more than a few years older than Violet. "Our teacher isn't here tonight. He broke his ankle and still isn't getting around very well, but we're praying for him."

Because of course, they prayed to God. Maybe even to the same God that Violet prayed to, just . . . differently.

Janelle invited everyone to sit in a circle on the floor, and Violet braced herself for a creepy chant, or a tirade against the government, or whispered plans to bomb a daycare center. But the group continued their small talk: the latest blockbuster movie, Tigers' box scores, Phil and Felice's new neighbors and their yappy dog. Apparently, no teacher meant no lesson.

Maybe a sliver of her wanted an extremist lesson. Knowledge of their beliefs would help her steer clear, maybe even help her know when to report someone else and when to shrug off their spiritual ideas as misguided but harmless. Austin would protest that, but he couldn't guarantee she'd never be in a similar situation again.

Just send the text.

She would. In a minute.

Her patience paid off about ten minutes later, when Janelle dug into her purse and brought out a leather-bound book with gold-edged pages. Smaller than the one hiding on top of Clay's bookshelf, and burgundy.

Clay gave a small gasp. "Janelle . . ."

"I thought we could read from it tonight, take turns, you know? I was going to write out verses on some paper, like Abe does, but I decided to bring all the verses."

"But we never . . ." Clay's voice faded into a sigh. Phil and Felice gazed at the book with some mix of fear and reverence.

Send the text. Violet's fingers curled around the faux leather handle of her purse, and its fraying edge dug into her palm. If they caught her, what would they do to her?

"Let's pass it around and read some of our favorite verses." Janelle flipped through the book as if she knew the exact page number she sought.

"Oh, awesome." Felice actually clapped her hands.

Violet slid her hand into an inner pocket and tugged out her phone. From inside her purse, with a glance downward, she started a new text message. Brought up the number Austin had given her.

Next to her, Khloe pulled her own phone from her pocket. Surely *she* wasn't texting her current activity to anyone. No, the intermittent movement of her thumbs didn't look like a text. Violet slanted her gaze at the phone. Pinball.

Did Khloe think Violet was doing the same thing? Demonstrating boredom and disrespect for these people? *Khloe, this is serious stuff.*

From Khloe's other side, Natalia's hand darted to the phone and snatched it away. She reached up behind her and set it on an empty shelf, in full view of the whole group. Then she did the same with Khloe's pink clutch purse.

Khloe's mouth rounded in protest, then snapped shut.

" 'Thomas said to him,' " Janelle was reading, " ' "Lord, we do not know where you are going. How can we know the way?" ' "

Oh, Violet knew this. Rick had read it a few weeks ago. *"Jesus said to him, 'Within you are the way, and the truth, and the life. Within you is access to the Father.' "*

Janelle's words didn't match Rick's voice in her head. " 'Jesus said to him, "I am the way, and the truth, and the life. No one comes to the Father except through me." ' "

Of course, this Bible was different. But it didn't sound . . . well, it didn't sound the way she'd expected.

Whatever. Details didn't matter. Not here,

not tonight. Violet's mission mattered. *5682 Apple Lane. J's Little Country Store.* She pressed a final key. Message sent.

8

Forcing them to come might have harmed his cause. Beside Clay, Natalia maintained an interested pose, sitting with her typical model posture and meeting everyone's eyes in turn. But her arm made the barest contact with his, and its rigidness betrayed her. She was scared or angry; he'd know which if he could face her for a second and read her eyes.

He pulled in a breath of stagnant storeroom air and sighed. Khloe's hostility was no secret to anyone in the room, not after the phone fiasco. Violet . . . What was in her head? She'd pulled her phone out first, but then she'd put it away. Maybe she was paying attention.

"Who else wants to read?" Janelle said.

"Pick me." Phil grinned and shifted his seat on the cool tile.

They each passed the Bible along until it rested in Phil's hands. His forehead crinkled as he searched, and the hoop in his left eyebrow stood at attention. "Here we go. This is from Isaiah. I love Messianic prophecies. They make you all in awe when you think about how many years this was before Jesus was born."

Messianic prophecy? Really? Natalia needed to hear something simple, something easily applied to her. *Okay, stop. The Bible's the Bible, right?* And he'd brought his family here to hear the Bible. Which he wasn't even listening to. *Focus.*

" 'But he was wounded for our transgressions; he was crushed for our iniquities; upon him was the chastisement that brought us peace, and with his stripes we are healed. All we like sheep have gone astray; we have turned — every one — to his own way; and the LORD has laid on him the iniquity of us all.' "

Natalia's discreet nudge conveyed her opinion of that passage. Clay elbowed her in return. *Just listen.*

"You want to read something, babe?" Phil held the Bible out to his wife still open, as if one wrong move could crumble it to dust.

"I wouldn't know where to start," Felice said.

Violet shifted her purse to her other side, out of Khloe's reach, and slid her phone into the pocket of her jeans. Next to her, Khloe leaked irritation like a sieve. What, had she tried to use Violet's phone after Nat took hers? Disappointment closed Clay's eyes. *I finally got them to come here. To hear the Bible.* Wasn't God supposed to act in this circumstance, somehow illuminate Himself?

"Maybe we could talk about what we've read so far," Janelle said. "Does anybody want to say something or ask — ?"

Bang-bang-bang.

The pounding on the door petrified Clay's body like an ancient tree, living tissues turned to stone.

"MPC, open up!"

Instantly, they all ceased to be people, became instead a ball of panic winding ever more tightly into itself. Frozen to the floor. Rounded, darting eyes. Then whispers pinged off the cinder block walls.

"We should've moved the location months ago, when —"

"But how do they know we're — ?"

Keep speculating, imbeciles, until they kick in the door. Meanwhile, Clay would do what he did best.

Run.

He'd already sprung to his feet. Survival instinct. He zipped across the room and tore down the black curtain that blocked light from the tiny window near the basement ceiling. He pried at the window. *Come on!* It fell open and left a stripe of rust across his palms. His wife's hand clutched the back of his shirt and trembled.

"Maybe they didn't surround the building." He interlaced his fingers and bent down to form a step.

Janelle's voice filtered through the roar of adrenaline. "That's right, hurry up, and don't make a sound."

Natalia's tiny sandaled foot hopped into the cradle of his hands. She leveraged herself up into the window with both hands and shimmied her way into the night.

"J-Janelle?"

Felice's shaky voice forced Clay to turn and look. Janelle had started up the stairs.

"Somebody's got to keep them out," Janelle whispered, "and I own the place."

"You have to come with us!" Phil said aloud.

"Without a diversion, they'll get us all. If I barricade the door, they'll spend manpower breaking it down. You keep quiet until you're a ways off."

While they debated, Clay vaulted his daughter up and through the window. *Run, baby. Find Mom and don't stop running.* The cops should have pounded on the door again. Should have battered it in by now. But maybe only moments had passed in this haze. He swiveled to find the final person for whom he was responsible.

"Violet, come on." Calm infused his voice, though his heart was trying to punch its way out of his chest.

Violet turned her saucer eyes on Janelle one last time, then stepped into Clay's hands and nearly pitched forward as he heaved her upward. Clay shoved against the soles of her shoes, and she disappeared through the opening.

Bang-bang-bang. "Open up in there! MPC!"

In the center of the room, Phil and Felice clung to each other.

"Come on." Clay beckoned them.

Felice's blank eyes blinked. "We can't just abandon Janelle to . . ."

No time. Janelle had reached the top of the stairs. They were all adults. Their safety wasn't Clay's job.

His slick palms gripped the window frame. He lifted himself up over the drawbridge of window and writhed into a rectangular opening that felt as big as a keyhole. His hands dug into parched grass and wispy soil. He braced his elbows in the dirt and twisted. Free.

A hand gripped his and dragged him up. Natalia. The girls hovered a few feet away. Voices drifted around the corner of the building on a storm-flavored breeze.

"They've got something up against the door."

"Careful, could be wired to something."

To flee, they had minutes. Maybe less. He motioned with one arm and dashed across the field behind the store. God must have provided the quilt of clouds that smothered moon and stars. Not that any of those agents would be looking away from Janelle right now. Clay glanced back once. *Come on, keep up.* The cushion of grass muted their hammering feet. Behind them, not quite reaching them, a weak light stretched across the field. Clay's feet dragged, and he turned back to look. The entire store was lit now, and . . . Another light slithered around the corner of the building. Green. Rotating pattern. Constabulary squad car.

A bitter taste raked the back of his throat. He ran. The muted footsteps behind him pushed his own feet forward. What were the Constabulary doing here? Was it a planned bust?

They'd come the first night Janelle had brought a Bible.

He led them across the first street, all but hurdled the curb, and dashed toward the street where he'd parked the Jeep. By the time the Constabulary organized a true search, Clay and the girls would be long gone. The Jeep waited up ahead. He didn't miss a stride as he tugged his keys from his pocket and clicked the unlock button.

"Okay." The door handle dug into his hand as he wrenched open the driver's door. "Everyone in —"

"Violet?"

The panic in Khloe's voice turned him around. She and Natalia stood there, both rotating in desperate search. Violet was . . . nowhere. Gone.

"She was behind me, just a second ago." Khloe's voice shook.

The Constabulary couldn't have grabbed Violet, not without getting the rest of them. If she'd fallen and twisted her ankle or something, she couldn't call for help.

"Get in. We'll circle the block."

"Absolutely no way, Dad."

Natalia gripped Khloe's arm and pushed her toward the Jeep. "He's right, get in. Now, Khloe Renee!"

The middle name had never dented Khloe's petulance before, so it must be fear that propelled her obedience now.

As soon as the Jeep was in drive, reality vetoed Clay's plan. "I'll take you home first. And then I'll come back for Violet."

"But, Dad, you said —"

"I know what I said." He drove down the street at an inconspicuous, residential-zone speed. Distance dimmed the store's light. "It's too dangerous to lurk around here."

"I'm not leaving my best friend for the con-cops."

"Khloe, I might have to search a little, and I don't want you ending up in the middle of this." Behind him came the sound of a door flinging open.

"Khloe!" Natalia shouted.

Clay's foot mashed the brake pedal to the floor. Something thumped to the ground. He swiveled to look back. Natalia sat alone. She stared at the open door across the seat, her mouth an oval of shock. She threw open her door and leaped out.

Clay jammed the Jeep into park. "No! I'll get her!"

Khloe had run a hundred feet before his first step. His longer strides could catch her, but she zigzagged like a soldier avoiding crossfire. Must have learned that from a movie.

"Khloe, stop." The words burst from him. Natalia gazed back over the field.

"Clay . . ."

He stood closest to the curb, so the tide of red and blue light stained him first. Ahead, at the end of the street, a squad car pulled around to block the way. An officer stepped out. Not Constabulary, just a regular cop. Flashlight in one hand, the other perched on his belt, one twitch away from the holster.

"Need any help, sir?" He walked toward Clay.

"Oh, no, officer, we're fine. Um, we lost our dog and . . ."

Lost the dog. At midnight. But the words were out now. Clay had to sell them.

"She looked like she was going to pee in the car, you know? So we went to let her out and she took off . . ."

The officer's flashlight beam and gaze pivoted toward the field. Nausea pummeled Clay, but the clearing stretched empty under the clouded night sky, void of fleeing teenagers.

"Sir, I have to ask you to leave the area. MPC asked for local backup, got a tip on an unlicensed gathering. Barricaded themselves inside, and we don't know exactly what we're dealing with right now. Just a block away. I need this area cleared ASAP."

"Oh, yeah . . . We saw the green lights."

"You're going to have to leave without your dog for now. We'll keep our eyes open. She got tags?"

"Yes, and a pink collar."

"Okay. Now I need you to get back in your car. You can go around my roadblock up there."

"Thank you, sir." Clay forced his legs to keep a leisurely pace back to the Jeep. Once Natalia had joined him inside, Clay turned the key to start the slow, confined cage. On his bike, he'd be gone in heartbeats.

He shouldn't have brought his family here.

He'd screwed up. Really, in a big way, screwed up.

He drove toward the squad car at a devastating, unsuspicious crawl. By now, they'd probably discovered Janelle's ruse.

"What are you doing?" Natalia's voice drilled into his racing brain.

"He told me to leave."

"Our daughter is out there somewhere, probably watching us abandon her."

Clay maneuvered the Jeep almost over the curb to make it around the police car. This close, the rotating lights made him squint. "I'll double back, but we have to wait, at least an hour. If they see us back here again, they'll know."

"We should tell them."

"Tell . . . the police?"

Natalia glared at him in the rearview mirror. "Obviously not the whole truth, that you're a Christian and pressured your law-abiding family into —"

"That's enough."

She barely paused. "If we explain that we suspected our daughter and followed her here, but she ran away when we confronted her about her philosophical indiscretions . . ."

Right, blame Khloe for his actions, his beliefs. Clay turned the Jeep onto the main road, and a fragment of his heart shook loose.

"Go back," Natalia said.

"Not yet."

Her hand shot between the front seats and gripped the steering wheel. The Jeep weaved.

"Nat, quit!"

"Go back, Clay. That's our daughter!"

"Text her. Tell her we'll be back for her as soon as it's safe." The quiet held a new tension. "What is it?"

Natalia's fingers dug into his arm. "Her phone. It's in the store. On the shelf."

A red light seemed to materialize a few feet ahead of him. Clay's foot slammed the

95

brake pedal.

"Their purses," Natalia said. "The police will have her photo ID, and Violet's."

"Not Violet's. At least, not her phone. Text Violet." Thank God she'd pocketed her phone.

Natalia was right. He had to turn around and go back. He could plow this bulky off-roader right over the curb, over the sidewalk, into the field. He could turn on the high beams and holler for Violet and Khloe until they emerged from their hiding places and ran to the Jeep.

But . . . no. It all smashed into Clay, how this would go down. The police would identify two minors at the scene of a terrorist meeting and inform their parents.

"She's not texting back." Natalia's voice was a rubber band about to snap. "She must've lost the phone. We have to go back."

"They'll never believe we were ignorant of our daughter's terrorist activities if we show up at the crime scene looking for her."

He had to keep driving. Get away now or there'd be no one to release the girls to later. He cracked his knuckles against his palm until the light turned green, then turned the Jeep toward home. *What kind of father are you?* He was leaving his little girl alone in the woods overnight, hiding on the fringe of a search radius. Hopefully, Violet would find her. Parental instinct told Clay that Violet would survive on her own just fine, would look out for Khloe if needed. But if the Constabulary began an earnest hunt . . . The image of Khloe cowering from a snarling, snapping search dog sent his pulse into overdrive.

Dear Lord, keep them safe and give them back to me. Soon. Please.

After a mile of straining silence, Natalia's voice came again, calm now. The sort of calm that stole over a landscape just before the touchdown of a funnel cloud. "If any of us end up in re-education over this . . ."

Janelle was probably already on her way there. *But they won't get us.* The promise stayed lodged in his throat. He had no idea if he could keep it.

9

Clay's taillights faded, and Violet lowered her forehead to her knees. Janelle, at least, was guaranteed re-education. Violet hadn't totally failed, not quite. But her primary responsibility was to Clay, not a bunch of Christian strangers. One blessing shone out from her disaster of a mission: Khloe wouldn't get shoved into re-education if her dad wasn't caught. But in light of everything else, that relief seemed shallow.

Oak bark prodded her back, but Violet didn't move from her knees-to-chest position at the base of the tree. She inhaled the dampening air and looked up into the foliage that rustled its disappointment. Even Phil and Felice might have escaped. Or maybe not. Her phone vibrated, and she pulled it out. Natalia. *Where are you?*

Temporary retreat had been smart of Clay. He wasn't abandoning them. He'd come back when it was safe. In fact, if she asked him to, he'd come back now. Miles away, thunder rumbled. He wouldn't leave her in the rain, would he? She hit Reply. She could say she was hurt. She could say . . .

Her thumb hovered over the phone. She'd done the right thing so far. She had to keep doing it.

Even if it cost her her best friend.

"Violet."

She jumped, scraping her back against the tree. Oh, no. Khloe. Crouched and picking her way forward, her yellow shirt a spotlight against the trees. Khloe half straightened and brushed her wind-whipped ponytail away from her face.

None of this was happening like it was supposed to.

Across the field, through a filter of ferns, sound and light drifted. Green lights rotating. Authoritative shouts. And once, a woman's husky-voiced shout in response. Janelle.

What made a person stay behind and let her friends go free? That had to be true brainwashing.

"Hiding out in the woods? Seriously?" Khloe whispered.

"What're you doing out here?"

"Finding you, stupidhead."

Dumb loyalty. Violet shoved the phone

back into her pocket. No luring Clay back. No "come get me" text to the con-cops. Not yet, anyway, unless she wanted Khloe to know everything.

"Oh. My. Gosh. Violet."

"What?"

Khloe swayed forward. Violet slid toward her through the ferns. "Hey, it's okay."

"Our purses. We left them."

Khloe's purse. On the shelf. Shoved behind a box, but they'd find it. Even if Clay escaped, Khloe couldn't.

"It's over. My life. All over."

Violet snared her hand. "We'll turn ourselves in right now. We'll explain to them that you had no choice, your dad made you —"

"I'm not going to re-ed, Violet. I'm not. Ever."

A chill washed over Violet, as if the rain had begun to fall. "They have your . . . our IDs."

"And they'll search our houses first. We can't go back there. We'll have to go . . . somewhere . . . until all this blows over."

Khloe folded forward, gripped her knees, and cried. Violet wrapped her in a hug and rocked her.

"Shh, okay, it'll be okay." Violet rubbed her back. She had to go find a con-cop and identify herself as their spy. But she couldn't walk away while Khloe clutched her shoulders.

"Dad and Mom, they'll look less suspicious too, if I disappear for a couple days. Then they can say they didn't know about me."

"And what'll we do, sleep in a tree and survive on fern leaves?"

Khloe shuddered against her.

"There's nowhere to go, Khloe."

Khloe pulled back. "This is going to sound crazy, but like a month ago, Daddy told me that if something ever happened . . . I think he meant something like this."

What in the world was she talking about?

"There's a house at the end of our block, with a big deck added on. He said somebody would come for me."

"Somebody." Good grief. Khloe wasn't talking about some random person's porch. She was talking about one of *their* porches. A resistance haven.

"They don't have to know I'm not a Christian."

No, they didn't.

"But if you want to turn yourself in, you can, Vi. They might go easier on you if you do, who knows how it works. I just can't start my senior year in re-ed. I can't do it.

By August, September, this will all be over. Things will be normal. We'll laugh about it."

In the distance, but not far enough, voices shouted to each other. Khloe hugged herself, and Violet glimpsed the two of them at ten years old, when Natalia was about to discover that they'd used her credit card to buy forbidden concert tickets online. Violet still couldn't say how they'd expected to get there, but their logic said that Khloe's mom couldn't deny them transportation once the tickets were purchased. Now, despite her speech seconds before, Khloe gave Violet that same stare, the one that said, *How do I survive this?* The one that said, *Please don't desert me now.*

The voices felt closer. Violet dragged Khloe several feet deeper into the trees, until Khloe started to run alongside her. Their fingers wove into a sweaty link.

Khloe was soon panting. "Can't we . . . stop? Climb a tree — or something?"

"No." Violet tugged her onward.

"Why not?"

"They could bring dogs in." A tree would be nothing but a trap.

They had to run as far as they could, as fast as they could. Violet's T-shirt stuck to her back. Feathery ferns and rough weeds tried to trip her. In the dark, she miscalculated distances, and her elbow left skin on a tree trunk.

Eventually, lights filtered through the trees before them. The voices had faded and then disappeared. Violet slowed, stopped. Khloe still clung to her hand, pressed the other to her side.

"Ow," she whispered.

The lights ahead blinked. No, moved. White lights, red lights, and that whooshing sound. Traffic. Probably a main road, judging from the speed of the passing cars.

"Violet?"

"Let's hope there's a street sign. We have to figure out where we are."

She set out toward the road. Rustling grass behind her assured that Khloe was following. She emerged into a gust of wind that dried the sweat on her back and raised goose bumps on her arms. The scent of rain filled the air around her. Perfect, if a dog tried to trail them later. *Come on, sky. Rain already.*

She jogged a hundred yards or so to the closest road sign, where a residential street butted up against the forest and intersected with this road.

"I know where we are," Khloe said behind her.

"Me, too." Mostly.

"I can find my street from here. And that porch."

Yes. This was it. God had sent Khloe back here to continue Violet's mission.

But Khloe would find out.

No, she won't. Violet linked her fingers through her friend's. Their charm bracelets clinked against each other.

"You're coming?" Khloe's whisper lilted with hope.

"Where else would I go?"

"Home, stupidhead."

Violet squeezed her hand. "Overrated."

10

His steps should echo through the foyer, down the hall, into the kitchen, but his tennis shoes were silent. Like the house. Like his wife, who slid away into their bedroom and shut the door. What Clay needed right now was the edge of a cliff to jump from, a plunge into water that would numb the silent screaming in this house. His keys dangled from his fingers. He rubbed the key to his bike, cold and ready. What he needed right now was an infinite blacktop carpet rolled out before him — curves and blind hills and speed.

He rushed to the rack of hooks hung across the room, below Natalia's calendar of waterfall photos. The keys jingled as he shoved them onto a hook. No bike. No running. He wasn't that man anymore.

This loss wasn't the one that tore holes in his dreams. Khloe was still alive, still healthy . . . and imperiled by his own stupidity. Clay wandered to the fridge and pawed for a Dr Pepper. The can chilled his palm.

Go back there and get her.

He popped the can's seal. Cool fizz sprayed his palm and tickled his throat going down. Maybe pop would settle his stomach. He gulped half the can before he noticed the blender parts in the sink. The glass container lay on its side, not even soaking. By now, the thin pink coat of strawberry smoothie had dried and crusted. Khloe had whipped up and gulped down one of her creations before they picked Violet up tonight for the Table meeting.

"Did you wash the blender or leave it in the sink?"

"I'm such an irresponsible teenager."

Clay turned the water on hot and squirted some soap onto the dishrag. Behind his eyes, something burned.

"Lord," he whispered. "You know I can't go out there and get her. So You bring her home."

"What are you doing?"

He didn't turn to face Natalia's brittle voice. "Praying."

"Ironic." She stomped to the sink and slammed the faucet off. "Do not clean that thing."

Clay angled a glance. Natalia's lips pressed into a thin, trembling line. He wanted to reach out and trace her cheekbone, her lips. He flipped the water back on.

"You detest dirty dishes left in the sink."

"She'll never learn to do things for herself if we're constantly —"

"That's your biggest concern for her at this moment, that she learns to wash the dishes?"

Natalia grabbed the blender jar's handle, and it slid from Clay's soapy grasp and smashed against the lip of the sink, fracturing the base away. Jagged pieces of glass dropped into the sink. Soap dripped onto the counter.

"You come home from dragging us there and making us criminals and then leaving your child to fend for herself, and the first thing you do is clean the kitchen."

Leaving your child. Clay's wet hand curled around the counter's edge. "That isn't what I did, Nat."

She picked up a sudsy sliver of glass and tried to find where it fit.

"You can't glue it back together."

She hurled the jar into the sink, and it shattered. "Fine."

"Natalia . . ."

She crossed the kitchen, snatched up his

keys, and offered them on an open palm. "Is this what you really want?"

No. Of course not. Clay fought for a deep breath. He dried his hands on the pale-green towel. Behind him, the keys rang against each other as Natalia shoved them back onto the rack. Her steps retreated down the hall, and a door shut.

Lord, I can't do this. Clay stalked to the back door, then into the garage. He shut the door behind him.

Crossing the garage left him breathing like a marathoner, smothering on the feelings that bubbled up as soon as he could be alone with them. He straddled the bike and gripped the handlebars.

His brain resumed working for the first time since he'd heard the *thump* of his daughter throwing herself from the Jeep. The Constabulary had her ID, and they would come here to interview her parents. A year ago, they would have come at a decent hour, likely dinnertime, when they could be more sure of catching interviewees at home. These days, rumor said they enjoyed showing up at random times. Just because they could. They could knock on the door right now.

They would question him. About his daughter. About their household beliefs.

Or maybe they wouldn't question at all. Maybe they'd simply inform him that his daughter was in their custody.

Clay bent forward over the bike but couldn't relieve the stomachache. "Lord, what are You doing?"

Minutes streamed away. Somehow sitting astride the bike held a hollow comfort. He wouldn't start it. He wouldn't ride it off into the predawn. These days, he was a man who stayed, and Natalia knew that. She was scared, that's all.

When his gut eased and his brain settled, he trudged inside. Silence tried to push him into the garage again, but he shoved back.

"Nat." He walked through the kitchen, the living room, the den, their bedroom. "Nat?"

Only after he'd searched every other room in the house did he admit that he'd known her location the whole time. He pushed Khloe's door open.

Natalia lay stretched out on the bed, hands curled around Khloe's sketchpad as it rested on her chest, staring at Khloe's gallery on the far wall. Pencil sketches, mostly people. Mostly strangers. An elderly woman she'd watched in the park. Twin boys chasing each other through the mall playground. But Violet's profile hung there too. And Clay's favorite sketch of all, Natalia pulling cookies from the oven.

She flinched as Clay stepped into view. Her head turned toward him. "You're still here."

Clay pressed his back against the door trim. "I was in the garage."

"Oh." She pushed herself up, reached over the edge of the bed, and set the sketchpad on the carpet.

"We need a plan, Nat, for when they come tonight, or tomorrow. What to say, and . . . you know."

Stiffness infused her as he spoke. She drew her knees up and huddled in the center of the bed. The nod barely came.

"I . . . Nat, I . . ." *I know this is my fault. I know I'm helpless to fix it.*

"I need to know now. What are you going to do?"

"Do?"

Her green eyes wouldn't rise to his. The rigid curl of her body pushed his mind toward the old panic. Two paths formed inside him. Leave or stay. He stepped into the room, across the indigo carpet. He sat on the edge of the bed, and Natalia's eyes remained on the lavender quilt.

"I'm going to find our daughter," he said. "That's what I'm going to do."

When his arms enveloped her, she didn't pull away, didn't shove at his chest, didn't impale him with verbal spears. She crumbled against him. She grasped the buttons of his shirt. He breathed in her mango shampoo, and his lips found rest in her hair. *Lord, You'd better help us. Soon.*

11

This mission was worth the possibility of Khloe's outrage. It was worth crawling under a stranger's deck and hunkering on a blue plastic tarp while rain dripped between the boards into her hair. But possibly nothing was worth a close encounter with the largest spider Violet had ever seen. She cringed against the house siding and tried to squelch the whimper between her fingers.

"Smash it, Khloe."

"With what, my bare hands?"

Violet shut her eyes against the spider's nearness. Its web hung just feet away. *It's not on you.* She could reason as long as she couldn't see the thing.

"Okay, Violet. Keep your eyes closed and scoot back along the side of the house."

Violet shuffled backward on her knees, off the tarp, hands squishing in layers of moist leaves that must have been gathering for a decade. Her head collided with a support beam.

"Ouch."

"Don't look yet."

A dull *smack,* then another that crinkled the tarp.

"He's smashed now. You're okay."

Violet's eyes opened and found the lifeless black blob at the edge of the tarp. She shuddered. "Um, thanks, sorry, I . . ."

"Freak out? Like that's news to me." Khloe slid her wedge back on. "If I'd known the future, I would've worn better shoes."

The moisture from the ground had begun to seep through Violet's jeans. She ducked the beam this time and crawled back to the tarp, although her hair was already dripping. She touched the phone in her pocket. Damp but not soaked.

She had noted their shelter's address as they sneaked through the front yard to the back. She'd text it as soon as Khloe surrendered to her drooping eyelids. When the con-cops arrived, Violet would feign shock and, once they were separated for questioning, defend Khloe the best she could. They'd owe her for her service.

Right.

She shivered as the rain continued to drip down her back. "If I'd known the future, I would have brought a jacket with a hood. And an umbrella."

"And a smoothie to go."

"Naturally."

They'd discovered a small cooler half buried in leaves, crammed full of bottled water and protein bars. But despite crouching there for a few hours, neither of them was hungry.

"I don't know how I can be sleepy and wet at the same time, but I'm getting there." Khloe leaned against the side of the house and tipped her head back.

Yes. Fall asleep. "Well, it's like four in the morning, and we've probably spent all our adrenaline."

"Yeah."

The pattering rain on the leaves of a nearby maple tree filled the next few minutes. At last, Khloe's lips parted in slumber. She looked even younger now.

Violet tugged the phone from her pocket and tapped the screen. *11317 Joshua Dr. Under the deck.*

If she hit Send, and if Khloe somehow did decipher the truth . . . The possibility tightened Violet's breath. Khloe was the one person in the world who'd always wanted her. But now Austin did too — in a completely different way. In a way that made Violet want back, a way that made love songs seem less cheesy. Success in this mission would fill his eyes with respect. Maybe he'd even realize she was adult enough to love him.

The scales tipped back and forth, Khloe on one side and Austin on the other. But when Violet added the weight of duty, of morality, to the scale . . . it crashed down on Austin's side.

She hit Send. Pocketed the phone. And waited.

In less than ten minutes, a quiet scratch came from the lattice to Violet's left. Khloe had been the one to find the section that could be tugged off and pulled back on from the inside. How did the Constabulary agents know where that opening was, and why the stealth? Unless . . . this was Clay.

The lattice popped off, and a man's silhouette filled the space. Not wiry Clay — this man's shoulders were almost too broad to fit through the opening. The dark obscured his features, but he jerked a beckoning gesture, so he must be able to see them. Then he disappeared. He couldn't be Constabulary. He'd gotten here too fast.

Khloe still slumped against the siding, eyes closed. Violet nudged her chilled arm, and she yelped.

The man's bulk blocked the space again. "Shh!"

He must be a resistance member. A terrorist. This was the kind of man who would strap on a bomb, stroll into a shopping mall with it, and set it off.

Khloe shivered and gaped at him.

"Come on." The man's whisper barely reached them over the drumming rain.

No, no, no. The mission had been over. Bust this house and go home. Violet couldn't go further. Couldn't follow this man and pretend to be like him, couldn't let him take Khloe.

"Who are you?" Khloe whispered, about three times more loudly than he had.

"Come on. No time."

"My dad's going to come here to get us, as soon as it's safe to come. He —" She scrambled back as the man dropped to his knees and pushed his way through the opening in the lattice.

"That's not. How this works." His words seemed to come in pieces, one-two punches to the air. "Nobody comes here. Just me."

"B-but . . ."

"And if your dad told you to come here, then he knows you'll be taken somewhere safe."

Khloe's lips pressed together, uncertainty

116

and hope clashing in her eyes. *Somewhere safe from re-education.* That's what she was hearing, and if she had to hang out with Christians in that "somewhere," then she would.

Violet pressed a hand to her pocketed phone. *Austin, what have I gotten myself into?* But if this guy thought she and Khloe were Christians like him, hiding . . . They'd be safe then. Christians didn't hurt each other.

Maybe this shelter *wasn't* the end of the mission. Maybe Violet was supposed to play a part, dig for information, truly infiltrate the resistance network. The concept sent a tremor all the way to her fingertips.

The man's gaze shifted to Violet and stayed on her, studying, waiting.

Khloe's hand circled her wrist and pressed her cold charm bracelet against her skin. "Vi, I think we should go with him."

Not breaking eye contact with the man, Violet nodded. *I'll go with you, all right. And then I'll turn you in.*

He backed from the opening and vanished again. Violet stuck her head outside, not expecting the rain to feel so wet. After all, she already was. She crawled forward and stood up. She sensed Khloe trailing behind her.

"Follow," the man said quietly. "No talking."

Without waiting for even a nod, he set out through the rain at a clip that forced Khloe to trot. She slid once on the wet grass, and Violet caught her arm.

"Jerk," Khloe whispered to the man's back, but he led at too far a distance to hear her. He zigzagged them through yards and down sidewalks. The path seemed random, but he moved too intentionally for that. In only a minute, he had robbed Violet of all directional bearings. She knew east only by the watery sunrise that winked around rainclouds.

In about five minutes, they reached a red pickup truck. The man opened the passenger door and motioned them inside. Khloe slid to the middle without hesitation. Hand on the inside door grip, Violet froze. She darted a glance over her shoulder. The man's face held no kindness, no smile, only an earnestness that burned like a torch behind his brown eyes. He looked ready to shove her inside.

She hoisted herself into the truck and pulled the heavy door shut.

After a few silent minutes of driving, the man pulled into the parking lot of a vacant strip plaza. Violet's mouth turned to sawdust. Her hand crept to the door handle. Without looking down, she reached for the lock button.

He parked the car but left it running. "Anything electronic on you?"

"No," Violet said.

"Your phone, stupidhead."

Violet elbowed Khloe, but not hard enough for the man to see.

He held his hand out, palm up.

"You drove us over here to steal my phone?" Violet shrank against the truck door.

"You can keep the phone. I need the battery and the card."

No way.

"Duh, Violet." Khloe elbowed back. "They could be tracking it. You want the con-cops to find us?"

"I'll turn it off."

The man rubbed his neck with one hand. "They'd still be able to track it. I can't take you any farther. Until you give me the phone."

"I'll take it apart and keep the pieces."

"No."

"Omygosh, Vi." Khloe shoved her hand into the pocket of Violet's jeans.

Heat surged into Violet's face, not embarrassment but a sudden desire to slap her best friend. She pushed at Khloe's wrist and shrank back until she collided with the truck door. She must have other options. She didn't have to give this man her only way to call for help.

"This is my job. Keeping you safe."

Either she pretended to trust him or she triggered his suspicion, which would be a lot more dangerous. Or she abandoned her mission and Khloe and took off across the parking lot. Not an option.

She willed her hand not to tremble as she relinquished the phone. The man worked for several minutes, first removing the phone's silicon case, then producing a tiny screwdriver from the glove box. His hands were quick and sure, and soon her phone was in three pieces. He returned only the lightless shell. The rest he shoved into a Ziploc bag, also grabbed from the glove box. He fetched out a black marker and scrawled her name on the bag, then pocketed it.

"Wait here." Mindless of the rain, he scrounged through the truck bed and got back into the cab with a black wand about a foot long, yellow letters proclaiming the brand as well as the function. *Handheld Metal Detector.*

"You're kidding." For the first time since the man had shown up, Khloe's voice quivered.

"You could have a tracker under your skin. They're getting more common."

That couldn't be true. He skimmed the wand a few inches over their bodies, without a chink in his matter-of-fact expression. He resumed driving only after stowing the wand back in the truck bed.

When Khloe shivered, he stripped off his rain-spattered green jacket and handed it to Khloe. "Here. It's dry inside."

Khloe spread it over her shoulders. "Thanks. We were under there for hours."

He nodded as if he knew, but how could he? They'd had contact with no one. Well, the owner of the house had walked out onto the deck once, in that first hour after they'd crawled under it. They hadn't been able to discern anything about the person except white shoe soles and a slight shuffle. But maybe he or she had been able to see them.

Khloe huddled closer to share the cover, but Violet couldn't drape herself in this criminal's coat. She sat up straight against the truck seat and crossed her arms. The man didn't seem to notice.

"You said your dad was coming to get you," he said. "I need to know what happened, the details."

And Khloe told him. Even the details.

Even her plan to hide until after the con-cops interviewed her parents, until things settled down when they couldn't locate her.

"You said they have your ID." He signaled a turn and veered onto an entrance ramp. The highway sign said they were headed north. Good to note, since his truck didn't have a compass.

"They do, but in a few days, I'm sure they'll have more dangerous people to hunt than us."

"Where's your church?"

"It's, um, in a storeroom, and —"

"The country store? On Apple?"

"Yeah, that one."

Quiet thickened, seemed to heat the air. The man's hands tightened on the wheel. "Who . . . do you know who got away?"

And who didn't? The desperation in what he didn't ask hung there, though he obviously tried not to show it. He knew those people. Violet continued to face the windshield but sneaked a glance at him as she spoke.

"I don't know about Phil and Felice. I know they arrested Janelle."

His left hand latched onto his neck and squeezed. A long minute passed while he drove one-handed.

"Okay," he finally said. "Anybody else —

that you know for sure? Who's your dad?"

"Clay Hansen," Khloe said.

His eyes darted over them as if seeing them for the first time. "I thought he just had one daughter."

"I'm his daughter. Khloe, with a K. Violet's my friend. She just came with us to church. Are we allowed to ask your name?"

"Marcus."

Violet forced herself to look fully at him, this terrorist who was also a person, a man with a name. A man who believed he was doing the right thing.

"Marcus what?" Khloe said.

He shook his head, but he had a last name too. A life, a job, friends, family. Maybe his parents had filled his mind with lies since he was old enough to read.

She turned her head to stare out the rain-smeared window. *Dear God, please use me to help him.*

"Well, anyway, Marcus." Khloe shifted beside her. "If you could help us hide for just a little while, that would be perfect."

"The Constabulary won't stop looking for you. I'll get you back to your parents. But it'll take time."

Time to gather evidence. Her mission glittered anew. She'd done the right thing, after all. Was still doing it, shivering here in this truck, across from a terrorist. A person.

"Violet?"

She jerked her attention back to Marcus. "Sorry. Wandering mind."

"Your parents. They weren't at the meeting."

"They're not . . ." *Come on, play the part. You can do this.* "They're not Christians. They'd turn me in, if they found out I was one." There, see? Not even a lie.

"Would Clay take you in?"

Wait . . . would he? Khloe was already nodding. "Of course."

Violet curled her hand around Khloe's. "Maybe."

Khloe gripped back. "And Mom would too."

Marcus nodded.

Violet watched his route and knew roughly where she was. She could stay for a few days, even a week, and report back to the Constabulary as soon as she had enough information.

Marcus exited the highway. Blacktop roads widened as the houses and plazas along the way grew sparse. The rain faded to drizzle, then stopped. He shut off the wipers and cracked the windows to let in a whir of storm-flavored wind. At last, he turned down a rutted dirt road. No houses on the left. On the right, they came with a quarter-mile of space between. Violet's breath tightened. No public place to flee to. No one to hear a scream.

At the fourth driveway, Marcus turned.

12

When they pounded on the door shortly after 6:00 a.m., Clay was awake and ready to lie. He hadn't managed to sleep longer than ten minutes, but Natalia jolted beside him in bed as if she'd been yanked from a dream.

"Stay here, remember?" He leaned close to kiss behind her ear and breathed in calming mango.

She stared at him as he pulled on his jeans and crossed barefoot to the door. By the time he got downstairs, the pounding had come again. He took a deep breath — *Lord, this might be wrong, but help me lie* — and opened the door.

A man and a woman stood on his porch, at least a whole foot of difference in their height though their hair was about the same length — less than an inch. They wore uniforms the color of campfire smoke and badges that caught the sunlight mostly concealed by rainclouds. A gray squad car lurked in the driveway. Clay's mouth turned to cotton. He'd unconsciously expected an unmarked vehicle, suits, badges they'd pull out and put away. The danger was the same no matter how they were dressed, but somehow this incarnation held a more visible threat.

"Mr. Hansen." The man took a step forward. "I'm Agent Naebers, and this is Agent Dell with the MPC. May we come inside, please?"

"It's six in the morning." Clay exaggerated a blink.

"Yes, sir, we're aware of the time. Do you know where your daughter is, Mr. Hansen?"

Even prepared for it, the question was a punch to the chest. Clay forced a frown of confusion. "Sure, she's in bed."

The agents exchanged a glance that nearly required Naebers to lean down. When they refocused on Clay a moment later, Agent Dell took on the speaking role. "If she's here, we'll have to speak with her. Why don't we come in, while you check on her."

"Why don't you wait here." Clay tried to glare at them.

Another glance, and then a nod from both of them.

Clay let the screen door fall shut and

jogged up the stairs. He passed Natalia hovering in the doorway of their room, shrouded in her blue silk bathrobe, arms crossed, face blank. As they'd planned, he stepped into Khloe's room long enough to "discover" her absence.

His daughter's essence caught him like an undertow, even stronger than it had been a few hours ago. He needed to hug Khloe. He shuffled across the carpet and stood in front of her gallery, grazed a finger over each sketch. Her hands had left these pencil strokes. Her eyes had seen these images and recreated them. Khloe.

"I'm going to be an artist, Dad."

"Looks like you're one already."

"No, I mean a real one that studies art in school and stuff."

None of the schools she wanted would take a student with a philosophical record.

Clay left the room with the long strides of a father whose concern is growing but hasn't morphed to panic yet. He called loudly enough for the Constabulary agents to hear.

"Khloe?"

Natalia wandered into the hallway. If the agents were peering upward through the screen, through the banister, they'd see her. She rubbed her eyes and yawned.

128

"What's going on?" Her slippers scuffed behind Clay.

"Khloe's not in her room. . . . Khloe! You'd better be in this house somewhere!" Real desperation seeped into his voice, unplanned, but if truth helped him lie, so much the better.

Natalia stilled as if she'd just become aware of the company her husband had left standing on the porch. She took a step toward the stairs, froze, and then hurried down, finger-combing her hair. *Nice touch, Nat.* Clay continued through the house, searching each room and intermittently calling his daughter's name.

Natalia's raised voice punctured his half act, half daze. "There's some kind of mistake."

Clay's heart rate spiked for real and brought him rushing before he realized she was cuing him. He burst into the foyer as the two agents pushed their way past Natalia.

"What do you think you're doing?" Clay planted himself in front of them. "You can't just come into my house."

"As of yesterday, yes, we can." Agent Naebers propped one hand on his hip. "Maybe you don't watch the news."

What? Natalia's gaze grasped for Clay's,

and she nodded. They could come in here uninvited, without a warrant? *Okay, calm down.* Right. Force nonchalance as these intruders stood in the foyer and conducted an impromptu interrogation. At least they couldn't search the place . . . right? He'd scoffed at himself for moving his Bible last night, but paranoia might actually save him. They'd never think to move the small refrigerator in the basement, no longer used, where he'd hidden the Book in the space alongside the compressor.

"Mr. Hansen," Agent Naebers said. "Your daughter's not here, is she?"

"She . . . she doesn't appear to be."

"And do you know where she was tonight?"

Avoiding the agent's eyes wouldn't throw suspicion on Clay. He'd only look like a father ashamed of possible negligence. And he could screen the guilt they'd surely see in his eyes. He dropped his voice. "I guess I don't."

"That's all right, because we do."

Naebers handed over a small, clear baggie from the pocket of his uniform shirt. Khloe grinned at Clay from the driver's license, red tints in her hair exaggerated by the photo's high color. He'd braced for this very piece of plastic, yet faced with it, he couldn't draw a breath. Almost as if they were the regular police come not to interrogate but to inform him of some awful accident.

"Mr. and Mrs. Hansen, I'm with your son, Clayton. He's fine, but I need to talk to you about your daughter. . . . There's been an accident."

Clay blinked. No time seemed to have passed. No one stared at him. The cold sweat didn't break out under his shirt. He wasn't eleven years old, and this moment wasn't about his sister. He was thirty-nine, and it was about his daughter.

"Where is she?" Natalia's voice trembled, and not in pretense.

"She attended an unlicensed gathering tonight, about five miles from your home. At least one Bible was confiscated."

"Where is she now?"

"It seems that several suspects got away, Khloe included."

"Then she'll come home." Natalia took the baggie from Clay's hands and cradled it, eyes glued to the photo.

"The bust took place almost five hours ago, ma'am. She'd have to be walking pretty slowly."

Natalia's fingers curled around the license, and the agent seemed to lean back from her glare. "I know my child, Agent Naebers, and

131

I'm telling you she is not part of whatever went on at that meeting, and she has no reason not to come home."

Agent Dell stepped forward, hands up, though her voice offered no surrender. "Mrs. Hansen, I know this is hard to take in right now. But sometimes teenagers surprise even their parents, start to explore dangerous philosophies —"

"What kind of mother do you think I am? If she were getting involved in that garbage, I'd know, and I'd put a stop to it, and I wouldn't need the help of the Constabulary."

Garbage. Clay pulled in a breath of composure. She was acting. That was all.

"I'm just trying to reassure you both," Agent Dell said. "You wouldn't be the first or last parents to be shocked by our visit. It doesn't make you unfit parents or even below-average parents. We'll be patrolling the neighborhood until Khloe's whereabouts are determined, so if she does come home, we'd appreciate a call."

"So you can lock her up somewhere?" He hadn't meant to snap. Now everyone else in the room was staring at him. Natalia looked ready to interrupt. *You've said enough, Nat.* "When our daughter comes home, we'll deal with her ourselves."

"Re-education for minors is mandatory." Agent Dell stepped forward several more heel-clacks. Her hands closed over Natalia's, over the bagged license. "I'm sorry, but I'll need this back."

Natalia stared down at her. An invisible tug-of-war ensued for the next few seconds. Clay stepped between them, severed both their grips, and caught the plastic card as it fell toward the floor. He held it out to Agent Dell, and a knife twisted in his stomach.

"Thank you." The license slid from view, into her uniform pocket. Evidence. His girl's smiling face was evidence. "Were you two home last night?"

So they were going to ask, after all. Clay nodded.

"*I* was home." Natalia stared at the wall.

"Mr. Hansen?"

"I was home for . . . most of the night."

"Most?" Natalia's eyes shifted to him, and even though she was acting, the look in her eyes dismembered him, piece by piece.

As if she weren't acting.

"Anything that might be helpful for us in constructing a timeline for Khloe?" Agent Naebers's dark gaze skated between them.

"No." *Agree with me, Natalia. Let's get them to leave.*

"Probably not. I'm not sure."

"Just briefly, then. Mr. Hansen, where did you go last night, and when did you arrive home?"

"Just a ride. On my bike." The script they'd agreed on. Surely she wouldn't deviate from it.

Agent Dell tapped a toe against the wood floor before seeming to catch herself. "Did you have a dispute? Did Khloe witness it?"

"Natalia broke the blender. And no, Khloe didn't know about it. We don't fight in front of her."

"We actually don't get to fighting. You're not here long enough."

Stop, Nat, stop. Heat washed upward from his neck to his hairline, bright as a sunburn against his sandy hair, he knew. All three of them could see it. "These agents don't need to hear about our personal —"

"So I threw the keys at him and told him to go for a ride, as if he needed to be told. He was gone for a few hours, at least. I don't know when he got home exactly. I'm a hard sleeper. And since it's going to be your next question, no, I don't know when Khloe had the opportunity to sneak out. I guess with her father gone, anything could have happened."

Clay barely heard the two agents offer Natalia their card and leave with a warning against the misconception that parents could deal with philosophical crimes. A bud of pain was slowly opening somewhere in his body, blooming outward in thorny tendrils.

He stood at the door, not seeing its painted white surface inches from his face, until Natalia's hand closed around his arm. He turned. She stood there, so close, so beautiful.

He buried the bedrock topic and dug into a safe, shallow one instead. "They can just walk into people's homes now, whenever they feel like it? I didn't hear about that."

"They recategorized philosophical crime. Terrorism."

"That's not new."

"I guess it wasn't part of the legal definition before. But anyway, it means they can enter any privately owned structure at any time, if they suspect . . . well, what they have to suspect is pretty vague."

His mind was absorbing only a portion of her words, distracted by the howling of the other, unspoken topic. He leaned against the front door, and seconds slipped away.

Natalia read his thoughts and sighed. "You said you were worried about pulling it off. So I thought, you know . . . method acting."

He swallowed, but the bitter taste lingered in his throat.

"Clay."

" 'With her father gone, anything could have happened'?"

"Did I say anything that wasn't true?"

The thorns converged in his stomach. "How about your use of present tense?"

She took a step closer, and the calm in her eyes flickered. "Poetic license."

"Or a little too much method."

"Do you even know what you did last night? You drove away without Khloe. You drove away from her."

Again.

Her legs folded until she drifted down to the bottom step. Her arms came up to cover her bowed head. "And I can't even think, so don't bother telling me I'm not being fair."

As if he had the right to call that one, anyway. "Natalia."

She wasn't crying, but she was curled so tightly on the stair, like a soft, wounded creature trying to become too small for any more wounds. Clay knelt beside her. *Look up. Look at me.* She didn't move.

Instinct swerved toward the only open path. He had nowhere else to steer. "I'll be back in a while."

"Have Khloe with you."

With his shield or on it. He stood, then bent toward her. He ran one finger over her hair, lightly, so that she couldn't feel it. So that she couldn't see him hold the sense of her close to himself, mango and shine, satin skin, green eyes that almost believed in him. In this moment, if she knew the precious-ness of those things, she might spit the knowledge back at him. Maybe he deserved no less.

He stood over her. *Say something, Nat.* She sighed and turned her head toward the wall, a quiet knot of self-preservation.

Everything crowded too close, even the ghost that had been silent for weeks this time. The Constabulary agents had awakened it with their somber, notifying faces. Hilary, her ten-year-old face waxy against the white pillow. The beeping machines. The tube down her throat. The panic in his chest when Dad pulled him away from her hospital door, when Clay came home from school to their impassive faces.

"Mom? Dad? Did she wake up yet?"

He walked to the kitchen and snagged his keys and could suddenly breathe again. Escape the present, if not the past. But pushing his sister's memory away only made room for everything else. Natalia and Khloe

137

and the man he was still trying to be.
He straddled the bike. Turned the key.

13

"You're going to catch cold in those clothes. Come on upstairs and grab something dry." Belinda, their new hostess, led Violet and Khloe through a spacious foyer with furniture that belonged in a museum. Red velvet–upholstered chairs with wooden feet, carved like the paws of some big cat. A dark wooden table. Someone had spent hours whittling leaves and flowers and vines down each table leg. A wide burgundy-carpeted staircase wound a spiral on the far side of the room. Halfway up, Khloe stretched out her arm and bumped Violet's bracelet with her own. Violet nodded at the soft *clink*. They were still together.

And nobody was going to harm Khloe or brainwash her. Not that this bottle-blonde grandmother seemed inclined to brainwash anyone, but personality and appearance couldn't override the Christian ideas in a person's head.

Their chauffeur had stayed only minutes after delivering them, which was just as well. Violet stayed at least three arms' lengths from his hulking frame and broiling gaze. Belinda sent him on his way with a travel mug of coffee and hugged him before he left, as if he were more teddy bear than grizzly.

Subconsciously, Violet must have expected some sort of military bunker or mobster penthouse, because her first step into this house had caused a ripple of surprise and relief. And Belinda didn't need a name to become a person. Her compassionate smile and Southern twang loosened the knot of fear inside. Violet could think more clearly now. Observe. Gather evidence.

The hallway Belinda led them down was narrow and ridiculously long, with rooms on either side. This house must have more than a dozen guestrooms.

"You'll sleep in here." Belinda motioned them ahead of her, into a room with ivory walls, two twin beds, and two old oak dressers. All the furniture looked to be about a hundred years old.

Someone had stenciled blue and red flowers over one wall, as well as a border around the whole room. Khloe reached out to trace the petals. Even when hiding from the

Constabulary, she couldn't lose her artistic self for long. She stepped closer to a floral painting on the far wall, probably analyzing its use of light or color or something.

"You'll want to sleep soon, but first things first." Belinda opened a walk-in closet and turned on the light. "Pretty sure this room's got both your sizes."

Someone had installed shelves on two of the closet's paneled walls, and stacks of clothing filled most of them. Violet picked up the nearest pair of jeans and unfolded them. Size five.

"Where did all this stuff come from?" Khloe's voice drifted over Violet's shoulder. She stepped around Violet to paw through a pile of bright T-shirts.

"Resale stores, clearance racks," Belinda said. "There's been a collection going for a few months now."

"You take money from people?"

Belinda's laugh was too loud for the small closet. "My heavens, no. My husband and I pick up things when we can. Marcus does, too. But most of it's from someone else."

"A resistance fighter like you?" Was that admiration in Khloe's voice? Surely she couldn't be won over with a closetful of hand-me-downs. But she browsed as if she were at the mall, slow steps from one shelf to another, touching every piece of fabric in sight.

Khloe, these people are not all as safe as your dad.

"Don't know that I count as a fighter. I'm just a hostess. But yes, from someone like me. She's well-off and wanted to use that somehow, toward the cause. Most of my closets are stocked like this one."

Khloe held up a hot pink shirt and tilted her head at the graphic, a blue tree with branches spreading up to the neck.

"Once you're changed, you looking for bed or breakfast?"

"Bed," Khloe said.

Yes. They needed to talk, and not in this woman's hearing. "Bed sounds good."

"One last thing." Belinda hefted about half a pile of sheets and quilts and moved them to the other side of the closet. She shoved the rest of the pile aside as well with a soft grunt. "Now where is it . . . ?"

Her fingers ran along the paneling. She pushed with the heel of her hand, then sat back a moment on her heels, lightly panting.

"Darn that man and his precautions, I can't even find it myself."

"Find what?" Khloe crouched beside her.

"It's right here. Used to have a little knob

to pull, but Marcus took it off and reset the door so it opens to the inside and . . . well, shoot, where . . . ?"

Her fingernail lodged in a seam between two panels, and a low door swung into the wall. Khloe gasped.

"Now, girls, we've never had a Constabulary agent search this house. Never even seen a squad car on our road. But if something ever happens, you hide here until someone tells you the coast's clear. Flashlights in there, water and snacks, not much elbow room, but you'd both fit easy."

Khloe brushed her hand along the paneling. "This is the coolest house in the world."

Violet folded her arms to keep from shaking some sense into Khloe while this Christian lady watched. Once Belinda was out of the room, though . . .

Amusement gathered in the creases around Belinda's smile. "About half the upstairs closets have rooms like this."

"Why?"

"It was built in the early nineteen-hundreds. We're guessing these are servants' quarters. My husband didn't want the walls paneled at first, but there's no other way to hide the doors."

Belinda chatted a few more minutes about

the history of the house and a tunnel in the basement that stretched several hundred feet to surface in the woods, which must have been used during Prohibition. She might have talked for hours, if Khloe hadn't yawned.

"Enough history lesson for now. Y'all get some sleep, and I'll make breakfast whenever you wake up."

Halfway out the door, she pivoted back to face them.

"I promise, this is the last thing. My husband, Chuck, he's off in some cabin with his fishing buddies right now. He'll be back tomorrow, and if you're still here, he might ask about . . . well, your faith. Please don't take it personal."

"What do you mean, our faith?" Khloe said.

Good question.

"Well, he believes there's a God out there somewhere, sure. I do too, most days. Used to be enough for us, but around the winter time I noticed a slow change, and now he questions pretty much everyone we harbor."

"But you're Christians. You're in the Christian resistance."

Confusion crinkled Belinda's face, then smoothed out. "Sugar, the resistance fighters, or whatever you want to call us — only

144

about half believe in Christianity. The other half of us just believe in freedom."

Violet took a step back. Something here didn't add up.

"You're tired." Belinda retreated a step too. "We'll have a chat in a few hours."

Violet nodded, Khloe shrugged, and Belinda disappeared down the hallway.

Khloe shut the door after her. "I'm definitely wearing this tree shirt in the morning. Let's see if they have any pajama pants short enough for me."

Violet grabbed some size-medium sleep shorts and a random shirt in her size, V-neck, salsa red. She turned toward the wall and stripped off her wet top and jeans. Khloe's voice rattled in the background of her brain.

If they weren't Christians, why did Belinda and her husband and half of these resisters do what they did? Either something *else* made Belinda as illogical and dangerous as a Christian, or she *wasn't* illogical and dangerous. But if Belinda was a logical, safe person, she wouldn't harbor dangerous people. Or work with dangerous people.

The shorts slipped from Violet's hand. She plopped down beside them on the bed. Her brain was turning into one of Khloe's smoothies. She had to sleep. In the morning, all of this would make sense.

In the morning. Friday morning. Austin would be texting her like crazy. Her fish would be hungry. She was scheduled to work a cashier shift, and tomorrow was payday. Good grief, what was she doing? She had a good, normal, everyday life. What would happen to all of it? She tugged on the cotton shorts and crawled under the covers.

"I think we're okay here," Khloe said. "Belinda's not even a Christian. And that Marcus guy knows my dad, so when it's safe again . . . My plan's going to work, Vi. I won't have to go to re-ed."

Everyday life had become, well, dispensable. Small. "You heard what he said about the con-cops. They don't give up."

"I'll be the one that got away."

Until her best friend turned in the people hiding her.

14

Only the most despicable husband would leave his wife in a hospital waiting room, waiting for their daughter to . . . Clay choked, huffed in a breath, and hit the accelerator. The car revved with its eternal death rattle. He jerked the wheel, and the back end skidded on slush. Four in the morning, and the road crews still hadn't cleared the aftermath of a blizzard that had ended six hours ago, or seven, or maybe eight. He hadn't been keeping track of the time when he charged through the hospital doors. He'd wanted the snowflakes to float around him and consume him in silence, save him from Natalia's gulped tears and Khloe's repeated gagging. Hearing his baby throw up didn't stab him so badly anymore. But the confusion of a five-year-old, the whimpers, the questions — they drove him down the corridor, to the elevator, to the doors, outside, just to hear the silence of the snow. And by then, of course, the blizzard had ended.

"Daddy, does hair always grow back?"

Finding his snow-covered car in the parking lot hadn't been planned. Nor had inserting the key and driving away. Natalia would awake from her bedside chair to discover Clay's absence, and a shouting match would probably follow, because she didn't understand. He could breathe here, inside the heated car, wipers streaking the windshield, away from the smells of disinfectant and his daughter's vomit. Away from the possibility of screwing up Khloe's final weeks. Days. Hours. The doctor wouldn't speculate beyond that, but soon. *Not rallying like we'd hoped, Mr. Hansen.* She'd die, and Clay would have to figure out how to live, a father without a child.

He didn't want to.

The car found its own way, the way his bike always did, some sort of unconscious, man-to-machine telepathy. Highway, highway, miles, miles, exit, streets, streets.

Snowdrifts piled against houses as if trying to knock them over. The houses huddled against the wind on either side of the street in uniform dilapidation. Weather and entropy had flayed white paint from the siding. Chunks of space gaped in brick foundations. Duct tape held a sheet of plastic to one door, where the screen should be. Probably not one whole car sat in the overly populated driveways. Tire gone here, window gone there, not a hubcap in sight. An entire neighborhood of missing pieces.

Clay coasted down the street in his clean, intact three-year-old car. Breaths came deeply now, rhythmic. Maybe some thugs would trickle down the porch steps from both sides, clenching baseball bats. Maybe they'd break a taillight. Maybe they'd drag him from the car and leave him stranded on the snowy street, or take the bats to his body. He eased off the accelerator again, down to twenty miles an hour. Fifteen.

Doors and windows didn't open to him. No one even saw. No danger here.

Was danger what he wanted? Was Natalia right when she called him an adrenaline junkie?

He slid through a stop sign and turned onto a new street. The car made its way back toward the hospital. Miles and highway again. His headlights speared snowflakes that dashed themselves to the ground.

Clay parked and slogged to the entrance farthest from the pediatric wing. In the building with his daughter, but not in the room. Closer, too close, not close enough.

He plodded past the information desk, down corridors. He'd been gone almost three hours. Had Nat noticed?

Or worse, had Khloe noticed?

He had to go back. Into that room. Sit and hold his baby and wait for weeks, or days, or hours. But his feet balked at the elevator. His hand refused to press the button. The door slid aside, and a petite brunette in pink scrubs rushed past him without meeting his eyes. He took one step before the elevator closed, then stared at the smooth door. *I can't.*

He didn't remember finding the chapel, didn't remember entering it. He had nothing to say to God. There likely wasn't a God in the first place. But his knees buckled right there in the aisle, hit padded carpet. He crawled to the front, to the table that bore a cross, a menorah, a Buddha, other statues he didn't recognize. All these ways to God. Assuming He was out there, and assuming He listened.

A burning ache seized Clay's stomach. He tried to get up, tried to go to Khloe, but his legs seemed paralyzed. Natalia said she needed him, Khloe would want him there, yet he couldn't move.

"Can I be of any help?"

The voice at his ear jarred him up from

his hands and knees. He pushed to his feet and gripped the shiny curved wood of the pew.

"So sorry." The man had been crouched next to Clay, but he stood now as well. Short, husky, black hair and brown skin. His tan suit jacket hung unbuttoned.

"It's fine." Clay squeezed the back of the pew. "I was just leaving to . . . to . . ."

"How is he? Or she? The person you're here for?"

"Dying." The word zapped the air with an electrical shock. He couldn't stay here with this kind-eyed man in this sacred place, with the truth he'd just voiced into existence. But his body quaked from inside out. He couldn't walk away.

"Sit, please. You look like you might —"

"There's nothing wrong with me." But Clay sidestepped into the second row and sat, hands still curved around the pew in front of him.

"Would you like to talk? Or pray?"

"I've never prayed before. And I don't . . . I don't think I want to talk."

The man sat down in the front row. "Up to you, of course."

"I think I want to die."

He must have said those words aloud, because the man's hands shifted in his lap.

And now more words came, unstoppable, an avalanche.

"She's not rallying, they said. Not this time. Fever and throwing up. A five-year-old shouldn't have to . . . She doesn't know why she's sick. She asks me, and what am I supposed to say? Is it God? Is it me, did I do something, did her mother do something? And there's no knowing when she'll go, the fever spikes and every time I think this is it, she's going, but she doesn't, and I need to be in that room, I have to be there when Khloe goes, but I can't. I can't."

His face pressed into his arms. He rocked forward.

"Oh, God, don't make me go in there. Don't make me go in that room."

Warm hands gripped his shoulders. "God won't make you."

By the time Clay realized where he was going, his bike's back tire had nearly fishtailed more times than he dared to count. He'd get a ticket if he passed a cop, but he couldn't seem to let off the gas. History flickered in and out of his head like a windblown candle. The chaplain pointing to the cross as superior to all the other relics on that table — a gutsy proclamation even twelve years ago — and an hour later, Clay's stilted prayer that mostly eluded his memory. God had delivered Khloe from the tumor, just as the chaplain had promised. Now He had to deliver her from the Constabulary's evidence against her.

Where was she right now? The June sun cast mirages over the pavement far in front of him, and his bike gunned forward as if trying to splash through one before it disappeared. He coasted onto an exit, and next thing he knew, he had parked on the third level of the cement garage, paid the admission fee, and stepped into the Sterling Heights Museum of Arts.

He power-walked the first level, past fiberglass cases of tarnished spearheads and grotesque dolls and crumbling pottery. Khloe preferred modernity. He took the marble stairs two at a time. Here. Level Three. The nineteenth and twentieth centuries, when artists depicted life as it was, not as they interpreted it to be.

"Slow down, Dad. Look. No, I mean seriously look."

"I'm looking. I just don't see what you see."

"You're such a nonartist, it's so tragic."

He stalked through long doorless rooms, one after another. The coolness seeped into his skin. He'd passed maybe a dozen people since he stepped into the museum. Maybe

153

some of them were teachers like him, not at work on a Friday morning in June. Art teachers, perhaps, planning the way he often did over the summer, though his version was usually to read a classic and develop essay questions along the way.

Khloe's favorite painting hung on a north wall in this wing. He passed through another doorway and halted. Here. Slow steps carried him closer to the painting, two girls sharing secrets and a handful of nuts that looked like white grapes.

"Okay, but Dad, the nuts don't matter. Look at the way her hair ribbon pokes up on the one side, and the dust on their feet. I wonder what they're talking about."

"They were real girls?"

"Maybe, but it's like . . . like they're all girls. And they're me and Violet."

He was standing too close now, just feet away. One of these girls was Khloe. One was Violet.

Violet.

Her parents hadn't called yet. No shock in that. They might not realize her absence for another day or two. But the Constabulary . . . Violet's ID had been left behind too, on the shelf beside Khloe's. Those agents should have asked about her.

Unless they didn't need to ask, because

they knew where she was. His stomach turned over.

They'd caught her.

She wasn't with Khloe. She was in custody. And Khloe was alone.

Clay turned his back on the painting. His two girls — really, Violet was more his daughter than Scott and Diane DuBay's, if you gauged that by the time she spent at her parents' house. Clay had lost Violet, too, not just Khloe, but the flood of guilt over Khloe always came first. Since she was born. No, since she was diagnosed at three with a tumor outgrowing her brain.

He had no business here, prowling a museum for memories. But he'd braced for death so many times that his heart tried to fit this new absence of Khloe into the "forever" category without fighting back. Unacceptable.

"With her father gone, anything could have happened."

Holing up in a museum counted as "gone." Clay strode from the room without another glance at the painting. He practically ran down the stairs and to his bike. Somewhere in those woods behind Janelle's store, Khloe had hidden. If he couldn't find her there, he would go to that house with the deck Marcus had told him about, at the end of the street. The deck he'd told Khloe would be a safe haven if she ever needed one.

Common sense didn't overtake him until he'd nearly reached Janelle's store. He wasn't supposed to know where Khloe's illegal activities had taken place. Biking there and searching the woods would be an admission, a stamp of guilt. The Constabulary had raided their meeting less than twelve hours ago. Agents would be prowling those woods for days.

He drove past Apple Lane with a sourness on his tongue and a burning in his stomach. Two Constabulary cars squatted in front of the store. Clay didn't brake. The squad car that passed him in his own subdivision flattened the last of his action-seeking panic. No, he couldn't look for his daughter — not in the woods, not under that deck, not anywhere at all.

Someone else could, though. Someone they weren't circling like vultures after carrion.

Clay parked the bike in the garage, and the reality of his uselessness nearly knocked him off his feet. He curved a hand around the handlebars and relaxed into the reassurance of his bike, the speed and autonomy. His eyes closed, and he breathed for a long minute.

He pulled out his phone, and it almost slipped to the cement floor. Oh. His palm was sweaty. He'd gotten a text sometime in the last hour. Omar.

Prof H, you seen Zena's newest argument? She sent it yesterday.

No, he hadn't checked email yesterday. Or pondered Willa Cather's writing motivations. Why had fiction ever mattered so much? He opened a reply to Omar, stared at the empty text, and hit cancel. He punched in a number instead. It rang, rang . . . *Formulate your clues. Let him know without letting them know.* Because of course, they were listening.

"Hello." Marcus's voice came over a faint whir of wind. He must be driving. Probably between contractor jobs.

"You have a minute?"

"Sure."

The silence dried Clay's mouth, worsening the sour taste. Something caught in his throat, and he cleared it with too much noise.

Marcus waited on the other end, silent and unhelpful.

"It's my daughter. Khloe."

If Marcus truly did lead the resistance movement, he had to know about the raid by now. He could help Clay decide what to do.

"What about her?" Marcus's voice betrayed no gravity at all, merely curiosity.

"She's missing."

An appropriate beat, a feigned shock. "You call the cops?"

"No, man, they came to me. The Constabulary. They said she's mixed up with . . . some pretty serious garbage."

"Dangerous."

Understanding clicked. The guy had asked about the cops, and now with this one word, Clay was being cued. And warned. All at the same time. Marcus knew exactly what Clay wasn't asking.

"Tell me about it." *Literally, Marcus, I need you to tell me about it. Please.*

"Well."

"Maybe tonight . . . If we could get some drinks and just . . . I don't know."

The pause hovered a moment, then released on a sigh almost too quiet for the line to pick up. "Where?"

"I was thinking that pub on Hamlin. It's not usually too crowded."

"I know where it is."

"So . . . maybe six or so?"

"Sure. Six."

"Thanks, man."

"No problem." The line clicked.

15

Thinking like a fugitive must take practice. When the doorbell rang, Violet's only thought was relief at the interruption to Belinda's bird-watching stories. A heartbeat later, Khloe's and Belinda's panicked, darting gazes reminded her that she was supposed to be scared.

"We'll hide upstairs, in the closet." Khloe scurried toward the foyer.

Belinda shot across the room faster than her age and figure should have allowed. She grabbed Khloe's shoulders and turned her toward the hallway on the opposite side of the kitchen.

"I left the front door open." She barely whispered the words. "Whoever that is, they'll see you go upstairs. Remember the tunnel I told you about? Down to the basement, center of the west wall."

Khloe ran. Violet trailed her down white-painted wooden stairs into cool, carpeted darkness.

"Where's the light? We won't find the door without the light." A small *thump* sounded a few feet ahead of Violet. "Ow! There's a couch or something. Watch out."

Violet stretched her hand along the stairway wall and flipped a light switch. The room was furnished with only the burnt-orange futon in front of her and a rocking chair in one corner. Violet's eyes roamed the room. This basement was some sort of gallery for antiques. She couldn't identify most of the rusted contraptions hanging on two of the walls. The other two were dark and paneled.

Khloe had already dashed to the farthest paneled wall and stood in the center, pushing at the seams. "This is west. Why won't it — ?"

A section of the panel caved under her hand as it swung open from the other side, a sort of revolving door. The opening couldn't measure wider than two feet or taller than three.

Khloe bent to enter the tunnel. "This is a new experience for me, ducking through a doorway."

Violet followed and pushed the door back into place. Darkness settled over them. Not a sliver of light reached through the door seams.

"We left the lights on out there," Violet said.

"If they come down here, Belinda will pretend she left them on, herself."

"Yeah."

Violet tried straightening up and bumped her head. She reached up, and soil grazed her fingers, then a timber support structure. She pulled away from a would-be sliver. The wood felt old. Or maybe the tunnel just smelled old. Moldy, for sure.

"Who do you think's upstairs?" Khloe whispered.

Violet stretched her arms and found the walls on both sides. "She said the con-cops have never been here."

"Always a first time."

"Or maybe it's a Christian come to visit."

"Let's hope so."

"You seriously mean that?"

Water dripped in the far distance. The new silence seemed to heat the space around Violet. But Khloe needed to hear this.

"Khloe." Violet blinked, but the tunnel's features didn't materialize, even dimly. "These people aren't safe. They should be in re-education, all of them. Even Belinda."

"And even my dad?"

"He's a Christian."

"So if it was your dad, you'd volunteer for re-ed. Just to save his brain from illegal beliefs."

The dirt walls absorbed their rising voices. Violet rubbed her thumb over a charm on her bracelet, bit her lip, then forced a whisper out. "I think I would."

"Actually, I was considering it," Khloe said. "I was thinking, 'Why don't I turn my whole family in and get a head start on re-ed? I'll be out the same month I graduate.' "

"All I'm saying is —"

"I could have two parties. A graduation party and a re-ed release party."

"These people are —"

"I could invite everyone from school. They could give me release presents, like graduation presents, only better. I could decorate with signs that say, 'You've been right all this time. I really am a freak.' "

"Khloe . . ." Wait a minute. All this time?

The dripping and the quiet rejoined them.

"I don't want you thinking you can trust Belinda just because she seems . . ." To care about other people, to risk herself for the freedom of strangers. "Just because she seems nice."

Drip. Drip. Was Khloe even listening?

163

Violet stepped forward into the black. "Khloe?"

Sticky strands draped her face. She froze. Something nearly weightless dropped onto her scalp. Leaves? Dirt? Moving dirt? Light and nimble, scampering over her forehead and down her cheek, grazing her lip —

The scream tore from her throat. She clawed at her face, snagged legs and furry body and tried to throw it, but where was it now?

"It's on me, it's on me, it's on —"

"Vi!" Khloe's hands clamped down on her arm, then her shoulders, and shook her hard. "Shut up!"

"Spider, Khloe spider, Khloe spider!"

"Shut up!"

Violet held her hands out at her sides and shook them. She stomped her feet and pawed at her face. Her skin prickled as if a hundred legs crawled over her. She brushed at her bare arms, her jean-clad thighs. Khloe smacked her shoulder, searching the dark, then found her hand and tugged.

"They might've heard you. Come on."

Violet was pulled a hundred feet or so before her brain rebooted. She jogged beside Khloe and used her free hand to skim the air in front of her. Better a handful of spider than a mouthful. She tried to stop

164

shaking.

"I'm sorry," she whispered.

"Tell me again when the con-cops storm in and haul us away."

Eventually, yeah. Violet swallowed a surge of tears.

As they ventured farther, the smell of dust and mold gave way to a richer scent, soil and some kind of foliage. A few more minutes of forward shuffling and Violet's hand skimmed a wall not unlike the ceiling above them — dirt and wooden beams.

"This is it." She stretched her hand from side to side and caught a length of rope, hung from somewhere above them.

"We should check it out." Khloe's hand settled above hers on the rope. "Even if nothing happens today, we might have to leave fast, you know? We should know how."

Violet shimmied up a few feet before colliding with a broad wooden square. After a minute of swaying on the rope, shoving with her shoulder and one hand, she budged the door a few inches upward. It lifted more easily after that, until it fell open with a muffled crash.

"See anything?" Khloe whispered from below.

"Hold on." Violet hoisted herself through the opening and into . . . not a forest. A shed, no more than six feet square.

Sunlight sifted through the grimy window and glinted off points of dirty steel hung on a pegboard, mostly trowels and shovels. Two rusty flat-tired bikes leaned against one wall. A green-and-gold braided rug had covered the trapdoor and now lay folded between it and the rough wood floor. There was a wheelbarrow, a watering can, white plastic bags of soil. An old hose was looped over a hook halfway up the far wall.

"Well?"

"It's a garden shed. Come on up."

Khloe squirmed up and over the edge of the trapdoor. "We escape the house to hide in a shed?"

"Someone probably put it here to hide the hole." Violet swiped a tendril of web from her arm. She stood and headed for the shed door. It shouldn't be locked from outside.

"Think we can see the house from here?"

"Let's find out." The knob gritted against her hand, left a layer of dust, and turned.

The steel shed crouched in a clearing along with a high blue pickup truck. Thick woods screened them on every side, but determining the direction of the house wasn't hard if you knew about the tunnel.

Khloe turned a circle, and sunshine

waltzed through the strawberry highlights of her hair. "Where do we go? If we're trying to escape?"

"Anywhere but —" Violet pointed back from where the tunnel had come. "Maybe the truck's a getaway."

No, definitely not. No license plate. She stepped over the uneven, weed-choked ground to the driver's side. Broken headlight, crumpled bumper, major damage all the way to the crushed doorframe. Whoever had been driving last didn't get out on this side.

Khloe rounded the front of the truck to the passenger side. "This side's fine, except the window's broken out. I wonder . . ."

She ran back around the truck and latched both hands onto Violet's arm.

"There's blood inside."

16

The bloodstain spread over the back of the driver's seat, about the size of a sand dollar. Violet stood on the running board, head poked through the broken-out passenger window, and tried to spot other clues. The truck looked normal inside, other than that brown stain. Her legs nearly buckled, and she locked her knees. *Keep it together.* Whatever happened here, it was over now.

"Somebody died in this truck," Khloe whispered from behind her.

"I think you have to lose more blood than that to die."

"Okay, so blood loss didn't kill him, the car wreck did. He was driving and someone shot him straight through his body and —"

"The windshield would be broken, then. Besides, there's no bullet hole in the seat." Violet hopped down from the running board.

Khloe padded over the grass as if someone

might overhear her steps. She wobbled on tiptoe and leaned toward the truck window but kept her hands balled at her sides.

"Okay, so they shot him in the back. And when he fainted and drove off the road and died, they hid the truck here."

"Khloe, who are we saying shot this person in the back?"

"I can't see Belinda doing it, so probably her husband. Or Marcus. He's kind of scary."

But a gunshot wound wasn't the only thing that could make a person bleed from his back . . . while driving and then wrecking his vehicle . . . Okay, yeah, gunshot did seem most likely.

Her thumb rubbed a charm on her bracelet. The starfish, painted red. Bright red.

She had to stop these people. She had to get to a phone.

"Vi? What're we going to do?"

Violet turned a circle, three-hundred-sixty degrees of indecision. The glassless window, the sunlight glaring on the chrome bumper blurred as if her eyes refused to see the evidence. She rotated slowly until she faced the edge of the clearing. The tree-fringed path pushed deeper into real forest.

"Something bad happened, obviously.

And if Belinda finds out that we know, she might . . ."

If Belinda would protect someone, even knowing they'd killed a person, then surely she'd have no problem threatening two teenagers who knew too much. Violet shuffled toward the trail that ended at the clearing. After ten feet, Khloe's hand clawed into her shoulder.

"Is that . . . a . . . ?" Khloe's voice pitched upward. "Omygosh, it is."

To one side of the trail stretched a slightly raised section of dirt. Nettles and a lone white wildflower had sprouted, and the ground had settled almost level, two feet wide and maybe six feet long.

Violet shivered in the thick heat and crossed her arms. "It's a grave. They buried someone out here." Killed and buried?

A blue jay squawked from nearby as if to prod her forward. *Look closer. Make sure.* No way.

"It's just some dirt," Khloe said. "Belinda didn't kill anyone."

"I'm not saying Belinda did it. Maybe the Christians did it and put the body out here."

"To frame her?"

"Or because it's somewhere nobody would look. Maybe Belinda doesn't even know."

They crept nearer until they stood over

the low mound. Mute seconds slid by. Violet bent to pluck the flower. The root system lost its grip on the loose soil, and she suddenly held the entire plant. She twisted the slender stem around her finger and pulled it tight. It pressed a ring onto her skin.

Khloe shook her head. "It's dirt. It's an anthill or something."

"Six feet long and wide enough for a person?"

"It's not a grave. It's not."

Violet's ice-capped thoughts were starting to thaw. "We have to call the cops."

The words seemed to paralyze Khloe. She didn't blink.

Violet put a hand on her back. "There's no way around it. If someone buried a body here . . ."

The end of the mission beckoned like a lighthouse. And there had to be justice now too, for whatever body lay eroding beneath the dirt. She'd call 911 right this minute if she had a phone.

"Violet, no. We can't. We don't know anything. Come on, we've got to go back before Belinda realizes we're gone."

"You'd do literally anything to stay out of re-ed, wouldn't you? Like, literally."

Khloe gnawed her lip and stared at the dirt.

They'd only been out here a few minutes, but that doorbell could have heralded the UPS man. Belinda could be on her way down that dark tunnel right now to give them the all-clear. And if the Christian resistance had hired her because she didn't *look* like a psychopath but was willing to do their dirty work . . .

That's really incredibly unlikely.

Still, she could call someone, send someone to find them. Someone with a car, while they plodded on foot. Someone who knew the woods better than they did. Where would they end up, if they started in any direction? Running off now, especially without a phone, would be stupid.

"Okay. We'll go back. But I'm going to find out what happened, Khloe, and if they killed somebody, then —"

Khloe's head shook, and her ponytail bounced around her face. Violet grabbed her shoulders, and she twisted away.

"Stop it. You want to get killed by a bunch of Christians?"

Khloe stilled her thrashing, but her whole body quivered. "They're not like that. My dad's not like that."

Maybe not.

Khloe grabbed Violet into a hug that, from anyone else, would crush ribs. "No cops,

172

not yet."

Even if that wasn't a body, Violet had to report to the Constabulary. Soon. *Tell Khloe the truth.*

Violet pulled away from the embrace and stalked toward the shed. Her legs trembled again. She looked away from the mound of earth as she passed it, but the truck drew her eyes. Shiny, blue, and crumpled up on one side as if punched by a giant.

If only Austin's friend could see this.

17

Clay hadn't meant to arrive half an hour early, hadn't done so with the hope that maybe Marcus would be early too. But he'd been here forty-five minutes. By now, he'd read every sign in the place, from the painted chalkboard announcing the beer specials to the bubble-lettered poster board tacked on a wooden pillar. *"Summer Concerts: Peace, Love, and Music Every Wednesday!"* He was waiting for his second Blue Moon as well as Marcus.

A table away, two gray-haired guys in greasy T-shirts had finished their chips and salsa and waited for their meals. Clay had opted for a table rather than the bar, but until Marcus arrived, privacy wasn't necessary. Maybe he'd go perch on a stool for a minute.

The door opened, admitting a burst of evening sun around a bulky silhouette. Marcus stood a second too long before crossing the threshold. Clay lifted one hand to shoulder-level as the man's gaze scoured the room for him, and Marcus beelined to the table.

Small talk would be in order. Clay squashed the questions he wanted to volley and nodded at the chair across from him, but Marcus was already pulling it out and sitting down. His gaze took in the building's whole interior in a few seconds, probably noting the exits.

Clay spoke over Sheryl Crow from the overhead speakers, clinking silverware from the back kitchen, and the small crowd's voices bouncing off the vintage brick walls and oak floor. "Thanks for coming."

"Sure."

Before Marcus could say another word, the buxom brunette server hustled up to their table. She set down Clay's drink with more flourish than the establishment warranted.

"Blue Moon, no fruit." She swiveled her gaze and her hips toward Marcus. "Nice of you to show up."

"What?"

"This poor, lonely man's been sitting here for an hour."

Marcus's eyes flicked between Clay and the girl as if he suspected a prank.

"Not that long," Clay said.

"Pretty close."

Hadn't anyone trained her on how to talk to patrons? Or maybe she was untrainable where tact was concerned. Khloe would be. Not that Khloe would ever work in a bar.

"Anyway," she said, "what can I get you?"

"Coke, please."

Her smile pinched at the corners. "One Coke, coming right up."

Clay hadn't even considered that Marcus wouldn't drink a beer with him, but it sort of fit the guy's personality. Marcus probably qualified as a control freak.

"You've been here an hour?"

"She's exaggerating. I was a few minutes early. No big deal." Clay ran his finger around the rim of the weizen glass.

Marcus looked skeptical, but after a moment, he planted his elbows on the oak-edged table. "Well. They're okay."

"You mean Khloe."

Marcus nodded.

Okay. She was okay. The miracle surged into Clay's throat, threatened to choke him up. He hid behind a long sip of beer and tried to focus more on the citrus-sweet flavor than on the gift Marcus had given him.

Screw small talk. Clay lowered the glass

and blinked hard. "It's been a long day."

Marcus's gaze sliced to Clay's glass, then cut away to travel the room. Another nod.

"So you've seen her? Talked to her? Is she scared, is she — ?"

"She's okay. And her friend. Violet."

Oh, Lord, You did more than I thought You could do. "When they questioned Nat and me, they didn't ask about Violet. And they had to know she'd been there. Her ID was at the scene. I thought they must have her, didn't need to ask."

Marcus met his eyes again with a sudden sharpness, leaned forward an inch or two. "How long have you known her?"

"Violet? Her whole life. Since she and Khloe were seven. Her dad works mall security, her mother's . . . Well, I don't know, Natalia's never liked her mother. I don't think she has much of a home life. She pretty much lives with us every summer."

The server hustled over and delivered Marcus's Coke with less fanfare than Clay's beer had received. "Enjoy."

"Thanks."

She was already heading back to the kitchen.

Marcus tugged the red plastic cup closer and took a sip, then sat back and . . . did

177

nothing, said nothing, simply sat there with a wrinkle between his eyes.

"Marcus, just tell me where they are. I'll go pick them up tonight. Now."

The unease deepened to a scowl. "No."

"I'll smuggle them home somehow, or —"

"No."

"I'm not an imbecile. I can keep my own child safe."

He shifted forward again and held Clay's gaze without blinking. "No."

So Marcus led a bunch of people in foiling the Constabulary. That didn't give him comprehension of fatherhood, of the power it lent even the weakest of men, the unreasonable reserves to do what needed doing. How dare he think he could protect Khloe better than Clay could?

"You're going to tell me where my daughter is."

"So you can tell them."

Clay pushed his beer aside. "That's —"

"They're already watching you. They could decide to take you in. Officially. We shouldn't be meeting at all."

"You're paranoid." Or maybe not.

"It's a good haven. The best one I have. Clothes, plenty of rooms, good people. They're safe."

"Who are they? The . . . hosts, or whatever

you call them." Yeah, not hosts. Sounded sci-fi, parasitical.

"Clay. No."

Clay braced his fists on the table as if they could anchor him to his calm, give him control of this situation. "I'm going to figure out where you're keeping her, and —"

"No." Marcus dug his knuckles into the back of his neck. "Listen to me. Nobody's being moved right now. Everything's frozen. You're watching the news, aren't you? Since the raid?"

He'd tried once and shut it off after about twenty seconds. "I didn't want to find out like that. If they had her."

"They don't. She's okay. But you've got to let me do this. Something's going on. They raided the store, and then — that house I told you about. You told Khloe about it?"

Clay nodded. *Make your point, man.*

"That's where I found them. A few hours later, she got taken too. The woman who lives there."

"So they know who you are. They followed you." Ice formed around Clay. "So you're the last person who should be protecting my daughter."

"I wasn't at the Table meeting. And I've been testing things all day. It's not me."

Vague, but Marcus's "testing" methods were irrelevant, anyway. Clay gulped his beer and stood, but Marcus stayed seated, eyed him without a hint of concession. Darn this guy.

"Clay, sometimes people try to . . . do things. Alone. Don't. It never goes right."

"I want the girls back."

"Not until I know what's going on."

Clay closed his eyes. If he forced himself to be objective, to be logical, it didn't make sense to take Khloe and Violet home. Not when Constabulary agents could pull up the driveway at any time. But he could keep them safe somewhere else, some other way.

Like what?

When Clay's eyes opened, the big guy still sat there, both hands gripping his neck, glaring into his Coke.

"Marcus."

He looked up, calm, distanced from desperation. He didn't understand. Clearly he didn't feel anything about this at all. Maybe his whole little network was nothing but a power trip.

No, Clay knew him better than that. Marcus was a good guy. A friend.

Still. These were Clay's children. "I'll give you twenty-four hours to deal with this. Tomorrow, we meet here again, same time."

"Not here. The mall, that outdoor one."

"Partridge Woods?"

"There's a fountain on the north end."

"Fine."

"I get detoured a lot. I'll call tomorrow. If you don't hear from me, don't go."

The greater part of Clay almost railed at Marcus. Nothing on this man's priority list should top returning Khloe and Violet to their family. Clay crushed the myopic tirade. There were other dangers. Other families.

"Fine." The word tasted like gravel. "But if you can make it, you'll tell me where they are, at the very least. The very least."

"If it's safe."

You'd better make it safe. Okay, that was unreasonable. Clay fumbled for his wallet.

"We can't leave yet. I just got here."

If a Constabulary agent had his eye on either one of them, a ten-minute conversation would raise alarms. He slouched down into his chair. "What now? Small talk?"

"Sorry."

Clay leaned back and let the chair hold him up. Twenty-four hours, but not the longest of his life. Those had just passed, when the question of Khloe's safety had beaten the drum of his chest. Still, this new waiting rubbed raw all the old places.

Marcus met the gaze Clay angled down at

him without looking away or saying a word. The voices of everyone else seeped around Clay instead. Their noise and Marcus's silence offered a sort of rest. Clay let his eyes close again. He could fall asleep right here.

"I'm pretty sure Janelle got arrested." The words slid out of him, mostly numb, as if he could feel horror for only one human's plight at a time, and Khloe would always head that list.

"Yeah. And Phil. And Felice."

"You know that for sure?"

"Now, yeah."

"Marcus, we're talking about my girls. If anything happens to my girls . . ." The conclusion of that thought burned behind his eyes.

For a long moment, the bar droned on.

"I'll keep them safe," Marcus said.

I'll take care of her, Mr. Hansen." The words of the physician who, a month later, retracted his promise. *"Not rallying like we'd hoped."* Khloe was alive today anyway. And for this blink of time, she was safe.

The girls weren't Marcus's responsibility, not really. But for a day, Clay had no other options. "Okay."

18

Violet had always thought people past fifty believed in that "early to bed, early to rise" thing, but Belinda was apparently an exception. Violet had lain wide awake and listened to Khloe's breathing for hours before sneaking downstairs. Incriminating items, whatever they might be, probably weren't left lying around. Searching the house was a risk, now that Belinda bustled around the kitchen making cookies from scratch. At eleven-thirty at night.

You'd think she would bake tomorrow morning, when her husband came home from his fishing trip. Violet hovered in a shadow at the base of the spiral staircase and glared at the light pouring into the foyer from the kitchen. But wow, the cookies smelled amazing. Belinda hummed off-key and let pans clatter. In a mammoth mansion, you could probably scream downstairs and not be heard upstairs.

Great thought.

Evidence wouldn't come to her, so she must go to the evidence. She headed down the hall to the right.

Belinda's tour had designated this room as her husband's study, but it didn't at all resemble Clay's. The rustic wall panels were a masculine touch — or an attempt to hide a door in the wall. The room held no desk, just a low bookshelf, a stuffed chair and coffee table, and a TV. A sleek gray fish hung on the far wall like a deer's head, above eye level and attached to a wooden stand. Its mouth gaped, and its eye watched Violet cross to the bookshelf, which contained about half movies and half books. The book titles were an interesting mix: ragged hardcovers by Mark Twain, recent paperback thrillers, and a slim collection of poetry by Robert Frost.

Violet flopped into the chair and made eye contact with the fish. "Am I wasting my time in here?"

Good grief, it looked like it blinked at her. She looked away to the coffee table. A slim, brass lamp stood on a woven doily. A cork-bottomed coaster depicted a guy and his dog in a fishing boat. And a leather-bound book just sat there, unhidden, like a dare.

Belinda's husband really was exploring

Christianity.

Violet picked the book up. Gold letters had mostly rubbed off the spine: *Holy Bible.* Holy? The new ones didn't say that. She opened the cover. A woman's handwriting filled in the blanks with purple ink. *"This Bible is presented to: James A. Cole. Presented by:"* Here, the woman had written a whole message, squeezing two rows of words between each line. She had to write smaller toward the end.

"To my second love and husband, who has finally met and embraced my First Love and Savior! I'm yours, and now both of us are His. Love forever and ever, Karlyn."

Violet's finger traced the names and trembled. James Cole. Karlyn Cole. Names from a news story, months ago, sometime last fall. Arrested Christians. They'd fought back when the con-cops came for them — violently, according to at least one news report. Violet wouldn't even know their names if her social science teacher hadn't given extra credit to anyone who wrote an essay on the Constabulary's latest success.

Where would Belinda's husband have gotten James Cole's Bible? Did they know him? Or did someone else know him, someone involved in the Bible black market?

She pushed away thoughts of the book's

previous owner and flipped to the first page of text. Genesis. *"In the beginning, God created the heavens and the earth."* That was the same. Well, she didn't have time to read the whole thing. She flipped forward to find one of Jesus' books. What did He say in this version? Did He promote violence and intolerance? Here. Matthew. This book would tell her.

Knock-knock-knock.

The sound came from the living room. Violet jumped up and ducked behind the study door. Her mouth turned to sawdust. She couldn't get back upstairs without crossing in front of the living room. Whoever that was, they'd see her.

Knock-knock-knock-knock.

A lock clicked, and the sliding glass door slid open.

If she was going to get caught, better not to be in this room. Maybe she could claim she was pacing the hallways, stricken by insomnia. She padded back toward the staircase but stayed hidden by the half wall. Too bad it didn't extend to block off the living room.

"Come in, come in," Belinda said. "No wonder I felt like baking — oh! What's wrong, what's — ?"

"I'm sorry. I couldn't call."

Violet cringed against the wall. Marcus.

"You know better than to apologize." Belinda's voice neared her. "Just fill me in as much as you can. Is she all right?"

"She needs somewhere to lay down."

"Right over here to the couch."

A new voice joined them, husky and low. "Thank you."

Violet reached the edge of the wall and peered around it. Belinda bent to switch on a lamp, and its warm glow filled the room. The male voice did indeed belong to Marcus, clad in jeans and a black T-shirt. A baseball cap's curved brim shielded the top half of his face. He carried a petite black woman to the couch and eased her down. Long braided extensions fanned onto the throw pillow. She kept her knees bent when Marcus withdrew his arms. Her clover-green maternity top strained over her belly.

Belinda sat beside her. "What's your name, sugar?"

"Please, I'm having contractions. He said you might know what to do to stop them."

"To stop them?" Belinda's face crinkled as she stared at Marcus.

Marcus ground his knuckles against his neck. "I thought — if she lays down and . . . I don't know, but —"

The woman pushed up onto her elbows.

187

"Sir, you've got to save my husband, whatever you have to do. Please."

"I will," Marcus said.

Belinda's attention bounced back and forth between them and rested on Marcus. "Can you tell me?"

"Her husband's driving home tomorrow afternoon. Business trip in Indiana. I've got to —"

"Get him and bring him here," the woman said. "Before they get hold of him."

"How?" Belinda clasped her hands together as if she'd suggest they all drop to their knees in prayer right there on her carpet. But no, she wasn't a Christian.

Marcus gripped the back of his neck and started to pace.

"All right, then. Tell me your name, sugar."

"Wren Thomas, Wren like the bird. My husband's Franklin."

"Wren, I'm Belinda, and don't you worry about a thing. Just lie back here and relax a minute while I talk to Marcus."

"He has to save my husband."

"That counts as worrying." Belinda patted her shoulder and followed Marcus from the room.

They headed to the kitchen. Violet ducked past the living room, unnoticed by Wren, and padded after them. *Go back to bed.* But

188

she might learn details, how Marcus planned to "save" this guy. When she peeked around the kitchen corner, Marcus was pacing in front of the fridge. Belinda propped a hip against the counter and watched him.

"I don't see how it can be done, Marcus. I mean, he'll probably get over the state line without trouble, but if she doesn't know what time or where . . ."

"I have to try."

"What'll you do, park across from his house and wait for him? You won't be helping anyone if you get taken yourself."

"The baby. You can help her? She said he's not supposed to come now."

"Could be false labor, could be stress. It might stop if she calms down, but I'm not a nurse."

Marcus shook his head. "No."

"I'm just telling you, if it's really labor —"

"No." His left foot dragged a step over the rug, and he reached a hand to the counter.

"Son?"

"I need coffee. Please. Black."

Belinda charged into his space and stared into his bloodshot eyes. "Oh my heavens, you haven't slept a wink."

"This isn't the time to sleep."

"And last night wasn't, either. Marcus, what were you thinking, getting behind the wheel with a pregnant woman depending on you?"

"That woman *is* depending on me. To save her husband. I need coffee. Now."

"You are not leaving this house. Not until you've slept."

Marcus glared at her like . . . like he could kill her? A shudder ran through Violet. He trudged across the kitchen to the coffeemaker, grabbed the carafe, and started to fill it with water.

"Marcus Brenner, you're not getting any coffee." Belinda stomped over and shut off the faucet.

Brenner. *Thanks for the info, Belinda. Keep talking.* Maybe he'd spontaneously confess.

"When Chuck gets back, he'll help you sort all this out."

"I won't be here when Chuck —"

A quiet groan from the living room broke into his words.

Marcus's gaze snapped to the doorway too fast for Violet to duck. She froze, as if he might not see her head poked halfway into the room. He jolted back a step, and then recognition relaxed his shoulders.

"Violet," he said.

"What are you doing up, sugar?"

"Couldn't sleep." Couldn't move while Marcus studied her.

"We've got another guest." Belinda steered Violet toward the stairs, seeming not to notice Marcus's eyes boring into their backs. Or just Violet's back. "Probably best if you go back to bed."

Wren moaned again, still quietly but a longer sound this time. Belinda rushed into the living room. Well, no one had *ordered* Violet to bed. She followed.

Wren sat upright now, doubled over as far as the swell of her belly would allow. Both her hands clung to the cushion. She lifted her head.

"It's coming again."

Belinda knelt beside her and rested a hand on her belly. "You're how far along?"

"Thirty-five weeks."

Belinda looked over Violet's shoulder, sending some message. Marcus blocked most of the doorway.

"This little one could be ready," she said, not to Wren but to Marcus. He stared at them both with something between concern and panic.

Wren rocked forward and back. "Not yet. Not yet."

"Anything we need to know? Risk factors?"

"No, but he can't come now."

"I think it's been four decades since a

child was born in this house. About time for another one."

They were all crazy. Nothing was worth giving birth without drugs, without a doctor. Belinda's hand moved on Wren's belly as Wren began to breathe harder.

Come on, somebody take her to a hospital.

When the pain ended, Wren sat there . . . crying. Soundless tears dropped onto her belly.

"It's labor, Marcus," Belinda said. "We're going to need Lee."

"Is Lee a doctor?" Wren's alto voice lilted upward with hope.

"She's a nurse, our go-to medical gal. I've got four children of my own, I know how it's done, but any sight of blood and I get dizzy as can be. Marcus, we've got to have Lee if we're going to deliver a baby."

From the kitchen, the coffeemaker gurgled. Marcus turned and left the room.

Belinda sighed after him, then looked to Violet. "Glad you're up, after all. He left his keys on the counter. I need you to swipe them for me as soon as he's not looking."

Prevent him from preventing a Constabulary arrest? Sure, she could do that. When Marcus reentered the room, cradling a steaming mug, Violet slid behind his line of sight.

192

Belinda's voice gentled even more than usual. "Son, I know you're worried right now, about all of us, and there's good reason for it. But please, you have to call Lee."

Violet slipped from the room.

The scent of coffee filled the kitchen. The carafe held about ten cups, kept warm on the coffeemaker's hot plate. Surely he didn't plan on drinking all of it. As Belinda had said, a key ring sprawled on the counter, only a few keys and a knife. Violet scooped them up and held them against her thigh to muffle the jingle.

Now to stash them. She stood in the center of the kitchen and pivoted a slow circle. Hmm.

She tugged open the lower oven drawer. Like Mom, Belinda stored her cookie sheets down here. Violet leaned down.

"What're you doing?"

She jolted upright. The keys hit her foot and bounced to the floor with a condemning *clink.*

Marcus's gaze bored into hers, traveled down to the keys, then back to her. His chest rose with a deep breath. Something crinkled between his eyes, some certainty or decision.

"What are you doing?" He took a step into the room and seemed to fill it.

"I — I — I —"

"Who sent you?"

He knew. He could probably see her heart hammering through her shirt. *Come on, girl, think.* She couldn't.

Another step, closer to her, his shoe almost soundless on the tile. Scents of him crowded too close — soap, wood, and clean sweat. She backed into the corner of the counter. Dead end. Literally. Because he knew it all, everything she'd done, and he was a Christian. The only reasonable thing for him to do was to kill her.

19

The cell phone's retro ringtone shrilled throughout the house, and *The Invisible Man* dropped from Clay's hand to his lap. He launched from his chair and the circle of lamplight, across the dark living room. The paperback slid to the floor. A corner of the cover bent under his heel. *Be Khloe, be Khloe, be Khloe* — the same mantra that had pounded in his head every time the phone rang this evening. Yul wanting to reschedule the bowling game. A photography client of Natalia's. A wrong number.

He glanced at the caller ID and took the call anyway, hoping he'd silenced the ring before it woke Natalia with that same stillborn hope. "Hi, Mom."

"Clayton, it's Dad. Your mother wanted me to let you know we got in okay. The flight was pleasantly boring."

"Great."

"And we're with Don right now, on the way to the house to see Tina. What's new with my favorite granddaughter?"

Clay's stomach bottomed out. He should have anticipated the routine question. He should have hit Ignore to silence the phone, not Accept.

"She's asleep at the moment."

Khloe probably was, somewhere. Curled on her side, the same way she'd slept since she was a toddler. Nestled in a stranger's bed. Clay trudged back across the room in the dark and kicked *The Invisible Man*.

"Oh, I'm such an idiot." Dad's voice distanced from the phone. "Honey, it's midnight in Michigan."

"Sure is." Clay stooped to pick up the book, and his body melted toward the carpet. He sat, knees up.

"Were you in bed, Clayton? I'm such an idiot."

"I was reading."

"Well, Tina's had a rough day. We're stopping to pick up all the ingredients for your mother's chicken noodle soup, and she's cooking for her tomorrow. Hoping this perks her up some."

Clay smoothed a new crease from the book's cover. "Sounds good."

"They're talking about hospice. It felt like

we were intruding at first, but Don seems relieved to see us. I guess we belong here."

"You don't belong here." Dad's voice, Dad's hands clamped around Clay's arms, pulling him away from the window in the door. Away from Hilary's face.

"People should be with her, to say good-bye." The words emerged like acid, burned the back of Clay's throat, but nothing in his tone gave him away. Nothing ever had. Not in the twenty-eight years since his parents told him they'd ended Hilary's life support while he was at school.

"Seems you're right. Don cried just seeing us. Caught both of us off guard and him, too, I think. Anyway, we might be here for a few weeks."

Mom's best friend, about to succumb to ovarian cancer. Would she put all the pictures away as if Tina never existed? Quiet lengthened over the phone line. Dad probably didn't notice. Clay stretched out on the carpet and stared at the ceiling.

Tap tap.

Clay jolted up as if cattle-prodded. Knuckles on glass. The sound couldn't be anything else. The lamp's reflection glared off every window in this room. Someone could be watching him through any one of them.

Tap tap tap.

No, the noise came from farther away. "Dad, I'll talk to you later."

"Of course. Sorry to bother you at midnight." The chuckle grated.

"No problem. Good night." Clay ended the call before his father could respond, but Dad probably wouldn't notice that, either.

He stuffed the phone in his pocket and crawled on hands and knees to the lamp. He reached up to shut it off, and a quick image of the bulb flashed on his retinas as the room blackened. But if the Constabulary were out there, they'd been listening to his conversation. They knew he wasn't talking to Khloe. And if they wanted in, they wouldn't knock on his window.

He stood in the dark and tried to step toward the noise.

Tap tap tap tap.

Helpful. It came from the guestroom, other side of the laundry room. No way to discover the prowler's identity or purpose before revealing himself. Not from inside the house, anyway. Clay detoured to the garage door and slipped outside, bare feet silent on the cement floor. He stretched his hands out for his bike and grazed a handlebar. He dodged before he could break his toe against the side stand.

198

Clay felt for the switch beside the door and turned off the motion-activated floodlight. He eased the door open and stepped outside. A wedge of moon peeked around a cloud, enough to see his own feet but not to scan for intruders. Clay's hands clenched. If he could identify this imbecile as a Constabulary agent, he'd try to get in one good punch, then claim he hadn't recognized the uniform in the dark.

The scent of honeysuckle filled the air as he rounded the side of the house. He crouched beside the bush and peered around the edge of the leaves.

Definitely a man. About his height. The moon emerged to halo a shaggy blond head. Low-rise jeans and a V-neck T-shirt instead of a uniform. Perfect. Maybe Clay could clock the guy in the teeth before he could call out his Constabulary identity.

He eased around the honeysuckle and crept closer, almost on top of the man before he turned, the whites of his eyes bright in the dark.

"What — ?"

Clay threw a punch at the whisper. The man ducked, grabbed Clay's arm, and half twisted it behind his back before letting go.

"Mr. Hansen."

Wait. That voice. Clay sprang back for another look. Austin Delvecchio.

20

There was no ducking around Marcus, no brushing past him, certainly no shoving him out of the way. The edge of the counter dug into Violet's back.

"You're a . . . spy." His teeth gritted against the last word.

Deny it. But words were missing. All of them. Thoughts evaporated in a flash of vision — Austin earning that doctorate in honor of a girl who'd disappeared, remembering at his graduation the night he'd sprawled on the grass beside a merry-go-round and caressed that girl's skin, the night she volunteered to make a difference for her society. And Dad and Mom, calling around when they opened the fridge and caught a whiff of week-past-the-date chocolate milk, which would happen before Violet's fish starved. And Khloe, knowing she'd been asleep upstairs while her friend . . .

"You," Marcus said. "You were at the Table. You were at Penny's. You're here, but — but I took your phone."

He stepped closer. He kicked the keys across the floor. They hit the wall and ricocheted. Violet closed her eyes.

"Look at me."

Her eyes sprang open and couldn't see around him. He'd closed the distance to only a few feet. He jabbed his finger in her face.

"You . . . did it . . . all."

Say something, make him believe you. Violet screamed.

Footsteps barreled in behind him. "What is the matter with this child?"

"I-I don't . . . I didn't . . ." His voice fractured with confusion, concern.

Belinda, don't listen to him!

Hands cupped Violet's face. She tried to wrench away.

"Sugar, it's Belinda. What scared you? What happened?"

Violet gulped for air, but the room had turned into a vacuum. "He-he was . . . going to —"

"Marcus, what on earth did you do?"

"Nothing."

Gray dots sprinkled her vision. If she fainted, he could kill her before she woke up. She reached out and caught Belinda's sweater. "Don't go."

"I'm staying right here. Just take some deep breaths. You're perfectly safe."

A minute or two must have passed. Violet's confetti thoughts slowly glued themselves back together. Her vision cleared, and her breaths came easily. Over Belinda's shoulder, Marcus stood against the far wall and sipped his coffee. Violet ducked his stare.

"That's better." Belinda rubbed Violet's arm. "Now, how about y'all tell me what went on in here?"

"She's a spy."

Belinda swiveled toward Marcus. "She's not even out of high school."

"She was hiding my keys."

"I asked her to."

He blinked, but then he shook his head. "She was at my church, at Penny's, everybody in the last three days —" His voice choked off.

Belinda bustled to him without a hint of fear. Her hand covered maybe half of his shoulder. "That don't make her guilty. You're not seeing this right."

Violet's mind finally shed the last of its stupor. She was exposed. She couldn't lie well enough to keep Belinda's trust. But in this moment, they both stood on the far side of the kitchen. If she could get out of the house, lose them in the yard, in the woods, in the dark . . . *Without Khloe?*

Marcus would realize Khloe's cluelessness after a minute of conversation with her, and besides, he wouldn't harm his friend's daughter. Khloe would be safe right here until Violet could get to a phone.

She dashed for the front door.

After about four yards, an iron arm wrapped around her midsection and lifted her off her feet. She twisted and kicked and jabbed an elbow into flesh.

"Stop," Marcus said in her ear.

Belinda stared at her as if Violet were a con-cop in full uniform. No hope to deny anything now. She stilled in Marcus's grip.

"Khloe doesn't know anything," Violet said. "You don't have to hurt her."

Their identical, frozen shock — no blinking, no breathing — couldn't be an act. As if neither one of them had ever considered inflicting harm, not only on her or Khloe, but on anyone. Marcus's brown eyes narrowed, and he set her down. Gently.

Her knees wobbled, along with the words that gushed out of her. "You have to believe me. She has no idea. Please, I won't tell the con-cops anything, but if you can't let me go, just don't hurt Khloe."

"That's enough hogwash." Belinda didn't step forward, but her voice softened. "No one's hurting you, and no one's going to."

Marcus didn't want her dead?

Fear had layers. The kind that robbed your breath and threw gray dots in front of your eyes when a Christian man three times your size backed you against a counter — that kind must be a tough, thick layer that took time to peel off. Because Violet's hands couldn't stop shaking.

"Violet," Belinda said. "We're not what you've been told we are. Marcus included, though he might fool you when he's riled up."

Marcus let out something between a huff and a growl and paced away from them.

"Son, you intimidate full-grown men. How do you think she felt?"

He faced the window, hands latched onto his neck.

Belinda's hand hesitated halfway to Violet's shoulder, then settled there with a sort of determination. "You're safe here."

"What about the grave in the woods?"

Confusion creased around Belinda's eyes. "When could you . . . oh, when my neighbor came over? Don't know what you found outside that tunnel, but there's no grave."

Words kept spilling. Violet forced them not to quaver. "It was the right length for a person. It wasn't brand new, but the ground was dug up and filled back in. Khloe and I both saw it."

"Whatever you saw, that's not what it was."

Marcus turned away from the window and trudged across the room. "I'll call Lee."

A few seconds after he left the kitchen, the click of a lock drifted from the living room. The glass door slid open and shut.

"He'll be outside awhile," Belinda said. "We can get some things said. First off, how did you — ?"

She broke off her own sentence as Wren plodded into the room with pinching lips. Another contraction? No, this was concern. "Is everything fine now?"

"Absolutely fine. Violet here just scared herself for a minute."

Wren's teeth flashed. "My heart rate took off like wild horses with that scream, girl."

"Sorry." Violet couldn't try to smile back.

"You go take it easy," Belinda said. "Give me one minute and we'll get ready for that little one, get you a nightgown and a room upstairs, clean sheets and towels."

"I think it was just stress. I'll feel awful if you call your nurse for no reason, especially in the dead of night."

"Don't you worry about that, sugar. Would you mind waiting in the other room for just a minute?"

Wren glanced at Violet, then nodded to Belinda.

When she was gone, Belinda motioned for Violet to follow her from the kitchen to the dining room. "Don't want her overhearing your story and getting upset. Go on and have a seat."

Since arriving, Violet and Khloe had eaten meals at the small white-painted table in the kitchen. This table stretched long enough for ten chairs to surround it, one at each end and four on each side. Violet took the closest one.

Belinda sat across from her. "Okay, now, you tell me exactly what happened."

Violet looked away from the puckering creases in her face, the hint of fear behind her eyes.

"I brought you into my home, and you put me in danger. Now you look me in the eye like a woman, not a little girl, and you tell me what you've done."

Don't make her mad. But the warning voice in Violet's head sounded scratchy, thoughtless, programmed. Belinda wasn't who the con-cops said she was. Who Austin said she was. Good grief, according to Austin and the con-cops, Belinda — a non-Christian fighting for Christian freedom — didn't even exist. Violet lifted her eyes.

"Violet, I know the Constabulary told you some hair-raising things about us."

"It's pretty much common knowledge."

"These days, I guess it is. And when I think it through that way, I've got less inclination to . . . well, there it is. What'll I do to you? Not a single blessed thing."

"How can you side with the Christians? You're old enough to be smart."

Belinda's laugh welled up and spilled out. "It's harder than that to hurt my feelings, young lady."

"I wasn't trying to."

Her humor slipped away. She leaned across the table, and her crinkled hands reached out to squeeze Violet's. "Then think on what you just said. I'm old enough to know how things were. How things are. Give me a little credit here, and things'll start making sense to you."

The words sank into Violet, like fish flakes drifting down through water. She tried to ignore them, but something inside her chased and gobbled them anyway. "Okay, explain it to me."

"You were, what, ten or eleven when the

Constabulary began?"

"Ten."

"The year you were born, so much of this was already in place. It's natural to you for people to go to prison for their thoughts, their beliefs, their prayers. When I was ten — my heavens, when I was twenty and thirty — a man could walk down the sidewalk with his Bible under his arm and not be breaking a single law."

"People can do that now, too."

"Oh, not that reinterpreted sham version the government's selling now. I'm talking about the actual Bible. The one that's over two thousand years old."

The Bible was that old?

"And I've got news for you, Violet. The people you've met who believe in that original Bible, the people you handed over to be jailed and brainwashed . . ." Belinda pulled her hands back and steepled them in front of her. "They're good people. Precious people. Not hateful, not dangerous."

A shudder seized Violet. "Not all of them."

"I'll admit, if you were a grown man, Marcus might have rounded your jaw. But he would never raise a hand to you."

"He was really mad. Really extremely mad."

"He's dog-tired, and he's grieving."

Grieving? Seriously? Belinda made it sound as if Violet had sentenced all those people to death. All they had to do was cooperate, and they'd be free again in a few months.

Belinda glanced toward the kitchen and sighed. "That's as much as I can say. But I'm sorry he made you feel unsafe. That wasn't right of him."

This wasn't a role Belinda had shrugged into. Her eyes held the same wide honesty they'd offered for the last day and a half. This was truth. Violet shut her eyes, and that breathless second hit her again, the collision of Marcus's arm and her stomach as he hefted her off her feet with no effort at all.

Faint words bubbled out of her, some deep well inside that didn't want to understand and couldn't help understanding. "He's a Christian?"

"No question about it."

"But you're sure he won't hurt me."

"Violet, the Christians I've met — the real ones — they don't hate. They love, or they try to. And most of them do it real well."

Violet stood up and pushed back from the table. Possibilities congealed in her chest until breathing took effort. Christians — some of them, at least — might be safe, loving people.

"I texted a con-cop with addresses. The church, Marcus's church. And that woman's house. Penny."

Belinda's steepled hands retreated to her lap. "You took their freedom from them."

I took their freedom. Violet tasted the words, swallowed them, and their rottenness choked her all the way down. But she'd done it for the good of others. Christians having freedom was dangerous. History had proved that, just look at her school textbooks. She backed away from the table, from the circle of lamplight that hung on an antique chain from the ceiling, from the first hint of warmth in Belinda's eyes since Violet had tried to sprint for the door.

"I would have texted your address too, but Marcus took my phone battery."

Belinda nodded.

"Khloe doesn't know."

Another nod. *Stop that, say something.*

"Her dad, he knows Marcus, he's a Christian too, and I thought . . . I thought it was the right thing to do."

Belinda's hands reemerged. She folded them and grounded them on the table, arms half-reaching toward Violet. "What do you think now?"

"I don't know."

"That's a start."

Maybe she should apologize for good measure, but the words stuck in her throat. She wasn't sorry. Not entirely, not yet.

Not yet. As if she would be in the future. *What's happening to my brain?*

"Belinda?" From the living room, Wren's voice pierced the pause.

Belinda pressed her hands against her forehead. They lowered a second later. "Not a word of this to Wren, now. She needs to stay calm. She doesn't want to believe it, but she'll be holding her little one by morning."

21

"Mr. Hansen, I didn't mean to freak you out. I was just looking for, um, for Violet."

Clay wasn't freaked out, he was mad. The kid had almost armlocked him. Adrenaline pulsed through his body and turned his heart into a jackhammer. He inhaled the cool, calming night.

"You're trespassing."

"I'm sorry, but is Violet here?"

"You know Violet?" *And you're looking for her at my residence, why?*

"From Elysium, sure. She's in my small group. A great kid." Austin's eyes darted to one side.

Oh, no way. The blast of adrenaline and anger turned hot in Clay's veins, then cold. He gripped the young man's arm and steered him to the porch and shoved him down onto the first step.

"How old are you?"

Austin rubbed his bare arms as if a breeze

had picked up, but the air around them remained still.

"For all intents and purposes, I'm that girl's father. I'm recommending you tell me the truth."

"I'm twenty-one."

Austin's shirt was balled in Clay's fist before either of them took a next breath. He jerked the kid forward, half off his feet. "Have you touched her?"

Austin's fingers pried at Clay's. "It's nothing like that, Mr. Hansen."

"Oh, is that why you're tapping on my window at twelve-something in the morning, because it's nothing like that? You feed me more crap and I'll shove it down your throat, Delvecchio."

"Violet is a thoughtful, introspective person."

"She's also seventeen years old." *And she's starving for love her parents can't be bothered to give her.* "And if you have so much as *thought* about —"

"I haven't. I haven't."

Clay breathed. Released the kid's shirt. Stepped back. Austin tugged at his collar, and his eyes darted toward the street, then fastened on Clay.

"I was hoping Violet would be here. She occasionally slips out this window to meet me, after Khloe's asleep. A few times, she's let me in." He lifted both hands before Clay could charge. "We talk, Mr. Hansen. About philosophy. And, yes, about what we'll do when she turns eighteen."

"Get off my lawn and do not come back."

"Do you know where she is? I don't think her parents do, but that didn't worry me."

"Violet's fine."

Miles above the motionless night air, a cloud shifted and bared the moon. Austin tilted his head, and a shadow appeared between his eyebrows.

"You don't know, either, do you? Is Khloe home?"

Promote a smart kid too young, and all you breed is arrogance. Elysium had done exactly that to Austin: let him lead a teen small group when he'd barely emerged from adolescence himself, given him a group of his own for the Saturday morning Fishers of Friends club. Now this barely legal, scholar wannabe faced Clay down on his own property. A ball of heat rose from the pit of Clay's stomach.

"If you don't leave in the next two minutes, I'm calling the cops."

He said it with all the conviction he could muster, but Austin glanced at the house and crossed his arms. At his wrist, bound there

215

with a black cord, something glittered. A charm . . . the silver fin of a shark.

"I could call your bluff," Austin said, "but I'm not sure what that would get me at this point."

"And I could call you a liar." Because Violet collected ocean charms. Because Violet held onto her heart, yet this guy merited a gift. Or a pledge.

Austin sighed and backed away. "Call me whatever you want, Mr. Hansen. Violet likes me. Violet talks to me. Violet asks me what to do when she finds out someone she knows is practicing illegal beliefs."

Clay's hands turned to ice. If not for the dark, Austin would see the pallor invade his face. *Better hit him. Better make a point.* But the ice traveled up his arms, down his legs.

"If Khloe acquainted herself with some Christians, like maybe the ones from that busted meeting two nights ago, how would you know? But you would. Parents always figure that kind of stuff out. I still don't know how they do it, but they do."

Clay pulled his phone from his pocket, showed Austin the keypad, and pressed 9.

"Which is why you won't finish dialing."

Who was this kid? The palms-up pleading from minutes ago had vanished, a stripped veneer. Clay pressed 1.

"No worries, I'm leaving. See you tomorrow." Austin turned and loped across the grass.

Clay didn't pocket his phone until Austin's car had pulled away and not returned for ten minutes. He slipped back into the house, locked and dead-bolted the door. Tomorrow. Right. Fishers of Friends day at Elysium. If Clay missed it now, Austin might congratulate himself on his intimidation technique. Might analyze this situation further. Clay couldn't haunt his own house, waiting for Violet and Khloe to skip up the driveway. He had to go . . . to church.

Irony in real life.

22

Violet padded barefoot down the upstairs corridor, past doors and doors and doors painted antique white. None of the knobs matched, but all of them held a dark, obsolete finish. Or maybe that wasn't a finish at all but rather the metal underneath, exposed by generations of hands. The night light at the far end cast her stick figure shadow on the ivory wall to her left. Ahead on the right was her room. Khloe's room. The one room in this house where she belonged. She should've sneaked in an hour ago, shaken Khloe awake, and confessed her dilemma. But her hand refused to reach for the doorknob. Her feet refused to shuffle inside.

She should go back to Wren's room at the far end of the hallway. She should watch and listen and make sense of these people. Anyway, if she didn't go back soon, Belinda's head would pop into view — "Don't go far" — then vanish back into the room. House arrest for a spy was understandable, but Belinda must have decided on room arrest.

Violet paused in front of an antique clock that hung at eye level. She touched the weighted pendulum, and dust speckled her palm. When she released it, it hung there, swinging a bit from the motion of her hand but not enough to run the clock. She pulled it to one side and let go. Restart.

She turned around and walked the wood floor like a plank. She paused at Wren's door. It cracked open to leak light and sound.

"Not here." Wren's voice wafted through the crack.

"Sugar, you know it's going to be here. You know it's got to be here."

"No. I don't want . . ."

Violet's fingers curled around her charm bracelet until it left indentations across each one, a starfish arm gouged here, a fish tail there, a rounded placeholder bead there. *"I don't want . . ."* Words her own mom might have said as she labored to give Violet breath.

"If it's here, you get to keep him. Think on that."

What was Belinda talking about?

219

Violet peered through the crack in the door. Wren lay on her side, knees tucked in. The pale pink nightgown strained tight over her belly, and only her feet poked from under the hem. Belinda perched near the head of the bed in an oak rocking chair. One of her hands was woven with Wren's, a white and black finger braid.

"Maybe Lee's on her way right now."

Wren stretched her legs and her back. "If there's something wrong, when he comes. If he needs a hospital."

"Don't go thinking that way, sugar."

"I don't want to lose him." Wren rested a hand on her stomach and closed her eyes.

So that was how she ended the sentence. Mom wouldn't have. *"I don't want to keep her. I want to give her up."* Everyone had stories from their childhood, and this one was Violet's. She'd been hearing it since she was old enough for language. *"But you were a good baby, Violet. I never regretted keeping you."* Wren already wanted her baby.

Movement from Violet's peripheral vision jolted her to face the hallway, almost bumping the door open with her elbow. Marcus headed toward her, followed by a thin woman in dark green scrubs. She carried a bulging leather laptop case over her shoulder. Or a medical bag, maybe. This

220

was obviously the nurse.

"Lee, this is Violet," Marcus said.

Lee's gaze measured her up and down, searching for something. After a moment, she nodded. Either this woman was an icicle to everyone she met, or Marcus had told her everything. *Betting on the second option.*

Lee moved like water around both of them and into Wren's room. Violet's gaze collided with Marcus's and locked. Behind her, voices filtered through the door.

"You're Lee? Oh, praise Jesus, praise Jesus for you, ma'am."

"I need to examine you." A latex glove snapped.

"It's good you're here." Relief eased the stress from Belinda's voice. "They're coming about six minutes apart right now."

"My baby, how is he, ma'am?"

Marcus didn't move, didn't break eye contact. His voice came quietly. "Why did you do it?"

Shouldn't be hard to guess.

"Did they threaten you?"

She should say yes. Make the con-cops out to be their common enemy. But everything Belinda had said ping-ponged around in her head. She'd lied enough to these people. She shook her head, and Marcus continued to study her.

Lee's voice came from behind her. "The heartbeat is strong."

"Praise Jesus." Wren's words caught on a sob.

"Remain calm, please."

"Yes, ma'am."

Marcus sighed, tried to rub his eyes, but his fingers only splayed over his face.

"Are you going home now?" Violet said.

His hand lowered to his side. His eyes narrowed at her.

Heat rushed into her cheeks. He thought she was probing for information. Well, of course he did. "You look tired, that's all. That's why I asked."

He turned and trudged toward the stairs.

"Are you leaving?"

No response, no pause. She didn't dare get in his way, but he might fall asleep halfway home and hurt somebody. She barged into Wren's room and froze. Wren lay on her back, knees bent and legs spread. Her nightgown was pushed up to bare her body from the waist down.

Belinda was nodding to Lee as the nurse recited some list. ". . . shower curtain, plastic garbage bags, and —"

"Marcus," Violet said.

Lee's gray eyes flashed toward her.

Belinda leaned forward in the rocking

chair. "My heavens, did he start the coffee again?"

"No, I think he's leaving, right now."

By the end of Violet's sentence, Lee was halfway to the door.

"I'll handle him, Lee." Belinda pulled herself to her feet. "You stay put."

"He won't listen to you."

"Him and me, we've come a long way these last few months. I know how to talk him down."

Lee stripped off her glove so fast it turned inside out. She tossed it onto the dresser as she left.

As if just realizing Violet's presence, Wren tugged the nightgown down over her thighs. She pushed up on her elbows and tried to roll to her side. "I think Lee's right, it's easier when I'm not on my back."

"Let me help you, sugar." Belinda rushed forward.

Violet backed toward the door. Not belonging here was an understatement. Half down the hallway, she was frozen by Wren's alarmed voice.

"Belinda?"

"Ooh." The little sound quivered.

Violet rushed back. Belinda sat on the floor beside the bed, ashen-faced. Bloody fluid smeared the white sheet under Wren.

Belinda must have gotten a glimpse.

"Belinda." Violet crouched in front of her. "Are you sick?"

"Blood," she whispered.

"I know, but are you okay?"

Belinda put a trembling hand to her own forehead as if checking for a fever. "Once I fainted."

Awesome. Violet bolted up and out of the room. A sleep-deprived guy really shouldn't rank on a nurse's priority list. Not compared to a woman in labor and a woman ready to faint. She padded downstairs and tried to listen for their voices. Words drifted from the kitchen, taut and low. Marcus.

"That's not what this is."

"It would be understandable," Lee said.

"I don't want a drink. I want to fix this."

Something clattered against the counter. Violet should barge into their conversation now, before Belinda passed out upstairs. But if they were about to discuss resistance secrets . . .

"You said yourself he isn't in immediate danger until he re-enters Michigan, and that won't happen tonight."

Keys jingled. Must be the keys Violet was supposed to stash. She shuddered.

Lee's voice came again, still impassive. "How long have you been awake?"

Silence.

She released a quiet sigh. "Marcus. Please."

Only a step away from the doorway, only inches from their sight, Violet pressed against the cool wall. This conversation wasn't revealing anything. A count to ten, and then she'd interrupt. One . . .

"It wasn't me." Marcus's voice barely reached her.

"If you're referring to your intimidation of a teenage girl —"

"No. It wasn't me. That they were using."

A floorboard creaked. The cuckoo clock chirped five times. Good grief, the sun would be up soon.

"You believed it was," Lee said quietly.

"Everything I did, the last three days, I knew — any day, any minute. They'd take me and . . ."

"You were wrong."

"I know, but I — I can't stop. Feeling it."

"You are . . . afraid?" She spoke the words as if they didn't belong together.

"I —" Trembling shattered the big man's voice. "Lee. I can't sleep."

Nine. Ten. The silence kept ticking.

Something Violet couldn't name existed between all these people, Marcus and Lee and Belinda and Wren. They shared a

225

camaraderie that only grew from fighting the world itself and winning together, from knowing what could send each other to prison and not fearing the other's knowledge. She peeked around the corner.

The growling grizzly was bowed over, elbows on the counter, head in his hands. Lee stood at his side. Care pulled her mouth, and her hand hovered at his back. But she lowered it without touching him.

Marcus shuddered hard. "I lost them."

"You're not to blame."

"I keep losing more of them."

"I know."

"There's not going to be anybody left."

Lee's eyes closed for a long moment. "I know."

He straightened up and pawed at his face with one hand, a tear-swiping gesture though his eyes were dry. "I'm sorry. I'm trying not to be . . . weak."

"Marcus, look at me."

He half turned, and Violet realized too late that she hadn't ducked. But his bleary eyes didn't see her.

Lee leaned against the counter, near his arm. "You are not weak."

His hand half rose to his neck, fell to his side again.

"However, you are exhausted."

His hands curled loosely.

"I'm going to deliver a baby tonight. Then I'm going home to bed. But I'll need to know you haven't stopped at a bar or fallen asleep at the wheel, trying to drive to Indiana."

After a moment, he nodded.

Her face softened into a smile. "Thank you."

In a few steps their path would collide with Violet's. Lee was on her way to Wren, so Violet didn't need to interrupt. She slid back along the wall into a shadow.

Not fast enough. They rounded the corner.

"Violet." Lee's eyebrows arched. Her eyes frosted.

Marcus's lips set in a thin line.

"Belinda, she saw the blood and got woozy. I came down to get you."

"And decided to continue spying instead," Lee said.

"I — no, just . . . I —"

Marcus growled. "I told Belinda to watch her."

"Clearly not the best choice."

They spoke as if Violet weren't there. She took a step back, toward the stairs.

"You'll be busy. I'll have to —"

"You're going to rest, Marcus. That isn't

negotiable." Lee folded her arms and tilted her head at Violet. "Are you squeamish?"

"Um, no? I don't think so."

"All right. You'll assist me, and you won't leave my sight."

The woman was somewhat tall but lean, not intimidating until she met your eyes. No, Violet wouldn't try to escape her. She nodded, and Lee motioned her up the stairs first.

The minute before they'd detected her had been her only chance. And she hadn't even thought to run for the front door.

Because Khloe slept upstairs, still unaware. Leaving her now, like this, would destroy their friendship forever.

And then there were all these raw, open people, none of whom fit into her mental box labeled *Christians*. Still, why did she care what happened to them?

She scaled the stairs ahead of Marcus and Lee and had no answer for that one when she reached the top.

23

Unlike Belinda, Khloe, and Marcus, Violet wasn't destined for sleep tonight. Hours after Marcus lumbered off down the hall and Lee dismissed Belinda from the birthing room, Violet stood next to Wren's bed. She used Lee's phone to time contractions as well as the intervals between. Essentially, she was useless. Not like Lee couldn't time contractions herself. But of course, this wasn't about Lee needing help. She treated Violet like a cobweb. Mildly irritating, not worth brushing from the room, but definitely not expected to talk.

Time crept by, even with Lee and Wren's sporadic conversations. Somehow, both of them were able to chat while Lee pressed Wren's abdomen and checked between her legs. By now Lee had asked about Wren's family (brother, cousins, husband), job (receptionist for a dermatologist), and hobbies (horses and gardening).

After an hour of telling her own story, Wren propped up on one elbow and tilted her head at Lee. "My turn. Which hospital you work at?"

Lee shook her head. "Don't ask about me."

The throbbing monotony of contraction, rest, contraction was wearing Violet's silence to the bone. She spoke for the first time in an hour. "Nothing dangerous, you mean?"

"Any detail could be dangerous."

"Favorite color." She shouldn't have said it. Lee would be annoyed. The pause lengthened.

"Teal," Lee said.

Over the next hour, whenever Wren moaned through her teeth, whenever she curled a hand against her belly as if to press the pain away, Violet asked Lee a question. Each time, her apparently random timing eased the tension in Wren's body, and once brought a smile in the midst of a contraction.

"Favorite food?"

"Mexican."

"Music?"

"Classical."

"Pets?"

"Definitely not."

Near seven-thirty, with a pink sunrise

striping the carpet through the blinds, Wren tensed and started to pant again, and Violet started the timer. Forty-five seconds to a minute, and then Wren would relax against the pillows that propped her into a half-sitting position. She would rub her belly and catch her breath, and then in four minutes, everything would loop. Again.

But this time, Wren arched away from the pillows. Her hands squeezed the sheet, and she turned over onto knees and elbows. The low moan that had become the morning's soundtrack rose to a cry. Something flipped over, low in Violet's stomach.

"Lee?" Wren rocked forward and wailed.

Lee slid a hand between Wren's legs. "All right. You're fully dilated."

Violet glanced at the forgotten timer. One minute, eight seconds.

"Ohhhhhhh."

"You're doing well, Wren," Lee said. "Breathe through it, the same way you did before."

"Franklin, I want Franklin. Ohhh."

"Breathe. Good. Good."

One minute, twenty-five seconds.

Wren curled into a kneeling ball, panting hard. Too soon, before her breathing leveled, she moaned again. Violet checked the timer.

"Lee, it's only been two and a half minutes since the last one."

Lee nodded. "All right. Wren, is this a comfortable position for you to push?"

Wren gripped the headboard in both hands and spread her legs.

Lee glanced at Violet. "Wash your hands."

"What?"

"Now. Thoroughly. Count to thirty."

Violet dashed into the suite bathroom and scrubbed her hands for thirty seconds. Longer than it sounded. She rushed back. Wren's nightgown was pushed all the way up her back, baring the lower half of her body. Violet focused on her upper half.

Lee knelt at the side of the bed, one hand between Wren's legs. "Push."

Wren's body strained. Her head drooped between her arms. "Ohhhh, dear Jesus, help me."

Violet stood by the rocking chair, ready with blankets and scissors and shoelaces, everything Belinda had compiled from Lee's list. She clenched her clean hands. Her own stomach cramped when Wren cried out. The next few contractions seemed to take longer than all the ones before them put together. If only Violet could help.

Lee, what's your favorite movie? But her voice couldn't penetrate the pain swaddling this room.

"He's crowning, Wren. Push."

"Ohhhhhhh!"

"Violet, come here."

Violet darted to the bedside and crouched next to Lee. Fluid and blood glistened on the sheets.

"Be ready to catch him."

Her heartbeat pounded through her whole body. Lee's face was a foot from hers.

"Violet. You have to look."

She mustered the gall to glance between Wren's legs . . . at the head of wet, curly black hair. "That's the baby."

"Yes," Lee said. "One more contraction, maybe two. Be ready."

"Aren't you going to catch him?"

"This is just a precaution. Hold your hands below mine."

Wren's body tensed, strained.

"Wren," Lee said. "It's time to meet him. Push."

Wren gave a loud sob, and the baby slid into Lee's hands, slick and wet, staring and silent. Violet never had to move. Lee directed Wren to turn over and lie back against the pillows again, while she cradled the baby. A creamy sort of membrane was spread over most of his dark body.

"Blanket," Lee said, and Violet grabbed

one from the rocking chair.

Lee wrapped the baby up and set him on Wren's belly. He thrust a ball of fist up from the blanket folds and screamed. Wren caressed his hand.

"He's here." Sobs shook her body.

Lee didn't pause from cleaning the baby and Wren. She didn't even look up from her task. "Yes, he is. Healthy and safe."

Wren slid her hands under the blanket to cradle the baby. "Timothy Franklin Thomas. Our firstborn son. We tried for so long. I couldn't tell you before. I was afraid if I talked about it, how hard it was, he might never come. But he's here. We won't lose him? The Constabulary won't take him?"

"You're safe here," Lee said.

"I need my husband. Oh, Franklin, we have a son."

"Marcus will do everything he can."

Wren rocked the baby in her hands. "Praise Jesus for all of you."

Violet stepped back from the bedside, from the stinging gratitude. Her senses prickled, and she glanced up. Lee watched her. The calm, clinical caring of the last hours dropped away from Lee and exposed that same cold Violet had felt the first time the woman looked at her. Then she crossed to the rocking chair and picked up another blanket.

In a few minutes, Wren moaned as the last contraction rid her body of the placenta. She settled the baby on the loose flab of her belly and closed her eyes. "Can I nurse him? I want to nurse him."

"Of course," Lee said. She helped Wren work the nightgown over her head.

Neither of them seemed to notice or care that Wren now lay on the bloodstained sheet wearing nothing but a bra. Well, Lee must see naked bodies every day. Violet averted her eyes. When she next glanced at Wren, the bra had been removed as well, but Lee had draped a blanket over Wren's torso.

"We'll wait ten minutes or so to cut the cord," Lee said.

"Thank you," Wren said without looking up from Timothy's suckling lips.

In another few minutes, Lee finished examining Wren and straightened, tired satisfaction in her eyes. "Violet, let's try to find a heating pack for Wren."

"Ohhh." Wren rubbed low on her belly. "That would feel so good."

Lee motioned Violet out the door without bothering to meet her eyes. If any breath of teamwork had blown through this room in the last five hours, it was gone again.

They found Belinda dozing in a chair in

the living room. Her eyes shone at the news of the baby's safe arrival. She microwaved a gel pack and handed it to Lee, insisting that Lee let her know if she could do anything else to make Wren comfortable.

"Do you understand what happened this morning?" Lee said as Violet followed her back upstairs.

A right answer and a wrong one existed for that question. *"Wren had a baby"* obviously qualified as wrong. Unlike most people, Lee didn't answer her own question when silence piled up like a snow drift. They reached Wren's room, but Lee stood outside it, studying Violet.

"Um," Violet said. "Wren had a baby."

"Yes, she did. Without pain medication or a doctor or a sanitized environment. Because if she delivered in the hospital, her child would be taken from her and raised by someone else. Someone chosen by the state."

"Or not, as long as she didn't preach at the nurses." *Good grief, Lee.*

"Hospitals require paperwork for admission. Patients have to mark their religious affiliation before they're treated, and Christians refuse to deny their faith."

Oh. Violet crossed her arms against the blast of cold from Lee's voice. Her own voice sounded small and stupid. "I didn't know that."

"The government has effectively denied them medical treatment. Or they can be treated and then transferred to re-education."

Violet closed her eyes, but she could still see it. Wren, a mother who wanted her baby more than anything else, crying as a man in a gray uniform carried him away. Or Britney, a friend from school, who'd fractured her arm last year so badly that pieces of bone broke through the skin. Violet had signed her cast. If her parents had been Christians, what would have happened to her?

Re-education, of course.

"If Marcus hadn't confiscated your phone, you would have texted this address to the Constabulary. Correct?"

Violet's voice wobbled. "That's what I was supposed to do. Yeah."

"Have you seen anything that would support what you've been taught about Christians?"

Violet opened her eyes. The steel-eyed statue in front of her hadn't moved.

"I've only been here two days."

"Long enough to observe. To begin basing your opinions on reality."

"You said . . . denied 'them' medical treatment. You're not a Christian, either?"

"I'm not."

"So why are you doing this?"

"It needs to be done." Lee reached for the doorknob of Wren's room but then paused. "Your small talk was helpful. You calmed Wren several times without knowing it."

"I knew. That's why I kept asking you stupid stuff."

The inscrutable eyebrows lifted, and the flash behind her eyes could have been respect, if Violet were someone else. Then it vanished.

"I'll keep one of the cordless phones with me and leave it on Talk, so you won't be able to call out. And we'll have to sleep in the same room, so I can rig the door from inside." At the last part of her plan, Lee's voice and expression withdrew more than usual.

Violet shook her head. "You don't have to do that. I'm not going to leave Khloe."

"You believe we would harm her?"

"You'd tell her what I did."

Lee studied her. "Eventually, she will find out."

"I know. But not yet. And I'm going to be the one who tells her. Not anybody else."

Not until Violet said the words did she

know their truth. She could never escape without her friend, even if Khloe was safe here and she wasn't. She'd dragged Khloe into the stickiest quagmire of their lives, and she owed Khloe more than abandonment.

"Besides," she said, as more truth filled her. "I don't leave my friends."

No, you just ruin their lives with re-education.

Lee nodded. "All right. I'll set my phone alarm to go off every thirty minutes and check on you."

"Lee, seriously, you can . . ." *Trust me? Right.*

"Go to sleep, Violet."

24

Violet tried to obey Lee's parting order. She slid into bed and stared across the room at Khloe's sleeping face. *Wake up, Khloe.* No. Better that Khloe kept up her summer habits and slept until noon. Or until Violet could tell her the truth. Every conversation they had from now until then would be a sort of lie.

The first time Lee leaned into the room, Violet met her eyes. Lee nodded and disappeared. After that, Violet dozed and dreamed a full confession after which Khloe hugged and forgave her. Around 10:00, she jerked awake and rolled over so that she no longer faced her friend.

Forget this. If she was awake, it was for a reason. Maybe she should search for more information. About something. Anything. *"It needs to be done."* Not that Lee would say that about this particular task. And she'd better not wander far, or Lee would sound the alarm when she wasn't in bed.

The house lay under a spell, bright daytime outside and slumbering people inside. Clocks ticked too loudly in the hall. Violet passed a room with a cracked-open door and peered inside. Marcus slept face down on top of the covers. The floor was strewn with all four pillows from the bed as well as his gray-and-black tennis shoes. She padded farther down the hall and passed Wren's room. Feeble fussing and Wren's quiet "shh" slid under the door.

Violet kept going, farther down the hallway than she'd walked before. She'd walk to the end, then return to her room. The weight of the dream should be shed by then. Okay, here, the last bedroom.

Wait.

Low crying came from the other side of the door. Violet opened it and stepped into the room.

Lee?

Under the brightly patterned quilt, she lay on her back. Her hands curled at her sides. Her breathing labored with dry sobs, but she was asleep.

"Lee," Violet whispered.

Lee twitched, whimpered, but didn't wake up.

"Hey." Violet crossed the room. "Lee,

wake up. Wake up."

She gasped and sat up. Her eyes darted around the room, past Violet without seeing. "Marcus."

Whoa. Had he done something to produce Lee's nightmare? But they'd been so unguarded with each other before.

"It's okay," Violet said. "You were dreaming."

Lee curled into herself, knees up. Her unblinking eyes saw something other than the dove-gray walls and the window blinds and the floral painting hung above the bed. She breathed too fast, inhaling almost before she released the last gulp of air.

"Hey." Violet sat on the bed next to her. Probably shouldn't touch her, though. Or maybe she should. *What do I do?* This wasn't a normal nightmare.

"Marcus?"

"Hey, Lee, I'm not Marcus. I'm Violet. Can you hear me?"

A blink. Lee's eyes found hers, and a lost crease gathered between them.

"It's Violet. You're at Belinda's house. You had a nightmare, you were sort of crying."

Lee jolted from the bed to her feet in a smooth motion that defied her rough breathing. "Go."

"Were you asking for Marcus?"

"No."

Violet stood and almost missed the flinch in Lee's shoulders. Way too jumpy. No way she was scared of Violet. The fear had to be leftover from the nightmare.

Violet backed toward the doorway. "Can I help at all? I could get Marcus."

"Don't wake him. Just go."

"Then I'll get Belinda. She'll know what to —"

Lee's eyes shot icicles. Her hands clenched at her sides. "I said no."

Okay. Privacy. Respect that. Violet nodded.

Lee nodded back and collapsed to her knees.

The carpet burned Violet's shins as she dropped and skidded closer. Lee thrust an open hand right in her face.

"Get out!"

The glare no longer fit Lee's face, like a poorly fitted mask that cracked at every seam when forced onto the person's true features. Yet Violet had almost believed it, almost walked out on this woman while she trembled and struggled to breathe.

A lump filled Violet's throat. "I'll only stay for a minute, until you're better, okay?"

"I'm fine."

"Which is why your legs just caved in."

243

"Please go."

"As soon as you can breathe again."

Lee tried to stare her down. The seconds piled on, and Violet held her gaze until Lee shuddered and turned away. She cupped her hands and breathed into them. Minutes crept along. Violet scooted back and sat against the farthest wall. Lee could have her space bubble. She just wasn't allowed to crouch there and hyperventilate all by herself.

Maybe ten minutes later, maybe a little less, Lee's hands lowered and spread open on her knees. Her eyes held a flat exhaustion.

"Lee?"

Her legs coiled beneath her as if to push to her feet, but she must have not trusted them. She leaned against the nightstand and stretched them out in front of her, one at a time. The movements were off somehow, floppy, the way Violet moved after a night of the flu, when pulling a shirt over her head took every ounce of strength left in her muscles.

"Please . . . go." The voice barely carried across the room.

"Okay." Violet stood, but Lee looked . . . well, like a different person. Shrunken and brittle. "Maybe if you told me about it, what you dreamed? It could help?"

Releasing a nightmare always helped Violet. She could sleep again after she gave the darkness words. But Lee's face froze, then blanked.

"Lee?" After five minutes of silence, Violet backed from the room. "I'll leave you alone now, okay? You'll be okay?"

Not even a blink. Violet retreated to her own room and crawled under the covers. Somehow, she had failed Lee. And for some reason, that mattered.

25

Tug-of-war between four seventh-grade boys produced a lot of grunting and a lot of sweat. Clay stood a few feet from his team of two and wondered if either of them had been taught to wear deodorant. He wouldn't be surprised if his own palms started sweating, embracing the elemental surge of survival that rooted his team's feet to the gym carpet. Their bodies angled backward, and their hands clamped around the rope that could burn their palms with one mistake.

"You've almost got them! You've almost got them!" the other team leader kept yelling, but Clay kept his eyes on his own team. Austin wasn't allowed to make Clay's palms sweat. Not over this trivial competition, not over anything else.

Gabriel lost his footing, skidded forward. Austin's team was going to tug Clay's right over the line of defeat.

"Hey!" Clay jumped into Gabriel and Cameron's line of vision. "Don't use your arms, use your whole body. Come on."

His words drowned in the cheering and jeering from the rest of his team, but Gabriel nodded and heaved back on the rope, and Austin's boys staggered toward the line.

"That's more like it." Clay stepped back.

Less than a minute later, his boys gave the rope a pull that yanked one of the other team members off his feet. Clay high-fived them both as they returned to their team line and the next two boys took their places at the rope.

Across the gym, two other teams battled through the same games. Which team played which was always random. Of course, this week, Clay had to oppose Austin. The kid's gaze had stalked him all morning long. But in fifteen minutes, Fishers of Friends ended. Two dozen seventh-graders would pour through the open gym doors and find their rides home, and Clay would escape to his bike.

If anything happened this morning, Natalia would text him. *Would you pick up some smoothie mix on your way home?* meant she'd heard from Khloe. She wouldn't, though, not with Marcus guarding their daughter's location like a Rottweiler. A request for pepper was a Constabulary emergency signal, but they hadn't worked out an exact plan. As if a plan could exist for one's imminent arrest.

Austin's team won the next round in less than a minute, as they did on every turn of Sean's. The kid was thin as string and had the soft, long-fingered hands of a piano prodigy. Too bad Clay's team's thugs-in-the-making had no appreciation for classical music.

"Why do we even let him play?" Gabriel stage-whispered.

Sean's face reddened, and he took his place at the end of the line. At that age, Clay might have volunteered to sit out, not from generosity but from shame. But Sean stuck out these pointless games every Saturday morning, all summer long. Had to step closer to serve the volleyball, got hit in the face with the dodgeball before he could catch it. Clay walked down to the front of the size-ordered line and faced Gabriel.

"If I hear that again, *you* won't play next week."

Before Gabriel could mouth off at him, Clay walked away. He stood at the corner of his team line and watched Austin across the gym. The kid grinned, high-fived, clapped boys on the back. A natural, really.

Austin spun on his heel and caught Clay with his eyes. He tilted his head, a question. Clay shrugged back at him. *What?* As if they didn't both know.

He never expected to enjoy himself when Natalia suggested, almost a year ago now, that he join an Elysium ministry. *"You know, to help you fit in as a sincere believer."* But normal Saturdays went by too fast. Turned out Clay enjoyed the connections he made with these kids, even the first session's classroom setting where he led them in a group discussion of whatever curriculum Elysium had meted out.

Today, the minutes couldn't melt fast enough. That silver shark charm of Violet's kept glinting in the gym's pale fluorescence. Every time it did, something like adrenaline spurted through Clay's body, some senseless rush that wanted to march across the game circle and rip the black cord off Austin's wrist.

The game leader finally blew the dismissing whistle, and Clay's boys gathered up their legal Bibles — the Progressive United Version, bound in paperback with multiple cover options. Most of his team preferred the adventure novel cover, but a few had the one that resembled a magazine. When they all clomped off, one PUV was left, set neatly against the wall. Clay stooped to pick it up and opened the cover, but teen boys didn't bother to write their names on things. He turned a chunk of pages to midway in.

In real Bibles, Psalms fell in the center, but so much of the Old Testament had been censored from these that the book opened to Luke. Clay skimmed. Jesus calmed the stormy sea. He fed five thousand people miraculously. The changes weren't notice-able until He started to talk.

"I tell you the truth, it is the will of God that you should save your life, not lose it. Do not deny yourself, for within yourself is access to God."

No, Jesus had said the opposite. This was where "take up your cross" was supposed to go. *Well, God, I think I'm doing that right now. Can't be much heavier a cross than isolation from my daughter and danger from the Constabulary.* He couldn't put words to himself and Natalia, though she had to be a whole beam of his cross. She hadn't said three words to him this morning, hadn't touched him once.

"What's that you're reading?"

Clay jumped. Dang it. This kid wasn't al-lowed to startle him. He shut the book. "Somebody left their Bible."

"You were engrossed," Austin said.

250

Clay held out the book. "Want to take it to lost and found for me? No name inside."

"Sure thing." Austin took the book with his left hand, and the shark charm dangled against it.

"Thanks." Clay headed for the gym doors. His hands itched for his bike's handlebars. *Be ready for me, baby, because we're going to ignite the pavement.*

"Why are you here?"

Clay turned back. "What?"

Austin shifted the book from one hand to the other. "I'd think you would be home as much as possible. Just in case they returned."

Oh. Crap. He schooled his face. "My wife's at home."

"You're not very worried, for a guy with a missing daughter."

"Of course I am."

Certainty sparked over Austin's face. "Maybe they're not missing. Maybe you know exactly where they are, and you know they're safe."

Clay half curled his fingers. Fists would give him away. So would open hands, trembling.

"Admit it."

"I don't know what you're talking about."

"Tell me Violet's okay."

251

Clay met his eyes, then lowered his gaze to Austin's left wrist. "Full disclosure is earned, Delvecchio."

He fled the gym without pause, even when Austin's voice followed him out the door. "Mr. Hansen, please."

A text vibrated his phone, and he tugged it out while jogging across the parking lot to his bike. Maybe it was Marcus, telling him what time to meet by the mall fountain. Heat rose from the blacktop and warmed his feet through his shoes. He swung a leg over the seat, and his whole body thrummed in anticipation of the engine's power to take him away from here. He read the text first, though. Natalia. He gulped the words in search of only two: *smoothie mix*.

I actually do need something from the store. I let myself run out of soy milk.

Curse Marcus.

Whoa, where had that thought come from? Marcus couldn't be blamed for Clay's judgment errors.

But he didn't own the girls. Khloe should be allowed to call home. There had to be a safe way.

Clay drove to the store at a less-than-legal speed and was securing the quart-sized carton in his bike's side case five minutes later. Truth waited until then to grab hold of his gut. Natalia had sent him on an errand to ensure he would return home before tomorrow. Something she hadn't done, hadn't felt the need to do, in ten years.

He sat on the bike but didn't turn the key. Ten years weren't enough to prove that he'd changed. Maybe nothing would be. Fair wages for every time he'd gotten in their car and driven hours away to flee the fears of a new husband, then of a new father. Fears for a sick child, then for a dying child. He'd run from all of it, and now, when crisis knocked their family down again, he expected Natalia to trust him to stay?

Yes. He did. Ten years should be long enough to earn trust back.

"Excuse me. Clay Hansen?"

Clay's head snapped up from his chest. Directly in front of the bike, as if daring Clay to run him down, stood a man in a gray uniform. Close-cropped hair, a few inches taller than Clay. Agent Naebers. Clay turned the key and revved the bike, and Agent Naebers took a step back. Nice.

Clay lifted his voice above the engine's growl. "Are you only allowed to interrogate me once a day, is that it?"

"This isn't an interrogation."

"Oh, good. I don't want the milk to spoil."

"I'm here with information for you."

253

"And you couldn't call? It's not like you can't get my number."

"My boss wanted you to hear this in person."

No. They were toying with him. They had to be. Clay put the bike in gear and coasted around Agent Naebers with more distance than necessary between them. No sense tempting the man to arrest him for endangerment of an agent on duty.

"We have Khloe in custody."

The words hit him in the back like sniper bullets, armor piercing, through and through, searing exit wounds in his chest. He braked, shut off the bike, kicked the side stand into place. His body pivoted slowly, one leg swinging around. Both feet touched the ground on the same side, but he didn't stand. Couldn't stand. Couldn't breathe.

"My daughter," he said.

Agent Naebers nodded. "She's being processed now, in preparation for —"

"Processed? She's not meat in a butcher shop!"

"Mr. Hansen, I'd like you to lower your voice, please."

Calm. Think. Stand up. His legs wobbled, but he stepped forward. Something was wrong here. "You're telling me you have my daughter."

"She'll be entering re-education by the middle of next week, Thursday at the latest."

Five days from now. Or less. They'd put her in all-day re-education for the summer, then evening sessions after school started. If her progress wasn't satisfactory, they'd put her in a group home for adolescent offenders. They'd turn her home, her family, inside out in search of the root of her criminal beliefs.

No, stop it. Think this through. *Something isn't right, something is . . .* "Where was she? How did you find her?"

Agent Naebers spread his feet apart. "I'm not at liberty to say."

"I think you're lying."

Naebers studied him a long moment, then reached into his jacket pocket. He held out a clear, square baggie. "I thought you might find this hard to accept, Mr. Hansen, but let me assure you, it's the truth."

In one corner of the bag lay a silver heart charm, a pink zircon in the center. Clay's heart seemed to stop. So this was the Constabulary now, kidnappers offering proof of abduction. His stomach balled up.

"What about Violet?"

"Excuse me?"

"Khloe's friend. Violet DuBay." Marcus

255

had said they were together. If the Constabulary had taken one of them, surely they'd taken both.

"I don't know anything about a Violet. I'm here to inform you about Khloe."

But this couldn't happen. Khloe was safe. Marcus's best haven, he'd said.

"She'll be released to you in a week or two, once re-education is in progress."

After they'd dug inside Khloe's head and begun to root out any truth Clay had managed to teach her.

"We'll be in touch with you, Mr. Hansen."

Clay must have nodded. Agent Naebers strode across the parking lot and got into a gray squad car topped with green lights. It hadn't been here when Clay went inside the store.

He shuffled to the bike. Straddled it. His chin hit his chest. Khloe. Taken.

Smart or not, he had to talk to Marcus. He dialed, but the phone only rang and rang. "Hi, you've reached Marcus Brenner. Leave a message."

Clay hung up. A sour taste filled his mouth. *I trusted you, man.*

No more.

He let multiple cars weave around him on the drive home. If he accelerated faster than forty, he might not stop accelerating. He might not stop for the red lights or the state line. He might not stop ever again.

But he did stop. Parked. In the garage. Trudged up the steps, through the door. Natalia bustled around the house, a dusting cloth in one hand and the polish can in the other.

Atta girl, make the house spotless for the Constabulary's next visit.

"Just put the soy milk in the fridge," she called without pausing.

Oh, soy milk, right. Cooking away outside. "Nat?"

"I vacuumed, steamed the floors, scrubbed the sinks and the bathtubs and even the walls. I know, it's ridiculous, but I can't stop. I keep finding other things to clean, like this can possibly help. Did he call you yet? When are you meeting him? If I didn't know she was with safe people, if I thought she was out in the woods somewhere, I think I'd lose it."

Clay barreled into the living room, into her space, and gripped her wrist to still the dusting rag. Her eyes darted up to his face.

"Clay, what . . ."

"I can't do this."

Wrong words. She stepped back, leaned back, and he tried to let go, but he couldn't.

"Nat, I . . ." *I let them take our child.*

257

"C-can't do what?"

"Come with me."

"Where? What're you talking about?"

"They're going to come here to talk to us, and I just can't be here waiting for them, I have to — I have to go and I want you to come with me."

Natalia backed into the coffee table and reached behind her to set down the polish. "Obviously, we can't disappear, Clay. When Khloe comes back home —"

"That won't happen. Not soon, anyway." The words made sense in his head, but in the air, they scrambled and fizzled. This must be speechlessness.

"What do you know?" Natalia whispered.

Now the words got stuck, somewhere between his mind and his mouth. What a strange, disquieting thing, the inability to speak your thoughts.

"Clay, what's happening?"

"They . . . have . . . her. I don't know how, but . . ."

Her fingers curled around the polish can. Her body tipped against the table.

"I thought she was safe," he said.

A bright blush erased her pallor. "How do you know this?"

"At the store. Agent Naebers, he walked up and . . . told me. That they had her. In custody. He had a charm from her bracelet. Khloe — she's going to re-education."

Natalia pitched the polishing can into the wall. It bounced off and clattered to the wood floor.

"I know," Clay whispered.

"I told you. No re-education."

"I thought Marcus was taking care of —"

"Marcus is not her father!"

The truth of the words kicked a hole in him. He turned away from her, vision blurring.

"You'll be next." She bent to pick up the can of polish and slammed it onto the table. "Your stupid, stubborn religion."

He took a step toward her. She withdrew and pressed her back against the wall. She seemed to shrink.

"The art schools," she said. "They might not want her."

"They might not."

"She'll say what they want her to say, and they'll let her out. But you . . . I don't know what you'll say. I don't know what you'll do. I never know what you'll do, until you do it."

Now that made no sense. Clay couldn't be more predictable. He rubbed his aching eyes.

He went to the bedroom and grabbed his

sports bag from the closet and filled it. Toiletries. Enough clothes for one night only. No sense tempting the inner coward.

Natalia stood in the doorway a long moment, a framed, cherry-haired sprite. Then she pulled her neon green duffel from under the bed and headed to the dresser.

"Nat?"

She tugged open her underwear drawer and pitched three silk panties into the bag. A bra. "I probably won't need socks, you think?"

26

Even if she weren't at the mercy of strangers, Violet should have wakened Khloe first
thing. They should have taken turns in the
shower, whispered plans or commiseration,
performed the bracelet-bump, and gone
downstairs side by side. Violet shouldn't
have crept to the closet for fresh clothes and
glanced over her shoulder to make sure
Khloe's eyes hadn't opened.

She showered in five minutes and pulled
on a blue V-neck shirt and a pair of Capri
jeans that sagged a bit at the hips. Whatever.
They wouldn't fall down, and she hadn't
seen any belts in the closet. Okay, now for
breakfast. Her stomach rumbled, but her
feet held back. She wasn't scared, not
exactly. Belinda wasn't going to poison her.
Marcus wasn't going to hit her. But facing
them prickled every nerve in her spine.
Violet pulled in a breath. They knew what
she'd done. She knew what they'd done,

were still doing. Go down and face them. Like an adult. And do what Lee had told her to do — watch and form her own opinions.

Lee was halfway down the stairs when Violet reached the top. She spotted Violet through the banister and waited for her. Her short black hair gleamed, still damp. Her jeans and crew-neck top fit too perfectly to be on loan from Belinda's closetfuls. Maybe she kept a change of clothes in her car.

"Good morning." The words held complete calm. This version of Lee didn't know how to hyperventilate.

Who are you really? "Hi, Lee."

Lee continued down the stairs. Violet was obviously supposed to follow. At the bottom, she halted again but didn't meet Violet's eyes.

"I would appreciate your discretion regarding what . . . happened to me last night."

"I don't really have anyone to tell. Marcus won't even look at me, and I won't tell Belinda, either, if that's what you want."

Lee's glance ricocheted off Violet. "Thank you."

They entered the kitchen without further words. The scent of bacon and eggs enveloped Violet along with Belinda's buoyant twang.

"You've got no reason to doubt my eggs. You've never tasted them before."

On one side of the stove, Belinda wore her orange apron over a flowered housedress and stood over a deep-bottomed skillet. At the other burner, clad in carpenter jeans and a fresh ivory T-shirt, Marcus bent his head over a smaller skillet.

"It's not doubt," he said.

"Get away from here." Belinda shooed at him with her free hand and flipped something with the spatula.

"I can flip eggs."

"I don't need you flipping anything. Just go sit at the table."

"And Lee likes them scrambled. Don't make them all for me."

"I'm not planning on over-easy for all of them. I got plenty of eggs, and I got plenty of kitchen savvy, so you go sit down and stop pestering me before I send you home with no breakfast."

He reached for the spatula.

"Marcus!" Belinda shoulder-bumped his arm.

He didn't budge. A smile creased around his eyes. "They're done."

"Go. Sit. I'm fixing this food, not you."

He turned, and his gaze landed on Lee

and Violet with a quick furrow of confusion, as if surprised to find an ally and an enemy side by side. "Hi."

"Good morning, though not morning for long." Lee pulled out a stool from the counter bar.

Marcus's mouth twitched. "Belinda wants us in the dining room."

"That's right. Everybody in the dining room, out of my kitchen. I'll bring the food when it's done."

Restrained amusement glimmered in Lee's eyes. Marcus glanced from her to Belinda with another twitch of smile. Violet followed them both through the kitchen to the connecting dining room. Lee crossed in front of Marcus, and his fingers curled at his side. Like last night, they were about to touch each other and then didn't.

Marcus sat, folded his arms on the table, and frowned. "You sleep? You look tired."

Lee sat across from him. "I'm fine."

He hesitated, then nodded.

"You seem rested," Lee said, and he nodded again.

A silence closed in, asking *"How do we talk with a spy standing here?"* Violet focused her attention on the closest item, a chair tucked into the table. Should she sit? She traced one of the swirling leaves carved into the back. On the far wall, the clock's second hand seemed to tick too slowly. Maybe the battery was dying. Maybe the seconds felt stuck because nothing filled them but bacon grease, hissing from the kitchen.

"How's the baby?" Marcus said.

"Seven pounds, two ounces, and nursing well."

"Wren?"

"Given a few days to recover, she'll be fine."

Belinda hustled in from the kitchen as Lee spoke. She carried a plate in each hand, one of eggs, half over-easy and half scrambled; the other of steaming pancakes and bacon. "You know she's welcome here as long as she needs."

Her tone held nothing uncommon, as if she and her husband often sheltered people for days or weeks. This must be how the network operated. Violet had expected Marcus to rush Wren to a new location immediately, but, then, he hadn't done that with her and Khloe, either. Maybe fugitives stayed here until they had a permanent place to go.

Lee pulled out the chair beside her. "Sit, Violet."

Robot legs carried her to obedience. She pressed her back to the chair and let it dig across her shoulder blades.

"We're about to discuss you," Lee said. "You should be present."

Marcus studied Violet too long, then sighed. He reached for the plate of eggs and slid three of them onto his plate, followed by four strips of bacon.

Lee folded her hands and hid them in her lap. "I made certain she didn't leave the house last night."

"You . . . I didn't think."

"You were past coherent thought. It was fine. But there are decisions to make now."

"We can't let her go, and we can't keep her."

Violet's mouth went dry, and her underarms began to sweat. They'd told her no one would hurt her. Belinda promised.

Belinda had started back to the kitchen, but now she turned to Marcus. "And why's it one or the other? Keeping her or letting her go?"

He poked his fork at her. "Keeping is kidnapping. Letting go is . . ." He shook his head and sawed an egg in half with a rush of yolk.

"That's what I'm trying to say, son. Both choices have some problems."

Oh, God, save me.

He grabbed a pancake from the stack,

curled it in his hand, and mopped up the yolk. "Well."

"There is no third option," Lee said.

"Wouldn't be kidnapping if Violet agreed to stay."

The fork in Marcus's hand froze halfway to his mouth. The bite of egg dripped gold back onto his plate. Lee folded her arms and cocked her head at Belinda, not curiosity but challenge.

"What?" The word blurted from Violet, and she pressed back harder against the chair. She'd been given no voice here.

"You don't know enough to understand," Belinda said. "Hold that thought, now. I've got a pan on the stove."

In the minute she was gone, Marcus consumed his eggs and bacon with unwavering focus. Violet breathed in and out, since she'd probably get to keep doing so.

Lee ignored the food altogether. "Marcus, there's only one option in reality."

"I know. I have to keep her here."

Before Lee could answer, Belinda bustled back into the room with a gallon of orange juice and three glasses, rims squeezed between her fingers.

"Lee, you eat up." She poured a glass of juice and offered it to Violet. "Now, what was I saying? Somebody needs to explain how things are, and why —"

"She can't be given more information," Lee said.

"She's a child, Lee."

"I'm aware of that."

She's sitting right here in front of you. Hadn't Lee told Violet to observe, to mold her own self, based on the truth? Maybe Violet's intrusion on her nightmare had somehow changed her mind. Violet ducked her head to hide the heat in her face.

"She's not responsible for the lies people told her." Belinda poured another glass and set it in front of Lee. "You're not giving her a chance."

"She's old enough to understand right and wrong."

"That's what I'm saying, she might could choose to do right, if we explain to her —"

Clank. Marcus stabbed an egg straight through to the plate. He pushed to his feet and paced the length of the table. "No."

Belinda froze with the orange juice gallon in her hand. "Marcus, I'm only saying —"

"I know what you're saying. I'm saying no."

Violet couldn't look up at any of them. She was pretty sure Lee's eyes were boring straight into the top of her head. She stared at the table. Marcus's egg was bleeding gold.

"Y'all are treating this girl like a Constabulary agent."

"She is," he said.

Yes. She was. Look what she'd done so far. *You took their freedom.* Exactly what she was supposed to do. She ignored the bitter taste.

"What'll you do with her, then? Keep her here until she's old and gray like me?"

"I don't —"

From somewhere across the house, a lock clicked and a doorknob rattled. A door swung open. Marcus's pacing stalled, Lee turned toward the threshold, and Belinda plopped down the juice gallon and scurried toward the sound. Her eyes shone.

"There he is," she said.

"Where's my Pearl, and what's she wearing? Not much, I hope." The booming voice lacked Belinda's accent.

Belinda giggled like Khloe. Barely into the living room, still in sight of all her houseguests, she rushed into the arms of a paunchy, olive-skinned man who swept her feet off the floor with his embrace. Silver crept into his black hair, starting at the temples. He leaned down to kiss her, but Belinda shoved at his chest.

"Behave, Chuck. We've got guests."

The man's gaze lifted, froze, then traveled

over each person around his table. It settled on Marcus. "Little early in the day for a powwow, isn't it? And who's this?"

"This is Violet," Lee said.

"She's a spy," Marcus said.

Belinda huffed. "I'll get the syrup."

Chuck grabbed a chair and sat. He eyed first the food, then the clock. "Better start at the beginning."

"The Constabulary sent her." Marcus sat back down, and his fork prodded his remaining egg like a hunter testing if his quarry was really dead. "She texted addresses to them."

Chuck hunched forward, and his dark eyes narrowed at Violet. "Not my address."

"N-no," Violet said.

"The church, then, Marcus's church? And that porch house?"

Violet dipped her head, half a nod, half submission.

Chuck shifted to shove a thumb into his empty belt loop. "So they're using children now. Can't quite get my head around that one yet. Give me a minute."

None of them understood, not really. Lee was the only one who credited Violet to make her own choices. Well, and Marcus, but he also wanted her locked in a medieval tower for the rest of her life. Violet heard her own throat clear before she realized that she had to talk. Suddenly, they all watched her.

"I'm seventeen years old, and I do have a brain." She traced the flower design looping over her empty plate. "Maybe all Christians don't need re-ed, but the ones who hurt people, I think it's a good thing to teach them how to . . . to think, and feel for other people, and . . ."

Marcus's fork impaled his egg, but he didn't take a bite. Chuck frowned at Violet as if she'd announced an ability to breathe underwater.

"For the moment," Lee said, "let's indulge that theory. Some Christians require re-education in order to grow past their erroneous beliefs and treat people properly."

Yes, exactly. Lee said it so perfectly.

"Violet, do you believe Belinda would be benefited by re-education?"

Carrying a glass pitcher of syrup in one hand and a butter dish in the other, Belinda froze three feet from the table. The butter dish trembled.

"She's not intolerant," Violet said, and the dish steadied.

"No, then?"

"Yeah. I mean, no." But that didn't prove

271

anything. Not really. Belinda was only one person.

Lee's chin tilted up, and the calm hardened. "Do I belong in re-education?"

"I don't think so."

"What about Marcus?"

Let me go and I won't turn anyone in. The words hovered in her mouth, tasting like a green apple, sour because of their truth or because of their lie. Belinda seemed to duck as she set the butter and syrup on the edge of the table. She shuffled back to the kitchen, and dishes began to clatter.

"Violet," Lee said.

Enough of this. She wasn't some dog learning tricks, reciting the proper response to buy her release. "He'd probably be a better person after."

If she hadn't ventured a glance toward him just then, she'd have missed his momentary flinch. Hurt that she saw him that way? Hardly. But fear didn't fit him, either, despite what he'd said to Lee when he thought only she could hear. He surged to his feet and paced again.

"A better person?" Lee ran a finger around the rim of her juice glass.

"Calmer, or safer, or something."

"All right." Lee's voice turned the room into an iceberg. If Violet *had* wanted to purchase her trust with a lie, she should have professed absolute faith in Marcus.

"She can't leave," Marcus said.

Chuck rocked his chair back on two legs. "What're you saying?"

"Nobody would be safe."

"Fair enough, but your plan is to hold her here? Are we taking prisoners now?"

Marcus paced, and Lee spooned scrambled egg onto Violet's plate with an indifferent command. "Eat."

"Marcus," Chuck said. "What you're talking about is the opposite of invisible. This girl has parents — you do, don't you?" He pointed at Violet.

Violet forked a bite of egg, perfectly salted. She still had to force herself to swallow it. She nodded.

"Okay, so the parents report her missing, probably by tomorrow if they haven't already."

Actually, that might take a week. Or two.

"The regular cops start a search, it comes out that she was on some kind of Constabulary mission, next thing you know her face is all over the news and she's presumed murdered by the Christian crazies. How's that for under the radar?"

"You want me to let her go," Marcus said. His feet slowed.

"It's not a great choice, but it's the only one."

"Chuck, I know — missing persons, the media, the cops — I know it could happen. But if she leaves, she'll talk."

"I can't keep her here."

"Well. You're going to."

Wow, Marcus knew how to overstep. This wasn't his house. Chuck and Belinda were adults — good grief, could be his parents. But Chuck didn't bristle at the order. Didn't seem surprised or even annoyed.

His chair thumped back onto all four legs. He looked from Marcus to Violet, then back again. "You're really serious about this."

"It's this or prison. For everybody."

"So to avoid prison, you're going to kidnap a child."

The pacing resumed. "We don't have a choice."

"This is not 'we,' Marcus, not for one minute. This is you. I have a choice, and I'm telling you, son, I won't follow you if this is the road you're taking."

Follow him? The slope of the debate had slipped right over Violet's head until this moment. These people had begun arguing as equals, but . . . they weren't.

"If I let her go" — Marcus's words bit the air with quiet steel — "they will lock us up."

"And if you lock her up, how are you any different?"

Wait . . . lock her up? Were they talking literally, throw her into some bedroom and board up the window?

Marcus dug his knuckles into his neck and drew in a deep breath.

"Marcus is different," Lee said, "because he isn't threatening or mocking or brainwashing her."

Chuck shook his head. "I know that, but it's still holding a defenseless kid against her will."

A long sigh lowered Lee's shoulders, and she turned to Marcus. "He's right."

"He's . . . what?"

"She'll escape if she wants to, unless you confine her, and you can't do that."

"Why not?"

"Marcus. You cannot physically force your will on her like this. You're not that kind of man."

Her words were a cool breath over the burning shield of his anger. He shook his head, but his shoulders caved forward.

"Nothing I decide is going to be right," he said quietly.

Belinda stepped into the room. She must have been standing behind Violet for a while now. She set another pitcher of syrup on the table. "Blueberry flavored."

Marcus rubbed his neck, then forked his last bite of egg and shoved it into his mouth.

"What happens now?" Belinda rounded the corner of the table and sat down beside her husband. They looked like some official council, Lee and Violet a few chairs down from Belinda and Chuck, all facing Marcus's side of the table.

Marcus sipped his coffee.

Belinda sighed and grabbed the fork from the plate of pancakes. "Someone had better eat these. I put wheat germ and blueberries in them." She stabbed two at once and deposited them onto Violet's plate.

"You won't keep her here?" Marcus said.

Chuck glanced at Belinda, who ducked her head and offered Violet the syrup pitcher. As if that were some meaningful gesture, Chuck leaned back from the table and hooked a thumb in his belt loop. "No, we won't."

"Okay." Marcus pushed his plate away. "I've got other places."

A stare-down ensued, and Chuck lost. He sighed. "All right, son."

Lee said nothing.

Violet's breathing pinched as she poured syrup over the pancakes. Her fingers stuck to a congealing drip on the handle. The syrup trickled over her plate, pooled in the center, and seeped under an edge of her eggs. She used her fork to push them clear.

If she bolted, would Marcus tackle her and tie her to a chair? Would the others let him?

In the quiet, Belinda made herself a plate of pancakes and drowned them in syrup and butter. Chuck wandered to the kitchen and came back with a mug of coffee. Lee finished her eggs and took her plate to the dishwasher as if she lived there.

Violet forced down bites of pancake for maybe a whole minute before courage took over. She set down her fork.

"What about Khloe?"

"Khloe stays here." Marcus picked up his dishes and crossed toward the kitchen.

"Who?" Chuck said.

"You can't take me away from Khloe."

Marcus pivoted with a glare that scalded her. "She'll be safer."

He assumed Khloe was a Christian. He assumed Violet would turn in even her best friend. *He's right, isn't he?* She shoved her plate, and it clattered against the pancake plate in the center of the table. Belinda jumped.

"Someone tell me what else is going on here," Chuck said.

Violet might as well be chained to her chair. She couldn't get up, couldn't get out of this room, away from these people.

"A lot's happened," Belinda said.

"Details, woman." He spread his hands on the place mat. "Who's Khloe?"

"That would be me."

Khloe stood on the cuffs of borrowed lounge pants, one foot on the dining room floor and one on living room carpet. She hugged herself, swallowed by the oversized sleep shirt. She didn't look at anyone but Violet.

"I'm Khloe." *With a K.* But those words didn't come. Khloe took another step into the room and shivered. "Violet, did you . . . do something?"

Eventually, yeah, Khloe was going to learn everything. Not like this, though.

Violet pushed her chair back and approached her friend. Khloe blinked at her like someone who'd just watched her house burn down. She didn't back away, though. Maybe she'd listen.

"Violet," Lee said.

Violet turned. "We're going upstairs. Marcus can wait."

She led Khloe back up to their room, shut the door, and sank onto the bed. Before Violet could open her mouth, Khloe planted her feet apart as if bracing for a fistfight and crossed her arms.

"You spill it, Vi, all of it. Marcus was accusing you of something down there."

Everything became inevitable, the way people described a car wreck. Why was she still pumping the brake, still turning into the skid of this friendship as if she could make it right?

"Khloe, I . . ." Her hands curled into the quilt.

"Come on, whatever it is, just tell me."

"When we were at the church meeting . . . and I had my phone out . . . I wasn't playing pinball."

Khloe's forehead furrowed. She crossed the bedroom and sat beside Violet. "Am I supposed to be following right now?"

"I was sending a text. 'Fifty-six-eighty-two Apple Lane.' "

"Uh . . . the address? Who would you text the . . . ?" Khloe's mouth dropped open. Her voice returned as a squeak. "Not the con-cops. You didn't text the con-cops."

Violet gulped a breath and steered them both through the guardrail. "I . . . I did."

They smashed through and plummeted forever, sitting side by side on Belinda's guest bed. Then Khloe was on her feet. Shaking. Shouting.

"You did not do this. You did not try to send my father to re-ed."

"Khloe, I did."

"You did not."

Violet doubled over and twisted her hands into the quilt. Her stomach hurt. "I did."

"No, Violet, no."

"The church raid happened because of me. Everything's happened because of me. I wanted him to get help, I wanted all of them to get —"

"No!" Khloe closed her eyes.

"I had to do it. Austin said they —"

Khloe stormed into Violet's space and shoved her. Another few inches back and Violet's head would have bounced against the wall.

"Austin? You turned my dad in for Austin? You ruined my life for Austin? Were you going to turn Belinda in too, while I was right here sleeping in one of her fugitive-Christian beds?"

Violet sat back up. "Khloe —"

"Were you going to even tell me about it, or just let the con-cops show up and play stupid while they hauled me off to re-ed along with a bunch of strangers!"

Something long simmering boiled up in Violet's chest. "Shut up. Shut up about you. This isn't about you, this is about everyone, this is about the whole country. I was trying to help these people, including your dad, and maybe if you end up in re-ed they'll teach you the world's bigger than Khloe-with-a-K Hansen."

Khloe whimpered, and her voice fell to a whisper. "You did know. That I'd go to re-ed. What was I, collateral damage?"

No. Of course not. And yes.

"My gosh, Violet. What kind of friend are you?"

Ten years of sleepovers and secrets and tears and laughter, Khloe's *I-know-you'll-save-me* gaze, a week's worth of Violet's clothes stashed in Khloe's bottom dresser drawer — all of it broke in Violet's chest, all at once.

Khloe shook her head as if to clear a daydream. "I heard a baby crying earlier, when I was getting dressed."

"Another fugitive came last night. She had a baby."

"I'm hungry. I'm going down to eat."

Khloe, I helped deliver him. He's so tiny and alive. And I don't want you to go to re-ed, and I'm starting to feel mixed up, and I think I need help to figure things out. "Belinda makes good pancakes."

Khloe ambled from the room. Violet shut the door after her and walked back to the

281

bed, smoothly, like water, like Lee. She slid down to the carpet with her back against the bedpost. Her knees drew into her chest. Tears clogged her throat, not because she hurt but because she should. And didn't.

27

They weren't escaping anything, not really. When they returned home in a night and a day, Khloe wouldn't be there. Clay pushed it out of his head, the image of where she was, would still be. *Lord, I asked You not to let this happen.* Beside him in the Jeep's passenger seat, Natalia hadn't spoken since they left. The open window ruffled her hair toward him, hitting him every so often with a breath of mango shampoo. He'd asked her where she wanted to go, but she didn't even glance his way. So he drove the highway and inhaled the freedom of speed. And prayed, though he was starting to wonder why.

Natalia shifted in the seat. "You're heading toward our old house."

"There's a hotel off exit Forty-One, remember?"

Only the wind responded.

"We skipped lunch." His thumb rubbed the steering wheel grip. "You hungry?"

"Drive-through. I don't want to sit down in some restaurant and have some person come inform me about the specials and expect me to smile and tip them and . . ."

"Agreed."

The conversation stalled again, until he'd filled up the Jeep's tank and bought sub sandwiches and taken a spontaneous exit that made Natalia finally look at him and keep looking. She knew where he was going. He waited for her to protest, but she didn't. The place drew him mile by mile until he turned onto the same dirt path they'd driven a hundred times, ten years ago. Through the same metal gate, into the same parking lot, paved now.

He wanted to ask her if this was okay, if he'd projected his own emotions onto hers. Maybe Clinton River Park was the last place Natalia wanted to be. He locked his jaw against the questions. Her silence couldn't last much longer, anyway.

But it did last. He grabbed the bag of sandwiches and locked the Jeep. She needed to say something. Anything. He led her toward the cluster of picnic tables canopied by century-old oak trees.

"Where to, Nat?"

She picked the table farthest from the family with a Lab puppy and two strollers and wow, five kids. Through a screen of foliage to the left, Clinton River glimmered, about fifty feet away.

Too close.

The kids across the picnic area provided most of lunch's soundtrack: shrieking and shouting and prompting barks from their dog. Farther away, out of sight, carousel music joined in counterpoint. But underneath the symphony of bliss roared the river.

Natalia found her Tuscan chicken, and Clay dug into his BLT. See, he could eat right beside the dragon. He didn't fear water, didn't even fear rivers. The sound simply didn't relax him. If she knew, Natalia wouldn't choose the table nearest the water, but she didn't need to know this. Didn't need to know he'd thrown out her *Wilderness River and Waterfall* CD, either.

Still she didn't talk. She took petite bites and studied the grooves in the picnic table, the paint chips that would have told Clay this wood used to be red, except he didn't need to be told. The paint job had been new last time they ate here. Last time Khloe had bounced on her bench and tossed her bread crusts to the squirrels.

Clay swallowed his fifth bite and threw

away his reserve. "I appreciate that you came."

Natalia's gaze jumped up from the table. She set her sandwich down on the plastic wrapper. "You thought I wouldn't?"

"I just don't take it for granted. That's all." He shouldn't have said anything. He bit into the sandwich.

"Where's my mommy?"

The squeaky voice came from over the table, behind Natalia. She swiveled on the bench, and Clay stood. The littlest from the nearby family, no older than four, stood with her small bare feet planted apart and her hands splayed open in front of her, a petition. Dark hair strayed from her ponytail, and her nose curved like Khloe's.

Shoot, she could have fallen into the water and . . . The river grew louder, or maybe he only thought it did.

"Come on, Clayton, don't be a chicken."

"I'm not, I just don't want to get wet."

Clay shook his head. The memories should know better by now. They weren't wanted. Weren't allowed.

Natalia practically jumped to her feet. "Let's find your mommy together."

"Okay." The girl reached for her hand.

Natalia latched on as another voice found them from across the clearing.

286

"Isabel! Izzie!"

"Oh, there's my mommy." The girl tore her hand from Natalia's and dashed toward the voice, though the woman couldn't be easy to spot from Isabel's three-and-a-half-foot vantage point. Natalia watched into the sun, until the girl collided against her mother's legs with an open-armed hug.

Clay sat back down, but Nat kept standing there, staring, her hand shielding her eyes. The child skipped alongside her mother for a few steps, then was scooped into her arms and wrapped in that smothering hug of released terror. One second, she's next to you. The next, she's nowhere. The next, she's back in your arms, and you vow never to blink again.

"Nat?"

She didn't face him, instead ducked her head and dabbed under her eyes.

"Oh. Nat." Clay was off the bench and beside her before he could think of a safer response. He cupped his hand around her face.

"Sorry, I — I guess she hit a soft spot. It's fine."

She backed away, and he let her. He could live a thousand years and never make this right.

Lord, You can't possibly want Khloe in re-

education. Why didn't You prevent it?

"Let's walk." His hand twitched at his side, but he didn't hold it out. Natalia stuffed their unfinished sandwiches back into the to-go bag and dangled it from her left hand. They strolled side by side, away from the river, across the picnic area, past Isabel and her siblings as they played frozen tag.

"Izzie, you have to stand still!"

"How come?"

" 'Cause Jamie tagged you!"

"Mommy, do I have to stand still?"

Natalia walked faster, and the debate faded before Clay could hear the verdict. If they'd been able to have more after Khloe, if even only that one time, when Natalia had been so sure she was pregnant . . . what if she had been? They'd have a thirteen-year-old too. Maybe a son. Maybe another little girl. Or if they'd been able to have as many as they wanted. If they could come to the park with a whole precious brood and play frozen tag.

The possibilities burned his eyes. He blinked fast, turned his head to watch a pair of Canada geese waddle down the sidewalk, single file. The one in the lead stopped before a dip in the pavement and eyed Clay as he and Nat crossed in front of them.

Once they had passed, the goose led his mate forward. Watching out for her. A dumb bird was a better guardian than Clay was. No wonder God hadn't given him more children.

The distant carousel score, the chattering squirrels, the random birdsong all mixed with the conversation clips of passing strangers. Yet it was Natalia's quiet that seemed to ring in Clay's ears. He had lost track of their direction. Maybe Natalia was heading somewhere specific. He let the park seep into his pores, memories thick as the scent of cut grass. Khloe's laughter trying to fill the whole park. Khloe's sticky kiss brushing his cheek. Khloe's dance in front of the carousel every time Clay handed her a bright blue ticket to ride her favorite horse.

The boisterous brass had been growing louder as they neared the park's biggest attraction. Clay veered toward it, and Natalia straggled for a few seconds, then jogged to catch up. Around a bend in the path, there it stood, a shiny rainbow of painted horses beneath the broad green top. It drifted to a halt as Clay and Natalia stopped at the metal gate. Hardly any line.

"Clay?"

"Let's ride it."

Her lips parted, and he held back the urge to touch them. She gazed at the kid taking tickets who had begun to stare at them.

"Y-you . . . want . . . to . . . ride . . . the . . . carousel?" Each word escalated, not in volume but in pitch.

To let the past cradle him for three or four minutes, to let it sweep him in circles until the world blurred around him, until his failure blurred too. Until he could hear his little girl laughing from the horse next to him, a sound the doctors had told him he would lose forever, a sound he had finally, this week, lost. Yes. He wanted to ride the carousel. He reached for Natalia's hand, tugged it to his chest, let her feel his pounding heart.

"Natalia."

Her fingers curled into his T-shirt and held on for long seconds. She stepped closer until her whisper fell against his chest. "Not without my daughter."

She let go. Stepped back. Walked away. Half of him wanted to watch her go, wanted to buy one ticket and ride alone. He jogged after her, caught her wrist, and let her pull away.

"I want to go home." Her words fell toward the concrete.

"Nat, they —"

"I have a wedding tonight, did you forget? A huge wedding, couple hundred people. The bride's Polish. She told me there'll be family there that she's never even met. And I . . . I need to do it, Clay."

A gray squirrel moseyed down the sidewalk ahead of them, a nut in its mouth, too heavy for scampering. Its tail was thin, chewed, as if something larger had attacked it and lost. Natalia stood still, watched it gain distance from them, then faced Clay with granite in her eyes — hard, beautiful, yet unable to withstand the strongest blows.

"I have to shoot this wedding. I have to do something . . . normal. Today. I don't know if that makes sense."

"So . . ." He cleared the sandpaper from his voice. "This isn't because of the carousel."

"It is, it absolutely is. I thought maybe you were right and we could run away, but even for a day — we can't. And I don't care if they come or not. They can question me. They've done it already and got nothing."

He pushed her hair back from her shoulders. She shouldn't be out tonight, alone in a crowd, feigning happiness. And he shouldn't be home tonight, alone in a house that echoed accusations and shoved him toward his keys, toward the door, toward the highway. He could reschedule the bowling game. He could call a spontaneous online chat for the Lit Philes.

He could act normal.

He leaned close to Natalia's ear. "I'm coming to the reception."

She stepped back. "You obviously can't do that."

"You said yourself the bride and groom don't know everyone."

"No, but I'm sure the bride's mother does."

"A couple hundred people? I can avoid the important ones."

"Clay, I'll be working. Even if no one figures it out, it's incredibly unprofessional to let my husband crash the —"

He settled a kiss on her lips, soft and salty, quick, but she closed her eyes and opened her mouth. Strangers passing on the path saw her hand on his arm and her hair in his hands and probably believed that Natalia loved him with abandon, that he could never hurt her. She pulled back from the kiss, but the granite had cracked a little.

"I guess you could be my assistant. You're pretty decent at holding things."

Despite everything, he smiled, and Natalia threaded her arm through his and walked

beside him to the Jeep, down the sidewalk
like an aisle.

28

After curling up on the bed for a while, Violet got up and opened the window. Birdsong floated in. Through the lattice roof of the deck, Khloe was easy to watch. She'd collected paper, pencil, and what looked like a hardcover coffee-table book for a lap desk. The porch swing moved in the breeze as Khloe bent her head over the paper. Her pencil scurried.

Someone tapped on the door. Must be Belinda. "Come in."

Chuck. He lumbered in and leaned against the wall.

"Time to go."

To go somewhere else chosen by Marcus. She'd jump out of his truck at the first red light, before she could become another grave in the woods.

No, she didn't really believe that. Willingness to kidnap wasn't the same as willingness to murder.

Regardless, she'd be out of that truck before he could stop her. The first chance she got.

When she didn't respond, Chuck joined her at the window. "She's an artist?"

Violet nodded.

"How about you?"

"Stick figures. Houses with inaccurate shadows." She'd never noticed her lighting errors until Khloe pointed them out. Sometimes, she still doodled while Khloe sketched, purposely creating top-heavy buildings so Khloe would give them the guinea-pig laugh.

"I told Marcus it's not right to separate sisters, but he said you're not."

Violet kept her gaze out the window. Khloe was shading now, broad sweeps of the pencil tilted almost sideways. "We're both seventeen. Khloe just looks young. Hormone deficiency."

"Now that makes more sense."

"She's staying with you?"

"For now. It was her choice."

Of course it was. Violet leaned her forehead against the screen, letting the wire mesh imprint on her skin. "Are you a Christian?"

He didn't answer for a moment. "Can't say I am."

"I went into your study. I found your Bible."

"How about that." Chuck ambled back to the bed and sat on the edge. "It's not mine, actually. Marcus gave it to me a few months ago, when I started badgering him about what it said."

"Is it really two thousand years old?"

He chuckled. "The physical copy? Of course not. The words? At least that old, and I guess a lot of the books in the first half are even older."

Two thousand years old. The Progressive United Version, government-funded and government-sanctioned, had been published in Violet's lifetime, or shortly before it. Repairing the ancient text. But everyone who'd lived before now, hundreds, thousands of years ago — they'd only had the ancient version. Had God's message to them been flawed?

Weird that she'd never wondered before.

"Anyway, yes, I'm reading it. And I'll make up my own mind in my own time, just like you have to do."

"I've already made up my mind."

Chuck pushed to his feet. "Seems to me, you don't have enough information yet for that."

She knew what her next question should

296

be. *So what do the old Bibles say?* But those words wouldn't come.

"Come on downstairs," Chuck said.

"Can I ask you one more thing first?"

He shrugged.

"You said you wouldn't follow Marcus anymore, if he did this. If he kidnapped me."

"That's not a question."

But the shifting from one foot to the other betrayed his answer anyway. And he knew she knew. *Austin, I did it. I really did it.* She had identified the resistance leader. Did the Constabulary know how organized their enemy was? That a chain of command had formed, led by some ordinary guy in his thirties?

Marcus's truck was running out in the driveway. He already sat behind the wheel. Violet climbed inside, and Chuck shut the door. She searched in front of her, craned her neck behind, checked both side windows.

Khloe wasn't here.

"I told her we were leaving," Marcus said quietly.

And she hadn't wanted even to say good-bye. Violet breathed through the threat of tears until her eyes no longer burned.

"What about Lee?" And Belinda. Not that Violet could say anything to them.

"Lee?" He put the truck in gear and started down the driveway. "She's okay. I think she's taking care of Wren and the baby."

Violet would never see any of them again. Not that it mattered.

A few miles from the house, now on blacktop but still in rural territory, Violet rested her elbow on the half-open window and watched him drive. He looked like he was gritting his teeth.

"Marcus?"

"Yeah."

"Where's the new place? How far is it?"

His right hand latched onto his neck. The only sound was the wind, rushing at the window and *whoosh*ing as cars passed from the other direction. Violet's body was coiled for the first red light, but every one was green. Or yellow, and Marcus passed under it just in time.

"You can't do this," she said. "You can't kidnap me and not even tell me where you're taking me."

No response.

Violet folded her arms. "You'd better tell them, whoever they are, that this is against my will and they're going to have to tie me to a chair and gag me and lock me in a closet."

"Stop." It was more a bark than a word.

Violet rubbed her thumb over her bracelet. They drove without music. Once, they had to brake for a tractor hauling a hay wagon. The guy in overalls — yeah, actual overalls — drove down the center of the road as if he weren't in the way. While Violet was still deciding if she could jump out of the truck without killing herself, Marcus sped up and passed the tractor. The sweet scent of hay filled the truck cab for a few minutes afterward.

They drove on M-53 south for miles. As they exited, Marcus gripped his neck again.

"I'm taking you to a public place. You can call your parents to pick you up. Or the police or the Constabulary, whoever you want."

"You're . . . letting me go? Why?"

He didn't speak again until he pulled into the parking lot of a long, flat plaza, starting with Kroger on one end and ending with Dairy Queen on the other. He parked the truck to face the stores, tailgate toward the road, and pulled a Ziploc bag from his glove box.

"You have your phone, right?"

She'd nearly forgotten it on the night-stand, useless as it was, but at the last minute she slipped it into her pocket. Her

299

name was scribbled on the bag from which Marcus shook the guts of the phone. Violet handed over the shell.

He made quick work of reassembling it with the same tiny screwdriver he'd used before. Before sliding the battery in, he put the screwdriver away and met her eyes.

"You've got no reason to do me a favor. But I'm asking."

Of course he was. He wanted her to walk away as if none of this had happened. Violet straightened her spine and tried to glare at him.

Marcus reattached the phone battery and waited for it to power up. "You said you don't think they need re-education. Belinda and Lee. Do you think the same thing about Chuck?"

"I . . . I guess not. I mean, I guess he doesn't."

His shoulders caved slightly. "Okay. Good."

Her phone vibrated and chimed again and again, texts and voicemails pinging in. Marcus tapped something on the screen.

"Don't read my —"

"I'm not." Another bark. He was typing a note. His thumbs were broad, and he had to backspace twice. He handed her the phone.

An address on Marina Street, wherever that was.

"My name's Marcus Brenner. That's my home address."

Violet's fingers trembled around the phone. "I don't get it." But she did.

"When you go to the Constabulary, if they ask where you've been, give them that address. And let everybody else —" His voice broke.

Violet looked up from the phone. His calm expression was betrayed by the death grip of both his hands on the back of his neck.

He cleared his throat. "Turn me in, just me. Please."

This was his favor. Violet gave a slow nod.

"You'll do it?" Marcus said.

"Yeah."

His grip eased around his neck, but his nod was stiff. Of course, he didn't fully believe her. He'd probably leave her here and rush to warn Chuck of the danger, if he hadn't already.

"Marcus, you said you wouldn't let me go."

"I know."

"But now you are."

"I know."

"Because of Chuck and Lee?"

"No. I mean, yeah, probably a little."

"Why else?" Why did she care?

He sighed. "I don't know. I guess mostly because of Jesus."

Uh . . . what?

Marcus jerked a nod toward the passenger door. "You should go."

She tried to answer, but her throat was too tight. She got out of the truck and walked toward the Dairy Queen. They'd let her use the phone, especially if she said she'd been kidnapped.

Except she hadn't been. And she didn't need to use their phone, because hers had been returned.

At the door, she glanced back. Marcus watched her. Two teen guys exited, releasing a chime from the bell above the door and a gust of air conditioning. They sidestepped her without a glance her way, and the door closed again. Its glass reflected the red truck as Marcus drove away.

29

The familiar ringback played in her ear, some elitist classical piece she'd always mocked that now flooded her eyes with tears. *Please pick up.* He should. He'd texted her nine times and left three voice-mails in the last two days.

"Violet?"

Thank You, God! "Austin."

"Where are you? Where were you? What happened?"

"Can — can you come get me?"

"Where? Are you safe? Are you okay?"

"The Kroger at the corner of Mound and . . . I think it's Twenty-Five Mile? I'm standing in front of the Dairy Queen."

"I'm on my way now. Babe, please, tell me you're okay."

"I'm good." She swallowed the tears that tried to block her words. No falling apart.

"Be there in ten minutes. Don't go anywhere."

"I won't."

But neither of them hung up. Violet sat on a wooden bench as two grade-school girls dashed up to the Dairy Queen window, one wearing a tank and shorts, the other smoothing her hand over her sundress.

"I want chocolate."

"I want caramel."

Maybe when they were older, they'd learn to appreciate fruit smoothies. A would-be sob crushed Violet's chest.

"Violet." Austin's voice shook. Think what he'd been through, not knowing if her mission had gotten her murdered by Christians. *Why does everybody believe they're all the same?* "Violet, talk to me."

"I'm good."

"I'm almost there."

His nine-year-old car was beige and squat and could only belong to a college commuter. His bumper stickers aided the impression. Violet had mocked him for all this in addition to his ringback tone, but his car pulled up to the curb worth more than any limousine. She flew to the passenger side and motioned him to unlock the doors before he'd fully stopped. The locks clicked. She threw the door open and leaped inside and slammed it shut.

And burst into tears.

Austin rubbed her back, and she leaned across the console, into his arm. Still, she wasn't close enough.

"Sorry, I don't know what's wrong with me, I just . . ." Stupid sobs, sticking in her throat.

Austin put the car in park. "Hey, hey. Talk to me. Tell me what happened to you."

Something had happened, all right, something that had torn her whole head apart. She knew she was supposed to turn them all in, was supposed to want to. But right now, all she wanted was to understand them, all of them, Marcus and Lee and Chuck and Belinda. They didn't make any sense.

"Okay," Austin said. "You want me to take you home?"

"No." The word shoved past her shaking and her tears. "No, not yet. I — I have to talk to someone. I have to talk to you."

His hand cupped the back of her head and caressed her hair. "Where to?"

Somewhere they could say anything. Nowhere public. "Your apartment. I've never seen it. I don't even know where it is."

"Violet . . ."

"We'll be safe there."

He regarded her a long moment, and he

probably would have said no in any circumstance but this one. Worry creased his face, and he was older today than the last time they'd been together. But so was she.

He sighed, a consent. "Okay. But you're safe with me no matter where you are."

Violet laid her head on his shoulder. "I know."

Austin's apartment was on the second floor of a brick complex that, even from the outside, looked as tidy and no-nonsense as he was. He led her up the foyer stairs, fumbled with his keys before finding the right one, and motioned her over the threshold with a smile that skipped her heartbeat.

Violet would have expected solid bookshelves along every wall of his one-bedroom unit, but the living room surprised her, split into half-study, half-gym. The bathroom furnishings included one set of white towels and one white rug. More like a hotel than a home.

They meandered into the living room. Austin sprawled in a beanbag chair and motioned her to the pillow-back couch. "Do you need anything? Lunch?"

"Later." She sank down onto the center

cushion, leaned back, and closed her eyes.

"Did someone hurt you?" Austin said quietly.

She shook her head. He stood and crossed the room to sit beside her, and Violet leaned into his shoulder. Maybe she didn't want to talk at all. Maybe she could stay here for a day, think things through, sleep on the couch tonight, and then in the morning . . . do what she had to do.

She did have to do it. Right?

"Violet?"

"You don't have to worry about me. Nobody hurt me."

They didn't move for long minutes. As tension melted from her muscles and sleep blanketed her, Austin's lips touched her hair. Then lowered to her neck. She burrowed closer, and warmth filled her.

"Yesterday," he whispered, "I had this thought that maybe you were dead."

She reached up to pull his head down. Their lips met, and she tasted coffee. Austin deepened the kiss. Closer, she wanted to be closer. Together. Safe. Wanted. Her breath was gone, but she didn't stop. She squirmed away from his arm around her back and grabbed his warm hand. *Here.* She pushed it under her shirt. He inched his hand up to her breastbone. Violet pressed against him.

He withdrew his hand and pulled back with a ragged breath. "Violet."

"Hmm?" She kissed him again, but he angled his face away.

"We can't," he said.

"I'm not a kid, especially not after this week."

"What?" The blue of his eyes seemed to darken. His hand clenched.

Oh, good grief. "I didn't mean like *that*. Just . . . that I've learned . . . that I've . . ." Why couldn't she tell him?

"Let's start at the beginning. Where have you been? Did someone take you? Did you escape?"

See, there, that was why. Because she didn't know how to answer any of those questions. Had she been at Chuck and Belinda's? Had she been at Marcus's house? Austin would never believe the resistance leader had let her go. Maybe she could distract both of them for now and deal with this later. She leaned closer for a kiss. He turned away. Again.

Violet pushed up from the couch and stood. "Why don't you want me?"

"You know I —"

"Just tell me what's wrong with me, maybe I can fix it."

308

"Are you serious? Violet, you're beautiful."

Oh, please. Outright lying was the last thing she'd ever expected from Austin. "If I'm so beautiful, have sex with me."

With a half groan, he turned away from her.

He didn't want her, not like that. Considering everything she'd learned and lost lately, this realization shouldn't have mattered so much, but it was a final weight, tossed onto the pile of things she couldn't carry for one more minute. She turned and rushed down the hall, past the bathroom to Austin's bedroom, the only other room in this place with a door. She locked it.

"Violet." The knob rattled. "Hey. Come on."

"You never should have dated me if you didn't want me."

A soft sliding sound, down to the floor. He must be slouched against the door. "You're misinterpreting all of this."

"It doesn't need interpreting, Austin. It's pretty clear."

Tears pushed for release. She swiped at them and smeared them all over her stupid face. Three crying bouts in two days, and she couldn't even blame hormones. A sob heaved in her shoulders, but Austin shouldn't hear her blubbering. She buried the mutiny inside and planted her feet apart until her legs stopped shaking. Until the tears stopped squeezing from her clenched eyelids.

She opened her eyes and noticed the four walls around her for the first time, the filled bookshelves, the lamp and nightstand hewn of a stained wood that belonged more in a resort cabin than an apartment. On one wall, a painting depicted the outstretched arms of two men. One reached slightly upward from the left, and one reached slightly downward from the right. In the center of the painting, their hands nearly touched.

"It's fine," she said to the closed door. "You can go date other people. Don't feel bad about it."

"Will you stop? I don't want to date other people."

Tears surged back at his frustration. If only she knew he meant it. But really, he'd never given her reason not to believe him. He wasn't the one who'd shaken her up like a snow globe. Maybe doubting one thing led her to doubt the whole universe. Violet stepped toward the door, then stopped. Seeing her tear-smudged face would make him feel worse.

"Violet?"

"Is there any Kleenex in here?"

The nightstand was bare, other than the lamp. Violet tugged open the drawer.

Her heart overturned.

A handgun. Small. Snapped into a holster with a folded strap. Not for a belt, then. She poked the holster strap, and it slithered to its full length. Cop movies were educational, after all: this was a shoulder holster.

Wait a minute.

Cop movies.

An edge of gold winked at her from under the shoulder strap. She pulled at it, and her thumb grazed the cold metal of the gun. She shuddered. Two fingers lifted the badge from the drawer. The badge with words embossed on a gold shield.

Michigan Philosophical Constabulary. US Department of Justice.

30

Assistant to the photographer was a mind-numbing job, but watching Natalia work was utterly engrossing. To Clay's surprise, the ceremony took place outdoors on a farm. The bride and groom escaped in a horse-drawn buggy to have their pictures shot around the red pole barn. A little after 9:00, dinner and dessert had been served — buffet style, plenty left by the time the vendors (himself included) got in line — and the tiki torches around the white reception tent were lit. The DJ powered out one R&B hit after another that sounded exactly the same and clashed painfully with the down-home country surroundings.

Clay, Natalia, and several octogenarians seemed to be the only ones not dancing. Clay sat at a deserted table strewn with flower petals, crumbs, and white cake plates that honestly did look like china. The geriatrics conversed several feet away in a huddle of cigar smoke.

Natalia had resumed taking pictures after wolfing down a plate of food. She might well have forgotten Clay was here the way she had re-submerged into work mode, artist mode. During the exchange of vows, she'd crouched in the center aisle, just behind the front row of white folding chairs, and angled her camera upward. She crept all around the silk-flowered arch and tilted her camera every which way, yet she never intruded. From an out-of-the-way corner, probably only Clay noticed her at all, though *noticed* was a feeble word for what he was feeling.

Dressed in a short-sleeved, black Oxford shirt and slim black jeans, her hair pulled back but loosened by the evening breeze, Natalia outshone the twenty-something bride without trying. Her lips pursed when she set up a new shot. A beam of success lit her eyes when she captured what she'd seen through her viewfinder or in her head. Clay could have stepped out from his corner, marched down the aisle, and demonstrated for the new couple exactly how to kiss one's bride. Now, hours and good food and fake conversation later, his final task was to guard Nat's camera case. He lounged back in a plastic folding chair and battled the

313

desire to drag her onto the portable dance floor.

A minute later, she lowered her camera to the at-ease position, level with her waist, elbows bent. White holiday lights fringed the inside of the tent, and colored lights rotated on the dance floor, constantly shifting the hue of the yellow bridesmaid dresses. As if someone had complained about the monotonous bass, "The Loco-Motion" started to play, and every dancer over fifty burst into applause. Natalia hovered at the edge of the celebration, face unlit. She lifted her camera, took a shot, lowered it again. Slipped around the edge where grass met floor and probably didn't realize she now faced Clay head-on. How could he have been married to her for nineteen years without seeing firsthand how her art absorbed her?

She raised her camera again but brought it down to waist-level too fast. Oh, must have seen him. Maybe she would approach him. No one would notice, at this point, if she did.

Nope. She took another few shots, sidling away from him. It was okay, it really was, or it would have been, if today had been any other day. If he knew that, had she not been on the job, Natalia would have danced with him to Grand Funk. At some point, though, he'd lost the answers to fundamental questions.

Someone's five-foot great-grandmother shuffled over to his table and plopped herself down. Her arthritic hands curled in her lap. "You here alone?"

"Photographer's assistant."

She laughed. "You're kidding."

"Nope."

"Never seen a wedding quite like this in all my born days. Horse and buggy, mostaccioli in warming pans, and the wedding party wearing yellow of all colors. Maybe those cops around back are the fashion police, eh?"

Fun. He got to entertain the delusional relative of strangers. "I'm sure that's what they are."

"That'd be why their uniforms are gray instead of blue. See, gray is a neutral color. Good color for fashion police."

Run! Clay shoved back his chair, breathed in and rocked back on his heels.

"And, see, that way they can judge anyone no matter what color she's wearing, unless she's wearing gray, of course. That might get a little sticky . . ."

The woman really didn't know who they were. Clay walked away, and she kept talking. Where was Natalia, why couldn't he find Natalia? He had turned both of their phones off. There was no one they needed to hear from other than Marcus, who wasn't likely to call now, since he couldn't have anything to say other than *"Sorry about that broken promise to keep your daughter safe."*

His body buzzed, senses tuned in. The evening breeze tingled the hair of his arms. Dance music pulsed in his ears. The scent of American gourmet had begun to dissipate: baked chicken, roasted potatoes, green beans, mostaccioli. He spotted Natalia and could breathe again. She knelt in a corner of the tent, lining up a low-angle shot of the dance floor.

He strode past her to the back of the tent. Not that it really had a back, but one end had been designated for the caterers, and they'd parked their trucks on the other side of the tent flap. He ducked outside, into the wavering light of tiki torches and a spotlight aimed in this direction from the barn. Guys in white shirts and black ties milled around, packaging food, loading their trucks.

Off to one side, out of the caterers' way, stood two stocky men in gray uniforms and utility belts. Badges, nightsticks, radios, sidearms. Clay backed away one step, then two. The one nearest him looked up and

316

met his eyes.

"If you're thinking we must be here without an invite . . ." The agent shrugged. Smiled.

In the stark shadows, swallowing nerves might be more obvious. For all Clay knew, his Adam's apple was all they could see. And if it was, then . . . *They don't know me.*

"Ending the honeymoon before it gets started?" His own voice sounded tinny.

"No, no. Would you believe it, here for the photographer."

"Oh, I think she's gone."

"They do blend in." The second agent scratched the side of his stubbly jaw. "GPS on the cell phone says she's still here."

Come on, Nat! Did she expect Khloe to call from inside re-education? *Don't look away. Calm down.* "Must be a very important person."

"We can't discuss that, obviously."

"Right, of course. But if you crashed a wedding for her . . ."

"It's just routine questioning. Needed an opportunity to talk to her alone."

Without Clay. Free to spill the burdens that anyone trained to read people would see in her every breath, her every blink. Her husband was a Christian, and her daughter was wrongly accused. They'd known

317

everything. All this time. Maybe they tacked on some clichéd assumptions, too, like Clay as an abusive husband who threatened her to keep her quiet.

Lord, if You're not going to make things right, then I am.

The prayer, the rant, the pushing back at a God who didn't bother to pull for him — it hung in the night and drifted away like torch smoke. But not before both agents zeroed in on something, maybe a flicker in his eyes, a twitch in his cheek, maybe just a breath that drew itself in deeper than the last one. They hadn't recognized his face, not yet, but they knew him. The almost fugitive. The man about to lose.

One of them stepped closer. "Clay Hansen?"

31

Stretched out in front of her, Violet's hands trembled, one on the doorknob, one gripping the hard metal shield. Her palm pressed the embossed words so hard, they would imprint onto her skin. She opened the door.

Austin nearly fell into the room. He scrambled to his feet. His wide eyes clung to hers. "Violet, I . . ."

Maybe she'd jumped to conclusions, maybe . . . What, maybe a civilian's nightstand drawer held a Constabulary badge and gun by mistake? She shoved the badge in his face. He actually paled.

"Crap," he said.

Violet dropped the badge at his feet. It hit the carpet with a gold glint. She hugged herself against the last truth she could ever have guessed. She'd come here to tell him everything. To trust him. To end the freedom of people she couldn't trust.

At least they all admitted who they were.

"Are you undercover?" The squeak sounded like someone half her age.

Austin bent to pick up the badge, and for a wild instant, Violet pictured herself shoving him off-balance and running out the door, down the lobby stairs, into the summer heat. He straightened. His eyes were blue pools of regret.

"Let's go sit down."

"Answer me first. Were you supposed to pretend you were in love with me, so you could convince me to spy on them?"

A scowl pulled his mouth. "Violet, who insisted on you spying?"

"Maybe you used some kind of, I don't know, psychological thing. To make me think it was my idea."

"Think about that. I didn't know about Khloe until you told me."

Khloe. Her arms tightened around her middle.

"Yeah, I know it was Khloe. The Christian friend you didn't want to turn in. She left her ID at the meeting we busted."

We. Ice trickled through her body. "Why, then?"

"You'll have to specify the question."

"Stop it, stop trying to sound all scholarly like — like — you."

The blink could have been a wince. "I'm not undercover. I didn't fake my interest in you. I met you at Elysium by chance. I thought you were attractive, and your introspection was refreshing. And you know I also thought you were older."

It sounded true, all of it. If only it was.

"Please come sit on the couch, and we'll talk."

Violet nodded, trailed him back to the living room, but sat across the room in his beanbag chair. He crumpled onto the couch as if a boulder had pushed him down.

"If you're not undercover, why didn't you tell me you're a con-cop?"

Austin rubbed his eyes. "Do you know that up to half the population knows of someone who's practicing Christianity and refuses to turn them in?"

"Okay, now's not the time to give me an education."

"The media wants you to think everyone agrees with the government all the time. Well, they don't. And the Constabulary . . . we're one of the least-agreed-on issues in the country."

"So . . . ?"

"So, no, I don't instantly tell acquaintances what I do for a living. Especially interesting female acquaintances.

About every third person I meet avoids me after they find out."

Weariness drew lines between his eyes. Violet pushed to her feet and stepped toward him, sat on the couch with a cushion between them.

"The buddy you told me about, the concop. You were talking about yourself. You're trying to find the resistance."

One hand fisted his hair. "What I did, hiding this from you. It wasn't to manipulate you into anything. It wasn't part of my job."

Violet twisted the edge of her T-shirt. She could forgive him. Unless . . .

"Violet?"

"That number I texted the addresses to. Was I texting you the whole time, on some government phone?"

He sighed and this time scrubbed both hands through his hair. For the first time, that flustered gesture didn't make her want to smooth away the mussed strands.

"You lied to me," she whispered.

He jumped to his feet. "Yes, okay? Yes. I lied to you."

"More than once."

"I was going to tell you, until that night in the park. You were so conflicted about Khloe, I didn't want to . . ." He scrubbed at his hair again. "To scare you off."

"So you used me instead."

"Absolutely not."

She sprang to her feet and poked her finger at his chest. It was risky, but she couldn't stop herself. "If I meant anything to you, you wouldn't have lied to me, and you wouldn't have let me go off trying to catch Christians when you thought I could be in danger."

"You weren't supposed to go off trying to catch Christians. You were supposed to text me one address. One. And then get out of there."

"I wanted to help —"

"Instead I get another text with another address, and I get no response from you when I ask what's going on. You vanished. I thought they were brainwashing you, I thought . . ." Austin gripped her wrist, pulled her closer. His cologne, his nearness, filled her head.

"You thought what?" she said.

His arms caged her. His mouth crushed hers. She couldn't breathe. He didn't let go.

Finally.

She melted closer. One hand held her, and the other was finding places he'd never touched before. He grabbed her hair, close to the roots, and his mouth followed her movement, kissed and kissed her, warm but hard. Wanting her, yes, but . . . A tear squeezed from her clenched eyelid. Her mouth felt bruised, and still he didn't let go. She whimpered around the kiss, pushed at his chest. Austin pulled back, and his breathing ruffled her damp hair. Violet shoved, but, crushed against him, she had no leverage. No strength. And then he was kissing her again.

This was being an adult. This was what she'd been asking him to do for months. *I don't think I want it. Wait, Austin, I don't think I . . .*

She let out a sob and beat her hand against his arm. He staggered back one step, but he would grab her again, force their mouths together again.

"Stop stop stop!" Violet planted both hands against his chest and shoved.

His eyes widened. He held up his hands. His foot tipped back, off-balance. Before Violet could stop pushing him, his head hit the wall and —

Blinking stars. A throb in her lip, in her teeth.

He'd hit her. With his fist.

He backed into the corner, hands raised in front of him, shaking. "Violet. Oh, no. No."

She ran to the laundry room and grabbed

her shoes. She headed for the front door.

"Violet, please, I'm sorry, please."

She didn't stop for his voice. She would never heed his voice again.

32

The agent's voice, not quite sure, snapped Clay from his paralysis. He ducked under the reception tent flap and dashed between tables, to the silent artist in black jeans amid the swirl of cocktail dresses and boldly colored ties. He grabbed Natalia's arm and jerked her to her feet.

"They're here. We have to go."

A few heads turned, but wine and music averted the rest. That and the desire not to see anything tonight that would ruin their celebration. Natalia ran to the table where Clay had been sitting and grabbed the camera bag. Clay dragged her through the tent, toward the open end. By the time they emerged under moon and stars, brightened by the distance from suburbia, she had gained her stride and ran beside him, fingers linked through his. A flashlight beam swung wildly behind them, lit the grass ahead. They dodged left, then right, together, no words needed to convey the path.

They reached the Jeep a hundred feet ahead of the agents. Clay leaped inside, waited for the slamming of the passenger door, and turned the key.

"Nat, you can go back. If you want to."

She gulped a quiet breath, as if he'd hit her. He was only trying to do the right thing.

"Drive," she whispered.

He jammed the Jeep into gear and floored it down the long dirt driveway, onto the dirt road. Headlights didn't appear in his rearview until he was about to turn, heading for the highway. He'd left them behind.

"Clay, we . . . just . . ."

"Became fugitives?"

Natalia curled forward, head in her arms. "I was going to be here for her. When she came home."

Why had she followed him, then? She could have stayed behind, waited for Khloe's release, stitched a new life around the hole of her runaway husband until the fabric mended itself. He tried not to press a hand to his stomach, but the ache had started to burn. He drove one-handed.

An anonymous hotel room was easier to book than Clay had expected, thanks to Natalia's quick thinking. The camera case contained an envelope of cash — the last half of Natalia's payment, offered with an apology from a member of the bride's family (*"and there's a little bonus for the delay"*). Clay gave a folded bunch of twenties to the hotel desk clerk and stopped before Natalia's maiden name came out of his mouth. The Constabulary would know that. Before his pause sounded like one, he blurted his mom's maiden name instead.

The luggage still in the Jeep held only one clothes change for each of them, but better than nothing. Once they got to the room, Natalia walked a slow perimeter, then collapsed onto the queen-sized bed and fingered the dark blue comforter. She gazed out the window into the darkness, where the traffic flowed below them. Clay crossed the room and blocked her view.

She stared at him, but their eyes didn't meet. For hours, she'd been slow-cooking words to a simmer, a boil. The tension of her shoulders, the tightness of her lips, promised a verbal volcano. He turned to lower the window blinds, then faced her again.

Natalia scooted farther back on the bed. "I'm not a criminal."

"I know that."

She stood, shuffled to the corner, lifted her suitcase and set it on the worn faux-wood desk. The folded stack of clothes didn't rise more than a few inches, but she lifted a top, refolded it, and tucked it into the dresser.

The room was too small for much physical distance. She stood just feet away, mango shampoo overpowering the faint vanilla room spray. With each fold of the fabric, a cord rippled in the back of her hand.

"Natalia, I —"

"I'm contemplating the rest of our lives. A year from now, we'll be a re-educated family. And either we'll have you home, or you'll be sitting stubbornly in custody, one of those re-education failure stories no one tells. Unable to be rehabilitated."

"That's not going to happen."

She refolded her Capri pants once, again, then pressed at a nonexistent wrinkle. "I don't know why I'm hiding out in a cheap hotel room when I should be turning myself in. Starting on re-education now. I could be finished the same time as Khloe. I could . . ."

Clay dropped onto the bed and bent forward, elbows on knees. Natalia couldn't possibly believe what she was saying. But if a person didn't believe in Christianity, didn't consider it the only absolute on which life itself was built . . . Well, they wouldn't evade capture forever. Turning themselves in might count toward clemency.

"You're not going to argue with me?" Natalia swiveled toward him and clutched the khaki fabric.

"You seriously want to go to the Constabulary and volunteer for re-education?"

"I don't think what I want has any bearing on what's going to happen."

"They'll turn your head inside out. They'll try to make you a good little citizen of the globe without any original thoughts or —"

Natalia tossed the pants back into her suitcase and turned her back.

Clay rubbed his stomach. "I'm not wrong."

Natalia unbuttoned her jeans. Whoa, wait a minute, that's not where they'd been heading two seconds ago. She perched on the edge of the bed to pull them off, still not facing him. Heat coursed through his body, but she pulled down the covers on the far side of the bed and crawled beneath them. Even with the air conditioning on, she'd overheat in ten minutes.

"Would you turn out the light, please?"

"Nat —"

"Whatever you're going to say, let's not say it."

But I need to tell you. You're right, I can't last forever. Before this is over, I'll be handcuffed, arrested, re-educated.

Minutes later, Clay lay on his back, weighted by the down comforter and every choice he'd made since he'd asked Natalia to come with him to a Table meeting. Since he'd brought Khloe home from the hospital for the first time, a seven-pound bundle of open eyes and open soul, and then for the last time, a gaunt six-year-old miracle. Since he'd asked a perky art major with strawberry hair to see the drama department's production of *A Streetcar Named Desire.*

A few feet away, lying on the same mattress, the girl who'd grinned up at him and flipped her loose curls — *"Thought I was going to have to ask you"* — drew her knees up and shuddered out a sigh.

33

Good thing Violet's parents were predictable in their sleeping patterns. Sneaking into the house before two in the morning risked discovery, should Dad still be up watching his TV comedians. But it was past three now. She crept to the back porch and slid her hand along the grill, up under the tarp. Here it was, the spare key.

She let herself inside, and the door whispered closed behind her. Another good thing — neither of her parents were light sleepers.

She hadn't seen Mom and Dad in three days. They probably had talked to Clay and Natalia by now, but of course Khloe's parents wouldn't tell them the truth. Wow, what *had* they said? That Violet was with them and fine, but she couldn't come to the phone? That the girls had taken Clay's Jeep for a joy ride and hadn't been seen lately? Well, no one would believe that. Khloe was still on her permit. Violet had barely put in any hours with her license. Her bike still felt safer than all those cars in the oncoming lane that she could crash into with one wrong turn of the wheel. It turned out to be a plus, though. If she'd driven her car over to Khloe's instead of riding her bike, her keys would have been in her purse, left behind at the raided store.

There was so much her parents didn't know about her now.

She could tell them the truth. Not about the Hansens, but about herself. She'd gone undercover for the Constabulary. They might even be proud of her.

Should they be?

She padded to her room and plopped down onto the edge of the bed. Her feet ached. The walk from Austin's apartment had been at least five miles. In ballet flats.

She'd left the aquarium light on last time she'd fed her fish, and no one had shut it off since. She hoped they'd been fed at least, but probably not. Violet sprinkled pellets and flakes into the water. Her gaze traveled the room half-focused. The last time she'd stepped over that threshold, she'd snagged her charm bracelet from the necklace tree on the dresser, clipped it on, taken a fortifying breath, and stared at herself in the mirror. Told herself that this mission for the Constabulary would help people. Told herself that Khloe would never find out about it, that someday they'd be two wrinkly ladies sitting on a park bench watching the young people make out. Laughing at how, no matter what life threw at them, their friendship kept coming back, a perennial flower.

Fluorescent light undulated over the carpet, and the darts and flits of the fish showed as thin shadows. Violet braved a look into the mirror now as if her face might have changed, eyes grown old, hair streaked gray. But she just looked like a tired, flat, makeup-less version of herself. She lay on her bed, the pastel quilt soft under her hands. Maybe she could stay curled up here forever. The Christians could wage their quiet fight. The Constabulary could pursue them. She'd root for neither side.

Except one side had to be right. Which made the other side wrong.

What she'd done — she needed to know if it was noble and right. She needed to know who deserved her trust. Someone who left a Bible in plain sight, or someone who hid a Constabulary badge . . .

Or someone who gave her freedom so she could take his away.

She sat up. Oh, no. If she didn't file a final report with the Constabulary, Austin would know. Might even suspect her of shifting loyalty. She fed her fish again, as if she wouldn't be back here in a few hours. She put on socks and tennis shoes and changed into a fresh shirt. She took her car keys from the kitchen wall rack, and her hand trembled. *Yes, you have to drive. Get over it.* She relocked the house behind her and left.

Maybe she was speeding, because the drive only took her eleven minutes. Not even 4:00 yet. Did Constabulary agents work in shifts, or would it be her and the custodians until normal office hours? She parked behind the one-level brick building, half the lot away from the cluster of cars at one end. Clearly not the whole crew. When she cracked the windows, a faint breeze drifted into the car. Maybe she'd stay here for now and watch the sunrise.

The tapping on the window jerked her from a dream she instantly forgot. She sat up and squinted. Red rays of sun poured through the windshield, heating the car already. The clock said 7:52.

"Miss?"

A face loomed in the window. A lean, frowning black face. Violet drew back as if the man might reach for her through the glass. *Jumpy much? Chill already.*

He held a badge up to the window. Agent Samuel Stiles, Michigan Philosophical Constabulary. "Everything all right?"

She'd only heard voices that deep from movie stars. She turned the key and rolled down the window. "I'm waiting for someone. To talk to someone."

"I see. What's your name?"

"Violet DuBay."

"Is that a fact? We've been looking for you, you know. Glad there was no need to worry."

His dark eyes shone with a kindness beyond the courtesy. The tension in Violet's back seeped away. "No, there wasn't."

"So, where have you been hiding?"

Violet opened the door and got out of the car. "I guess this should be official. You know, an interview."

Agent Stiles nodded, straightened up taller than six feet. "Follow me."

She expected to be taken in the front doors, but Agent Stiles led her to the side of the building and swiped an ID card to enter. She trailed him down a narrow hallway with glass windows and doors spaced along one side. On the wall beside each window hung a phone. The first few rooms were empty. Then they passed one that wasn't.

Janelle.

Violet hardly knew her feet had stopped. Janelle's hands were cuffed to the table. She faced the window but stared past Violet. These must be the window-mirrors used in cop shows. Violet could see into the room, but Janelle saw only her own reflection. Or not. Right now, she looked blind. And about ten years older than she had three nights ago, shoulders stooped, salt-and-pepper hair stringy against her head. Her head sagged, and her right hand tugged at the restraint. She bowed over and rested her forehead against the desk. A slow, hot churning started in Violet's stomach.

"Your text messages at work." Agent Stiles's voice sounded even deeper when the hallway echoed it back.

"That's Janelle," Violet said. As if he wouldn't know.

"Janelle Beers, arrested three nights ago, thanks to your mission for us."

"Did she attack someone?"

"Oh, the cuffs? She's obstinate, that's all."

But re-education was like school, not jail. Re-education involved classes. Therapy. Groups of people talking through the hate they'd been raised on until they could understand love instead.

Love. That growing ache seized her throat. Love like staying behind and barricading a door you knew your enemy would breach eventually, so your friends could escape even if it meant you would get chained to a table.

"Do all Christians . . . I mean, is this . . . Is Janelle in re-education right now?"

"She is. Sometimes, people cooperate right away. They're given a four-course meal and a shower and a bed to sleep in, in one of our group homes. They're kept for a few months, of course, but the treatment plan for them is more pleasant than the plan for someone like Janelle."

"But . . ." Violet tried to look away, but the woman on the other side of the glass gripped her and wouldn't let go. So weak, bent over like that. So strong, silent when she knew what the con-cops wanted her to say.

"Do you want to ask any questions before we begin your interview?"

Violet stepped back from Agent Stiles and tilted her gaze up. His eyes didn't waver from hers, unbothered by her reaction. Was it safe to question him?

Of course, it was safe. Violet wasn't a Christian, wasn't a criminal. She was a citizen who'd accomplished a mission for the government. She could ask anything she wanted.

"I didn't know re-education was this . . ."

"You know the statistics, don't you?" Agent Stiles pulled a pen from the pocket of his suit jacket and walked it through his fingers, one twirl at a time. "We're very successful. Eventually, Janelle will give up on her faith. She'll be re-educated."

"I know." Violet turned from the window. "Where do we do the interview?"

Agent Stiles led her to the room at the end of the hall that smelled like lemon-scented cleaner and had no windows, just a door. He promised a quick return; as he disappeared from sight, Violet propped the door open with one of the two chairs. Waiting room chairs, with wooden legs and gray upholstery. Janelle likely hadn't been given a chair this comfortable. Violet claimed the other one and pulled it closer to the low, foldaway table. A white counter stretched across one wall, ending against a half fridge. Weird room for an interview.

Before Violet could check the contents of the fridge, Agent Stiles strode back into the room and moved the chair from where she'd wedged it into the doorway. A grin split his face for only a moment. He settled into the chair, across the table from Violet, and pulled a tiny voice recorder from his pocket.

"Are you ready?" he said.

Of course. She nodded.

He nodded back and pressed a button. A red light began to blink on the side of the recorder.

"Agent Sam Stiles, interviewing Violet DuBay," he said. "Okay, Violet, just tell me what happened in your own words, everything you can remember, starting that night after the raid on the church meeting."

Violet opened her mouth. The red light blinked. And blinked.

"Violet?"

Say something. Say something to help them. But what if she wasn't helping?

"Did you meet any Christians, after that night?"

She nodded and forced herself to meet his eyes. His face showed no expression at all now, not even the gleam of compassion from before. Professional distance. He didn't want to influence her responses.

"Did anyone hurt you, or threaten to hurt you, if you turned them in?"

"No one's hurting you, and no one's going to."

Violet blinked away the memory of Belinda's kind eyes. "No. Nothing like that."

"You ended up at the home of Mrs. Penny

Lewalski, hid under her deck and texted her address to us. By the time we arrived, you had left."

Violet nodded.

"I need you to tell me the rest." Agent Stiles leaned back in his chair. He must be stretching his legs under the table. He reached one hand to the table's edge and tapped out a brief rhythm, then went still.

"A man came, thought I was a Christian." They knew about Khloe. Austin had said so. But if Agent Stiles didn't ask about her, Violet wouldn't volunteer. "He took me to another house. I was supposed to stay there until . . . I don't know. But I left. I, um, hitchhiked back, and here I am."

"Why didn't you text the new address to us?"

"The man took my phone, so you couldn't track it."

"What's his name?"

Her lips fused at the memory of him sitting at Belinda's table, the flinch in his shoulders, in his face, when Violet had told Lee he would be a better person after re-education. And his shaking voice: *"I can't sleep."* He knew what was being done to Janelle, to others. He wanted to stop it. You couldn't just leave a person handcuffed to a table for three days. Were the "obstinate" ones allowed to eat, to use the bathroom? They had to be.

"Violet, did this man tell you his name?"

"Turn me in, just me. Please."

If their Bible didn't brainwash Christians into killing people, then Marcus was right. To save people. From the Constabulary. A wave of calm slid over her. She looked up from the half-curled hands in her lap.

"He said no one was allowed to know his name."

Agent Stiles barely leaned forward. He scrubbed his coarse black hair with one hand. "Describe him for me."

He was trained to read people. She needed to feed him some truth. Good thing Marcus's basic features were ordinary. "Brown hair, brown eyes."

"Physical build?"

"Big."

"Do you mean tall?"

"Not really. I mean, not short, but not really tall, and not fat. Big like a wrestler. You know, muscles."

"Distinguishing features?"

Left-handed. And those knuckles were noticeably scarred. Too much detail. "You mean like a birthmark? I don't remember anything like that."

Agent Stiles nodded, sighed, and leaned

342

back in his chair. If only he'd look around the room for a minute, but his eyes were glued to Violet's face.

"And where's this house? Who owns it?"

"It was his house, but I don't know where . . ."

She was lying to a con-cop. As if he couldn't see straight through her. But he didn't seem to. *Keep talking, be like Khloe, sell the story.*

"Sorry," she said. "I'm just tired."

"You're doing fine. What can you tell me about the house?"

"He blindfolded me on the way there."

"But you ran away, didn't you? What direction was it?"

Oh, right, of course. If her lying skills didn't improve fast, she deserved to get caught. But she might not have to lie about this.

"I know I had to go south. But I was scared, and I didn't see landmarks. I walked along M-53 until someone picked me up."

"North of here, off 53. Okay, that's a start. And you met no one but this one man?"

"Right."

The tapped rhythm of Agent Stiles's fingers sped up. He blinked a few times but didn't break eye contact. Violet's pulse pounded over the whirring of the refrigerator. All she could do was gaze back at him and wait for him to accuse her of withholding information.

"Can you tell me anything else?" he said.

She shook her head and told as much truth as possible. "He was careful about information. Maybe he didn't trust me for some reason."

"I'll put some agents on a search for this house, but if you don't even know the name of the street . . ."

"I'm sorry," she said to everyone but Agent Stiles.

"Thank you for coming in, Violet. We'll be working on this, and if any other details come to mind, let us know." He stood, pulled out his wallet, and handed her a business card.

Violet shoved the card into her pocket and kept her hand inside. When she stood up, her legs nearly buckled.

Agent Stiles shut off the recorder and tucked it into a pocket of his suit jacket. He opened the door for her, ushered her back the way they'd come. Violet tried not to look in the windows as they passed, but her eyes caught movement halfway down the hall. A tall redheaded man in a black suit stood over Janelle, emphasizing whatever he was saying with a slicing gesture of one hand.

"Keep walking," Agent Stiles said.

He escorted her all the way outside to her car. Just before she closed the door and drove away, he leaned down and gripped the handle.

"One last question."

"Are you lying to me?" Violet steeled her spine and waited for the lethal words.

"We're keeping tabs on a woman we think might be involved. We couldn't prove anything six months ago, but we're still trying. Maybe the man mentioned her. Lee Vaughn."

Violet's heart stopped.

Agent Stiles cocked his head. He must have been delaying this question on purpose. Must be reading recognition and panic shouting from Violet's face. Must be getting ready to handcuff her and haul her back into the building.

"No," Violet said, and her voice didn't even wobble. "Like I said, he was careful about names."

Violet smoothed her expression, stuck her key in the ignition, turned it, and angled a quizzical look up at Agent Stiles. He tapped his fingers on the roof of the car until she wanted to shout at him to stop. He stepped back, and his look resembled that of her science teacher when she got 110 percent on a pop quiz. Somehow, she'd passed this man's test too. Maybe God had helped her lie. Maybe God had blindfolded the Constabulary agent.

If she credited God with keeping the Christians safe, she had to acknowledge He was on their side.

"Violet," Agent Stiles said, "thank you for the interview. You've been a great help today."

"You're welcome."

Agent Stiles nodded and gave her a two-fingered salute. He turned and loped back into the building. Violet pulled out onto the road and sighed with relief at the red light, as if an extra minute would be enough time to know her new destination.

Her mission for the con-cops was over. Time to go home and be her normal self, whoever she was now, stripped of the comfortable ignorance. Stripped of a friendship more than ten years old. Stripped of her beloved Hansens, her adopted family. The thought of driving home to Mom and Dad, drifting past them with the least contact possible, for as long as it took her to save up for an apartment . . . Her whole body felt empty.

A car beeped behind her. She hit the gas as the green light turned yellow. *Sorry, dude.*

She turned left into the library parking lot and parked. Her forehead rested against the warm steering wheel. The sun instantly turned her car into a greenhouse. She lifted her head and people-watched. A white-haired woman held a cane in one hand and a cloth book tote in the other. A couple of girls, no older than ten, tugged a red wagon brimming with books toward a minivan.

Books. The sight of them rebooted Violet's brain. Her next step was so obvious. She had to know if the Christians were indoctrinated with violence. Observing and forming her own opinions, just like Lee told her to do.

She locked her car and jogged up to the library. Through the double doors, quiet wrapped around Violet, a blanket that comforted and stifled all at once. Anyone could keep a secret in a library. Except online. But she wasn't searching for anything illegal, and no one had reason to monitor a search like this one. She walked around the labyrinths of oak shelves to the computer bay, claimed a kiosk, pulled up a maps page.

First, search for the library's address. Quick and easy. Then route directions from here to 86594 Marina.

In minutes, Violet tucked the printed,

folded map into the pocket of her shorts. Not even noon yet on a weekday. Marcus must be at work. She cleared the computer's online history and searched the library catalogue. Biology. Marine life. See, anyone could kill time in a library.

After a few minutes of browsing, she carried an armful of hardcovers to the kids' area and sat down in a three-foot-tall wooden-backed chair. Against her thigh, the map seemed to burn. She opened the first book, a history of oceanography, and glared at the words that wouldn't focus. Maybe her brain was on overload. Maybe that happened when a law-abiding person made the decision to commit a crime.

34

Just a day in this cheap little room, one day to hide and plan, one day to let the Constabulary ransack their home and waste manpower scouring the streets for the Jeep. Clay could handle one day in a hotel room, even with a wife whose moods pitched like the sea. Still, the thought of his bike impounded by the Constabulary made him want to hit someone, preferably someone dressed in gray.

They'd both slept in as if on purpose, to slog through time with the least interaction possible. Then they'd had a breakfast of vending machine trail mix and odd-tasting tap water, the combination of which triggered Clay's gag reflex. Natalia washed their shirts and undergarments in the sink while they wore nothing but white bath towels and avoided touching each other. She spread the light cotton articles side by side over the old AC unit under the window, and everything dried faster than Clay expected.

They didn't talk. Natalia turned on the TV shortly after she woke up, and Clay read every word of the *Reader's Digest* someone had left behind. Then he paced the perimeter of the room until he could close his eyes and not bump the walls. Every time he attempted a conversation, Natalia's back stiffened, and she stared at the TV as if soap operas engrossed her.

Well before 5:00, Clay progressed from cabin fever to claustrophobia. He found one shoe by the door, the other under the bed, and tugged them on.

"You can't go anywhere," Natalia said to the TV.

Oh, now she'd talk. He'd have put his shoes on five hours ago, if he'd known. "Maybe you haven't heard my stomach growling. It's getting obnoxious."

"You just wore socks down the hall before."

"If I try to swallow any more trail mix or Snickers bars, I'm going to throw up." He grabbed the keys from the TV stand and crossed the room in six steps. The lock clicked too loudly, misaligned, when he turned the bolt.

"Clay." Her hand seized his, the one holding the keys. "We have to stay here."

"Hey." Her shoulder trembled beneath the brush of his fingers. "There's fast food literally across the street. I saw a Taco Bell. I'll get us some tacos, fresco with the tomatoes. Chips and mild salsa."

"We have to talk. Make a plan."

"We will, Nat. Over dinner."

She dropped her hand to her side and nodded. She blinked away the momentary glitter in her eyes. Fear?

"I want a chicken taco. And chips and salsa."

"Coming right up."

"And a burrito, the one with rice and that sauce."

She was so beautiful. More so because she didn't know. He ran his thumb down her cheek, stopped on an oversized freckle at her jawline that she always covered with makeup. As much of herself as she'd taken back over the years, sometimes he forgot all that she'd given. Still gave. Before he could say the wrong thing, before he could sweep her into his arms and feel her push against his chest, Clay jingled the keys and smiled and slipped out the door.

By the time he returned to the hotel, he'd convinced himself twice that he was about to be arrested. A Constabulary squad car in the parking lot — no, wait, just a gray sedan.

351

An agent in an unmarked car, behind him in the drive-through — no, a layman wearing a blue suit, hollering on his cell phone. Clay let himself into their room and slid the bolt on the door, and his body caved onto the bed.

"Thanks for not locking me out," he said.

Natalia grabbed the cardboard tray of drinks and one of the food bags. "Cherry coke?" She punched a straw through its wrapper and took a sip. "You do love me."

She was blurting a cliché to avoid deep conversation, didn't mean it literally, but the words still hit Clay in the gut. He lay back on the bed.

Natalia attacked her taco like a teenage boy and spoke around bites. "We won't be off their radar unless we cross the border."

"Canada? Khloe doesn't have a passport."

"The state line, I mean. Ohio would do the job. That House resolution about making their jurisdiction national still hasn't passed."

"Not yet, but the federal-audit thing did."

"I didn't hear about that."

"It was on the news. A few nights ago." Clay propped up on one elbow and pulled the second bag of food closer. "And apparently they don't need warrants anymore, either. Who knows what else was in that bill."

Natalia sat across the bed, holding her pop steady on one knee. "We can relocate in three months. Maybe less, even. Anyone who interviews Khloe will figure out pretty fast that she's no Christian."

"Three months is still protocol." Clay shoved a warm bite of quesadilla into his mouth. A whole portion of his head had stepped back from this conversation and watched it with the interest of a psychologist diagnosing his patients. *Way too calm in the face of disaster. Delude themselves into making a "plan."*

This was his Natalia, though. She hadn't been able to pound his chest hard enough to pulverize the situation, and shutting down for a day hadn't erased it. Time to stand to her full five-foot-three and face it down.

"Fine, three months, then. We can survive three months. When she gets out, she'll call me."

"At which point we drive over to pick her up?"

Natalia hurled her balled-up taco wrapper. It bounced off the TV screen and fell to the carpet.

"We might have to cross that bridge when

we come to it," he said. Now who was hiding behind a cliché?

She crunched down on a chip and stared at her bare feet.

"In the meantime, we'll have to dodge them. Maybe between now and then, we'll be able to —"

Her head whipped up. "I am not leaving the state without her."

No matter what else transpired between them, always back to this. Clay pushed the half-eaten quesadilla off his lap and shoved to his feet. "And I'm chomping at the bit to abandon her, of course."

"Clay —"

"Don't try to take it back, Nat."

She leaned over to set her pop on the nightstand. "I don't know why I said it."

"Obviously, you thought it was necessary to say."

"I need her here."

And he didn't? He walked the perimeter of the room, and the old hiss started in the back of his head. *Nothing to offer here.*

"That girl in the park." Natalia folded the Taco Bell napkin into ever-smaller squares. "I'm seeing Khloe everywhere. As if she's dead."

Clay's knees liquefied. He wobbled to the stuffed chair in the corner, its dark blue tweed worn down on the arms. The room that narrowed around him, the catastrophe he couldn't fix, faded as memory flashed. Each curve of his baby's face the first time he held her, the swelling understanding that he was no longer going to be a father — he *was* a father. He'd wanted in that first minute to hold her for the rest of her life and his, to let her grow up in his arms. He'd looked down at her mother whose petite body had labored fourteen hours to give her breath, and Natalia had reached a hand toward them both. *"Clay, look what we did."*

Her voice drew him back to the present, quiet and a little lost. "You'll think I'm crazy, but it was her nose. She had Khloe's nose."

Clay shook his head. Not crazy. Nine months plus fourteen hours plus seventeen years. Khloe had molded them across a timeline they'd never considered could end. Her absence — a three-month anomaly? More? Less? But they had to live those three months. Had to ache through each day without verbally knifing each other, without escaping.

"You're right," he said. "It curved up at the end."

The slow motion hours didn't click back into normal speed after their pseudo-

Mexican dinner. They still didn't talk, not really. Clay was sprawled, Khloe-style, in the shabby blue chair, rereading the book excerpt feature of the *Reader's Digest* — a true account of one man's rodeo adventures complete with silver buckles and bull gorings — when Natalia switched off the TV and started making the bed. She'd run out of brown paper napkins to fold. He set down the magazine.

What's wrong? qualified as the stupidest question he could ask. *Do you want to talk?* ranked a close second.

"Nat?"

"I need to know something. I've been trying not to go there, but I can't help it, I have to know." She tugged the flat sheet up to the edge of the mattress and smoothed it down.

"It might help to look at me."

"Have you prayed today?"

His gut filled with cement. "You probably have too."

"Don't do that, Clay."

"Do what?"

"I'm not talking about legal praying. I'm talking about the kind of praying that made this situation in the first place."

"What if I'm doing that right now?"

She hopped up on the bed and reached to

pull the sheet forward. He'd never understood why she knelt on the sheet to do this, but she always made it work. She didn't face him, but the petite stretch of her body tugged at something visceral that made him want to shield her, hold her, touch her.

"Nat."

"No hypotheticals. Just answer the question."

"I don't know the answer."

She glared at him over her shoulder. "You don't know if you've prayed today."

"I've talked to God, yeah. I think the last thing I said was, 'Why are You letting this happen?' "

"And what did He tell you?"

"Nothing."

The word wasn't supposed to come out like that, a sharpened knife, a crushing weight. Natalia swung to her feet and stepped toward him as if the floor could collapse beneath her. His pulse pounded. He didn't move, even when the caution dropped from her face.

"Clay, are you still waiting for God to fix this?"

Faith did that. Waited. Believed. He wanted to know, to trust, with the same unquestioning fervor that had lilted in his chest the day Khloe's final test results were in. Healthy. Healed. But trust was born of a track record, and God had been on a cold streak for the last four days.

Natalia caressed the back of his hand, and a tremor zipped up his arm.

"They weren't supposed to get to Khloe," he whispered. "God wasn't supposed to let them."

"You believe sometimes He lets things happen." Accusation, barely veiled, layered the words.

"Not this." He withdrew his hand. "He wants devotion? Exclusivity? He wants me to — to take up my cross? Well, I did. And look what happened."

Natalia searched his eyes for something. She wasn't shielding herself now. No preemptive strike of verbal darts. She stood close and tilted her face to him.

"Clay." Her breath ghosted along his neck. "Tell me what you're saying."

He clasped his hands together until they stopped trembling. Outside the room, the icemaker clanked and clattered, and clomping footsteps faded. He stared down at the stain-absorbing brown carpet.

Lord, we're falling apart. Please make things right.

"I don't know what I'm saying."

"When we go home," Natalia said, "do you know where we go from here?"

"Not yet."

"Clay, I need you to know. Pick anything and just know it."

"I know I'm not going to say what you want me to say if it isn't true."

Her eyes flickered, then closed. Her hand hovered between them, rested on his chest, then moved under his arm and pressed each fingertip against his back and drew her against him, close, close, closer. She tipped her face and parted her lips.

Silken hair in his hands. The curve of her back. Then layers of cotton stripped off by his hands and hers until skin and skin made heat. Until they breathed the air from each other's lungs. Until this moment boiled in his body and erased all the things he didn't know.

35

Around 6:00, with the cloudless sky still brighter than sunset, Violet drove past the decades-old taupe bungalow. Marcus's red pickup truck sat in the driveway. At least he was home. She parked one street over and walked back. Her spine kept prickling, sending a shiver straight to her toes, but when she glanced over her shoulder, no one followed her down the street. Not Austin, not a gray uniform, not Agent Stiles. She braved the walkway to Marcus's porch as if it were made of hot coals.

She knocked on the green front door. A deep bark rushed closer, then continued from the other side of the door. That wasn't a dog. That was a monster. Violet inched back.

The door opened before she could slink to her car. Marcus's eyes darted over her shoulder as if she might be leading a squad of con-cops. He flicked a hand at the German shepherd behind him, and the growling stopped.

"Come in." He stepped back and opened the door wider.

The last man she'd accepted that invitation from had slugged her in the jaw. "I just wanted to ask you something."

"We can't talk on the porch."

"Nobody followed me, as far as I know."

His eyebrow quirked at her, the message plain. He wasn't trusting her ability to spot surveillance. Well, he shouldn't. Agent Stiles might have pondered her interview and decided to bring her back in or observe her from an invisible distance.

"Violet."

She slid through the door sideways, out of his reach and the dog's, into a small foyer furnished by nothing but a throw rug over the wood floor. The dog padded forward as if to sniff her, but Marcus's hand swept a short, downward motion, and it sat, then settled at his feet.

He shut the door. "What're you doing here?"

"I, um . . . I was hoping maybe you would help me with . . . something."

His left hand latched onto his neck, and weary furrows dug deeper into his face. "Come in."

Violet followed Marcus, and the dog followed her, into a sparse beige living room. Clearly, a guy's house. Not a figurine or family picture anywhere, nothing soft but the furniture itself, two stuffed chairs and a couch in matching fudge-brown microfiber.

She'd expected her palms to sweat in the house of the Christian resistance leader, in the house of the grizzly who'd already proved he might corner her and roar into her face. But he wasn't only a criminal leader or an angry bear. Her legs rubberized and lowered her to his couch. She could rest here and be safe. On the cushion beside her rested a squishy gel pack, appearing tossed aside. Heat emanated from it.

Marcus ignored it and didn't sit. "Why'd you come here?"

"I thought you might be able to get me a . . . a Bible. An old one."

There it was, out of her mouth, into the air. Marcus went still.

"If you can't, just tell me now, and I'll leave, but you gave one to Chuck. So I thought . . . you must be in the black market or something."

"Why do you want one?"

"I just want to know what the big deal is, why Christians think the old ones are right and the new ones are wrong, and I don't

362

know anyone who'll be objective about it. So I thought I'd just read it, the actual book."

He paced, stopped, searched her face for something. "That's the best way to learn about it."

"So you can get me one?"

"I don't know."

Of course. Black market, not black giveaway. She rubbed her arms and stared down at herself as if her humiliation could conjure a hundred-dollar bill into the pocket of her shorts. Assuming Bibles weren't worth more than a hundred dollars. Good grief, she didn't even know the going price.

"I don't have any money. Not on me, anyway. I could go home and get some."

"Violet —"

"Wait. Here, I have . . ." She fumbled with the latch on her bracelet. "The charms are stupidly expensive. I don't know why I pay so much for them. They're real sterling silver, they don't tarnish ever, and you can sell them online or . . ."

She dangled the bracelet between them, her lifeline. Why was Marcus staring at her as if she'd sprouted fins? Was she insulting him by offering something other than money?

Her voice wobbled. "Is it not enough? If

you charge like thousands of dollars or something —"

"Charge . . . I don't . . . Violet." Marcus's knuckles dug into his neck. "I don't distribute."

Oh. She lowered her hand, fingers numb around the bracelet.

"But if I did . . . The Bible's not — I wouldn't — some people do make money. But they shouldn't. And most of them don't. It's not that kind of thing."

"So people give people Bibles . . . for free?" Seriously?

"Yeah."

"Why?"

"Because. People should be able to have a Bible. If they want one."

Okay, sure, maybe, but anyone who would offer something so unobtainable and not charge for it . . . Gifts came from people who wanted something in return.

Or from people who loved other people.

"Is this because of Jesus too?" she said quietly.

"Yeah."

Violet ducked her head and put her bracelet back on. "But you can't get me one."

"I . . ." A soft sigh leached from him. "Wait in the kitchen."

"Why?"

"I'll be there in a minute."

Nothing dangerous in that request. He nodded toward the next room, which pretty much melded into this one. More wood floor, more neutral walls, but the kitchen held a small oak dining table and stainless steel appliances. The counters were black granite. Marcus disappeared in the direction of the living room bookshelves.

Nothing in this kitchen disclosed that a Christian lived here, cooked here, ate here. Not that she'd expected it to. She wouldn't open the fridge and discover that he liked to feast on the livers of non-Christians. Still. She'd never stood in a Christian's house before — Clay's house, sure, but Khloe and Natalia lived there too. Part of her, especially a week ago, would have expected hostility to ooze from this house, the walls, the floors, the ceilings.

Something wet bumped her hand, and she jumped. The dog had followed her.

"Hi." Violet tried to pet its head, but it ducked her hand. "Sorry. I know I'm intruding. Thanks for not biting me."

"She won't." Marcus lurked against the far wall, a black leather book in one hand. "You'd have to break in or threaten me."

She coughed a laugh. "Right, me threaten you."

He shrugged. "If you had a gun, sure."

'Right, sure.

"Here." He crossed the kitchen and offered her the book.

So he did distribute Bibles, after all. His first lie to her, as far as she knew. "You had to make sure I wanted one for a good reason?"

"You need to leave."

He didn't trust her. If she could explain, if she could . . . She reached out and took the Bible on open palms, held the weight of it, illegal and intriguing.

"You don't have a purse," Marcus said.

"Um, not anymore."

"You can't carry it like that."

He wrapped it in one plastic grocery bag, then shoved the bundle into another one. He walked her to the front door, and she let the bag swing at her side, though instinct wanted to hide it under her T-shirt. Yeah, that wouldn't look suspicious. Marcus started to open the door, then stopped.

His eyes burned straight through her, but she didn't let herself look away. Her hold rustled the plastic bag handles.

"Violet, I . . . I know what you did."

"And you let me go anyway. I didn't say

thanks before."

"No, I mean, I know what you did. For us. For — for me. You talked to a Constabulary agent this morning. But you didn't tell him anything."

Wait a minute. "How'd you find out?"

"Doesn't matter."

"You know what they do," Violet said. "You know what's happening to Janelle right now, and to other people."

He nodded.

"No one told me. If that agent hadn't walked me past the window, I still wouldn't . . ." Pieces fell together. "Do you know Agent Stiles?"

"Don't, Violet."

Don't ask questions. Okay. "For all I know, this thing —" She jerked and rustled the bag — "is full of mistakes and teaches intolerance and —"

"Well. Just read it."

"I'm going to."

"Good. And thanks."

A silence lingered between them and rooted itself in some crevice inside Violet that she'd never known was empty. This was respect between two people. Two adults.

"Marcus?"

"Yeah."

"I need to know something." Risk shuddered down her spine.

Marcus closed the front door but didn't lock it, didn't lean against it. "Okay."

"I need to know who's buried in the woods."

He breathed in and seemed to keep the air in his lungs. "I can't tell you that."

So it was a grave. "Did you kill him, or her — the person?"

For only a second, his mouth seemed to tremble. "No. But if I'd . . . done things differently . . . she'd be alive."

"Did she get shot?"

"What? No, she — you saw the truck? In the woods?"

Violet nodded.

"She was driving it."

"What about the blood?"

His knuckles dug into his neck. "It's my truck. And that's my blood."

"You just said she was driving."

"That happened a couple days before. I — I had a cut on my back. She — I wasn't in the truck when it . . . It hit some ice. Went off the road. When I found her, she . . . She was already . . ."

Khloe's tendency to weave tales had educated Violet on spotting them. People tried to tell a lie in order, tie everything together, give plenty of convincing details.

Marcus's story didn't make enough sense to be untrue, especially not rehearsed.

Grieving, Belinda had said. He didn't look so massive right now, only tired and bent and barely guarded.

"I'm sorry," Violet said. "I shouldn't have asked."

"No." He dragged in a deep breath. "If you thought I . . . well, I can't prove anything, but it's good you asked."

"I believe you."

That brought out a crinkling around his eyes. "Thanks. Now, you've got to leave."

"Okay. Thanks for the Bible."

"Sure."

He opened the door for her, and she hurried down the walkway, down the street, following the curb. The plastic bag in her left hand wasn't heavy enough to dig into her palm, but she still felt ready to drop it all the way back to her car. She *should* drop it. But she couldn't, because Marcus should have kidnapped her and didn't. He shouldn't have opened his door to her, but he had. And this book might be the reason.

36

By the time Violet dredged up the audacity to drive back home, the sun had gone to sleep, and a crescent moon floated out the passenger window. She parked in the driveway and slipped into her parents' house with the spare key again. They weren't likely to notice she'd lost her purse. She shoved the key into her pocket and clutched the Bible to her chest, nestled in the white plastic bag. Four days, nearly five — a record sleepover at Khloe's, especially without letting Dad know first. One hope gleamed: that he hadn't worried enough yet to call the Hansens, that Violet's story didn't have to match anyone else's.

At the mudroom doorway, she crouched to untie her shoes and tug them off. Now to stash the bag in her room. Then she could double back to the mudroom and announce her presence. Voices came from the living room, Dad's easygoing baritone and Mom's clipped vowels. Playing cards, maybe one of those close games that sounded casual until you watched their eyes darting from their own cards to their opponent's face. Violet ventured into the kitchen.

"I'll peek at your cards." Mom would never use that warmth for her. Violet paused to listen anyway.

"And spoil your own victory? Never."

Not even a second to hide, plan, panic. Dad rounded the corner and froze.

"Violet. Well, what do you know."

"Hi." Shrug. Make distance. Amble toward her bedroom, business as usual, all quiet on the home front.

"I saw your car was gone. Thought about calling your cell."

"Oh, Khloe and I went to the mall today, and I thought it would be good to do some driving." She tossed the words over her shoulder. Almost to her room. They'd never bother to trespass.

"What's in the bag?"

Her heartbeat pounded her calm veneer to a pulp. If she faced him, he'd read everything, not because he was some gifted face reader, but because he wasn't blind.

"Charms. For my bracelet."

"And you're not wearing them yet? They must not be that great."

Somehow, in the last four days, Violet had shed herself like a lizard skin. Stepped clean out of that girl and forgotten how to wear her. Of course, new charms should already dangle from her bracelet. She should be spinning them, wandering to the living room to angle them beneath the lamp glow.

"I'm putting them on right now." She slipped into her bedroom and closed the door.

Now she could hyperventilate in peace. She pressed the bag closer to her chest. She took a breath and tried to will her pulse to steady. If it didn't in a few minutes, she'd try Lee's trick of breathing into her hands. She sat on the bed and watched her fish. Then she drew the Bible from the bags and let them fall to the floor.

God, I don't know what You want me to learn from this, but please don't let any messed up ideas get into my head. Thanks.

She opened the cover to the dedication page. A handmade bookmark lay against the spine, braided ribbons in various shades of pink. But if this Bible had belonged to a name in the news, she'd never know. No one had written on the dedication page. The leather hadn't softened like that on its own, though. This book was far from new.

So many books in the Old Testament that

she didn't recognize. Foreign names, and one called Job. As in, good job? Never mind all these added books — well, not added. This Bible was the original. But first things first. She found the book she'd never gotten to read at Chuck's house. Matthew. She needed to find some words from Jesus.

And this Bible made that crazy easy. It printed everything He said in red. She scooted back on her bed, turned the lamp to its brightest setting, and propped herself against a pillow and her headboard. Her fish seemed to eye her from across the room, which was impossible, but she had to restrain herself from throwing a beach towel over the aquarium.

I am breaking the law. I could end up handcuffed to a table for days.

No, she couldn't, because she wasn't like Janelle. Something pricked in her chest. She'd never believed in anything the way Janelle believed in this book.

Hours melted. Her back stiffened. Even through the pillow, her headboard pressed soreness into her backbone. Her hand fell asleep until she realized she'd leaned all her weight on it and shifted position. Her fish darted and drifted. And Violet read the red letters.

The Christians were right. This Jesus was

different.

At first, she couldn't find a word for the change, but she finally did. Tough. Then she found another one. Passionate. Yeah, this Jesus was tough, and this Jesus was passionate for the truth as He saw it. Good grief, as He saw it? He was obviously God. He even said so Himself. So He didn't see truth, He was truth. Or made truth. Or both. This Jesus grabbed a whip and chased the money guys out of the temple like some kind of Old West sheriff who rode into his town and saw that no one cared about the laws anymore. This Jesus called the Pharisees some pretty gross names when they lied to people. But this Jesus had so many feelings, too. Sometimes, Violet could picture Him smiling at the people around Him. And when Lazarus died, His tears made Violet want to cry too.

She didn't cry then, though. She didn't cry until He got Himself arrested, and the palace guards started hitting Him and pulling out His beard and whipping Him. Then her tears dripped onto the Bible's thin pages. She held it out in front of her — it wouldn't be right to leave drop-marks all over a Bible — and she sobbed for Him. He'd loved the people, healed them, fed them, but He'd also told them truth they didn't want to hear, so they yelled for His death until they got it. She hated them.

Jesus, I'm so sorry they did this to You. Are You this Jesus? Did You say these things?

She wiped her face on the hem of her T-shirt and kept reading. The crucifixion seemed like the same scene, though maybe some of the details were different. She should boot up her computer and pull up a PUV Bible online to compare the two, but the story tugged her forward, page after page. She'd have to compare details later. When He rose from the dead and called Mary by her name, Violet cried all over again, but this time the tears dripped into her smile. Jesus was so kind. So good. In this Bible, He wasn't a fluffy teacher guy. He was a whole person. He could be angry or stern, not just happy.

And the things He said were so different. He never once told someone that they hadn't sinned. He forgave them instead. The story of the hooker was similar, but not really, because at the end, Jesus didn't tell her to go in love and gladness. He told her to go and sin no more.

Elysium speakers echoed in Violet's head. They taught that Jesus loved everyone, which was true in both versions of the Bible. But they also taught about rewarding oneself, understanding one's true nature and potential for goodness. If they met the Jesus in this Bible, they wouldn't like what He had to say.

A knock on her door nearly jolted Violet off the bed. She shoved the Bible under a pillow and lost her place.

"Food out here, if you're hungry."

She sniffed hard against the leftover tears. Her stomach had been growling for the last hour, but it was almost midnight now. "What's for dinner, Dad?"

A chuckle wafted through the door. "Made some nachos. Come on out and have some."

Violet shoved off the bed and padded toward the food. The tang of salsa filled the kitchen, and two paper plates of topping-slathered chips sat on the counter.

"So." Dad pulled a whole section of chips onto a new plate and added sour cream. "I keep trying to concede the night, but your mother wants one more round. She's going to sweep me. Must be off my game."

Violet snagged a random chip that had missed all the toppings but the melted cheese. Mmm. Good stuff. "She's savoring the victory."

"She'd better savor it. I'll mop —"

"The floor with her next time," Violet finished for him. "How'd it get to be just you two?"

"Oh, yeah, Hursts and Kowalskis were supposed to be here, but there was food poisoning and a flat tire in there somewhere, so your mother and I just decided to play like the old days, one on one, and . . ."

She tried to keep listening, but the small, irrelevant conversation pressed and trapped her like a house on fire. Dad didn't understand that life was serious, that the decision for life or death hung before every person ever born, that Jesus was real and He was God and He wanted allegiance.

Follow Me.

Those two red words hovered in her head. She'd heard them before, at Elysium, and she'd thought she agreed to them. But she'd had no idea what they meant. Maybe still didn't.

"Thought you were hungry." Dad shoved the plate at her.

"Why'd you make nachos this late?"

Footsteps clomped toward them from the hallway. From . . . her room. Mom. Stomping her feet ranked on the rarity scale with throwing dishes. A yearly-or-less occurrence.

"What is this?"

An arctic lake couldn't have been colder than Mom's voice. Violet didn't have to turn to see her mother. She knew. What her face looked like. What was in her hand.

"What the . . . ?" Dad's eyes jumped from Violet to Mom and back again.

When she turned, Violet would see it. The curl of Mom's lip, the pleat between her eyes. She'd finally made Mom regret being a mother.

"English Standard Version," Mom said, and Violet braced for the tirade.

Instead, Mom said just two more words. She threw the name of God's Son like a grenade, like garbage. Violet whirled. Charged. Grabbed the book. Clutched it to her chest, the leather cover and the translucent pages. The red letters.

"Don't say His name like that," Violet said.

Dad rounded the counter, stood shoulder-to-shoulder with Mom, blocked Violet in and gaped at her.

"You're not a . . . are you?"

They couldn't even say the word? And no, of course she wasn't a Christian. She was just reading the Bible, trying to understand it, trying to . . . "Why were you in my room? You're never in my room."

Mom stared at the Bible in Violet's hands as if she wanted to snatch it back. She shook her head.

"You were gone five days," Dad said.

"Without calling. And then you took the car. And when you came in the house, you went straight to your room with that bag, and . . . We were thinking pot, pregnancy test."

"We definitely weren't thinking Bible." Mom crossed the kitchen and picked up her cell phone.

"Dee, what're you doing?"

"The only reasonable, legal thing to do. She clearly needs help, and I'm not going to be one of those irresponsible mothers who ignores her child in crisis."

The laugh burst from Violet's mouth. "Are you serious, Mom, are you really serious? You're going to start parenting me? Now?"

"Dee, put the phone down. We have to talk about this."

"There is absolutely nothing to talk about. She's going to re-education."

"This is Violet we're talking about."

"This is someone who brought illegal contraband into our house, Scott."

Someone. Violet took a step back from them. *Dad? You're going to say something, aren't you?*

The silence screamed, sliced Violet open at her oldest seam and tore out their place inside her. This wasn't like losing Khloe. This was a wrenching in her chest that threatened to double her over. She stayed upright to meet their eyes. She'd been the best daughter she could be, donned the invisible cloak, fended for herself. Well, she wasn't see-through anymore.

"Go ahead," she said. "Call them."

Mom pressed three digits and held the phone to her ear.

"Dee." Dad wandered to the table and sat, folded his hands and sighed. "You're not going to do this."

"Hello, I need a Constabulary agent at my house as quickly as possible. My daughter's in possession of an illegal Bible, and — Diane DuBay. My daughter's name is Violet."

She might have only minutes. She ran to her room, dug her overnight bag from under her bed, and threw things inside. First, the Bible. Then clothes — underwear and another bra, socks, shirts, shorts, jeans. Then the envelope from her underwear drawer labeled Cash Stash. She'd count it later, but it held at least a few hundred bucks. She grabbed the pillow from her bed and pushed it through the duffel handles. Now she could carry everything she owned in one hand.

Dad stood in the doorway. "Violet."

"Get out of my way, Dad. Unless you're

going to lock me in my room till they get here."

"Why would you bring that thing into our house? You had to know we couldn't let this happen without —"

"No, actually, I think part of me had this fairy-tale idea that parents protected their kids and —"

"Your mother is protecting you. From yourself. You don't get that now, but you will."

"Daddy." Her voice trembled. "I'm asking you. Let me have a head start on them. Because I'm your daughter."

"I don't know if that's best for you."

"It is. Please. I wish I could explain it all, but — have you ever talked to God?"

Suspicion leaped into his eyes. He shifted against the door jamb. "If you're going to start proselytizing me . . ."

"No, no, Dad. Just, God is important. Learn about Him, ask Him for help to show you what's right, not what's legal."

He stepped aside. "You'd better go."

Violet leaned down for one crazy moment and waved to her fish. "Bye, guys." She stood up. "Would you do one other thing for me?"

Her dad waited.

"Don't flush them. Take them to a pet

store, okay? Somebody will buy them."

She couldn't expect a committed answer. Maybe he'd do it. Maybe not. They were only fish. She hoisted her duffel and her pillow and marched down the hall, past her mother, who still held the phone to her ear.

"Violet, did you . . . ? They're telling me you were involved in some kind of . . . ?"

Violet swiped her keys from the counter, stepped into her tennis shoes, and stood in the doorway. She'd never lived in any other house. Her best memories were at Khloe's, not here, but this was the base she returned to, involuntarily as a tetherball.

She glanced back. Dad hadn't followed her. Mom hadn't followed her. She ought to be grateful. Or maybe they were falling back on the only mode they knew. Maybe the easiest thing for them to do with her was to look straight through her.

She shut the door behind her, climbed into her car, and stowed the duffel in the back seat. Maybe they would come to the door and watch her drive away. She backed down the driveway under the soft moonlight. If the door so much as cracked open, the light from inside would show.

It stayed dark.

Violet drove away as if she had a destination. As if someone, somewhere, would see

her little blue car coming down the road
and rush out to meet her.

37

Clay didn't dream, or if he did, his mind blocked the mess of his subconscious the moment he surfaced in a hotel bed under a down comforter. The AC rattled under the window. Sunlight slanted through the blinds. He squirmed, stretched, and reached toward his wife. That side of the mattress was cold.

He sat up. Two seconds' glance confirmed she wasn't in the room. She'd tugged her half of the sheets wrinkle-free. He padded barefoot to the bathroom.

"I've been thinking," he said, "we're going to need to trade the Jeep or . . ."

She wasn't here, either. His stomach tightened. He turned in the doorway, and his eyes roved the room as if he could conjure her. They snagged on the ivory sheet of hotel stationery propped against the TV screen. Five steps crossed the room. His fingers swiped the paper — papers.

Several sheets. The cheap black ballpoint had dried up on her a few times on the first page. She'd had to scribble a loop in the margins to get it writing again.

Dear Clay,

No. His eyes snapped shut.

She'd taken the Jeep to get some breakfast. She was coming right back. *Read it, imbecile. That's all it says.*

Three sheets of stationery for a breakfast run. Right.

He was going to throw up before he read another word.

Coward. Read it.

His hands quivered. He opened his eyes.

Dear Clay,

You're going to be shocked, I know. You don't think I have it in me. I've known for a while now that I do, that this kernel of action is lying in my chest waiting for something to water it. Something finally did, the night our baby jumped out of the Jeep and we didn't stop her. And since that night I've been trying not to do this and trying to believe in us because I want to, I really want to. You're my husband. I pledged myself to you. I loved you. I do, still.

We should have said things to each

other. Part of me wants to rip this up and wait for you to open your eyes, so I can say all this to your face instead. But I don't think I can. It hurts to give you pieces of me and watch you drop them on the floor and walk over them because you don't know what to do with them. So you do nothing. I know it isn't your fault. I know if you could, you would be the husband who stays with his wife through everything, not just with her in the room, but really with her. Not because it's what I need but because it's what you want.

I have tried for days not to compare past and present. Not to remember every night I stayed up waiting for you to find it in yourself to come home and face life again. Come home and make us a team again. I guess it really isn't fair, but when I think about that night, leaving Khloe behind, it's like in that second you made me like you. You have no idea how many times I've vowed never to let her feel abandoned.

Clay doubled over on the bed. The next sheet was wrinkled at one edge with drop marks. Tears. A little sound pushed up from the pit of him and bled into the air. He forced his eyes to the page.

I don't want to leave you right now. I can see in your eyes that you're lost, you're hurting, just like I am. But you let hurt drive you, Clay. You're going to keep leaving, whether by your choice or the Constabulary's. Last night, when I asked you about prayer, it was because I need to know what I'm facing. I need to know, if we get caught, whether I'll ever see you again or whether you'll cling to your version of Jesus for years. Right now, I think I would lose you.

It's not an ultimatum. Please, please don't see it that way. I just have to give myself a little time away from us. You said you don't know where we're going from here. I don't either. I just know that the last week has torn us up and I don't think we can deal with this if we're stuck together in a little room.

I took a taxi and half the photo money. I have my phone. Don't call me today. I'm not going to turn myself in. That's a promise. Not for at least a week. I don't know if I will eventually or not. What I'm asking is that both of us figure out what we want and how much we want it.

Clay flipped to the final page. The tear marks on this one warped the center, right on top of the words.

Clay, I love you. I think if I loved you less, I could watch you grab your keys and head out the door and I could just wait for you to come home and not feel a thing. Maybe if I loved you less, I'd be a better wife. I'm sorry. I'm so sorry. I'm still sitting here with you. You're sleeping just a few feet away, hair all mussed and your arm stretched toward me. I feel as if I'm going to be leaving half my body and all my heart in this room, but I have to do this for me and for you, too.
   I want to come back to you. I think I can. Not today, but maybe soon.

Forever,
Nat

The pages slipped from his numb fingers. He rocked and held his stomach. His vision washed gray. Time passed.
   When he could think again through the howling inside, he straightened up and pulled on the jeans he should wash soon. Where would she have gone? Another hotel? Somewhere she linked to Khloe? She was too smart to go home. A taxi was risky,

though. Someone had seen her face in his rearview mirror.

Lord, don't let her get recognized, don't let her —

Wait. Wait a minute. What was he thinking? His voice spurted at the ceiling.

"What is wrong with You? I prayed. I believed You. I tried to be a witness for You, like You wanted, to my family, and You just stand back and watch while they . . . while I . . ."

He kicked the sheets of paper, and they flew up around his feet like startled birds, then drifted back down.

"I can't do this anymore. I don't want to do this anymore. I'm not doing this. Anymore." His knees hit the carpet. "You don't keep Your word."

He turned on the TV and found a local channel. If Natalia had been arrested this morning, the media would be highlighting the event for at least a day. For the next eight minutes of news loop, he hid his hands in his lap to keep from shutting it off.

The blonde anchorwoman paused to shift her notes on the table in front of her. "And now for our last local story, the Michigan Philosophical Constabulary has been —"

Bile rose halfway to his throat.

"— recently made suspicious of an

389

organized movement created to thwart them. Members of this movement are unidentified at this time, but they're suspected of aiding and abetting Christian fugitives, including some of the most dangerous criminals on the Constabulary's wanted list. We interviewed MPC Agent Larry Partyka earlier today regarding the steps the Constabulary is taking to apprehend these suspects."

Clay swallowed, breathed, and sat back against the bed frame. This had nothing to do with Natalia. Unless they tacked her arrest onto the end as a reassurance to the public that the Constabulary was still on top of things.

The camera cut to a tall redheaded agent in a black suit, standing beside the same news anchor but obviously at a different time, in a different location. She angled her microphone toward him and flaunted her perfect teeth.

"Agent Partyka, can you explain for us exactly what civilians can do to aid the Constabulary in this . . . ?"

Partyka grinned, or grimaced, or something. "The suspects taking part in this resistance movement are considered erratic and dangerous, and we're starting to believe they're more organized than originally thought. The most important thing — the only thing we're requesting from civilians — is information. Stay safe, avoid a confrontation. Leave that part to law enforcement."

The camera cut back to the blonde anchor. Her words blurred, but that calm voice coated the room and let Clay think again. The news looped a minute later. No Natalia.

Syllables filtered back into his brain. *"Recently made suspicious of . . ."* Not likely. They'd known about the resistance for a while, he would bet on it. They'd wanted to nab the offenders quietly, then pop up on the news with a surprising success story. Clearly, that wasn't working, and they'd resorted to enlisting information from the public.

No wonder they couldn't find anyone. Clay knew Marcus personally and still hadn't known . . .

"Unidentified at this time."

No, the resistance leader wasn't unidentified.

What would Clay's knowledge be worth? Not that he'd ever use it.

Marcus was worth a lot more to them than Khloe. She was only one harmless teenager, and she wasn't even a Christian, and they knew that by now.

He wasn't really considering this.

Would *they* consider it? Would they honor a deal?

Marcus was a friend.

A friend who'd lost Khloe and Violet and not cared enough to contact Clay, to fix this failure.

The Constabulary might say they agreed to his terms with no intention of letting him or Khloe go. But the hollowness of this room and the pain in his gut and the crumpled letter on the carpet beside him . . .

He had to try.

He shut off the TV. Pulled on his shirt. Stuffed his wallet in his pocket, grabbed his keys and his shoes. He'd be there for Nat. He'd learn how to hold the pieces, if she'd give them again. He'd get their daughter back.

He'd make everything right.

38

Assuming the con-cops had her license plate number, her description, and everything else ever officially recorded about her — work records, medical records, school records — Violet's best bet would be to go live in a forest as a hunter and gatherer. Make her clothes from squirrel skins and live on . . . *Fern leaves.* The memory squeezed her throat. Running through the woods, Khloe's hot hand in hers. She shoved it away and put her car in park. Maybe she ought to leave it here, grab her duffel bag, and start walking. Somewhere.

For now, though, she rolled down the window and sat in the parking lot behind a mostly vacant strip mall. A non–chain ice-cream shop occupied one end, and next to it sat a used book store. Every other window in the strip sported a For Lease sign.

She'd driven almost an hour from home, north on M-53 and then west on a random mile road. Based on her memory, she shouldn't be too far from Chuck and Belinda's house. From Khloe.

Maybe she was stupid to park here and think she could relax. She was probably really stupid to unzip the duffel and dig through her clothes until her fingers grazed cool leather. But she needed to read more. She needed to be sure about the decision that had been nudging inside her all night, all morning.

She'd finished Matthew and Mark. She was halfway through Luke. The tiny differences in the stories fascinated her. He was the same Man in every one of them and did the same things, but the different men who'd known Him noticed different details about Him. They told some things in different order, which she didn't get. Maybe someday she'd have the opportunity to ask someone which story was chronological, and why all of them weren't.

And she'd discovered why Marcus let her go, recorded in Matthew and Luke. Jesus had said it multiple times.

"Love your enemies."

"Do good to those who hate you."

"Pray for those who persecute you."

Though she hadn't hated the Christians, she was a persecutor. The word was a nettle in her heart, but she couldn't deny it. Had Marcus prayed for her?

She opened to the place she'd left off, the pink ribbon bookmark. Strange that it was pink, because the few instances of handwriting in the margins were definitely a man's. Black ink, small and neat letters. Beside Jesus's words on the cross, *"It is finished,"* the man had written, *Nothing left to pay.* And every time Jesus told someone, *"Your sins are forgiven,"* the words were underlined. She found even more underlining when she reached the book of John. Mentions of persecution or tribulation, being hated by the world, being free when set free by Jesus — all of these things, the man had underlined. She flipped through the Bible at random, searching for more underlining, and found a lot of it, mostly in Romans and Hebrews.

If this man was like all the other fugitive Christians, then Violet could begin to understand them. Their hidden hearts beat in every careful line of black pen, in the verses this man held closest to him, the ones about persecution and difficulty and trusting that Jesus would overcome whatever happened to a person here on earth. He believed with as much certainty as Janelle. He knew he had sinned, but he also knew the sins were paid for.

Were Violet's sins paid for?

She thought so. She hoped so.

She stretched out her legs across the car, and her heels bumped the passenger door. She rolled the windows down further, but the air hung like a veil today. Sweat darkened her top. At least she had extras now, though who knew when she'd be able to do laundry. She read pages and pages, the rest of Luke, the whole book of John. This was the end of the Jesus books. It was time to talk to Him.

Her eyes closed. Her hands shook a little. Because the Jesus she spoke to wasn't the easygoing, tolerant, inspirational teacher. To really speak to Jesus, she would have to address the Man who confronted, who loved, who healed and scolded.

"Nothing left to pay."

Nothing left to do, except talk to Him. She rested her forehead on the steering wheel.

"Um. Jesus, I'm so sorry. That You died. I wish You hadn't been hurt like that, but — but thank You for paying. I — I had some things screwed up, and I did some things —" A sob ripped her chest. Her shoulders heaved to keep it in, but Jesus had cried too. So it was okay. "Jesus, I'm sorry. I thought I was doing good. But they're Your followers, and I — oh, God, Jesus, Janelle. I'm so sorry about Janelle."

She held the Bible to her chest and rocked it. The tears came too hard to talk out loud, so she prayed inside.

Please let my sins be forgiven too. I love You, Jesus, now that I finally know You. I'll keep this Bible safe. And the guy who had it before me — if he was free, he would never black-market his Bible. So if he's handcuffed to a table somewhere, be with him, please.

Slowly, the tears dried. Violet breathed the stuffy car air, in and out, and lifted her head. *Nothing left to pay.* To be forgiven? No. But to make things right with the people she'd wronged, the best she possibly could . . . she had to do something.

"Jesus, if You would, please be with me." She turned the key and pulled onto the empty road, back toward the highway. "I'm scared to death."

39

"So Clay Hansen comes to us." The shoulder seams of the man's blue suit jacket strained as he stuck his hand across the table to Clay. "Agent Lopez. I'll be conducting the interview."

Clay sat back in his chair and blinked. Surely the man didn't expect a handshake. After a moment, Agent Lopez settled into his own chair and nodded to the voice recorder that sat between them, winking its red light.

"Obviously, this has to be recorded, but I'm hoping we can keep things on some level of civility."

Sure, why not.

They hadn't even handcuffed him, just checked him for weapons and escorted him to this room, white walls on three sides and a broad, dim window on the fourth, beside the door. No way to tell how many people watched him from the other side of that window. All he saw was his own reflection. He breathed in deep, let his body loosen. They'd honor the deal, or they wouldn't.

"You mentioned you had something to offer us," Agent Lopez said.

"This resistance movement you're all panicking about."

"The Constabulary doesn't make a habit of panicking."

Of course not. "I know their leader."

In the moment before the professional mask settled, Lopez's eyes flickered. Impressed. Curious. Hungry for this morsel of information. No, not a morsel. Clay was offering him the whole meal, and they each knew the other one knew it. Lopez's hand made it halfway up from his side before he lowered it again, preventing some giveaway gesture. He cleared his throat.

"You have the leader's name?"

"I know the leader. Personally."

Lopez waited, nodded, and sighed when Clay didn't break the silence. "Please do tell."

This guy must think Clay was stupid. Well, maybe only stupid people approached the Constabulary for a deal. Numbness crept into his hands. *What am I doing?* He battled his lips into a firm smile.

"First, I get to see my daughter. Then you

release her, permanently, clean record. You stop looking for Violet, clean record for her, too. Then I give you the name, and then you release me."

"And Natalia?"

Her name speared him straight through. The guy had to see it. Roll with it, bounce back, smile. "She's not here, in case you missed that. She's not a Christian. She hasn't done anything illegal."

"She fled a crime scene."

"There wasn't any crime at the reception. Those agents didn't have anything on us, they just wanted to talk, and we didn't feel like talking."

"We? Did you ask your wife if she wanted to talk to them, or did you intimidate her into coming with you?"

Clay shoved his chair back but stayed seated. He inhaled the clean cotton scent of the air freshener. Come on, get control. See the humor. He'd bet his bike he'd never intimidated a soul in thirty-nine years.

"But if you're not concerned about Natalia, then I'm not either, for now. About Khloe, though. You won't be seeing her today. She's in a group home about half an hour from here."

"Looks like an impasse to me."

Agent Lopez stood, leaned over the table.

"Except you're the criminal, Mr. Hansen, and I'm law enforcement."

On the wall, hung between the door and the mirror-window, a red phone rang twice. Lopez hastened to it, listened for about fifteen seconds, and then hung up.

He turned back and shrugged. "You've got a deal. My boss will release you and your daughter."

"And Violet?"

"How we deal with her will depend on Violet."

What did that mean?

"But before anything else happens, I need that name."

"No way."

"Mr. Hansen." Lopez sat across from Clay and spread his hands flat on the table. "You're not getting a reunion or a release or anything else without that name."

Even Clay's arms had gone numb now, as if the blood were receding from his limbs and damming up in his torso, weighting him to the chair.

"So." Lopez folded his arms.

"How do I know you'll honor the deal?"

"You don't, but we will."

In the last week, Clay hadn't ever controlled a single thing. He'd simply been funneled by fate toward the moment he

401

gave the Constabulary what they wanted and lost his freedom in return.

I tried, Nat.

"All right." Clay balled his fists in his lap. Never let them see you shake. He shifted in the chair, and it suddenly felt harder. If they could prove Marcus's role in the resistance, the man wouldn't go to re-education. He'd be imprisoned for the rest of his life.

"You're doing the right thing for your family, Mr. Hansen."

If they kept their word, that was more than Marcus had done for him. More than even God had done.

"All right."

"The name?"

"Marcus Brenner."

Lopez's eyes darted to the window.

The door sprang open. Another agent charged in, lean and no taller than five-foot-nine, probably shorter. His coarse, sandy hair was mussed on top. Lopez shut the door behind him and stood against it. New point man in the interrogation. This must be the boss.

The new guy's eyes, blue and hard, drilled into Clay. "Did Brenner put you up to this?"

Whoa. What? "Uh, no, of course not."

The man approached the table but didn't sit. He leaned toward Clay, pushing into his personal space with the scent of cinnamon gum.

"You just said you know him personally."

"And it follows that he told me to turn him in?" Clay leaned back in his chair.

Satisfaction flickered in the man's eyes. He straightened but didn't step back. "Agent Mayweather. Mr. Hansen, if Marcus Brenner were leading a resistance movement, why would he tell you about it?"

"He trusts me."

"Why?"

The Constabulary wasn't supposed to challenge his story. He folded his arms against the chill in the room, or maybe against the chill inside him. *Yeah, Marcus, why would you trust me? Look at me now.*

Agent Mayweather rounded the table and perched on the edge of it, a foot from Clay. *Back off, why don't you.* But Clay wouldn't retreat again. This guy could touch noses if he wanted to, as long as he believed Clay, as long as he honored the deal.

Apparently, Mayweather wasn't going to shoot further questions until this one got answered. "I guess because I'm . . . well, family."

"No, you're not."

Impossible that this guy could know that. Unless . . . maybe they had a whole file on him, on Natalia and Khloe. They could have researched his whole family tree.

He shrugged anyway. "Suppose we're cousins?"

"Brenner doesn't have family, hasn't since his mother's death thirteen years ago. And when you lie to me about one thing, I assume you're lying about everything else, including whether he put you up to this. Not the way to reunite your family, let me tell you."

They didn't have a file on Clay. They had one on Marcus. And Agent Mayweather knew that file so well he could spit out biographical details without checking his notes.

"We're not blood relatives, but the last church you busted — that was his church too. He called us his family. All of us."

"Really. So he's the sentimental type."

"No, just . . ." How to explain the guy? Clay shrugged. "Loyal, I guess."

"Loyal enough to divert us with a ploy that he's the leader?"

"I sincerely don't know what you're talking about."

Mayweather studied him another long moment. "Lee Vaughn."

He shook his head. "Never met him."

A slow nod, a twitch of the mouth, as if

Clay had said something amusing — but Mayweather seemed to believe him. "Well, Mr. Hansen, you're going to call Brenner and arrange a meeting. Give him a reason you have to see him, today. He can pick the time and place; you just sell the emergency."

Sure, easy. As long as Marcus picked up the phone. As long as he wasn't "detoured."

If only Clay could think of Marcus as a bargaining chip instead of a person. Instead he'd carry this conversation for the rest of his life, a tiny, putrid seed to fester in his gut along with every other rotten day that he couldn't spit out and leave behind. The drive in the snowstorm while his daughter lay small and sick in the hospital. The pieces of Natalia he'd trampled without knowing it. The salt of his tears as he stood outside his sister's hospital room, not trusted or worthy or something, not allowed in. *"Wait outside, Clayton. I said go. Don't be here right now."*

He swallowed this new day, and it wasn't as bitter as he expected. In a way, Marcus had earned this. Clay settled his hands on the chair's smooth armrests. "When do I call him?"

"We're ready now."

40

No way Clay could pull this off. He clenched his hands between his knees and leaned forward on the weathered wooden bench. Bikers, runners, and power-walkers passed him, then rounded the curve of the walking path, out of sight behind a fringe of trees. Marcus had described this bench and the flower garden across the path as if he'd been here hundreds of times. *"I'll come to you."* Sure, and the moment they made eye contact, the guy would read everything in Clay's face, in the fidgeting of his hands and feet. *Sit still. Calm down.*

One thing Marcus wouldn't see was a wire. Agent Lopez had suggested one, but when Clay refused — no telling what would happen to the deal if Marcus mentioned Clay's stint as Toddler Transporter — Agent Mayweather shrugged, and no one brought it up again.

No one had informed him what would

happen after he shook Marcus's hand. As far as he knew, the Constabulary team was limited to Mayweather, Lopez, and an Agent Tisdale, whose version of street clothes included camouflage fatigue pants. He was built like a bouncer. All three agents probably hid in the shrubs somewhere, ready to handcuff Marcus the moment Clay identified him.

Which didn't make any sense. Mayweather had far too much information on Marcus to be missing a physical description. Or a home address.

Clay stood and stretched his arms, paced the grass. No one had come by in a while. Where . . . ? There. Marcus jogged down the track toward him.

He slowed as he neared Clay. Sweat darkened his red T-shirt. The shorts weren't exactly workout shorts, but they were a lightweight khaki with minimal pockets. Marcus had already planned to be here and simply tacked a meeting with Clay onto his scheduled run. A fact that wouldn't faze Clay under normal, low-stress circumstances. Right now it felt like an insult. Really illogical considering what Clay was here to do.

"You're going to have a heatstroke." The idiotic words popped out of his mouth as soon as Marcus entered hearing range.

Marcus jogged in place for a minute, then joined him on the bench. "Weather like this, you just slow down a little."

In weather like this, you could overheat standing under a tree. *Focus.* Clay's neck shivered, but he didn't turn to look. Where were they? Why didn't they just step into the open and read the man his Miranda rights?

"So," Marcus said. "What's going on?"

Persuade him to show up. That was the sum of Clay's role. A cover story had never entered his head. But he did have something to say. "Why didn't you tell me?"

Marcus rubbed his neck. "What?"

"When they, when you —" He pressed his fists against his knees. For one scorching second, he *wanted* this man in prison. "However it happened, I should've known about it. Right away."

"Clay. What're you talking about?"

So this was his choice, to play stupid. No. "Khloe. However they got to Khloe."

However you failed her.

"I couldn't call you before. Things happened. But Khloe's okay. I just saw her yesterday."

"Where is she, then?"

Marcus sighed. "You know where she is."

408

"I sure do. She's been in a state foster home since Tuesday, and you didn't think this was something her father should know."

"No."

"They informed me. Officially. My daughter's in custody, after you —"

"Clay. She's not. They're lying, to — I don't know what they're trying to do, but she's safe." His voice lowered, although no one had passed in the last few minutes. Had the agents cordoned off the path? A hundred yards away, even the swing set and the old merry-go-round were empty. "You know where she is. You've been there. But I need you to stay away for another few days."

Clay scrubbed at his hair, shifted on the bench that still dug into his back. "The agent showed me proof. Just admit it, Marcus, admit they have her."

"You've got to trust me." Marcus dug knuckles into his neck.

He'd tried that once. And if he defected on this mission . . . jail was a given. Khloe might be in custody, or she might not be, but either way, he couldn't get to her without buying his own freedom.

I tell you the truth: it is the will of God that you should save your life, not lose it. Jesus hadn't said that. Well, probably hadn't. But for today, it applied. And even if this wasn't

God's will . . . this was Clay's.

He held out his hand. "I trust you."

Marcus's eyebrows rose, probably at the formality. Then he reached across the bench and clasped Clay's hand. The half smile and the warmth in his eyes sent ice all the way up Clay's arm. *He's a bargaining chip.* No. He was a man. A loyal man.

"Freeze!" Lopez and Tisdale appeared around the blacktop curve behind Marcus, hands on their sidearms.

Marcus's grip loosened. Shock blanked his face, and his breath caught. As Clay withdrew his hand, Marcus stood and stepped back from the bench. He was going to run.

"Hands up! Get down on the ground!"

Marcus turned and faced them. Measured them.

Lopez drew his weapon and leveled it inches from Marcus's chest. "I said, on the ground."

Marcus blurred. Flashed to the side, clear of the gun, and threw an elbow that knocked a grunt from Lopez. That gun would go off. Or Lopez would intentionally shoot him. *Marcus, don't be an imbecile. You've lost. Go quietly.*

Marcus's fist smashed into Lopez's face. The gun dropped into the grass.

Agent Tisdale charged and tackled from the side. Marcus's body seemed to bend sideways at the knees, maybe at only one knee. They fell together. Tisdale scrambled up to his knees. Marcus tried to. He crumpled back to the grass, facedown. He rolled to his right side, swung his left leg at Tisdale's knees, threw fists and elbows until Tisdale swiveled and brought his heel down to gnash Marcus's right knee into the ground. Marcus roared. Writhed. Curled one hand into the grass. Lay still.

Tisdale grabbed Marcus's arms, pinned them behind his back, and hoisted him to his feet. His right leg buckled, but Tisdale's hold kept him upright. Their breathing, rough, labored, pulsed against Clay's ears.

"Marcus Brenner." Lopez wiped blood from his nose and stepped back while his partner clapped on the handcuffs. "You're under arrest on suspicion of harboring fugitives, aiding and abetting the distribution of materials violating MCL seven-fifty-one-oh-six, suppressing evidence of said materials, obstructing justice, and resisting arrest."

A grimace pulled Marcus's mouth. His voice rasped. "This guy. I don't know him. He doesn't know anything."

Guy?

Oh.

Marcus's eyes flickered to Clay, then refocused on Lopez. "Let him go."

"We're planning to." Lopez holstered his weapon and turned to Clay with half a smile. "He earned it. Thanks, Mr. Hansen."

No. No, no, no. They'd never rehearsed this. Clay fought to look away, but Marcus's gaze fused to his, wouldn't release him, flashed disbelief, then realization.

"You?"

Clay's face must have affirmed it, because Marcus flinched. *You'd have done the same thing, man. Freedom's expensive. You were the only asset I had.*

"Let's go." Agent Tisdale pushed Marcus forward.

His face crumbled into pain. He would have collapsed if Tisdale hadn't held him on his feet, but he stiffened against Tisdale's shove.

"Stop resisting."

Marcus stared past all of them to the tree line and the swirl of clouds above it, as if trying to wake up from all this.

Or praying.

"Come on." Tisdale shoved harder, and this time Marcus didn't fight. His head drooped, and Tisdale half-dragged him back the way the two agents had come, following the edge of the running track. They shrank into distance and vanished around a bend.

"Right," Lopez said, maybe to himself. He rubbed his hands together as if to scrub them clean. "We'll debrief you as quickly as possible, Mr. Hansen, but I need you to come with me."

Clay's heart pitched. "You're supposed to let me go. That's what you said. That's what we agreed to."

"Of course. As soon as we've debriefed you. This was something of a covert mission."

The ragged puzzle pieces refused to fit. "Did you have any pictures of him?"

"Well, of course we . . ." Lopez cocked his head. "Observant."

"You could've gone to his house and arrested him. You didn't need me."

"To identify him? To arrest him? No. Didn't need you for that." Lopez hit a button on his radio and half turned away from Clay, a pointless shield for his words. "He's in custody. . . . Well, I think he sprained his knee or something, you want a doctor to . . . ? Of course not. We secured the area first. I'm bringing Hansen back."

Clay stood. *Run. Now. While you can.*

Lopez paced the grass and didn't seem to care if Clay dashed away. Maybe because he couldn't outrun bullets. Clay sagged back

413

onto the park bench.

"Jason, if this gets — I'm telling you, it's highly — No, actually, I was going to say highly explosive, but you spin it however you want. We got him. They'll fall apart without him. . . . Yeah. Twenty minutes, tops."

Spin it. Right. The media would report that Marcus had been armed and deadly. They might even mention Clay, though not by name — from philosophical criminal to Constabulary informant. From Christian to whatever he was now. Whatever God considered you when you figured out He wasn't as reliable as He claimed to be.

Lopez clipped the radio back to his belt and turned to Clay. "You did fine, by the way. Exactly what we needed you to do."

"Why was I here?"

"You can ask Agent Mayweather if you want. He's the one who set this up, and he seemed to have reasons."

If he could secure Khloe's release, he hoped almost to God that she'd never know what he'd done today, trading freedom for freedom, choosing himself. Yet the burden was already lighter now than it had been minutes ago. He'd strategized, he'd acted, he'd carried out a plot to keep his family.

He pushed back to his feet. "After this

debrief, I'm free to go?"

"Sure thing."

"Lead on." He gestured an open path to Agent Lopez and followed him to an unmarked Constabulary car. He forced himself to duck inside, not to balk at the metal grid between the front seat and the back. He wasn't under arrest, and he never would be.

If he could redo this day . . . His stomach soured at the truth, but lying to yourself was pointless when you knew you were lying. *Face it. You're not noble. That's why you're not in handcuffs.* And when he considered the last few hours, he couldn't think of anything he'd do differently.

41

The house stood taller than she remembered, throwing an evening shadow across the yard. Finding it had eaten four hours, three-quarters of a tank of gas, and most of Violet's trepidation over driving. Anybody who could drive for four hours straight without wrecking her car must not be too bad at it, after all.

If a con-cop had tracked her to the highway, they lost her for sure the third time she turned around and drove the other direction. Maybe they thought she was some brilliant, two-faced spy with training in how to ditch a tail. Nope, just a girl with a pathetic memory for directions. She'd found it, though — not only the correct exit, not only the correct road, a stretch of dirt that needed grading — the house itself. Here she was. Drawn curtains hid any inside movement. The porch steps loomed steep as mountains. Violet's hand shook, and a chill snaked down her back as she pressed the doorbell.

A long minute. Another one. Someone must have peeked through a curtain. No admittance to the spy.

Violet bit her lip, twirled a charm on her bracelet, and hit the doorbell again. *Please, I need to talk to you.* She should have prowled around the house and knocked on the sliding glass door. Chuck and Belinda would've thought it was Marcus.

Maybe God didn't want her here in the first place. Three steps toward her car, she froze. Where did she think she was going? Depending on what Mom told the con-cops, her face might be a news item by now.

She sat on the porch step and faced the road. Chuck and Belinda's front yard unfurled down a gentle hill, with more space between it and the road than every backyard in Violet's neighborhood put together.

"Um, Jesus, if this is the wrong place, then I don't know where You want me, because I . . ." Her throat tightened. No more crying. "I don't have anywhere to go."

Behind her, the dead bolt clicked, and the door opened. Someone stepped outside.

"Violet," Chuck said.

She stood and turned to face him, pulled in a deep breath that tasted like the ap-

417

proach of rain.

"You want to tell me what you're doing here?"

If he ordered her off his porch . . . She rubbed her arms and stood straight. She would be alone, but solitude was fair punishment. *"I am with you always."* Red letters cloaked her against the chill. *Thanks, Jesus.*

"You'd better answer me." Chuck hooked his thumbs on his belt loops and stood with feet apart, but nothing in his tone threatened her. Of course not. She had to learn to stop looking for danger from these people.

"I'm here to . . ." He would laugh at her. The word was so lame. "To apologize."

Chuck rocked on his feet and frowned. "What for?"

"For everything I did. And would've done."

"Uh-huh. You even know what you're apologizing for?"

Heat rushed into her face. "For getting people arrested. For planning to get *you* arrested, and Belinda, and Marcus, and Lee, and Wren. I really would've turned you in."

"But?"

"But I know now. What re-education is. And what you're trying to do. Fighting. For

418

freedom."

Chuck motioned her to the porch swing swaying gently in a breeze that had blown away the humidity. She sat on the red-and-orange-swirled cushion and traced its design. No. She lifted her head to meet his eyes, specked with gold and green and brown. She didn't look away again. The minute of scrutiny felt like a year.

"Belinda wants me to invite you in for apple pie."

Oh, Belinda. Violet shut her eyes before he could see the tears. "No, it's okay, I shouldn't, I just wanted you to know —"

"For crying out loud. You have to run home all of a sudden?"

Words wouldn't squeeze past the rock in her throat. She shook her head.

"If you're here on some new mission, you'd better tell me. Right now."

"N-no. I'll never work for them again. Never."

"Well, then." Chuck opened the door and gestured her inside.

She'd taken three steps over the threshold when Khloe galumphed down the stairs with more noise than her body mass should make. She planted herself in front of Chuck and mimicked the resolute spread of his feet.

419

"You seriously let her in the house?"

Chuck's eyes flashed. "My home, my decision."

"I'm not going to talk to her. Or look at her."

"Fair enough."

Khloe bounded halfway back up the stairs before she stopped, turned, and headed back down. "Wait a second, Violet."

They faced each other like strangers. No, like enemies. Soldiers from opposite armies, unarmed for now but not forever. Khloe laced her hands behind her back.

"Go ahead," Violet said.

Khloe grabbed Violet's wrist and yanked at her bracelet. "My charm. It was a pledge. I want it back."

The knife wound Khloe was trying to inflict barely stung. Violet removed the whole bracelet for the second time this week, and her wrist felt less naked this time, more free. She held it up.

"Here, take it."

"And wear it? To remind me of the best friend that wrecked my life?"

"Khloe, I'm —"

"Marcus made us leave in case you brought con-cops here. He only let us come back this morning. I slept in a car last night."

So did I.

Khloe popped the amethyst pansy off the bracelet and dropped it. The rug softened the jingle of the bracelet's impact. "Stay away from me."

This time she stormed all the way upstairs, down the hall, out of sight. A door slammed.

A year ago, a month ago, Violet would have scurried up the stairs after her. Mollify. Make amends. She scooped up her bracelet and shoved it into the pocket of her shorts.

"Apple pie?" Chuck said.

"You guys had to sleep in a car? Because of me?" Chuck or Belinda might have a back problem or something. Old people shouldn't be sleeping in cars.

Chuck's thumb hooked in his belt loop. "Softer than the fishing lodge bunks, I can tell you."

"All of you in one car? And — and Wren just had a baby. She should've been in bed."

"Oh, Marcus took them with him. I don't know where they are now, but he told us they're okay, the whole family. Now, you sticking around for pie or not?"

She didn't deserve pie. She should leave. But they wanted her to stay. "Please and thank you."

He actually smiled, motioned her ahead

of him into the kitchen. The smell of apples and cinnamon watered her mouth. Her stomach growled. She'd eaten nothing since yesterday, holed up in her car afraid to show her face even to a drive-through.

Belinda stood at the counter and poured a glass of milk. On the plate in front of her sat a ridiculously enormous piece of pie. She carried both to the kitchen bar and waved at Violet to sit.

"Here, now, eat up. I know you already told my husband. Now tell me. What brings you back here?"

More of the story poured out to Belinda. You could set a clock by the interval of her clucks and croons and *mmm*s. When Violet told her about Mom's phone call to the Constabulary, Belinda patted her hand. Still, she couldn't talk about Austin.

Out the window, sunlight faded and rain-clouds rolled in. Drops pattered the window by the time Violet's words dried up.

"You know you can stay here, don't you?" Belinda said.

She shook her head. "That wouldn't be right."

"Why not?"

"I didn't come to . . . and anyway, Khloe —"

"Aw, Khloe." Belinda carried Violet's plate

and glass to the dishwasher. "She's young, that's all."

"We're the same age."

"Only by the calendar, and you know it."

No matter how final their severing was, Violet wouldn't let Belinda misunderstand. "Khloe went through a lot when she was little. Hospitals and stuff. And she . . . until I betrayed her, she was a good friend to me."

Belinda shut the dishwasher and returned to the table. "Good for you, holding onto the good stuff. Now, you going to spend the night here at least? Has to be comfier than your car. Oh, and go park around back of the house, just to be on the safe side."

With no other options, Violet stopped arguing. An edge of injustice still grated, yet her lungs seemed to fill with forgiveness, as fresh as the raindrops she ran through to grab her duffel bag and pillow from her car. She locked it and tossed her keys into the duffel.

Headlights.

She crouched behind a tree. A car pulled up the driveway. Crunching gravel stopped. The car must have parked. The engine and headlights shut off. Rain started to dampen her hair. Her heart thudded. She'd been here almost three hours. If she'd led con-cops here, they wouldn't have waited so long.

Violet peered around the trunk. They shouldn't be able to see her.

The car was small and silver. The porch light at Violet's back didn't reach far enough to illuminate the driver. He must be studying her car right now. Recognizing it, maybe. Calling in her location. But that didn't look like a Constabulary vehicle, even an unmarked one. The driver's door opened.

Lee.

Violet could have jumped up and hugged the woman, icy glares and all. Instead, she ducked. No way Lee would offer apple pie and sympathetic clucks.

Lee approached the house, then stared up at it. The rain fell harder, slicking her black hair and spattering her olive green T-shirt. Her feet dragged the next step, and the next, as if shackled. One more step. Then she doubled over and retched into the grass. She gripped her knees, dry-heaved twice more, then straightened. And saw Violet.

Standing up, stepping toward her, had simply happened. Violet didn't even remember doing it. Lee blinked through the rain as if Violet could be a ghost.

"You," she said.

"Lee —"

"He was wrong. All this time, it was you."

She grabbed Violet's arm and shoved her up the driveway, up the porch steps, through the door.

Belinda's voice drifted down the hall, coming closer. "You must be wet through by now, what took you so long?"

Lee wrenched Violet's bag from her hand. She threw it onto the rug, knelt, and unzipped it.

"Lee? What in heaven's name — ?"

"Clearly, you offered her bed and breakfast." Her words held the inflection of a digital voice. She pulled the clothes from Violet's bag, one article at a time. Shirts, jeans, panties. "You didn't think to question her, simply opened your arms despite her stated intention to —"

"The girl's had a change of heart."

"That is highly unlikely." Lee yanked out each sock, one at a time, and hurled it to the floor.

Belinda approached her from the side, as if Lee might be physically dangerous. "What do you think you'll find in there?"

Lee's hand stilled inside the bag, then drew out the Bible. Her eyes widened, frosted. "What is this?"

"Marcus." Violet sidled closer to Belinda but felt no safer. "I found his house and

went there to — to ask for one. Chuck said
he gave him one, so I knew he distributed
them."

Lee opened the Bible, flipped pages as if
looking for something. Toward the end, she
stopped at a page and stared at it. The book
trembled. She snapped it shut and dropped
it on the floor.

"Okay now." Belinda's voice couldn't
patch the holes ripped in the air by Lee's
every movement. "I know what she's done,
Lee, but the girl's learned a lot of lessons.
You're too riled up."

Lee glanced up and pushed to her feet.
One of Violet's socks drifted from her lap to
the floor.

"Why don't you tell us what brings you
over here," Belinda said. "Something's going on?"

The silence throbbed.

"Lee? Sugar?"

Lee blinked and seemed to detach from
the room. That morning after her panic attack, she'd donned a mask. This was more
like a suit of full body armor, complete with
the face-hiding helmet. She stepped past
Belinda, toward the kitchen.

"Chuck should be present," she said.

"I'm right here." From the living room,
the TV clicked off. Chuck lumbered into

the kitchen, and then they stood there, a loose square with three corners of uncertainty and one corner of ice.

"I'm unsure how to say this." Lee took a small step back and laced her hands. "Late this morning, my Constabulary contact found out about a planned operation later than he should have. It was apparently kept covert until the agents involved were successful."

"Spit it out," Chuck said.

"Someone gave them the identity of the resistance leader. Their operation succeeded in apprehending him."

Chuck's head bowed, and a long sigh spilled out of him.

Oh, no. "Lee, it wasn't me. I swear it wasn't me."

"That is not a black market Bible." Lee glanced back to the disemboweled duffel bag in the foyer.

"What?"

"That is his personal Bible. His handwriting. He would never part with it."

Oh, gosh. No wonder Lee suspected her. "I asked him for a Bible, and he gave me that one. I haven't seen him since yesterday, Lee. I swear I didn't turn him in."

Belinda gave a tiny gasp. "No . . . you're saying . . . Marcus? They arrested Marcus?"

"Pearl." Chuck circled his arm around her.

"Oh, no," she whispered. "He can't live in a jail cell, Chuck. He can't. He's got to be free, he's got to be outside under the sky."

No, Jesus, not Marcus. I did the right thing finally, but what good was it if he goes to jail anyway? And he doesn't deserve it. You know he doesn't, Jesus. Violet's arms and legs felt packed in ice cubes, but the river of prayer kept flowing while she stood silent.

Lee stared at Belinda and seemed to stop breathing.

Belinda hugged Chuck's arm, and her words gained speed. "Lee, that inside man of yours, he has to do something to get him out, he has to free him somehow, someone has to —"

"My contact was unable to locate him after the arrest. Sometime later, the Constabulary's official report was filed on the operation. Their suspect escaped."

If he escaped, why did Lee look like she might throw up again?

Belinda rocked up on her toes and leaned into Chuck's arm. "There it is, I knew it. He's on his way here right now."

Lee stepped back again, only one step, but now she stood apart from their square. "He is unreachable."

"He's hiding," Belinda said. "He'll contact

us as soon as the coast is clear."

But Chuck cocked his head at Lee. "Out with it, all of it."

"The arrest took place nearly ten hours ago. The alleged escape was shortly after that. He would have found a way by now to contact me. We have multiple methods set up for emergencies."

"So he didn't escape," Chuck said.

"I don't believe so."

"But if he didn't, they should be gloating about the capture. It should be all over the news."

"And they should have a case file on him. According to my contact, no paperwork has been filed."

"So either way, they're not making sense." Chuck took one of Belinda's hands and rubbed his thumb over her knuckles. She glanced up at him, eyes wide and watery, but his focus didn't waver from Lee.

Silence howled through the house. Lee backed up until she bumped against the table. She flinched, a ripple in the armor.

"You're sure about this," Chuck said.

"I am." She laced her fingers in front of her.

Sure about . . . Oh. There was only one reason a Constabulary agent would report a false escape.

No no no. No, Jesus. Please.

When the rest of them stood paralyzed, Violet forced herself to say it. "He's dead, isn't he."

42

Debrief. Such a deceiving word. It should be *unbrief* or *anti-brief* or *not-so-brief*.

They were frying his brain.

So many hours had passed. Clay couldn't count them, but they had to be adding up. Maybe darkness was falling outside this room, the same nondescript room with the reflective window. Or maybe the night had already worn away. Maybe the sun was coming up.

Agent Lopez squeezed the bridge of his nose. Must have ticked Mayweather off to get stuck with the stubborn Christian-turned-informant. "Mr. Hansen, I really don't want to repeat myself again."

"Release me, then. All I'm asking is for you to honor the deal."

"So you got desperate enough to turn in a fellow . . . believer." His mouth pursed around the word. "Before you're released, we need to be certain of your philosophical standing."

He couldn't answer that, not when he himself wasn't certain. He rested his head on his arms, the way Khloe did when she was done with the world. He spoke down to the tabletop.

"I want to see my daughter."

"We've talked about this. Over and over."

"Yeah, well, you're not getting any answers without her."

"You mentioned that."

"Still true."

If Clay were a less civilized man, he'd have decked this guy hours ago. Lopez deserved decking. But Clay embraced the self-control that had lasted this long. If he stood up from this chair, even to stretch his legs, he might get too close, be tempted to take a swing. And that would get him nothing but a spot on the re-education list. He hunched in his chair and crossed his arms.

The red phone rang. Lopez huffed and ambled to the window wall to pick it up. "Yeah." Pause. "You think that's going to accomplish anything?"

Was Mayweather on the other side of that window?

"Fine." Lopez hung up the phone and resumed his seat across the table. "You mentioned that Brenner said we didn't have your daughter."

"I know what I mentioned." Hours ago, when they'd first herded him into this room, when he'd had energy to challenge them.

"Well, when I said he was lying, *I* was lying."

Clay's wrung out brain had to replay those words. Twice. "You don't have Khloe."

"Never did."

The chair crashed behind him. His hands flattened on the table as he leaned toward Lopez. "Where's my daughter?"

"If we knew, we'd have her in custody."

"That charm, the silver heart."

"We have multiple sources of information, of course. Someone knew your daughter collects them."

He spun, kicked the chair, waited for the handcuffs to emerge while it skidded across the carpet, but Lopez didn't move. Clay dug his knuckles into his eyes. The right thing — he'd lit it on fire and watched it turn to ashes.

"You're still searching for her?"

"Actually, while we do lie sometimes, we also tell the truth sometimes. All depends on what we want. Your bargaining chip scored big, I'm sure that doesn't shock you. Agent Mayweather had the search called off for Natalia and Khloe. And for Violet."

Weariness, relief, maybe even gratitude wobbled his knees. He righted the chair and fell into it. *Have to get out of here.*

"He's willing to honor the rest of the agreement as well." Lopez glanced at the window as if he could see outside.

"The rest of the agreement?"

"Your freedom too, Clay. It's just not unconditional."

"Whatever you want."

Lopez twirled the stirrer in his coffee mug. His voice shifted to recitation, like a kid who knew the words by heart but couldn't define them. And didn't care to. "I want you to admit that God doesn't pick and choose who gets to heaven. That He doesn't dictate which path we follow to get to Him. That sin is less about God and more about how we condemn ourselves."

Elysium dogma. The stuff he used to mock, the stuff he used to pray wouldn't sink into the minds of his wife and his daughter. But really, did it matter?

"If you cling to your Christian beliefs, then we obviously can't let you go."

Okay, God, they didn't get Khloe. Maybe You did keep her safe. But You also let Natalia leave me. If he gave God credit for one thing, he had to hold Him accountable for the other. The scales tipped back and forth.

He closed his eyes, shut out the walls, the phone, the window, the table. Inside him, a storm cloud spun.

"Mr. Hansen, at this point, what happens next is up to you."

Maybe it always had been.

Clay opened his eyes, lifted them to the white ceiling tiles, the fluorescent lights. In the far corner, a light panel flickered. They'd have to replace it soon.

God, it's time You did something, really did something. If You kept Khloe free, if You really did heal her ten years ago, if You've been with me all this time and I haven't just wanted You to be . . .

"Mr. Hansen?"

Get me out of here. Clay waited. God could do it however He chose. Call Agent Lopez away and leave the door open. Cause a blackout so that Clay could sneak through the doorway, down corridors to a generator-powered exit sign. Shoot, an earthquake would be fine too.

The light panel hummed.

You see me, don't You? But You're not going to do anything for me.

"All right, Mr. Hansen, we'll be moving you to a secure facility where you'll be enrolled in re-education for no less than ninety days."

"Forget it."

"Excuse me?" Lopez's dark eyebrows crinkled.

"I've given God the last ten years. He doesn't get the next three months. I'm not going to re-education."

"If you're going to give a recanting statement, we need it in writing."

He was ready. The end of something throbbed in his chest, but when he told it to stop, it did. This would be a new life, free from the helpless pleading that God would come through. Free from the obligation to trust and obey.

Clay held out his hand, palm up. "Just get me a pen."

43

Maybe Violet should be crying like Belinda, whose weeping overflowed from the dining room. Chuck had shepherded her in there when she looked ready to fold over. But instead of sorrow, a numbness spread from the center of Violet, stretching toward her toes and fingers. *They killed him.* She angled a glance at Lee, who still stood framed by the bay window. Fingers laced behind her back. Poised like a sculpture.

"Lee?" If anyone should be crying . . .

Lee pivoted toward her, stiff but dry-eyed. "Yes?"

"I'm sorry. I know you . . . I mean, obviously, he was your friend." At the very least.

"Thank you."

"Is Belinda . . . Will she be . . . ?" *Okay* was a stupid word to use in this situation.

"He made her dining-room set."

The sturdy table, the carved chair backs. Violet tried to picture the time and care

437

required for a project like that.

He was really gone? None of them would see him again?

"Lee, maybe she's right. Maybe Marcus got away."

"I can't logically account for his silence in that case."

"Well, what if he got hurt somehow and he's in the hospital right now?"

"The Constabulary thought of this. According to my contact, only one patient admitted in the last day has matched his description. It was not him."

"Okay, so maybe he —"

Khloe skidded into the room and froze. "What in the world? What's wrong with Belinda? Did somebody die or something?"

"Yeah," Violet said. "Marcus."

"Wh-what? How did . . . What — just now?"

"Today, yeah. They arrested him and then they killed him."

The words sank in at last, through layers of denial. Images burned in front of her eyes even when she shut them, the different ways they might have killed him, his eyes open and glazed. Her stomach churned.

"But . . ." Khloe plopped down on the kitchen rug. "He's dead? He's actually dead?"

Lee swept past her and headed for the front door.

Violet trailed her down the hallway and ignored Khloe's quavering "Violet?"

Lee stood before the open front door. Rain poured now, pelted, the kind of drops that punched ricochet marks in the dirt. It poured down one side of the porch awning with a waterfall sound that mingled with the storm of Belinda's crying.

"Um, Lee."

No movement, no response.

Violet stooped and picked up the Bible, fallen to the floor next to her mostly empty duffel bag. She stepped around the mound of clothes, stayed to one side of Lee and held out the book.

"Here. This isn't mine. He — he would want you to have it."

Lee spoke to the rain. "He gave it to you."

"But he didn't know this would —"

She blinked once, slowly.

Nothing Violet said was helping. Good grief, nothing anybody said would help right now. From the dining room, Belinda quieted. Violet held the Bible out to Lee again, and not only because it belonged to Marcus.

"I think you should read it."

The mask rippled. Lee half turned. "You

have experienced a conversion."

"I . . . well, I've been reading. I started in Matthew. I got to Acts."

"You are a Christian."

"What? No, I . . . I mean, I'm . . ." Her breath caught on a searing in her chest. It wasn't a government label. It was what the true followers labeled themselves. So, if she was following the true Jesus, then . . . "Okay, yeah. I guess I'm a Christian."

Past the porch, tires ground on gravel. Violet ducked from the doorway, but Lee stood still. Violet reached for her hand and tugged her out of the way. Lee jerked her hand back, eyes sparking with some emotion that she quenched before Violet could name it.

"What if it's con-cops, Lee, what do we do?"

"It isn't."

Violet peered around the doorway. A red Jeep came to a halt halfway up the drive. Clay stepped out and traipsed through the rain, up to the house. He didn't look as tall as he had a week ago. His eyes landed on her, and he broke into that rolling lope, up the steps, right into the house. He lifted her off the floor in a strong hug that smelled like soap and tasted like tears. Her tears.

44

"Where's Khloe?" Clay's whole body waited for Violet's answer — his breath, his heartbeat, the arms he'd wrapped around her. His other daughter. She wouldn't be here unless Khloe was here too. But in her pause, he still couldn't breathe.

"Dad?"

Khloe's high voice pierced him straight through. She barreled down the hallway, would have crashed into them, but Violet stepped out of his hug and to one side.

Khloe latched onto him like a toddler. "Dad . . . Dad . . . Daddy."

Her arms squeezed out his breath, and she sobbed into his T-shirt. She stood level with his chest, but in his arms she was a bright pink infant, still wrinkled from her watery first home, testing her lungs with a scream. She was a four-year-old who couldn't stop screaming with the pain of an enlarging tumor in her head, and she was a five-year-old throwing up on his shirt and smelling like a hospital even when she was home, and she was a healthy first-grader who could run and laugh and demand rides on the park carousel. She was a middle schooler in high heels and makeup because she wanted to look older, and you couldn't say no to that when half of you still feared she'd never *be* older.

"Don't leave, Daddy."

"No, no," he whispered to her. She gulped away tears. "Never, baby."

"Where's Mom?" She peeked around him, beyond the open front door.

He rubbed Khloe's back to keep from scooping her up in his arms. "She didn't come with me."

"But where is she?"

"She'll be with us soon."

Khloe pulled back from his arms and stared up into his face. Her lower lip quivered. "Re-ed?"

"No, Khloe. She — she decided she needed a little time. It was — it was really hard, baby. Without you."

"She doesn't know you came to get me?"

"Not yet."

"Okay, let's call her." Khloe grabbed his hand and tried to pull him down the hall, toward what looked like the kitchen.

"Not here." A cold female voice snapped through their blind reunion.

A woman around thirty stood against the far wall, black hair layered short, gray eyes watching without expression. Had she been standing there the whole time? Her eyes brushed over Clay, frosty with . . . warning. Then she pushed away from the wall and left the room.

Khloe's grip tightened around his hand. "It's not like the con-cops are bugging the phone."

"No, Lee's right." Violet grimaced as if she'd said something wrong.

Khloe's glare sliced her like a laser, and Violet glanced toward the wall. He'd sort the details of their falling out later. Or better yet, Natalia could. Not the first time she'd forced them — well, usually Khloe — to "talk it through."

"We'll call her on the drive."

The woman must be a resistance member. Why she and Violet had been standing in the open doorway as if waiting for him, why the owners of the home — Chuck and Beverly, was it? — hadn't shown their faces yet . . . Clay tried to be curious, but the gaunt truth was that nothing mattered. Not the resistance, not its leader who probably sat in some interrogation room being pressured to sign a recanting of his faith. Not any of these people, only *his* people.

"Are you ready to go?"

Khloe nodded hard, as if she had to convince him. He turned to Violet, but she stepped back.

"No," Khloe said. "Violet doesn't come."

45

A moment of hope had buoyed her while she stood in the comfort of Clay's hug, the same hug he'd given her since she was nine and fell off her bike. They could go back, all of them. She could keep them. Clay and Natalia would take her in. But the idea itched like dry skin. She fidgeted inside it. No. Going back wasn't right. Could even be dangerous for them. Still, she might have done it, had Khloe crossed the room, reached out, and clinked their bracelets together. Except Khloe couldn't do that, because Violet's bracelet was shoved into her pocket.

"Khloe." Clay's forehead wrinkled with confusion and weariness. "Of course she's coming with us."

"I don't want her to."

He shook his head. "Baby, whatever you guys are fighting about, we'll sort it out."

"It's my fault." Violet backed against the

wall where Lee had been standing. "I'm sorry, Uncle Clay. I reported the church meeting to the con-cops."

His eyes widened. His mouth opened and closed.

"Violet . . ."

She pushed her hand into her shorts pocket, and it jammed against the bracelet.

"You did this? How could you do this?" He cracked his knuckles.

Violet's fingers curled up, hidden inside her pocket. "I didn't know —"

"You didn't know we'd go to re-education? You didn't know I would lose my daughter?"

Not daughters. "I thought it was the right thing. For everyone."

"So you did know, then. You knew exactly what you were doing."

His voice lurched between calm and fury, but Violet could absorb it, could wait him out. He was Clay. He wouldn't hate her, especially not forever. She pressed her palm to the cool wall, stenciled with roses.

Khloe marched to the mostly refilled duffel bag in the center of the room and kicked it. It skidded across the floor and bumped Violet's ankle. Khloe kicked a stray shirt, and then, before Violet could step forward to intercept, she kicked the Bible.

Clay didn't scold her.

"Dad, if you take her with you, I'm not coming."

He scrubbed at his eyes, fixed them on Violet, and let the silence sting.

46

She was only a kid. She couldn't be blamed for media propaganda. But when Violet's eyes met his, Clay couldn't hold her gaze. However irrational or despicable it was, he wished his daughter had never met her.

Khloe turned back to Clay and hooked her thumbs in her back pockets. "I'm not exaggerating."

"Go wait in the Jeep." Whatever he was about to say to Violet, Khloe didn't need to hear it. Or interrupt it.

"Dad, I —"

"Khloe. Go."

She didn't flounce off with flourish, didn't stomp. She walked outside, arms wrapped around herself. *I'm not choosing her, baby.* Her glance back never landed on Violet.

The moment Khloe disappeared past the doorframe, Violet knelt on the floor and righted the duffel bag. She stuffed clothes inside, then the Bible. What was she doing with one of those, if she'd made it her mission to send people to re-education?

He was only going to talk to Violet, not bring her along. But now that she crouched in front of him, piling what might now be everything she owned into one bag, he couldn't cast her aside.

"Violet, we're going home. All of us can go home, and . . ."

And what? Violet had spit on everything Clay and Natalia had ever tried to give her. A voice at his core whispered forgiveness, but it sounded distant and untouchable, part of God's standard, not his. How had he followed to his own detriment for ten years? *Let's try a compromise, God. You show me how forgiving this girl will benefit me and mine. Then I'll bend to Your rules.*

Violet zipped the duffel and stood up. "I can't. My mom found the Bible, called the con-cops."

So that was an emergency stash of clothes in the bag. Parental alarm zipped through him despite everything. But wait. "I made a deal with the Constabulary. It included you."

She passed the duffel from one hand to the other. "A deal? How?"

"You'll have a clean slate with them from here on out, as long as you don't commit any further crimes."

"But why would they go along with that?"

A question he would never answer. Ever. "Listen, Violet, if you can't go home, then we've got to come up with somewhere you can go."

He should take her in. Had to.

"I don't think Chuck and Belinda will throw me out."

Great, but she sounded unsure. "We should . . . I don't know, ask them."

"Not now. Uncle Clay, I want you to go. Really, I do. Khloe might run away or something if I come."

"She'll come around."

"Not anytime soon, and I don't blame her. Look what I did."

He was trying *not* to see it right now, and she shoved it into his face anyway. He steeled his jaw against the grimace.

A smile's ghost drifted over Violet's face. "Thanks."

"For . . . ?"

"For trying to want me anyway."

Oh. He cracked his knuckles against the palm of his other hand. "Violet . . ."

"No, really. It's okay." She shrugged. "Maybe I'll see you guys again, and it'll be better. And I feel almost like . . . like God wants me here for some reason. Maybe I can do something right."

Good girl. She always had been. A better person already, at seventeen, than Clay had been so far in his life and maybe ever would be. Not everyone could be noble, but the ones that pulled it off . . . He crossed the room and wrapped her up in one last hug.

She stiffened at first, then dropped the bag and hugged him. A shudder, a quick sob, and then she stepped back.

"I understand," she whispered. "I hope Aunt Natalia comes back, and I understand. They're your real family, you have to put them first."

"You were our family too." The betrayal wouldn't hit so hard otherwise.

"You did a lot for me, and I'll always love you guys." Violet dug into the pocket of her shorts. "Listen, if Khloe can ever . . . get past it. If she ever misses me. Would you give this to her?"

The silver charm bracelet. Clay took it, held onto it for a moment, warm and light in his hand. He shoved it into the pocket of his shirt.

Violet's eyes filled. "Um. I hope I see you again."

"Me, too," Clay said, too muddy inside to know if he meant it or not. He gave her a last quick hug and ducked outside into the rain. He jogged to the Jeep and climbed behind the wheel.

Khloe sat with her knees up, shoes on the seat, breathing steam onto the passenger window. Clay left the silence alone while he backed down the gravel driveway, while he navigated back to the highway.

"Daddy?"

"Yeah, baby."

"She was my best friend." She hid her face against her knees and cried.

Clay pulled over to the shoulder and parked. "Khloe, do you want me to go back?"

"I want you to fix it. So that she never texted the con-cops. So that I never had to be so scared and wet and cold in the rain, and alone and scared."

He rubbed her back and felt again the mortal wound of fatherhood, the inability to make everything go away.

"I'm sorry, baby." He rubbed her back. "I'm sorry you were scared."

"I hate her, Dad."

For Khloe's sobs, he could hate Violet too. Still so muddy inside, but at least one part of him felt that clearly. He tried to bury it. He pulled his phone from his pocket. For the last three miles, he'd squashed this desire. It wasn't time. Not yet. Natalia had said so. But he couldn't hold himself in any longer.

"Khloe, here. Call your mother."

She took the phone and cradled it in her hands, as if it were a rare diamond — better, an unlimited credit card. A smile tugged his mouth.

"But what about the con-cops? What if they hear us talking? What if —"

"I took care of it."

"You did?" Her teary eyes lifted to his, and in them he was a strong rescuer, worthy of trust. Every grubby thing he'd done this week was washed spotless. "How?"

"However I had to, and that's what matters. The Constabulary won't ever bother us again. We're free."

Khloe had already dialed. "Mom, it's me. I'm okay, and I'm with Dad, and he fixed everything."

Natalia's voice burst over the line, a repetition that sounded like their daughter's name.

The distance was going to kill him. He thrust his right hand toward Khloe. "Let me have the phone."

She offered it to him without hesitation, without a whine. This week had changed them all.

"Clay?" Natalia's voice quavered over the

line. "You fixed everything?"

Her voice mended all his gaping holes. He didn't need to run, didn't want to, even when the feelings surged into his throat. "We're coming to you, Nat. Where are you?"

But she didn't tell him. She simply wept into the phone. His hand flexed on the steering wheel. She wanted them to come, didn't she? She wanted him?

"I'm in Rochester. Downtown. I went to the doll store where —" Sobs kept interrupting her words. "Where we took her for her tenth birthday. I was trying not to . . . but I can't . . . Clay, please. I don't know what's wrong, I don't know how to keep us, but . . . but I want us."

His face was wet. Khloe was staring at him.

"Daddy? Are you . . . um . . . crying?"

He wiped his face on his arm. Not in front of Khloe. "Nat, I'm coming. We're coming."

47

As long as Lee's car was still here, she had to be here too. But Violet had searched the whole house. Well, other than Chuck and Belinda's bedroom, but Lee wasn't in there for sure. A little while after Clay and Khloe left, the couple had emerged from the dining room, braced against each other, and sat on the couch. Silent except that every few minutes, Belinda still moaned softly, like a person in deep physical pain. Soon Chuck half carried her upstairs to bed, then disappeared into his study.

When the basement proved empty too, Violet went to the study, tapped on the door, and pushed it open.

He wasn't here. The Bible sat on the floor beside the overstuffed chair, open to the book of Romans.

He must have gone up to check on Belinda. Violet took the winding stairs two at a time. Halfway to their door, she stopped.

Belinda was crying again. Maybe Violet shouldn't intrude.

She had to tell them where she was going, at least.

The tap on the door sounded too loud. Belinda's tears floundered, quieted. The door opened to Chuck, stooped and crinkle-faced.

Violet spoke as fast as she could. "Lee's not in the house and I'm going outside to look for her and I wanted to let you to know where I was."

Violet looked past him into the room. Huddled under the covers, Belinda pushed up to one elbow. "L-Lee's gone m-missing?"

"No, she's probably just outside." Violet backed away from the door. "I won't bother you guys anymore. I'm sure I'll find her."

"Oh, Chuck. How could we forget Lee?" Belinda sat up and shoved the blankets aside.

"You stay here, Pearl."

She pushed her hair back from her face and took a deep, shaking breath. "That girl's hurting bad. Laying here feeling my own hurt don't help no one right now."

Downstairs, Chuck grabbed his shoes, and Belinda pushed her feet into a pair of ragged blue house slippers. The three of them marched out into the dark. The rain had stopped, but the grass squished under Violet's tennis shoes. Good thing she'd brought these shoes and left the ballet flats and sandals at home.

She should probably try to stop thinking of her parents' house as home. Or the Hansen house, for that matter. Or anywhere.

They circled the whole house and nearly missed Lee. On the far side of an overgrown spruce tree, Belinda had cultivated a garden of wildflowers, bordered in stone. The flowers spilled over the rocks and crowded each other, a blooming rainbow riot that left no space in the garden to walk. The porch light didn't reach this far, but a floodlight was set up several feet away and aimed at an antique-looking sign on a post: *The Vitales.*

Lee sat in the grass, knees up, staring into the garden. She'd been here since before the rain stopped. Her hair clung to her head, and her T-shirt was saturated. The rain hadn't brought the temperature down much, but she still had to be cold.

Belinda shuffled close and stood over her. "Lee, sugar, come inside. You'll catch your death."

Not even a flinch of response. Violet circled to face her. Lee's eyes held no focus.

Violet perched on a stone seat, her back to the flowers. "Lee?"

457

She could have been a robot, shut off with the flip of a switch.

Belinda squatted to her eye level. "I know it hurts real bad right now. It's —" A tiny sob broke through. "It's hurting inside me too. I can't hardly let myself believe it. But you can't sit out here all night. You'll get sick, and anyway, it won't help the hurts. Come on inside, and I'll make us some tea. You want something to eat, maybe?"

Lee hunched tighter over her knees.

Violet shifted her seat. The stones were making her backside sore. "Lee, should we leave you alone?"

No response.

"I'm not leaving you outside like this, sugar. You might as well come on into the house."

Chuck stood apart, thumbs hooked in his belt loops, out of Lee's sight. He shifted on his feet.

Violet rubbed her arms. Maybe Belinda was right to push. No matter what Lee wanted, she couldn't stay out here all night.

"Please look at me, Lee," Belinda whispered, and a tear dripped down her cheek.

Finally, the blank eyes blinked and focused. "You fail to grasp nonverbal communication."

Hurt flashed into Belinda's face. "What's that mean?"

"Like, 'if I ignore them, they'll go away,' " Violet said. Lee's gaze flickered to her and stayed there. Progress, maybe. "If you wanted to be by yourself, you could have driven off somewhere."

"I did not wish to endanger other drivers. My concentration is somewhat lacking." No inflection.

"Well, um, why don't you come in? And you can drive home in the morning? It's only a few hours until then, anyway."

The weave of Lee's fingers whitened. She was clenching her hands, but the way she folded them hid the tension. Unless you were close enough to see that her fingers had gone bloodless.

"That's a good plan, Violet." Belinda stood up with a tiny grunt and held her hand out to Lee. "What kind of tea do you like? I've got lemon and honey, too."

Lee's eyes sputtered like a wind-ravaged candle. Her hands spasmed tighter.

Belinda wasn't doing this right. Violet breathed in deep and blurted the only thing she could think of.

"Lee, could I drive you home?"

The motionless, flat figure in front of Violet gave her no way to guess if this was a helpful idea or not. Except for those clench-ing hands. A bit of pink seeped back into her fingers.

"We don't have to talk. If you want, I won't talk at all, all night. Do you work in the morning?"

Lee blinked. "Yes."

"Okay, well, I'm homeless anyway. If I need to hang out at your house until you get off work, I can. And then you can bring me back here for my car."

Another blink. A breath that raised Lee's frozen shoulders.

"Is that what you want, Lee?" Belinda's voice wobbled. "To have Violet drive you home?"

Lee pulled her hands down to her lap. "Yes. Please." Her eyes found Violet's again. "Thank you."

"Yup." Violet sprang to her feet. "I'll go grab my stuff."

48

Around Clay, the world of night rasped and chirped and rustled. Cicadas, crickets, maybe a rabbit in the bushes beside the patio steps. He shifted against the hard Adirondack chair and leaned his head back. He'd sat here less than a week ago and listened to Khloe and Violet's sleepover chatter and thought of how he'd escaped danger. Escape, yeah. So he could dive back into it and drag his girls down with him and . . . *Stop it. You dragged them down and pulled them back up. Can't change it now, but you did something about it.*

The sliding door whispered open, shut. He turned his head.

"She cried herself to sleep." Natalia took the chair across from him and drew up her bare knees. She'd changed into a fresh shirt and khaki shorts. "She keeps asking me if Violet's okay."

"Violet's fine."

"I'm sure she is." Natalia stretched her legs and met his eyes. That hadn't been sarcasm.

"You don't think I'm a monster for leaving her with those network people?"

Natalia shook her head, but her eyes strayed past the glow of the porch light. Tires squealed from miles away, and Clay's body tensed, waiting for a crash, but the night carried on without one. A tree frog trilled.

Nat's sigh seemed to push out into the dark and fade away. "She made a choice, Clay. Thinking it was the right one . . . doesn't make it the right one."

He nodded.

"And Khloe will be fine, but it's hard to . . . to hate someone. And love them. At the same time."

What was she saying? Clay's breath drew in too loudly. She had to hear it. She stood up, wandered to the wooden patio railing, leaned her elbows on it and faced the night. Her back shuddered.

Say something. She's waiting. "I don't think Khloe noticed the lock."

He was truly stupid.

But Natalia turned around. A headache dug a furrow across her eyebrows. Clay's hand twitched. He could rub the stress away. She'd always said so, all the way back to college.

"I'll, um, I'll buy a new doorknob and everything tomorrow, first thing. Should be able to handle that."

"No pun intended?" A smile lifted her mouth.

Pun . . . right. The grin took over his face. He nearly stood up and gathered Nat to his chest. But the levity winged away a moment later. He had to talk to her, and he had no idea what he was going to say.

"Have you checked the news today?" Natalia said. Maybe she wasn't ready to talk, either.

Clay shook his head.

"Texas seceded."

"They . . . what? Can they do that?"

"We'll find out, I guess. They've talked about it before, you know."

"Right, but they were just being Texas. Protesting the erosion of the Constitution, maintaining their individuality among the states . . . It'll never be allowed."

"Time will tell. But they're going to become a fugitive sanctuary, if they don't close their borders fast. They disbanded the Constabulary."

No way it would last. The country was centuries past the idea of civil war, but somehow, the federal government would stop them.

"After this week, I have to admit, the end of the Constabulary might be a relief. But it'll never happen here." Natalia looked over her shoulder, toward the front of the house. "I'm surprised all they did was force the lock. I expected crime-scene tape and ransacking, but . . . well, I can't even tell they moved anything."

"Maybe they didn't." But if they had . . . and then put it back . . . The shiver ran up and down his spine again as he pictured agents roving his house. "Maybe the lock's a message."

"They're not the Mafia, Clay."

Close enough sometimes. Making deals, agreeing to leave certain lawbreakers alone on certain conditions . . . Maybe he was crazy not to care that his front door wouldn't lock right now. Crazy to leave a chair shoved under the doorknob. But after the past five days, he couldn't trust a locked door any more than an unlocked one. He'd sleep in his own bed. Burglars and Constabulary agents and everyone else could go to oblivion.

"Anyway." Natalia paced back to her chair and curled up. "I should be grateful, I guess. They could've done worse."

A lightbulb, cobwebbed and flickering, came on in his brain. "You feel okay here? I mean, would you have wanted to stay somewhere else?"

"Oh, it's fine." But then she stared at him. "What?"

"You just asked . . . how I feel."

Had he? "I . . . well, sure, I ask that . . . sometimes. About some things."

"You don't, Clay."

He squirmed, stood up, paced to the edge of the patio and wanted to keep going. No. No, he didn't want that. He wanted to live the rest of their lives without giving his wife another reason to write a note and walk out the door. But getting that message to his feet, his legs, the weight in his chest — none of them wanted to listen.

"I think I'll go to bed," he said.

Back indoors. Walls to keep him where he needed — wanted — to be.

"Clay?"

Her voice barely reached his back. Soft. Seeking. His pulse hammered. What did she need? What if he couldn't give it, didn't have it to give?

"I . . . I feel like maybe . . . something's . . . different? About you?"

Turn around. *You undeserving dung heap of a husband, turn around.* Clay's body

465

fought his brain every inch of the way, and his heart — did he have one? Which side was it taking?

"What happened? How did you manage to . . . Why did they let us all go?"

"I . . ." He faced her at last. Her eyes glimmered under the porch light. A moth fluttered past the back of her chair. "I gave them something they wanted . . . more than us."

"Something?"

"I did what I had to, Nat. I finally did what you — what we all — needed me to do, and that's all I'm saying about it."

A slow nod, but she kept studying him. "Is this problem . . . could this . . . come back . . . in the future?"

That wasn't a general question. "I signed a statement."

Her eyebrows lifted with surprise. And hope.

"It's over. I recanted."

"Were you lying?"

He was pitiful, because after all this, he still didn't know. Which version of God was real, which version of Jesus had walked the earth, which one had heard his prayers in the beginning, which one had recently developed deafness. Well, one thing he did know. *Whichever one You are, You didn't deliver us. I did.*

"No," he said.

Natalia stared at him, a bright-haired pixie statue. "Thank God."

"Look, Nat, I . . . I don't know . . . I know I'm . . . I might not ever be the person you need, and I don't know —"

"Shut up." Tears filled her eyes, magnified their green glimmer. "Please shut up about that and talk to me."

"About what?"

"I feel — I feel like I can't get anywhere near you."

A quaking started somewhere, maybe in his feet, maybe in his chest. Feelings. Curse them. Not now. Too much to process with his Nat standing here. She crossed the patio, and the porch light danced through her hair as she walked directly under its glow. She wrapped his hand in both of hers and tugged him toward the closest chair. His pulse drummed in his head.

Natalia pushed at his shoulder until he sank into the chair. She leaned down and kissed him, and a sweet caution flavored her lips. She pulled back before he could return the kiss and settled on his lap.

"Clay?"

Right, go ahead, say it. *I feel fill-in-the-blank.* "Nat, I . . ."

467

Why did she suddenly want his feelings out in the open? Even when they were dating, the early weeks of breathless discovery, of kisses like fireworks and hand brushes like lightning strikes, Natalia had never asked this of him. Never once asked how he felt. About anything. As it should be.

"Please say something, anything," she said.

She tilted her head onto his shoulder and rested her hand on his chest. She breathed against him. A tear dripped onto his T-shirt. She huddled, the same soft, beautiful thing that learned to shield herself, but she offered herself again now. Right now. If he maintained the silence, he would be throwing away everything she gave.

This was what he'd asked for. Another chance.

But not this kind of chance. Not the kind that asked for pieces of his heart. Natalia lifted her head. Her hand curled into his shirt, then let go.

Silence was safe, but so was Nat.

Natalia shifted her feet to the porch, and her tears reflected the light. "I guess I should . . . Clay?"

He caged her in his arm. Pulled her close. "What is it?"

Just give me a minute.

"Clay, what — ?"

468

"I had a sister." Clay trembled. Of all the words to burst out of him.

Natalia pushed back, sat up. "What are you talking about?"

"In Ohio. When I was a kid."

"I don't understand. You've never talked about her. Your parents have never talked about her."

"She drowned. At a park. Like Clinton River. We were insect hunting and she saw the stepping stones and we didn't know, we didn't know the water was so fast. She fell. In. And I couldn't get — I couldn't — I couldn't get to her —"

"Shh."

Her arms enfolded him. He hid his face against her neck. His tears filled every silence, every space.

"Shh, Clay."

"They resuscitated her, but she never woke up. She was comatose until . . . for weeks until . . . I was at school when Dad and Mom decided. I came home and she . . . They never let me in the room. I saw her through the door. And then I never saw her again."

"I'm sorry."

"They never said that. They never said anything at all. It was like they never had any child but me. We moved and their new

469

friends didn't know her and they never told anyone about her. So I couldn't, either. She's locked inside me, and I want to believe she's locked inside them too, but I've never seen her in their eyes. I don't know if they even remember their daughter."

"You could have told me. When we first met, you could have talked about her right then."

"I knew I could. But I couldn't." He tried to stop the rest of the tears, but they poured. Those few drips in the car with Khloe — they should have warned him more were coming. He never cried halfway. But on his bike, tears dried too fast to count. He'd never known how many he had.

"Have you ever cried for her before?" Natalia whispered into his hair.

He nodded against her neck. "Sometimes I have to, so . . . so I go off by myself for a while."

"Clay, is this what you do? Not just for your sister, but . . . is this what you do?"

"Cry excessively? No, I — I don't —" He gulped air. "Not normally."

"I mean, when . . . when Khloe was sick. You weren't running away from it. You were running to it. To a place you could let it out."

What? Did he do that?

Natalia rocked him. "Listen to me, we're going to figure this out. You are my husband. I want . . . I want to be that place you run to."

Clay sat up, shifted, pulled her into his arms instead. Her forehead was warm under his lips. He should wipe the tears, but she'd already seen them, and it was all right.

"Nat, I know I've got . . . things. To prove."

Natalia kissed him, deep and long, salty and sweet. "You've proved a lot in the last day or two."

His heart stung, but then it eased. It had been so long since he felt . . . clean. Open. Ready for whatever might come next. He kissed his wife and saw the unfurling flag of the future. Khloe growing up with a clean record, going to the best art school in the country. Him and Natalia growing together, slowly at first, then twining so close they forgot how to cut each other, holding each other into old age until death at last parted them. And what could he ever need again besides these things?

"I was thinking the three of us should go up to Mackinac next weekend," he said.

Natalia smiled. "Reclaiming us. Let's do it."

"Hilary." He stood up and scooped Nat

471

into his arms. "My sister's name was Hilary."

"Do you have any pictures?"

"No."

"Do your parents?"

"I don't know. Maybe."

"Let's ask for one."

Maybe he could. He dropped a kiss on Nat's forehead. "She liked waffles with whipped cream. She wanted to be a veterinarian."

Natalia's hand curled around his neck and tugged. The kiss tasted like honey and a vow.

49

Lee didn't speak during the drive other than to give Violet directions. Violet didn't speak either, only nodded that she understood where to turn next. Her heart pounded for the first few miles because she had an actual passenger, someone she was responsible not to kill with her driving. But by the time they reached Lee's, she could relax enough to lift a hand off the steering wheel when the air vent blew a hair in her eyes.

Lee let them both into the house and dropped her keys on the kitchen counter. Without a glance back, she disappeared into the bedroom at the end of the hall.

At least going to sleep would be good for her. It was after midnight by now. But Violet was wide awake, and she should try to be available in case Lee needed something or had a nightmare. *Because you were so help-ful last time that happened.*

Lee hadn't restricted her to a single room

473

or anything, so Violet gave herself a tour. The house was small but not cramped, surprisingly . . . well, cozy. It was the only word Violet could think of. She'd anticipated white walls and carpets, chrome and glass. All-around Spartan spotlessness. But the living room was painted in warm browns. The guestroom was Lee's favorite color — cool, ocean-inspired teal — and the comforter was patterned with seashells. Her kitchen was actually yellow. Not obnoxiously cheery, though. A calm, soft yellow that didn't bring to mind lemons or bananas or canaries but rather the golden top of a perfectly baked loaf of bread. The rug in front of the refrigerator was patterned with sunflowers.

Lee lived here?

The living room bookshelves would probably take Violet a lifetime to get through, assuming she had any desire to get through them. She'd seen some of the literary classics on Clay's bookshelves, read a few of them in school — who would own *Moby-Dick* by choice? — but the nonfiction titles stymied her. She read through them for the heck of it, though she had no idea what most of them were about.

The Two Treatises of Government. The Wealth of Nations. Reflections on the Revolu-

tion in France. The Federalist Papers.

Okay, she did recognize *The Constitution of the United States of America.* Wait, had Lee actually read it?

She wandered back to the classics. Lee had them arranged by topic or something. Her edition of *The Glass Menagerie* was the same as Clay's.

Violet tugged it from the shelf, cradled it in both hands, and knelt on the plush carpet. She traced the title letters and let the ache in her chest break off inside, float away, an island that used to be connected to the land. Her wrist felt suddenly naked.

What were they doing right now? Had they met up with Natalia yet?

"God?" she whispered. "Um, do You want me to go back to them? Khloe — will she forgive me someday?"

A couple tears fell onto the book's cover. Violet swiped them off.

She had no idea what she was doing here, why in the world Lee had agreed to this. Violet didn't know Lee. But the way Belinda tried so hard to help in all the wrong ways, and the way Lee shrank further inside herself with Belinda's every attempt . . . someone had to rescue them from each other.

Still, this hardly felt like her first step in

truly serving God. She lay back on the carpet and stared up at the bookshelves.

Economic Harmonies. On the Origin of Species. Democracy in America.

"I really don't get it, God. I don't get what I can possibly do for You here. Am I supposed to tell Lee about You? Am I supposed to leave Marcus's Bible for her when I go . . . wherever?"

She shut her eyes, opened them to the books again. *The Civil War. Survival in Auschwitz.* Sleep crowded in, wrapped around her without the aid of a pillow or blanket or even an actual bed. Yeah, she was going to fall asleep right here on the floor . . . with *The Glass Menagerie* propped on her chest.

Sunlight warmed Violet's arm and neck and the side of her face. She turned her head and squinted. Definitely morning. She stretched, and her arms grazed something too rough to be a sheet. Carpet. She sat up too fast, and the bookshelves reminded her. She was at Lee's house.

Violet stood and padded to the kitchen. Clatter hadn't wakened her because Lee was like a ghost in her own house. Her hair was mussed from towel-drying, and she wore the same green scrubs from the night

Wren had the baby. Her gaze flicked off Violet without pause, and she left the kitchen for the bathroom. The hair dryer came on, the first sound of the morning.

Violet stood just outside the closed door. "Lee? Anything I can do? I could make breakfast."

"No."

"Did you eat?"

No response.

"I'll make something light, then."

Still no response, so Violet returned to the kitchen and scrounged the fridge. Eggs, check. Oh, and a loaf of wheat bread. She could make toast. She wasn't turning into Belinda, really, but Lee hadn't eaten since she'd thrown up. By now, she had to be starving.

Violet threw four slices into the toaster and shoved down the levers. The frying pans hid in a cabinet under the counter, three different sizes. Mom only had one frying pan.

Mom. Violet opened the place inside her where her parents had always been, a place that was better off locked. She waited for tears to come, the way they had for the Hansens, but . . . No. Nothing. So Mom had called the con-cops on her. Well, she shouldn't have brought a Bible home.

477

The toast popped up while she was trying to scramble the eggs. See, she truly wasn't turning into Belinda. Just look at her pitiful version of eggs. She snatched up the hot toast, threw it on a plate, and slathered on butter.

The dryer shut off, and the bathroom door opened down the hall. Violet shut the burner off and found two plates for the eggs.

"You did make breakfast."

Violet jumped. Couldn't the woman shuffle a little or something? She turned to face Lee. "I was hungry, that's all. I left the toast plain, with butter."

"No, thank you."

Violet grabbed herself a fork. "Okay, whatever."

Lee left the kitchen again and came back wearing her tennis shoes, keys in one hand and a small, matte black purse over her arm. "I'll be home around eight tonight to return you to the Vitales."

Violet nodded and took another bite of eggs. They might look too brown, but they tasted okay with salt.

"Thank you for driving me."

"No problem."

Lee nodded, stood still for a moment, then crossed the kitchen to the plate of toast. She picked up one slice and took a petite bite.

"Promise I didn't burn it." Violet tried to smile, but Lee's eyes didn't look much more alive than they had last night.

She took another bite and nodded. "Thank you." Keys in one hand, toast in the other, her footsteps faded toward the back door.

So maybe Violet was a little helpful. Not that Lee needed help exactly, but . . . The footsteps rushed back. Stopped in the bathroom.

Lee threw up. Over and over, though the first time would've gotten rid of a few bites of toast. When the sounds stopped, Violet approached the door, which Lee hadn't bothered to close. She sat on the rug, knees up, back against the wall. One hand still clutched the uneaten half of the toast. She glanced toward Violet, then down, and noticed her crushing grip on the bread. She pushed it away, across the tile.

"Lee, can I — ?"

"No."

"I know you don't talk about yourself, but maybe it would —"

"No."

Dear Jesus, she does need help. What do I do for her?

"I'll be late now." Lee threw the toast into

the toilet, flushed it, and brushed past Violet without touching her. The footsteps didn't return this time. The back door shut.

Violet sat on the bathroom rug and drew up her knees. She leaned her head back against the cabinet and tried to figure it all out. Why did God's plan feel so unsafe? So awful?

"Jesus, You didn't have to let all this happen. So why did You?"

No voice spoke to her, but His red letters talked about this. In the world, there was trouble. But He overcame all of it.

"How're You going to overcome this? He's dead, and Lee can't even eat. And I can't go back to Chuck and Belinda's house and leave her here with nobody, but she'll take me back anyway."

Or maybe Violet could convince Lee to let her stay. If that was what God wanted.

"Please show me what to do, Jesus. And help me do it right."

EPILOGUE

Windowless walls. Roughly six feet by six feet. Light from the gap under the door. Cracked, dirty tile. Never the cage Marcus pictured. He'd expected iron bars. A miniscule window too high to reach. Room to pace. Not that he could right now. He'd tested weight on his right knee and nearly blacked out, catching himself before his face hit the far wall. Lee would tell him to put his leg up, but the only prop he had was his other knee. Too vulnerable a position when they came back. So he sat against the wall across from the door, his left leg bent, ready to push himself up.

Judging from the light — and then lack of it — under the door, a whole day and night had drained away. At some point, he'd slept for a little while, though he tried not to. Hunger gnawed, and his head throbbed. A day and night without coffee. He imagined the soothing bitterness of an Americano, but he would down a cup of gas-station mud without complaint.

Of course, his brain latched onto its need for a fix in spite of the real dangers here. After the arrest, protocol had disappeared. The agent had driven past the Constabulary admin building, down a street of vacant houses that backed up to the Constabulary lot. State-owned, probably. Marcus was hauled from the car and shoved across an overgrown front yard toward a dilapidated house. Handcuffed, unsteady on his knee, he'd rammed a shoulder into the agent's chest and nearly twisted free. Until the taser. Three times. Must have ticked the guy off.

He was dragged into a house, down the basement stairs. Handcuffed to a metal support pole. Left there for a while until the white hot, quivering shock of the taser wore off and he could think again. The man retrieved Marcus from the basement and then tased him once more before tearing the dart from his back and throwing him into this room on the main level. Neither of them spoke. No need to.

Marcus's knee prevented him from working his cuffed hands to the front, so he'd backed against the door to explore it. The hinges were sturdy. The knob had been reversed to lock from outside, maybe by the agent while Marcus was cuffed to the basement pole.

Now, a day and night later, he slouched against a wall of the dark pantry and breathed in the rankness of his own sweat. *God, please help me.*

He'd faced it only days ago — the reality that he'd soon be locked up. He'd set Violet free because he had to honor Jesus, whatever the cost. But he hadn't been strong, hadn't been ready. No, he'd gone home and collapsed on the floor, spasms twisting in his shoulders and his neck, the headache like claws in his skull. Indy had guarded him for hours, her head on his chest, until he could sit up.

For some reason, Violet hadn't turned him in. He'd started to breathe again.

He shifted his swollen knee. *God, I need to get out of here. Back to my family.* He prayed for them, name by name, as he'd done a thousand times. For the ones taken from him, locked up. For the ones still free, the ones he had to protect.

Clay.

The name punched a hole in his chest. He clenched his fists against the ache, clenched his eyes against the burn. He'd been fighting for hours to understand. How.

Why. But the hole inside just kept bleeding. *He's my brother. Family doesn't do this. Janelle said family doesn't do this.*

A shadow crossed in front of the door. The knob rattled.

Marcus braced both hands on the wall, pushed up with his left leg. On his feet. Ready.

Sunlight flooded in, and Jason Mayweather stepped through the door. Marcus's body coiled, pulsed with instinct and adrenaline. He'd only have one chance.

Jason's cologne overwhelmed the little space. His blue eyes glittered. He planted his feet across from Marcus as if they were guarding each other in a basketball game and he expected a charge. *In a minute, Jason.*

"So." Jason tilted his head. "It really is you."

Marcus curled his fingers against the wall. What did Jason want, a confession?

"You're a Christian, aren't you."

"Yeah."

"Right. And I've spent six months chasing the wrong half of you. No wonder I couldn't get anything on Lee. When you said she was innocent, you weren't lying. There's the kidnapping thing, but compared to all the crap you pulled . . ." Jason shrugged.

Maybe he did need a confession. No, Clay's testimony should be enough. And there'd be evidence, now that they were looking for it. They couldn't trace the burner phones, but they'd find something. Nobody committed as many crimes as Marcus had without smudging a fingerprint somewhere.

Jason stepped closer until Marcus couldn't help breathing his breath. "I'd have just turned you over, if you were someone else. I want you to know that."

Okay.

"You know what else? I should be getting a commendation. Instead, I had to file a report on your escape. My colleagues have been burning midnight oil to track you down, and they're pretty disgusted with me."

Now.

Marcus rushed, didn't allow himself to favor the knee, and if it hadn't been torn before, it was now, but Jason was off balance and the threshold of the cage was inches away.

Shock. Heat.

The dart was in his stomach this time. Jason tore it out and ignored the blood, hauled Marcus to his feet and shoved him against the wall.

Jason holstered the taser. "Just so you're aware. Too many jolts from this thing could stop your heart, though it's inconclusive as a cause of death. Of course, you won't get an inquiry either way."

Marcus shivered in the overheated room. Nobody knew he was here. *God, Jason's going to kill me, isn't he?* Right here in this room. This tiny, stale space. He tried to picture the sky, sunshine and blue and clouds, the way it looked on his last day outside.

Jason spoke against his ear. "I chose this instead of a commendation, Brenner. I chose this. Because the cost is going to be worth it."

Marcus's nerves tingled. His muscles tensed. His wrists ached as his hands strained against the cuffs.

Not another shock. Not a bullet between the eyes. Jason hit him. Close and hard. Like a boxer. Again and again. Marcus doubled over, couldn't help it, but Jason caught him by the chest and forced him upright. The next punch hit his right ribs and knocked his balance to his right knee.

The floor came up. Smacked his face. He rolled to one side, tried to see.

A steel-toed boot blurred past his face and bashed into his chest. His arms jerked but couldn't shield the pain. He tried to curl in on himself. The next kick came to his stomach. He wheezed. His breathing was too loud. But it didn't drown Jason's voice, calm with a burning thread of fury.

"You came into my house."

Kick to his back.

"You infiltrated my house."

Kick to his shoulder blade.

"You had every intention of influencing them. My wife. My son."

Kick. Kick. Kick. Kick. Kidneys. Stomach. Ribs. Chest. *Lee, he's breaking things.* Cold floor. He was too hot. He was shaking.

He had to shield his head. Getting kicked in the head could kill you. He wasn't supposed to die yet . . . or maybe he was. He couldn't see anymore. Just gray and black, drifting over his eyes.

"See, Brenner, this — is — worth it."

It was. The people he'd saved. They were worth this. And Jesus. He was worth this.

Marcus shut his eyes and tried to see the sky.

ACKNOWLEDGMENTS

I'm writing this in December. My first book, *Seek and Hide,* has been out in the world for ninety days, and I have so many people to thank, not only in the writing of this book but in the reception of that one.

To the first readers of *Found and Lost:* Andrea Taft, Emily Stevens, Heather MacLeod, Melodie Lange. For catching typos, critiquing characterization, solving plot, and everything else.

To *Seek and Hide*'s advance reviewers, for your time and enthusiasm: Andrea, Chris, Emily, Hannah, Jessie, Jocelyn, Julie, Melodie, Stephanie C, and Stephanie R. To each blogger who hosted me, for your hospitality. And extra thanks to those of you (you know who you are) who have spread the word about my series to essentially everyone you know. You are an author's best blessings!

To my sweet coworkers for the release-day party (I still have the banner and the framed picture; the chocolate and popcorn is long gone): Angela, Cindy, Dawn, Debbie, Diane, Janis, Mary, and Sally. And to everyone else at work who bought a book.

To Cornerstone Baptist Church for hosting my first book signing and to Ruthanne O'Brien for coordinating it.

To Emilie Hendryx for answering my "what would a photographer do?" questions.

To Jocelyn Floyd, for the prologue's legal language (which I forgot to mention last time), fake penal codes, and the continued suggestion of meteors.

To Jess Keller, for We MUST Write reminders and general cheerleading and traveling companionship on the writing road.

To Melodie Lange, for romance-flavored story encouragement and soul-baring Panera nights.

To Andrea Taft, for the fan club and *Treasure Island* and not laughing when I cry over a song that reminds me of Marcus.

To Charity Tinnin, the greatest of critique partners, for challenging Marcus's (and my) ethics, loving Violet as much as I do and talking me off my Clay ledge, line edits including my overuse of *just,* character therapy, and everything else.

To my marvelous agent Jessica Kirkland, for continuing to challenge me and believe in me and for liking this book so much.

To Nick Lee, for now two ominously beautiful cover designs. I still stare at them both.

To the David C Cook team and editor Jon Woodhams, for your continuing dedication to excellence.

To my siblings Joshua, Emily, Andrew, and Emma, for memories and laughter and love.

To my parents Bill and Patti, for everything I said last time, plus your excitement to tell everyone about this book your daughter wrote. Thank you for wanting a Haven Seekers billboard on I-94. For wanting me to succeed and believing that I can, and for raising me in "the nurture and admonition of the Lord."

To the only wise God and King, Father Son and Holy Spirit. May the words of my mouth and the meditation of my heart and the stories of my pen be acceptable in Your sight, O Lord, my Rock and my Redeemer.

ABOUT THE AUTHOR

As a child, **Amanda G. Stevens** disparaged Mary Poppins and Stuart Little because they could never happen. Now, she writes speculative fiction. Holding a Bachelor of Science degree in English, she has taught literature and composition to home-school students. She lives in Michigan and loves books, film, music, and white cheddar popcorn.

The employees of Thorndike Press hope you have enjoyed this Large Print book. All our Thorndike, Wheeler, and Kennebec Large Print titles are designed for easy reading, and all our books are made to last. Other Thorndike Press Large Print books are available at your library, through selected bookstores, or directly from us.

For information about titles, please call:
(800) 223-1244

or visit our Web site at:
http://gale.cengage.com/thorndike

To share your comments, please write:
Publisher
Thorndike Press
10 Water St., Suite 310
Waterville, ME 04901